THE
YELLOW COTTAGE
VINTAGE MYSTERIES

BOOKS 1–3

J. NEW

The Yellow Cottage Vintage Mysteries
Books 1–3

Cover illustration © Albatross / Alamy Stock Photo
Cover design: Stuart Bache, Books Covered
Interior formatting: Stephanie Anderson, Alt 19 Creative

BOOKS BY J. NEW

The Yellow Cottage Vintage Mysteries in order:

The Yellow Cottage Mystery (Free)
An Accidental Murder
The Curse of Arundel Hall
A Clerical Error
The Riviera Affair
A Double Life

The Finch & Fischer Mysteries in order:

Decked in the Hall
Death at the Duck Pond

CONTENTS

AN
ACCIDENTAL
MURDER

An Accidental Murder

ABOUT THE BOOK

WHEN A STRANGE CHILD FOLLOWS HER HOME ON THE TRAIN FROM LONDON, ELLA BRIDGES FEELS BOUND TO HELP HER. HOWEVER, SHE SOON DISCOVERS THE CHILD IS NOT WHAT SHE SEEMS.

Having recently moved into a large home on Linhay Island, affectionately known locally as The Yellow Cottage, Ella finds herself at the centre of a murder investigation thanks to a special gift from the previous house owner.

Along with her unusual sidekick, a former cottage resident, Ella follows clues which take her to the heart of London.

As the mystery unravels she is forced to enter the lion's den to solve the crime and stop the perpetrator. But can she do it before she becomes the next victim?

FOR MUM. WITH LOVE.

CHAPTER ONE

I t was a particularly chilly and damp Saturday afternoon in September, and I was taking a momentary break from the unpacking of boxes to have a quick sandwich and a cup of tea. I'd already laid and lit the log fire and now sat, sleepy and content, in an overstuffed armchair, watching the flames dance and flicker in the grate. And listening to the wind whistling down the chimney like an irate ghost.

I'd only been living in the cottage for a few short weeks, but it felt as though I'd lived there all my life. From the moment I stepped inside at the initial viewing, it had wrapped itself around me like a second skin and I knew I'd come home at last.

It had—or so I thought at the time—been a spur-of-the-moment decision to come back to the island after so many years. But it seemed now as though fate had conspired to steer my actions.

As a child, my family had chosen the island as a holiday destination for two weeks each summer. And one year—the last as it happened—I'd seen and fallen in love with The Yellow Cottage. Coming back so many years later on a whim, I had discovered it was for sale and, to cut a long story short, I bought it.

As I sat there drinking my tea, remembering the rather strange circumstances in which the cottage had become my home, the cat came in. Not a particularly interesting event in itself, I'd agree, except this cat walked in through a solid wall.

I'd idly been wondering why he always chose that particular spot to enter from the back garden, but once I knew the answer it was obvious. I was cleaning the small snug area under the stairs a couple of days ago, having decided it would be a perfect place to use as an office.

Going through the bookshelves, I'd come across a large hardback book, and folded inside were some of the old building plans. Looking closer, I realised that the current door to the back wasn't the original. That had been bricked up and a new opening made further along. Phantom, as I'd named the cat in a particularly unimaginative moment, was using the old doorway. The same one I expect he always used when he'd lived there as a flesh and blood companion.

Phantom was a legacy from Mrs. Rose, the previous owner. She and I had met when I first came to view the cottage a few months ago, and we had chatted briefly whilst simultaneously saving a swan from *'death-by-fishing-line.'* It wasn't until I returned to the cottage and Mr. Wilkes, the patiently waiting estate agent, that I found out she'd already been dead for seven months.

As it turned out, Phantom wasn't the only thing Mrs. Rose had left me. But it wasn't until the phone rang and set in motion a series of extraordinary events that I realised just how strange the rest of my life was going to be.

It took a minute to find the phone, entombed as it was under a pile of linen and, for some bizarre reason, three odd mittens and a teapot. But eventually I pulled it free and picked up the receiver.

"Hello?"

"Ella, it's Jerry. How are you settling in? Everything unpacked?"

I laughed. "Not exactly, Jerry. That's why I was so long answering the phone actually. I'm still knee deep in boxes and can't find a thing."

"Well, you certainly sound happy about it."

"Like the proverbial pig in muck. It's wonderful. You and Ginny really must come and visit, especially now I'm so much closer to London. You could get the train and be here in under an hour. I can't remember the last time we were all together."

"Actually, that's why I'm calling. Ginny is pining for her sister-in-law and wants you to come for lunch tomorrow. Can you make it?"

"Of course I can make it, I'd love to come. Just so long as you don't expect me to dress up. Considering how the unpacking is going I may turn up wearing my dressing gown and Wellingtons."

"Well, I doubt Ginny and I would bat an eyelid. We're used to your odd little ways—not sure how Peter would feel though." He laughed.

"Oh, very funny, you make me sound like some eccentric octogenarian. Wait a minute … who's Peter?"

"Oh, didn't I mention he was coming too?"

"Jerry, you know very well you didn't." I sighed. "Promise me you aren't matchmaking again. You know what an utter disaster your last attempt was!"

"*Moi?* How could you think such a thing of your dear brother?"

"You really are the most awful liar, you know. Please don't, Jerry. It makes me feel so uncomfortable, and it's not necessary. I'm perfectly happy as I am. More so since I moved here actually. If it happens then it happens, but I'm not going to force it. And I'm certainly not going to be paraded in front of your friends like a prize heifer, no matter how well-intentioned you are."

"Oh, Ella, I'm sorry. I really didn't mean to upset you. I just want you to be happy. It's been a few years since John died and I don't think you've been on more than three dates the entire time. I just worry about you, that's all."

"Jerry, I'm not upset, truly, and I *am* happy. I know you worry, but everything really is wonderful. In fact, I've already made a new friend. Her name is Mini. She lives just up the lane and she's a potter! Can you imagine? She makes the most glorious things and looks like a film star. She's away visiting relatives at the moment, but I'd love for you and Ginny to meet her. You'll see tomorrow that I'm perfectly fine. We'll chat then, all right? I'll get the 11:00am train and should be at your door just after noon."

"I'll meet you off the train, Ella."

I smiled at his concern. It was hard to believe *I* was the elder of the two of us.

"Jerry, you live a fifteen-minute walk from the station. I'll be fine."

"Darling, if you're going to wander the streets of London in your dressing gown, then I need to be there to prevent you from being carted away and thrown in a padded room. I'll be there waiting. You'll recognise me by the rose in my lapel and I'll be carrying a copy of the Times."

I grinned. Jerry wrote spy thrillers and he loved the clichés.

I dropped my voice to a whisper, "What's the password?"

"Snowmen in winter are a wondrous sight, but beware the yellow one."

I laughed out loud. "Silly ass. I'll see you tomorrow," I said and hung up.

I spent the next two hours sifting through boxes in an attempt to find something suitable to wear. I would have loved to turn up in my dressing gown—the look on Jerry's face would have been priceless and he'd have appreciated the joke—but with a stranger at lunch, I thought better of it.

Eventually, I found a suitable dress, a wrap and boots. With those items set aside, I searched for and miraculously found, in less than half an hour, my jewellery case, and the ensemble was complete.

I was looking forward to seeing Jerry and Ginny again and a Sunday lunch sounded divine. I'd barely made a dent in unpacking the kitchen items since moving in. As long as I had the necessities like tea, I considered it a job well done. I just hoped that this Peter chap wasn't expecting it to be more than it was.

But as it turned out, that was to be the least of my worries.

CHAPTER TWO

I adore train journeys. There's something soporific about the constant clickety-clack of the wheels on the track, the gentle swaying motion, and the speeding by of minute life outside the window.

My carriage was very quiet; there were only two other passengers besides myself. A gentleman with his head stuck in a newspaper and a woman with a cat in a basket on the seat beside her.

Seeing the woman with the cat reminded me of Phantom. One of the many bonuses to having a ghost for a pet was that I hadn't had to arrange for anyone to come in and feed him. As far as I could tell he didn't eat; well, not on my plane of existence anyway. He also didn't leave half-eaten presents for me on the doorstep. He didn't leave hair everywhere or cough up fur balls either, which was a blessing.

I hadn't found it at all odd when he'd walked through the wall that first time. I suppose it was because I'd almost come to expect it, especially after the stories Mr. Wilkes had told me, along with the fact that I'd had a perfectly normal conversation with a woman who had been dead for several months.

I suppose I should have felt more rattled than I did, but for some reason I didn't. It all seemed perfectly ordinary and I found I could just accept it for what it was.

What I did find curious, though, was that Phantom could choose to be solid almost at will. He'd curled up on my lap last evening and let me stroke him and he was as solid as I was. I could feel his weight on my knee and his soft fur under my fingers. I could even feel the gentle vibration in his chest as he purred contentedly, although all of this was done in complete silence. Ghost cats obviously didn't make any noise.

Then, hopping off a little while, later he took on a sort of transparent quality and disappeared through the wall into the garden. I wondered if all spirits could do that. And if they could, were we surrounded by ghosts who appeared to be just as alive as we were yet we didn't know it? I don't suppose we'd know until they decided to walk through a wall.

I hadn't told anyone about Phantom or Mrs. Rose. The only one that knew was Mr. Wilkes, and seeing as though he'd had some unexplained experiences himself, I knew he understood.

I had toyed with the idea of mentioning it to Mini, but as the friendship was new, I didn't want to ruin it by talking about spirits and have her run for the hills. It would be nice to have someone to talk to about it though.

I was still pondering the mystery of it all when the train pulled into the station.

As I walked up the platform, I could see Jerry beyond the barrier. He was wearing a rose in his lapel and carrying a copy of the Times under his arm. I couldn't believe it; I should have worn my dressing gown after all.

As I approached, I sidled up beside him facing the opposite direction and said in a most serious voice, "Snowmen in winter are a wondrous sight."

"Yes but beware the yellow one," he replied.

Unlike the carriage, the station was very busy, and we were awarded several bemused glances as we burst into raucous laughter and made our way outside.

Linking my arm into Jerry's, I said, "So ... tell me about your friend Peter. What does he do and how did you meet him?"

By the time we reached the apartment I knew as much about Peter Clairmont as Jerry did.

He'd not known him for long, just a matter of weeks actually. They'd met via a mutual acquaintance—at a fund-raising dinner that Jerry had attended—and found they had something in common, namely Jerry's books. It turned out Peter was a fan, and not only that but he was also an aspiring writer and had picked Jerry's brains all night.

As we stepped through the apartment door, I was engulfed in a perfumed hug.

"Ella, it's wonderful to see you. It's been far too long. I'm thrilled you could come to lunch."

Ginny, as always, was impeccably groomed. The only child of minor aristocracy, she and Jerry had fallen in love quickly and passionately, much to her father's chagrin. Jerry's books were being published by a small independent press at the time and consequently his income wasn't much. Ginny's father felt she could and should do better, but Ginny was adamant she was going to follow her heart.

For the first couple of years they lived on Ginny's trust fund and with the time and freedom to write, along with the support, belief and encouragement from his new wife, Jerry produced not one, but two best-sellers, and their future was assured. Needless to say, Ginny's father had a complete turn-about of opinion and became one of Jerry's staunchest supporters. To hear him talk now you'd think *he'd* been the one to launch Jerry's career.

"Ginny, how lovely to see you," I said. "It really has been too long. A Sunday lunch is just what I needed. I've barely unpacked the kitchen at the cottage."

As she took my wrap and hung it in the closet, I walked down the hallway and entered the kitchen with Jerry and Ginny on my heels.

"Oh!" I said as I spied a ball of fur curled up on a cushion. "You've got a . . ." I froze. It was a cat—but not just any cat—it was Phantom. What on earth was he doing here? I knew Ginny would never have a cat—she had allergies.

I realised I was mid-sentence and they were waiting to see what I would say, so I foolishly pushed on regardless, "Lovely view," then looked up to see the ugly wall of the adjacent building staring at me from the window.

I could feel the heat of the blush suffusing my neck and rising to my cheeks. *Ella, you idiot, how are you going to get yourself out of this one?* I was just about to open my mouth and dig the hole a little deeper, when Jerry saved the day by bursting into laughter.

"Sarcasm, Ella? You must be feeling better. I agree the view is appalling from this window but the rest are wonderful. It's a small price to pay for the location, though.

Come, let's go through to the drawing-room and I'll pour us some drinks."

Following Jerry, I glanced back at Phantom, who had extricated himself from the chair and was now padding along silently behind me. If I had any doubt the others couldn't see him it was allayed when we entered the drawing room. He jumped up on to the table right in front of us, and nonchalantly walked its entire length as though he owned the place before settling on the window ledge. Neither Gerry nor Ginny flinched. They really couldn't see him.

I was just hoping that I wouldn't make more of a fool of myself than I already had when the doorman buzzed up to say their guest had arrived. It was time to meet Peter Clairmont. I could only hope Phantom would remain invisible to everyone.

CHAPTER THREE

I hadn't really given a thought to what Peter Clairmont would be like, but as he entered the drawing room with Jerry, I caught Phantom out of the corner of my eye. He was standing with his back arched and his fur on end, his mouth open in a silent hiss and teeth bared menacingly. I glanced back as Jerry made the introductions. Peter seemed harmless enough and was quite pleasant both to look at and in his manner, but Phantom obviously didn't like him at all. I wondered if this was some sort of warning. Could Peter be the reason Phantom was here?

As we all took our seats in the dining-room and the first course was served, the conversation turned to how Jerry and Peter had met. I hadn't realised Ginny hadn't met Peter either, although like me she knew the circumstances of their meeting.

"Well, of course Jerry was extremely generous with both his time and his money at the fundraiser, you know," Peter began. "I must say we raised a terrific amount for the orphanage that night; it was more successful than I dared to hope and will keep us going for a good few months. Jerry was actually the one that got the ball rolling with the first donation. After that it was simply a matter of collecting the loot, so to speak."

Ginny patted her husband's arm and smilingly said, "Well, of course he was, he's the most generous man I know."

"How did you get involved with the orphanage?" I asked, studiously ignoring Phantom, who had taken up residence at the foot of Peter's chair and was staring at him, unblinking.

"Actually, it was my home for a short while. I felt it only right when I reached adulthood to I gave back to those who provided a roof over my head when I needed it most."

Phantom bared his teeth. I ignored him. What on earth was the matter with him?

"Well, that's very commendable, Peter, I must say. We could do with more people like you in the world," said Jerry.

As the dishes were removed and the next course set, I asked Peter what sort of books he wrote.

"Nothing like the fabulous spy thrillers that Jerry pens. I write historical novels mostly, although I'm sure he told you I've yet to actually publish anything."

"Well, I'm sure Jerry would be only too happy to help in that direction, wouldn't you, darling?" Ginny said.

"Of course. Let me know when you're ready and I'll put you in touch with my agent. I can't promise anything, mind you, but it's worth a shot."

Peter smiled, obviously pleased, as I would be in his position.

"That's very kind of you, Jerry. I'll certainly take you up on that offer when I'm ready."

As the main course was taken away and the most fabulous Pavlova arrived in its place, talk moved onto more mundane things and I switched off as I attacked my dessert with gusto. I had always had a sweet tooth and this was one of my favourites.

Phantom had barely moved since we sat down and was still giving Peter the stink-eye. He was like one of those Egyptian statues and I just caught myself in time before I mentioned it. Honestly, it was quite hard work pretending everything was normal when I was the only one who could see the spirit of a cat walking about.

I looked up, having finished my Pavlova, to find everyone staring at me.

"What are you all looking at? Do I have cream on my nose or something?"

I started furiously dabbing at my face with my handkerchief just in case.

Ginny squealed with delight. "No, of course not, silly. Peter was just asking about your cottage and you were ignoring him."

"I wasn't ignoring him, Ginny! I didn't hear him, that's all." Turning to Peter, I said, "I do apologise. I was miles away. What would you like to know?"

"Come on, we'll have coffee in the drawing-room and you can tell Peter all about the cottage," said Jerry.

Comfortably ensconced on the sofa, with Peter at a polite distance next to me and Phantom perched on the arm, still staring at him with complete and utter hostility, I told him the story of how I had come by the cottage and bought it, long after Jerry and I used to holiday there as children. I made it all sound as normal as possible, no mention of ghostly owners or exploding pantries, and absolutely no mention of spectral cats. This must have annoyed Phantom as he shot his paw out and caused me to spill hot coffee all down my dress.

"Oh, Phantom!" I exclaimed as I jumped up.

"Now there's a curse word you don't hear every day," laughed Jerry. "I'll have to remember that for my next book."

At that, we all burst out laughing. To be honest, I still felt like a prize idiot but Jerry, as usual, pulled the embarrassing attention away from me, for which I was very grateful.

After managing to clean up as much as I could in the cloakroom, I returned to announce that it was time for me to catch my train home.

"I'll walk you to the station," Peter said, standing. "I'm heading that way. That's if you don't mind?"

So, with that settled, we thanked Jerry and Ginny for a wonderful lunch and departed with promises we'd get together again soon. Little did I know it would be sooner than I expected.

"So you and Jerry used to holiday on the island when you were children?" Peter asked as we made our way to the station.

I nodded.

"I remember one time at the orphanage we had a day trip down there. It was the first time many of us had seen the sea."

"Do you mind me asking how you ended up there?" I asked. I didn't want to appear nosy, especially if he didn't like to talk about it, but I was dying to know.

"No, I don't mind you asking. I don't normally make a habit of discussing it, but you're actually very easy to talk to," he smiled. I blushed, thinking that he was actually quite a nice man. Not good looking in a movie star sort of way, and slightly on the short side, but he had a kind face.

Phantom, trotting beside me, turned and hissed at him again as though he were reading my thoughts. I ignored him and turned back to Peter as he continued.

"My parents were killed in an accident when I was nine. My only next of kin were an Aunt and Uncle, but they'd moved to Ireland before I was born. I didn't know them, although I had heard my mother mention a sister. I think they must have been estranged, as I'd never known them to be in contact. It took the authorities a while to trace them, and during the interim period I was sent to the orphanage to live."

"How long were you there?"

"Just short of four months, but it was summer and we were allowed to play outside a lot and it wasn't as cold inside as it is in the winter. Part of the funds raised recently will go towards an overhaul of the heating system. Plus we had a day trip to the seaside when funds would allow. I think I went twice during my stay which was unheard of. Although after the last one the visits were stopped for a while."

"Oh? What happened?"

He sighed, and his face took on a sad cast.

"One of the girls waded out too far and a rip-tide took her. There was nothing any one could have done."

I stopped, my hand on my heart. "Oh, Peter, how awful. That must have been so traumatic for you and the other children to witness … and that poor girl."

"Well, that's part of the reason why I help. If there had been someone there with training, then I'm sure she could have been saved."

By this point, we'd reached the ticket collector and would have to part ways. "I'm terribly sorry if I opened up old wounds, but thank you for sharing your story with me, and I'm glad you finally found your extended family," I said.

"Well, that's a story for another time," he said with a frown. "It's been a pleasure, Ella. Perhaps we could do it again sometime?"

I sighed inwardly. I hated being put on the spot like this. He'd been a perfect gentleman all through lunch, so I was inclined to believe Jerry when he said he wasn't matchmaking. Even so, there was something holding me back. A niggle of doubt like an itch I couldn't scratch. "Well that's very kind of you, Peter. You never know. Perhaps we'll have lunch with Jerry and Ginny again," I said, smiling and shaking his hand as I presented my ticket to the guard.

I left Peter at the barrier and made my way down the platform. A quick glance down told me Phantom was determined to accompany me on the train.

As I got on and turned right to enter the carriage, he shot in front of me and sat in the doorway preventing me from going any further. Well, even I understood that message, so I turned around and went in the other carriage.

Phantom jumped up on one of the seats and looked at me.

"No, I can't sit there. I have to have my back to the engine otherwise it makes me feel queasy."

"I know what you mean, dear," said a voice.

Oh, good grief. I must have spoken out loud. I looked over and saw the voice belonged to a lady a few seats down. Nodding and smiling, I took the seat opposite Phantom and popped a mint in my mouth. Hopefully that would help me to keep it shut.

Just as the first whistle blew, a child no more than eight years-old shot into the carriage and scrambled under the seat in front of me, obviously hiding. I looked down the aisle, but saw no one chasing her. Glancing out of the window, I saw that all was perfectly quiet on the platform too. I looked back at her, opening my mouth to speak, but she put a finger over her lips to shush me. The pleading look and abject fear in her eyes made me keep quiet.

The carriage began to fill up as people took their seats, but the girl was well hidden, tiny as she was, and luckily no one noticed her. I was having second thoughts about keeping my mouth shut when the train began to pull out of the station. It was then that I noticed Phantom had disappeared.

CHAPTER FOUR

The girl remained hidden the entire journey. As people got on and off the train, the sea of faces in front of me changed and I was awarded a glimpse of her periodically during the brief moments when the seat was empty. She lay there as quiet as a mouse and perfectly still. She'd look at me every now and then and each time she raised a finger to her lips. Eventually, I watched as her eyelids grew heavy and she fell asleep, no doubt lulled by the swaying of the train and the sound of the wheels on the track.

I took this chance to examine her in more detail. Her dark trousers were homespun wool and, although clean, were far too big for her and had been rolled up several times at the cuff. Her shoes, whilst looking to be the correct size, were scuffed and worn through so her sock could be clearly seen through the sole of one. Her navy coat was the right size and looked warm, which was a blessing, but I thought she could have done with a hat as it was bitterly cold out, especially at this time of night. I wondered what her story was. She was obviously either from a very poor family or she was homeless—a runaway perhaps? I wondered what sort of tragedy would befall a family to result in a tiny child like this having to curl up under a train seat. She should be home, tucked up safe and warm and sleeping the sleep of the innocent.

My station was the last on the line and by the time we pulled up the carriage was empty. As we stopped, the girl opened her eyes and then carefully unfolded herself from beneath the seat. With a brief look at me, she left the train.

By the time I'd got off, gone through the small ticket booth, and begun to walk up the lane home, she was standing there waiting for me.

I don't know why I should have felt so surprised. She'd crawled under the seat in front of me, I was the only one who knew she was there, and I'd kept her secret, so it would seem natural for her to trust me. But what on earth was I supposed to do with her?

All the way back to the cottage, I tried to engage the girl in conversation, but she remained as silent as she had been on the train. I didn't even know her name. Glancing at my watch, I noted it was a quarter past seven. We'd probably be home by half past and I'd get her some food and a warm drink and then make up the spare room for her.

There was still no sign of Phantom and I wondered if he would be at the cottage by the time we got there.

Fifteen minutes later we arrived home. It was cold so I put a match to the fire that I'd laid that morning and set about things in the kitchen whilst it slowly infused the room with warmth.

Placing hot milk, toast, jam, and a few biscuits on the table for the child I went upstairs to make her bed.

On my return I found the empty dishes in a pile on the draining board and the girl crouched on the floor in front of the fire.

I took my tea and sat in a chair next to her. I'd tried to put my arm around her shoulders on the walk home, but she'd immediately shied away. I wanted to offer her some sort of physical comfort—she was so obviously lacking in affection—but, by the same token I didn't want to frighten her. I supposed I'd just have to be patient and let her go at her own pace.

"You know I don't even know your name," I said. She looked up at me with huge brown eyes, but still said nothing and then turned back to gaze at the flames.

"Well, I can't very well call you child. I'll call you Poppy for now if that's all right with you, just until you're ready to tell me your real name?"

At that she nodded briefly then rose and stood at the foot of the stairs, apparently it was time for bed.

As I stood to accompany her, Phantom appeared.

"Oh, so you've decided to come home, have you?" I said. At that Poppy turned and looked at me. I'd forgotten once again to keep my mouth shut, and was about to open it again to explain when to my utter amazement she reached down, scooped Phantom up in a hug and carried him upstairs. And Phantom was quite happy to let her do so.

As I entered the bedroom I found Poppy already fast asleep in bed, her shoes set neatly at the foot and her coat folded on the chair. Phantom was also asleep, curled up on the eiderdown with Poppy's arm hugging him close.

So I wasn't the only one who could see this ghost cat. I'd heard tell that children were more open to these sorts of encounters with imaginary friends and suchlike, but I was a little perturbed. For some reason I couldn't help but feel there was more to this encounter than met the eye, and what I initially thought of as coincidence wasn't one at all.

CHAPTER FIVE

Monday morning came bright and early, and as I opened the curtains I was greeted with sunshine and a pale blue sky. It promised to be a glorious autumn day and I wondered whether I should continue unpacking inside the house or venture out into the garden. Or even take a walk along the beach. Then I remembered!

Grabbing my dressing gown, I hurriedly put it on whilst dashing to the spare room down the hall. It was empty and the bed made up neatly. Had I dreamed it all?

Scrambling downstairs in a most unladylike manner, I was relieved to see both Poppy and Phantom curled up together in a chair.

"Good morning," I said cheerfully as I made my way to the kitchen.

"I hope you slept well, Poppy. I'll make you some breakfast and then I thought perhaps you'd like to go and play in the garden. The front is quite safe and has lots of magical things to find if you look closely enough."

As I set to scrambling eggs and making toast, Poppy wandered out to the front with Phantom on her heels and sat on the stoop. I could see her looking around the flowerbeds to see what I meant by magical things; then suddenly she spied something and off they went.

I'll never forget the first time I had seen the cottage garden. I was a little older than Poppy and had peered over the gate drawn to the promises beyond the high hedge.

It was like a fairytale with all the flowers in bloom, and I'd made up stories as to whom it could possibly have belonged. I rather fancied the idea of Cinderella living there with her stepmother and sisters. Or Hansel and Gretel after they'd escaped from the wicked witch. I'd spied several things that day under the foliage: a ring of toadstools, a giant's boot and a huge dragonfly nestling in the apple tree.

I had of course added to the wonders in the garden myself since moving in. Several ornate butterflies, a family of frogs, and a number of miniature houses were all carefully hidden unless you knew just where to look.

I stood at the window eating my toast as I watched Poppy and Phantom searching, and smiled when I saw the look of amazement on Poppy's face as she discovered the next wonder.

"Poppy, come in and eat your breakfast now, it's on the table for you." As she came in and seated herself I said, "I'm just going to dress. I'll be upstairs if you need me."

She looked at me and gave her usual brief nod but remained silent. I was beginning to wonder if she'd ever speak.

Once dressed, I went to Poppy's room and opened the curtains to let in the sunshine. Turning, I spied something stuck down the side of the chair cushion. It was a gentleman's wallet. It must have fallen out of Poppy's pocket when she'd taken her coat off last night. I wondered what she was doing with a wallet. Could it belong to her—a gift from her father perhaps?

Well, I had to make sure, so I opened it and got the most awful shock. It belonged to Peter Clairmont! I sat on the chair whilst I contemplated what this could mean, but no matter how hard I tried I could only come up with one explanation: she had picked his pocket.

Opening it again, I saw there were various pieces of identification. These all showed that Peter was obviously the owner, but there was also a tidy sum of money in it. So whilst Poppy had stolen his wallet, she hadn't removed the money and thrown away the incriminating evidence, which is what I would have expected a thief to do. The more I thought about it the less sense it made. There really was nothing left to do except to go down and confront her.

I found her still sitting quietly at the table. Her food was gone and the crockery once again was stacked on the draining board.

I took the seat opposite her and then slowly pulled the wallet from my pocket, laying it on the table between us. She looked at it, then at me and smiled. Of all the things she could have done—run from the house, burst into tears, snatched the wallet back—that she would smile never crossed my mind, but what did it mean? Did she want me to find it?

"Poppy, did you steal this wallet yesterday at the train station?"

A shake of the head, no.

"Well, was it given to you?"

Another no. I sighed, trying to extract information like this was wearying but I had to know the truth.

"Do you know the person it belongs to?"

A nod, yes. We were starting to get somewhere.

"Did you find it?"

Another nod.

"At the station yesterday?"

No.

I thought for a moment, trying to work out the next question. "Well, did someone else steal it and perhaps drop it and then you found it?"

No.

I couldn't think what else to ask. None of it made sense. She hadn't stolen the wallet, it wasn't given to her, she knew who it belonged to and had found it, but not at the train station yesterday when I knew for certain Peter had been there and when Poppy came rushing into the carriage as though the very devil were on her heels. Obviously with the wallet in her coat pocket, otherwise it wouldn't have been on the chair this morning.

"Poppy, you do realise that I also know the owner of this wallet, don't you?"

Yes, she nodded.

"And that I must return it to him?"

At this she nodded enthusiastically and grinned. I was completely confounded. It was as though this was what she was waiting for me to say—that I had every intention of returning it. But what could it mean?

"All right. Well, I'm afraid I can't leave you here alone. You'll have to accompany me back to London and I'll return the wallet to Mr. Clairmont."

I stood and went to the phone with the intention of calling Jerry to obtain Peter's number. As I lifted the phone to dial, Phantom shot out of nowhere and batted the receiver from my hand.

"Phantom, for goodness sake, what on earth has got into you?" I glanced over at Poppy as she walked to the phone and returned the receiver to its cradle, and then shook her head.

"You don't want me to contact Mr. Clairmont?" I asked. "You want me to just turn up unannounced and hope he's at the orphanage?"

Poppy nodded solemnly. It was obviously important to her that I do it her way. She'd made no secret of the wallet particularly and she was both understanding and accepting that I had to return it. She was also prepared to accompany me. I looked at Phantom, who sat on his haunches next to Poppy with a patient look on his face. I was definitely outnumbered.

"Fine, I'll do as you ask although I don't understand it." Grabbing my bag coat and keys I said, "Come on then, if we get a move on we'll make the ten-fifteen."

Thank goodness, I thought later, that I had no idea what I was about to discover as I hurried down the lane with a small child skipping beside me and a ghost cat leading the way.

CHAPTER SIX

As I began to climb the orphanage steps I glanced back at Poppy, who had stopped at the bottom and was clinging to the rail. She obviously wasn't prepared to go any further. I nodded to let her know I understood and, looking back, I couldn't say I blamed her. The building was a Gothic horror. Overwhelmingly huge with towering parapets and monstrous-faced gargoyles.

Large as it was, it blocked out all the light and left the area in dark foreboding shadows. Soot-blackened bricks gave it a menacing aura and small grimy windows, that I doubted had ever been cleaned, gazed out like sightless eyes.

Taking a deep breath, I made my way inside and was greeted by a woman in uniform whom I assumed was the Matron.

"Can I help you?" she asked.

"Yes, I'm here to see Mr. Clairmont. Is he available?"

"Do you have an appointment?"

"No, I'm afraid I don't, but if it's not convenient I'd be happy to call another time."

"I'm sure that won't be necessary. He's in a meeting at the moment but I'll let him know you're here. You can wait in there," she said, pointing to an open door behind me. "He shouldn't be much longer."

"Thank you," I said and made my way to the indicated room.

It was as dispiriting in here as it was outside. Dark wood paneling on the walls rose from floor to ceiling of the cavernous space, and although there were a number of table lamps lit they couldn't compete with the gloomy decor and barely made a difference.

The rugs on the blackened floor were dull, dusty and frayed, as were the covers and cushions on the meagre supply of chairs. Works of art adorned the walls but again were filthy and the subject matter either thoroughly depressing, like the seascapes and landscapes, or positively frightening, like several of the portraits and the religious scenes, which seemed to focus on the hellfire and damnation aspects of religion.

I shuddered involuntarily, how could any child survive in surroundings as bleak and joyless as these? It seemed to me that no matter how much fund-raising was done, the task to bring warmth, love, light and happiness into this place was nigh on impossible.

At the end of the room was a large built-in bookcase with glass-fronted doors and internal lights and as I moved closer, I realised it was a display of some kind.

Various photographs adorned the shelving, along with more personal items like books and dried flowers, and in one instance a tortoiseshell comb. At first I couldn't work out what it meant, but as I studied some of the photographs, and saw a small sign of remembrance for those that had been lost, it dawned on me what I was looking at. I was so stunned that I didn't hear the footsteps behind me and nearly jumped out of my skin when a voice spoke.

"Ella! What a lovely surprise. I didn't expect to see you again so soon." It was Peter.

I turned to face him and forced myself to smile. "Oh yes, well neither did I. Actually I'm sorry to have turned up unannounced."

"Oh, it's no trouble at all. It was a good excuse to leave a thoroughly boring meeting."

I nodded, then looked back at the display. Peter obviously saw the look of distress on my face and moved closer.

"I'm sorry you had to see this alone," he began. "But we feel it's appropriate to remember them in this small way. It was my idea actually."

"I understand, of course. It was just a shock when I realised what it was. Can you tell me about them, how they died?"

There were at least two dozen photographs, all of them children who had resided at the orphanage at one time or another, and all who had met their deaths far too early. They'd barely had time to live and what life they'd had must have been so difficult and lonely.

"Well, some of them were before my time, of course, but I'll tell you what I can." Pointing at one of the images he said, "This was Cedric. He contracted pneumonia and after a short illness passed away in his sleep. He was six years old."

I looked at the photograph of a tiny, under-nourished looking boy in a too-large jacket and a cap. He had an adorable cheeky face and a gap-toothed smile. I doubted the tooth fairy had ever visited him.

"This was Elizabeth. She was a little older than Cedric at nine. She ran into the road and startled a horse and carriage. The horse reared and brought his hooves down on her head. She died instantly. There was nothing anyone could do, it happened so fast." Another beautiful innocent child smiled back at me from the grainy black and white portrait.

As we moved up the display Peter stopped in front of a photograph of a beautiful dark-haired girl. "This was Mary. She was the one I told you about."

"The one that drowned?"

He nodded and I noticed him grit his teeth and clench his hands into fists. "She was only twelve."

I'd moved up almost to the end and was looking at another young girl. "And this one?"

"That was Millicent. She was only seven."

"What happened to her?"

"She slipped and fell in front of an oncoming train."

I gasped. "Oh, how awful. Was it recently?"

"Well, more recent than the others, but it was over a year ago. Why do you ask?" He said with a frown.

Just as I was about to answer, the Matron came in with a box and interrupted us. "A lady just dropped these donations off, Mr. Clairmont. Where would you like them?"

"Just put them in my office for now, Matron, thank you."

"I'm sorry, you must be busy," I said. "I'll leave you to get on with your work."

As I started to leave the room, Peter called after me.

"Ella, was there something in particular you came to see me about?"

Oh, I'd forgotten all about the reason for my being there in the first place! Luckily, the Matron's previous interruption had planted a much-welcomed seed in my mind. I turned, and for an instant swore I saw a look of disdain on his face, but then it disappeared to be replaced by a smile. I must have imagined it.

"Of course there was. It completely slipped my mind. As you know, I've moved recently and I've now far too many belongings. I wondered if you'd like me to donate them to the orphanage."

"Well, that would be very kind of you, Ella. We can always use more donations, thank you. Did you come all this way to ask me that?"

I smiled. "It wasn't a special journey, if that's what you mean. I had to come up to the city for an appointment, so it seemed prudent to pop in and ask at the same time."

He nodded. "Well, that explains it."

"I must dash if I'm to catch my train home. It was nice to see you again, Peter. I'll get those donations packed up soon. Bye for now," I said as I turned on my heel and waved over my shoulder. I forced myself not to run but it was a challenge, I just wanted to get away from the horrible place.

By the time I'd reached the bottom of the steps I found Poppy was nowhere in sight, I could only hope she wasn't too far away and would see me leaving. Glancing back, I saw Peter staring at me from the doorway, but this time the look on his face was unreadable.

CHAPTER SEVEN

As I dashed through central London in my eagerness to get as far away as possible from Peter Clairmont and the orphanage, I literally ran smack into a woman coming the other way.

"I'm terribly sorry, I wasn't looking where … Oh, Ginny, it's you. Thank goodness."

"Ella! Heavens above, what's happened? Is someone chasing you?"

"No, nothing like that. I was just in a rush to get to the station before I missed my train."

"Darling, I have to say you're not looking at all well. In fact you look like you've just seen a ghost. Are you all right?"

I burst out laughing, I couldn't help it. *'Seen a ghost!'* If only she knew.

"Well, that settles it," Ginny announced. "You're obviously hysterical, something must have happened. I insist you come home with me and have a cup of tea, or possibly something stronger. Then you can tell me all about it."

And with that she linked arms and steered me towards the apartment.

As we rounded the corner I happened to glance at the small park that sat opposite Jerry and Ginny's building. Sitting on one of the seats was Poppy, with Phantom next to her. Oh, thank goodness. She waved and indicated that she would wait for me there. I thought that would be for the best under the circumstances, so after a quick nod I followed Ginny into the foyer.

In the apartment Ginny divested me of my coat, hat, gloves and bag, then proceeded to the kitchen to ask the maid to make some tea.

In the drawing room she poured us each a small sherry and then, making herself comfortable in an armchair, she asked what on earth was going on.

"Oh, Ginny, I don't know where to start," I confessed.

"Well, I always find the beginning is as good a place as any. Of course, if you want to begin by telling me why you were racing down the high street as though being chased by a pack of hell hounds, be my guest."

"Actually I'd just come from meeting Peter Clairmont at the orphanage."

"Oh, Ella! He didn't molest you or anything awful, did he?" she asked, shocked.

"No, Ginny he did not, and please don't jump to conclusions like that. I went to return something to him but had second thoughts. Actually that reminds me, do you have any spare clothing, books or children's games, or perhaps bedding? You know, things you no longer need?"

"What? Ella darling, you're not making any sense. Here, have some more sherry. Now what do you mean do I have bedding or games? I say, are you planning a slumber party with Peter Clairmont? How wicked, Ella!" she said, laughing.

"Ginny, really, of course not. I idiotically happened to mention that I had some unwanted items to donate to the orphanage, but the fact is, I haven't. Of course, I can't let Peter know that otherwise he'll think I was there for some other reason altogether. Which of course I was, but I can't let him know that, otherwise he'll know I'm onto him, don't you see?"

"Not really, no. Could you explain?"

As I was trying to gather my thoughts into a more cohesive pattern the maid came in with the tea. Pouring, Ginny said, "I think it would be better if you started at the beginning, Ella. I can't make any sense at all of what you've said so far, darling."

I took a deep breath. "Ginny, do you believe in ghosts?"

"Oh, I see, this is about your cat?"

"What?"

"Your cat. You know, the black apparition that came to lunch with you yesterday."

I was astonished. "You mean you could see him?"

"Well, I certainly saw him sitting in the kitchen chair, and I knew he was the one who caused you to spill your coffee."

"Why didn't you say anything?"

"Dearest, when exactly have I had time? I could hardly say anything at lunch lest both our guest and Jerry thought we'd gone mad."

She did have a point I supposed. It seemed much longer considering all that had happened to me, but it was actually less than twenty-four hours.

"Do you have some sort of special gift, Ginny, and does Jerry know?"

"Sadly I have no particular gift. It happens very rarely and usually when I'm in the company of an adept such as yourself. It's a legacy from one of my Romanian ancestors."

"Really? How fascinating. I didn't know your history was filled with such colour," I said in awe.

"Heavens, that's just one branch darling. I'm fairly sure one of my great-great-grandmothers on the maternal side was burned at the stake. It's a wonder I'm here at all."

"And is Jerry aware?"

"Of course he is. Jerry and I have no secrets. But because it's such a rare occurrence it's not something we've discussed in detail. But never mind me. We need to talk about your sudden ability. It is something that has only happened recently, correct?"

I nodded. "Yes, it all started when I went to view the cottage for the first time."

"How interesting. Start again and tell me everything." And so I started at the beginning, when I felt as though I'd been steered by an unseen hand to discover the agent who was selling The Yellow Cottage.

By the time I'd got to the part where Poppy had rushed into the carriage and scrambled under the seat facing mine, Ginny was in raptures.

"Good heavens, Ella. What happened to her?"

"She fell asleep until it was my stop, then she got off and was waiting for me halfway up the lane. What else could I do but take her home?"

"So where is she now, back at the cottage?" Ginny asked.

"Good heavens, no. I couldn't leave her there alone. I brought her with me. She's waiting for me in the park across the road."

Ginny stood up. "We can't leave the poor girl there. I'll go and bring her in."

"No, Ginny, honestly it's fine. She really didn't want to come in. She's not spoken a word yet and I don't want to overwhelm her." I rose and went to the window overlooking the park. "It's all right," I said, giving a small wave. "She's still there."

"Well, of course, Ella, whatever you think is best. So, what happened next? Why did you go to the orphanage?"

"Oh, yes. Well, when I went into Poppy's room this morning, I found a gentleman's wallet on the chair. I thought it strange so I opened it, and guess who it belonged to."

Ginny shook her head. "I've no idea, who?"

"Peter Clairmont."

"No!" she exclaimed. "How extraordinary. How did she get it?"

"Well, I thought she must have picked his pocket at the station last night, but now I know that's impossible. It…"

"Darling, I'm home. Where are you?"

It was Jerry.

"In the drawing room, Jerry."

Jerry walked in. "Hello, Ella, I didn't expect to see you here. Guess who I bumped into on the way home?"

I glanced up just as Jerry said "Peter," to see the man himself walk in. Oh no, how much had he heard?

"Ella, what a surprise. I thought you were rushing to catch your train," he said as he came and sat in the chair next to me. It may have been my imagination but I could have sworn he made that sound like an accusation.

AN ACCIDENTAL MURDER

I'd frozen. For some reason I couldn't think of a single thing to say. Luckily Ginny, cool and calm as always, answered for me.

"Oh, she was. I bumped into her as she'd almost got to the station but insisted she come home with me. We so rarely get girl-time together and it was a perfect opportunity to catch up properly. We've had a lovely afternoon discussing the cottage and the island. In fact, I've decided I'm going to go back with Ella this evening to spend a few days down there. I think the sea air will do me a world of good. That's if you don't mind, Jerry?"

"Of course I don't, darling. You go and have some fun. I'll be perfectly all right. I'm working on my new manuscript anyway. No, I think it's a wonderful idea. When were you thinking of going? It's five now," he said, glancing at his watch.

"We were just waiting for you actually. We thought the six o'clock if you were back in time and could drop us off. I do so hate dragging my luggage down the street."

Jerry laughed. "Of course I'll have the car brought round. Peter, I shan't be long, old boy. You're more than welcome to join us, or you can stay here if you'd prefer?"

"Thank you, Jerry, that's very kind I must say. Yes, I'll wait for you here. Perhaps I could have a look at some of your books whilst I wait?"

"Certainly. I'll show you through to the library and if you need anything just ask the staff. I won't be long."

Ginny and I briefly caught the other's eye. I was concerned that Jerry was getting too friendly with Peter. I would have to warn him somehow without giving the game away.

Ginny turned and said, "It's very nice to see you again, Peter, but if you'll excuse us, I need Ella to help me choose some suitable attire for life on the island."

43

I almost rolled my eyes. It was an hour's train journey away, not Antarctica. Heaven knows what she was planning on packing. I hurriedly said goodbye to Peter and Ginny took my arm, almost dragging me down the hall.

"For goodness sake, Ginny." I whispered, suppressing a smile. "Don't you think you're going a bit overboard? He'll smell a rat for sure if you keep this up."

"Nonsense. Men are clueless when faced with either beauty, or damsels in distress. He won't suspect a thing."

Whilst I understood her reasoning—in fact I had seen her womanly wiles in action to great effect on a number of occasions—I wasn't so sure it would wash with Peter Clairmont. There was something about him that just didn't ring true and I was determined to find out what it was.

CHAPTER EIGHT

As Ginny and I were settling into our carriage for the journey home, I spied Poppy entering one of the others. She obviously didn't want to be seen, but I was extremely relieved to know she was there.

Ginny and I had barely had a chance to discuss that day's events, and as the train was full to the gills we decided to wait until we got home.

Back on the island, Ginny flagged down a taxi. She really *didn't* like dragging her luggage, and looking at the amount she'd decided to bring, it would have been impossible for just the two of us anyway.

I'm not sure how long she was planning to stay, but I thought four hat-boxes, three suitcases, and a carry-on a little extravagant. But that was Ginny to a T and I couldn't help but love her for it. I must admit the motor car was a pleasant change from walking, although I did miss the scenery along the coastal path.

Half an hour later, we were warm and cosy in the cottage and I was just waiting for the kettle to boil when I spied Poppy in the garden. She was obviously waiting to enter but not prepared to do so whilst Ginny was there. I had to think of an excuse to get Ginny out of the room in order for her to sneak in.

Whilst I was contemplating what to say, Ginny in an uncanny act of prescience said, "Well, are you going to give me the tour, darling? I love what I've seen so far."

"Of course, we can start with your room and take your luggage up too," I said.

Staggering up the stairs under the weight of Ginny's belongings, I noticed Phantom sitting in the hall. I guessed that meant Poppy wasn't far behind. Entering the largest of the four bedrooms I said to Ginny, "I thought you'd like this room the best. It's the largest and the one with the most closet space."

"Oh, you know me so well, Ella dear. I must say it is rather beautiful." And it was. I had barely done anything to the decor myself; just put a few knick-knacks around the place, but it was very grand. The four-poster bed with its lemon yellow floral canopy and eiderdown, lent a cheery ambience to the room, and the fabric had been mirrored in the other soft furnishings. The chaise longue at the foot of the bed was done in deep green velvet, as was the stool at the dressing table. But my absolute favourites were the small chandelier with its tear-drop crystals and the matching lamps on either side of the bed.

"Thank you, Ginny, plus it has a wonderful view of the back garden all the way down to the river. Now I'm afraid I'll have to leave you to unpack. I haven't had chance to find a daily as yet."

"There's no need to worry about that, Ella dear. I'm used to roughing it a little sometimes, you know. And I want no argument from you but I insist on helping you with your unpacking. Now come along and let's finish our tea and you can tell me what happened today. I'll have a look around the rest of the place in the daylight."

We made our way back downstairs, but not before I took a chance to check in on Poppy. She was fast asleep in her room with Phantom by her side.

Once again settled in front of the fire, I said, "Now, how far had I got Ginny?"

"You were just about to tell me about the wallet."

"Oh, yes. Well, first I need to go back a little bit. You see when I got to the orphanage, the matron showed me to a waiting room, a huge dark and dismal place with barely any light, but at one end there was a display cabinet and inside were around twenty or so black and white photographs of children, along with books and dried flowers and other keepsakes. At first I couldn't work out what it was, but then I realised it was a sort of shrine."

"A shrine … whatever do you mean?"

"It was a way of remembering all the former orphans who had died whilst living there."

"Oh, Ella, how terribly sad."

"I know, isn't it? Then Peter came in and saw me looking. It was his idea apparently to remember them all in that way. But that's not all. I asked him to tell me how they had died."

"Heavens, Ella, don't you think that was a little … macabre?" asked Ginny.

"It was a gut feeling, Ginny. I just felt I needed to know for some reason. Anyway he proceeded to tell me about several of the children. One died of pneumonia, a little boy aged just six, another was killed by a rearing horse when she ran out into the road, and Mary—Peter had already told me about her when he walked me to the station on Sunday evening—she was drowned on an outing to this very island, Ginny. Peter was there at the time too. It was when he was living at the orphanage for that short time."

"It's all so very heartbreaking, isn't it, Ella? So is that when you told him about the wallet?"

"Oh, no, he doesn't know I have it. I'd obviously gone there to return it but you see he gave himself away when he was telling me about the children. That's why I made up that nonsense about the donations."

Ginny frowned. "But how did he give himself away? He didn't have anything to do with those three deaths, did he?"

"Not those three, no, but he told me about a fourth, a seven-year-old girl named Millicent. She died at a train station, Ginny. She fell on to the track seconds before the train pulled in."

Ginny covered her mouth and widened her eyes in shock. "You don't mean … ?"

I nodded. "Yes, I do. Poppy, the girl who came home with me, is Millicent, and she died over a year ago."

"Oh, I say! That means Peter must have been there at the time, otherwise how would Poppy, I mean Milly, have got hold of the wallet?"

"Exactly, Ginny. So you see now why I couldn't return it to Peter."

"Yes, I do, Ella. But whatever are we going to do now? Peter must be involved in the death of that child in some way, would you agree?"

I nodded. "He must have been. Whether it was a tragic accident like he said or something altogether more sinister, he was definitely there. Why else would Milly come to me? I think it must have happened at that train station. It fact, it could have been that very train, at that very time, just a year prior. I think it was Phantom that led her to me and now I must solve the case in order for her to find peace."

"Well, thank heavens we warned Jerry not to get too close," said Ginny.

"I say, do you think Peter had anything to do with the girl that drowned?" she asked.

I thought about it. "I'm not sure, Ginny. I do hope not. He did seem genuinely upset when he spoke about it." I frowned as something else dawned on me. "More than the others actually, and he was angry."

"Well, perhaps they were related in some way. Cousins, or brother and sister, perhaps?"

I stared at her. "Why, Ginny, I do believe you may be onto something."

CHAPTER NINE

There was nothing more we could do that night, so Ginny and I went to bed, having decided to sleep on what we knew so far and make plans the next day.

Rising early, I was in the kitchen preparing a light breakfast for the two of us whilst waiting for Ginny to wake up. There was no longer any need to prepare something for Milly, not now I knew who she was.

I should have seen it sooner. I'd fixed food for her but had never actually seen her eat and the dishes were empty and stacked on the draining board each time, I just assumed she'd eaten it.

I shook my head, thinking how easily we take things at face value. Believing what we see as opposed to delving a little deeper for the truth, rather like seeing a magician's trick. We know the lady isn't really sawed in half but accept that she is, and then watch as she is miraculously made whole again. It's just a trick of the eye, a sleight of hand, smoke and mirrors. *Probably because we want to believe*, I thought. Or more to the point because we don't want to believe the alternative.

"Good morning, Ella, what a marvellous night's sleep I had. That room is absolutely divine. And the peace! So much different to waking up to noisy London traffic," Ginny said, coming down the stairs at a light trot.

I smiled and handed her a cup of tea. She looked absolutely impeccable as usual in grey wool and cream cashmere. I on the other hand was in my drab working clothes. I couldn't see the point in getting dressed up to unpack boxes. But perhaps Ginny had something else in mind.

As we took our seats at the breakfast table she said, "I've had an idea, Ella, about how we can solve this case of yours. I think we need to get a confession of some sort out of Peter Clairmont. We need to know for sure the depth of his involvement before we start making accusations."

"Oh, I agree, Ginny, I was thinking the same thing actually, but how do you suppose we go about it?"

"Well, I think we need to get the police commissioner involved."

"Oh, Ginny, really!" I exclaimed. "Why on earth would the commissioner be interested in what we have to say? Especially as we have no real evidence at this point and only a ghost child and a phantom cat as witnesses." Goodness, it sounded even more ridiculous when I said it out loud.

"Because, dearest, Uncle Albert will do anything for his only god-daughter," Ginny said with a wink.

After breakfast, whilst I washed up the dishes, Ginny made a telephone call to her godfather. I had no idea what she told him but she bounced back into the kitchen with a look of glee.

"Well, that's settled, Uncle Albert will be here at two so shall we crack on with those boxes of yours whilst we're waiting?"

I must give Ginny her due. She certainly knew how to crack the whip and get things in motion.

An exhausting four and a half hours later the boxes were unpacked and everything assigned a home, although not all put away, but it was lovely to be able to see the floor again. As I pottered about making some lunch, Ginny went upstairs to change. I supposed I should do the same considering the importance of our guest. Plus of course I wanted to appear as credible as possible. I still didn't know what we were going to tell him but I'm sure Ginny would have a plan as she usually did.

At two-o'-clock on the dot I heard the gate creak and Ginny went to the door to greet our guest. I hadn't realised Sir Albert Montesford was the Police Commissioner now. I'd met him very briefly when Jerry and Ginny had married but we hadn't really spoken at length. However, I recognised him as he waddled up the path and enfolded Ginny in a huge hug. He was quite easily the largest man I had ever seen.

As they came inside I offered my hand to shake, but to my amazement he waved it away and instead engulfed me in a hug as big as the one he'd given Ginny. "Isobella, it's lovely to see you again, my dear. Now what's all this about you seeing murdered ghosts?"

I sighed. Well, there went my idea to introduce the concept gently. The clever plan I assumed Ginny had hatched was obviously to tell him everything at once, no matter how ludicrous it sounded. I couldn't begin to fathom whether or not he believed a word of it, but he was here and prepared to listen, which was a start. Now we just had to convince him.

I decided something a little stronger than tea was needed, so as we moved into the drawing room I went to the drinks cabinet and poured us all a snifter of whiskey. As I was arranging the glasses and decanter on the tray I saw Milly and Phantom descend the stairs.

Once we were all seated Albert spoke. "Now before we get to discussing the case in more detail you both need to understand something. No doubt Ginny has told you how I am wrapped around her little finger," he said, looking at me with a twinkle in his eye.

I smiled thinking, *yes, something like that.*

Albert continued, "Of course to some extent that is perfectly true, however first and foremost I am a policeman and a former solicitor. I deal in tangible truths and evidence; things I can see with my own eyes and prove exist within the scope of the law."

Oh, dear, my heart was sinking with each word he spoke.

"That said, I know you, Isobella dear, we are practically family after all, and as Ginny so rightly pointed out on the telephone, you are level-headed and not one for hysterics. To that end I am here and prepared to listen to your story objectively." He paused.

"But?" Ginny asked.

Albert nodded. "But I would like to see some evidence of the girl. A demonstration of some kind perhaps?"

I had no idea whether Milly would be able, let alone agreeable to, providing a demonstration. I glanced over at her questioningly. She sat chewing her lip. Then, after what

I could only assume was a signal from Phantom, nodded her head.

"Yes, I think that would be possible." I said. "Although, you must understand I have never asked her to do such a thing before and I can't guarantee what will happen, if it works at all."

"Is she in the room with us now?" Albert asked.

"Yes, she is," I said, but omitted mentioning she was sitting beside him.

"Very well, let's begin. Do we need to close the curtains and dim the lights?" he asked, perfectly seriously.

Ginny burst into peals of laughter. "Oh, Albert really, that nonsense is for charlatans and crooks. Ella is the genuine article, aren't you, darling?" she said, patting my hand. "There's really no need for theatrics. So what did you have in mind in order to convince you?"

Albert thought for a moment, then said, "Well, moving an object would seem to be the best solution. Perhaps the candelabra on the mantelshelf there? Would that be possible?"

I glanced above the fireplace. The candelabrum was solid silver and although it was heavy I felt sure Milly could lift it. However, there was a more immediate problem. She was too short to reach.

I was just about to voice my concern when Phantom nimbly leapt upon the shelf and swatted it with his paw. Such was the force of his swing that it flew through the air, scattering the candles to the four corners, and came to rest with a resounding crash in the middle of the table. I was exceptionally glad at that moment that Albert had not chosen my grandmother's crystal vase.

"Good God!" he exclaimed, pale-faced. After a moment or two of silence he held out his empty glass in a slightly shaking hand and said, "Be a dear and fill it up, would you?"

After dutifully refilling his glass, I sat back and watched as he very carefully examined the candelabrum. He then rose to examine the mantelshelf. I assumed he was looking for springs or something that would indicate it was a gimmick.

Seated once again, he said, "Well, I must admit that was an extraordinary display and I can see no obvious trickery involved, but I would like to see more."

"Of course," I said. "What else would you like to see?"

"That book on the shelf behind you, the green one with the bookmark just peeking out, can she bring it to me?"

I watched as Milly rose and went to the book in question, then turned back to observe Albert's reaction. From his perspective it would look as though the book were floating through mid-air.

Closer and closer it came, wobbling slightly as Milly strained under its weight. It was rather a large tome. As she neared Albert, she held it out in front of his nose and moved it slowly from side to side. I nearly laughed at her cheeky antics, especially as Albert's eyes were practically crossed in an attempt to keep it in view. Then Milly raised it as high as she could and let go. It landed with a resounding thump in his lap.

He sat staring at it, mesmerized, his hands in the air. I could see he was more than a little shocked so I leaned over and moved it. Placing it on the table seemed to break the spell. "Albert, it's just a book, really."

Glancing at Ginny I saw the look of shock and concern on her face too. I know she believed wholeheartedly in

Milly. She had also seen Phantom with her own eyes. But still, I supposed it was a different matter altogether seeing demonstrations such as these in broad daylight.

"Are you all right, Ginny?" I asked.

She nodded, her eyes still glued to the book. "Yes, I'm fine, Ella. It just makes it all seem so real, you know, seeing it like this. We really must help her."

I turned to Albert. "Have you seen enough, Albert?"

"Yes, I rather think I have," he said, reaching for his whiskey glass.

At that moment Phantom sprang up from the floor. In midair, for a split second, he materialised into his solid form for all to see, and then on the downward arc, he vanished.

I looked at Albert. "That was Phantom, my ghost cat," I said. Then I rose to get him a cloth to wipe the whiskey from his face.

CHAPTER TEN

A lbert decided to stay the night in order for us to formulate a plan. He'd already made some telephone calls to ask his men to find out as much as possible about one Peter Clairmont.

He'd also called Jerry, and once he'd explained the situation had asked that he get the next train down so he could talk to him face-to-face about what he knew.

Now Ginny was upstairs making up a room, whilst I was in the kitchen preparing dinner.

Shortly before six Jerry walked in, shaking out his umbrella and removing his sodden top-coat. I hadn't noticed but it had started to rain quite heavily.

"Why, Jerry, you're soaked! There's a fire lit in the drawing room. Go and get warm, and help yourself to a drink. Albert's already in there. He can tell you about today's events," I said.

"Thank you, Ella." He looked round appreciatively. "I must say I can see why you fell in love with this place, although it's certainly bigger than you led me to believe." He bent and gave me a quick kiss on the cheek. "You should have told me about the ghosts, you know. I would have understood."

"But would you have believed me? They're two quite different things."

He shrugged. "I most probably would have wanted proof like Albert. Perhaps you could organise that for later, do you think? I must say I'm rather intrigued."

"Well... I can't promise anything. I'd have to ask Milly. She's not a performing monkey, you know." Although Phantom was another story entirely, I thought. That last display surprised even me.

"I'll see what I can do. Now run along and get dry, and keep Albert company. He won't admit it but I think he's had rather a shock today."

As I was getting the roast out of the oven, I heard Albert say, "Jerry, good to see you, old boy. Thanks for coming down at such short notice. Got ourselves a bit of a mystery here which I'm hoping you can help with. I thought we'd discuss it properly with the girls over dinner. By the way, I got that latest book of yours. Fabulous stuff, and I didn't see the woman being the murderer."

"Well, that's a terrific compliment coming from the Police Commissioner, I must say," replied Jerry.

At that moment Ginny came waltzing down the stairs in yet another outfit and went to greet Jerry. "Darling, how good of you to come. It's so lovely to see you. And what do you think of the cottage? Marvellous, isn't it? Wait until you see our room, it's simply glorious. Now if you boys would deal with the wine, I'll help Ella with the food." A second later I heard the telephone ring and

Ginny call out, "Albert, it's for you." I assumed that meant there was some news.

Once we were all seated Albert got straight to the point.

"That was Detective Inspector Wilkes on the phone and he's found out a very interesting little tidbit about our Mr. Clairmont. But before I tell you more I'd like to hear what Jerry knows."

"Well, to be honest," Jerry began, "I think I know the least of all of us. However, I'll tell you what I can. Ginny, could you pass the salt, please, darling?"

Just as Ginny stretched out her hand the saltcellar rose from the table and travelled through the air before depositing itself in front of him.

Jerry shot up like a bullet from a gun, knocking his chair over in the process. "Bloody Hell!" he swore, backing away from the table.

"Yes, that was my reaction too," intoned Albert, glaring in disgust at the faint whiskey stains still visible down his shirt.

"So that was Milly?" Jerry asked, looking at me.

"Yes. I haven't quite perfected the art of levitating objects myself yet."

"You can sit down again now, Jerry, your dinner is getting cold," said Ginny. As if on cue, which of course it was, Jerry's chair rose and sat itself upright in front of the table once again. Then Milly went to sit on the window seat. The demonstration was over.

"It's all right, Jerry, you can sit. That was the demonstration you asked for. There'll be no more," I said.

He slowly moved back to the table and tentatively sat down.

"Well, I never," he said, shaking his head. "I don't suppose I really believed until I saw that."

"That's how I felt, darling," said Ginny. "Now we really must help poor Milly find peace. Let's not forget she's the reason we're all here. Tell us what you know about Peter."

Jerry nodded. "As you know, it was at the orphanage fundraiser where I first met him. You had a prior engagement so couldn't attend with me, if you remember? Well, he kind of latched onto me, said he was a fan of my books."

"And you believed him?" asked Albert.

"Well, yes. To be honest, there was no doubt in my mind. We discussed at length two or three of my books and made reference to more; it was obvious he'd read them. Then we went on to discuss his own writing."

"He's a writer, you say?" Albert said, making notes in a little black book.

"Well, he said he was although he has yet to publish anything."

"Yes, he said that at lunch on Sunday, didn't he?" Ginny said. "Historical novels, wasn't it?"

"That's right. He said at the fundraiser that he had one manuscript almost completed, set in Ireland, I believe."

"He told me that too when he walked me to the station," I said, nodding. "He went to live in Ireland after leaving the orphanage. Apparently he had an aunt and uncle on his mother's side and he was sent to live with them after his parent's death," I said.

"Did he say anything else to you, Ella?" asked Albert, pen poised at the ready.

I paused, thinking back. "He said that he was nine when his parents died and that he was at the orphanage for around four months whilst his next of kin were being traced. He also mentioned day-trips the children took, down here actually. He came a couple of times but the last time one of the girls drowned. The trips stopped after that."

"How did he seem to you when he relayed that incident?"

"Certainly upset. He did say that was the reason he worked for the orphanage, to help raise the money to employ qualified staff. He's of the opinion that had there been someone there that day who was trained, the girl could have been saved."

Albert was nodding and making notes.

"Ella and I wondered if the girl could have been his sister," said Ginny.

"And why would you think that?" asked Albert.

"He pointed out her photograph to Ella and she thought he seemed … how did you put it, Ella?"

"He seemed to take it more personally. He was quite angry about Mary actually, more so than the others, but of course that could just be because he witnessed it. I said at the time how traumatic it must have been for him and the other children."

"Her name was Mary, you say?" Albert asked.

I nodded.

"No other names, I suppose?"

"No, he just said Mary. Although the orphanage will have the details, I expect. In fact it may be written in the display cabinet somewhere and I missed it."

"Do you think they could be related, Albert?" asked Jerry.

"It's possible. I'll have one of my men find out her full name and details surreptitiously. We don't want to tip our hand too soon. However, she certainly won't be related to Peter Clairmont."

"Whatever do you mean, Albert? I thought you just said Peter and this girl could be related?" said an exasperated Ginny. I must admit I was thoroughly confused myself.

"Oh, the girl and our man could be related, but I'm afraid the real Peter Clairmont died in a suspicious house fire in Yorkshire some eighteen months ago."

"What?" we all exclaimed in unison.

"Oh, yes. DI Wilkes was adamant," Albert said.

"But how do you know it's the same man that our Peter Clairmont is impersonating?" Jerry asked.

"Because of the information left in the wallet that Ella found. It contained, amongst other things, a National Identity Card."

Of course, I remembered now. I'd seen it when I was first looking through the wallet. I'd not taken much notice of what it was at the time, I'd been too shocked to see Peter's name on it.

"Really? I thought those things were scrapped after the war," said Jerry.

"Exactly, Jerry. You've hit the nail on the head so to speak. Considering they were first introduced in 1915 and put to sleep in 1919, this would mean our man would be, at a minimum, thirty-two years of age."

"Well, I don't suppose that's outside the realms of possibility. Although I must admit he does look considerably younger," said Jerry.

"I agree," Ginny said, wrinkling her nose in protest. "He doesn't look a year over twenty-five, if you ask me, but that still doesn't prove anything, Albert."

"Not alone of course, however my man Wilkes did some extra digging. It turns out that the NIC number on the card was registered in 1916 to a Mr. Peter Clairmont, age thirty-four."

"Oh, I say, that would put him at fifty-three today then," said Jerry.

"Precisely," said Albert. "The same age as the deceased incidentally."

"I'd wager he's taken other documents then. I mean, *if* he's taken on the identity of this man, then it makes sense to go the whole hog, as it were and take the lot," said Jerry.

"Heavens, he probably took his money as well," exclaimed Ginny.

"Aren't we forgetting one vital piece of information?" I asked, looking at the faces before me. Jerry and Ginny waited but I could see Albert knew what I was going to say.

"If our Peter has taken this man's identity and goodness knows what else, then he must have killed him to do it. The Peter Clairmont we know is a murderer."

I glanced over at Milly who had been silently listening to our exchange. "But I think we knew that already," I said softly.

CHAPTER ELEVEN

"So what exactly are we proposing to do now?" asked Ginny as we settled in the drawing room with coffee. I glanced at the mantel clock and saw it was already nine-thirty. It was going to be a late night.

"Hmm, we obviously need to flush him out somehow," said Jerry. "Wouldn't you agree, Albert?"

"I would indeed, but it's paramount he doesn't suspect anything. I've already got a man on his tail to see where he goes and who he contacts, and I've dispatched another up to Yorkshire to see what he can discover up there. What we need, as a matter of some urgency, are the details of the drowned girl. I believe once we have that information we'll find out who this man really is."

"Do you have someone looking for information about Mary?" I asked.

"I do," Albert said. "However, I've told him to steer clear of the orphanage at present, just find out what he can from other sources. If we go in there and start asking questions our man will smell a rat for sure, and if he runs we may never find him again."

I thought about that for a minute. I'd been ruminating over an idea ever since Albert had revealed that Peter Clairmont was actually a fraud. And not only a fraud, but a probable murderer too. I glanced once again at Milly and made up my mind.

"Well, of course I could go in there. He's already expecting me with the donations, remember?"

"Absolutely not, Ella," said Jerry immediately. "You'd be going straight into the lion's den. It's too dangerous."

"Jerry, he doesn't know that we're onto him," I said. "What would seem more suspicious is if I didn't go when I've already said I would."

"Oh, dear, Ella is right, Jerry. She's going to have to make good on that promise sooner or later," Ginny said.

Jerry got up and started to pace back and forth, running his hand through his hair. He was terribly worried, I could see that, but I also knew I was the only one who could get close enough to Peter to find out the truth.

"He told me he found me easy to talk to, Jerry. Now that may very well be a ruse but I have to take that chance."

"I don't like it, Ella. You'll be vulnerable and alone. I can't let you put yourself in harm's way like that."

"But I won't be alone, Jerry," I said. "I can hardly carry the boxes myself. I'll need assistance." Turning to Albert I asked, "Albert, do you have a man who could help? Someone who could be undercover to accompany me as a chauffeur and delivery boy?"

Albert stood. "Ella, I do believe you've hit on a way to get the information we need. And yes, I do have a man perfect for the job. However, I echo Jerry's concerns. This could be dangerous. If he suspects for even one minute why you are really there, it could turn nasty and we don't know what he will do if cornered."

"And we certainly know he's capable of murder," said Jerry.

Ginny leaned over and took my hand. "Ella, are you absolutely sure about this, darling? It doesn't have to be you, you know. I'm sure given a bit of time we could work out another plan."

"Honestly, I'll be fine. I'll have Albert's man with me, I'll be in the orphanage where there are other staff and children and I promise I won't do anything to put myself at risk."

I looked up at Jerry and Albert, then back at Ginny.

"So does that put everyone's mind at ease?"

Jerry finally sat back down and leaned back, saying, "The only thing that would put my mind at ease would be if you weren't going. But I can see yours is made up. However, I'd like some assurances from Albert that there will be someone other than his undercover chap looking out for you."

"Of course," said Albert. "That goes without saying. I'll post several of my men in the vicinity."

"Good," I said, standing and addressing them all. "I suggest that we do this as soon as possible. Ginny, I'll need your help with some donations. I have some items I can get together, but not nearly enough."

"I have more than enough, Ella. Jerry and I can go back tomorrow and sort out some items. All right, darling?"

"Yes, all right. I'll throw in a signed copy of my latest novel too. I doubt he has it, as it's only just been published."

"Jerry, that's an excellent idea," I said. "I'll say it's a gift for him personally from you. That should get him thinking we are all friends, and stop him suspecting anything."

"And I can have my men ready as soon as you give the word," confirmed Albert. "I'll send Jimmy, one of my best officers, with you as chauffeur. When did you have in mind?"

"How about the day after tomorrow? We should have everything boxed up by then," I said.

Everybody nodded.

"Right, well, Thursday it is then. Now if you don't mind, it's been rather a long day and I'd like to head up to bed."

Ginny rose too. "I think we'll all benefit from a good night's sleep actually. We have a busy day ahead of us tomorrow."

"Yes, and possibly a perilous one after that," Jerry warned.

It wasn't until much later that I remembered Jerry's words and realized just how much we'd all underestimated Peter Clairmont.

CHAPTER TWELVE

Even though we'd all gone to bed late the night before, the next morning found us all up, dressed, and having breakfast by six-thirty.

I for one had slept solidly for two or three hours, and then had found myself wide awake, at four am. I dozed on and off for a while, during which time my mind ran through everything we had planned, over and over in a never-ending loop. This had left me feeling groggy. Consequently, my head felt as though it were stuffed with cotton wool, and I could feel the onset of a headache.

Looking around the table, I could see that Ginny and Jerry were feeling the same. Albert, on the other hand, looked as he always did. I supposed it was because he was used to dealing with nasty business like this, whereas the rest of us were complete novices.

As he began to liberally spread his toast with butter, topping it off with strawberry preserve, he looked at me.

"Ella, how are you feeling about everything this morning? Still wanting to go ahead? I know how different things can seem in the cold light of day, and I want to make sure you're not taking on more than you can handle."

"I'm determined to see this through, Albert. I admit to being nervous, but I suspect that's perfectly normal considering the circumstances."

"I'd be more than happy to go in your place, Ella," Jerry said.

"I know that, Jerry, I really do, and I appreciate it. But I think he will be more open and forthcoming with a woman. All I'm going to do is to engage him in conversation and get Mary's full name. It's not as though I intend to go in and accuse him of murder. I can't see why he would suspect anything from that. Then I simply pass on what I've found out to Albert."

Jerry sighed. "Well, when you put it like that, I suppose it's simple enough. But promise you won't do anything foolhardy."

"I promise," I said. "Now, what are the plans for today?"

"I think the best thing is for us to help you pack up your donations here. Then we can all head back to London. I'd feel much happier if you stayed the night with Jerry and me. We can sort out what we intend to give this afternoon. Then we'll be ready in the morning. Does that work for you, Albert?" Ginny asked.

"Yes, that would work out particularly well. I motored down here, so I'll give you all a lift back then head to the yard and apprise DI Wilkes."

"I'll need to telephone Peter to let him know I'll be there tomorrow," I said. "I don't want to just turn up. We need to be sure he's not otherwise engaged. Jerry, do you have the telephone number?"

Jerry rooted through his wallet and brought out a card. "Here it is."

"I must say, I think you're awfully brave, Ella," said Ginny. "Even if poor Milly were an accidental murder, Peter is certainly guilty of doing away with the real Clairmont."

Jerry chuckled, and swapped an amused glance with Albert. "Ginny, there is no such thing as an accidental murder. It's either one or the other. I think the term you're looking for is manslaughter."

"Well, I think that's just splitting hairs, Jerry. The point I'm trying to make is that this chap is dangerous, and capable of doing the most awful things. To go and knowingly confront him, as Ella is doing, takes a lot of guts. And I admire her tremendously."

"Of course, you are right, Ginny. We all admire what Ella is doing," agreed Jerry.

Glancing at the clock, I noticed how early it still was. "I'll call at a more reasonable hour. In the meantime, Ginny and I can make a start on the packing."

A couple of hours later, Ginny and I had managed to scrape together a couple of boxes, mostly linens with a few books and games, and a few toys that had belonged to Jerry and me as children. It really was a paltry offering. I was glad Ginny had volunteered to see what she had too.

"Well, I suppose it's time I made that telephone call," I said.

But before I could do so, it rang. It was DI Wilkes for Albert. Ginny, Jerry and I stood in the background listening to one side of the conversation.

"Hello?"

"Ah, Samuel, what's the latest?"

"They can't?"

"No, I see."

"Good idea. Yes, see what you can find and we'll go from there."

"Of course, will do."

"Yes, I'm heading back shortly and will update you then. It'll probably be tomorrow. Just awaiting confirmation."

"Of course. Cheerio."

Albert replaced the receiver and turned to us all, notebook and pencil in hand.

"That was DI Wilkes with an update. Our man in Yorkshire wasted no time upon arrival. Talked to the local constabulary and the witnesses, and visited what was left of the crime scene." He paused, sighing.

Ginny had her arms crossed and was impatiently tapping her foot. "Uncle Albert, please just get on with it. Was it him?"

"Actually," I said, "would you mind if I made that call first? I'd rather do it before Albert tells us what he knows."

"Of course not, you go ahead and I'll make some tea. We can meet in the drawing room shortly." Then she turned on her heel toward the kitchen.

I took the card Jerry had given me and went to the telephone. Taking a deep breath, I dialled and waited for someone to pick up. I had expected a secretary to answer so was surprised into sudden silence when I heard Peter's voice boom in my ear.

"Peter Clairmont, good morning."

"Hello? Is there anybody there?"

Gathering both my wits and my courage, I managed to answer.

"Peter, it's Ella."

"Ella, hello. Well, I must say I didn't expect it to be you. Are you well?"

"I'm very well, Peter, thank you. I hope I'm not interrupting anything?"

"No, not at all. Just some paperwork. How can I help?"

"I just wondered if it would be convenient for me to come tomorrow with the donations?"

"Goodness, that was quick work. I didn't expect you to have it done already."

"Oh, well, it was good timing for me actually. I'm still unpacking, remember, so it was no trouble."

"Ah, of course. Well, I'm tied up in meetings in the morning but I'm free around noon if that works for you. Would you like me to come and get them … save you the journey?"

"Oh, no, that's quite all right, Peter, I've already arranged for some help. Noon is fine. I'll see you then."

"Yes, all right, see you then."

I hung up and leaned against the wall for a moment. I hadn't realised how nervous I would be and my heart was pounding. I just hoped I'd sounded sincere and calm. Although, if that was the result of a simple telephone conversation, it didn't bode well for my meeting him face-to-face.

I shrugged the thought off. No point worrying about it now the appointment was made and the plan was in motion.

Moving into the drawing room, I sat and helped myself to tea. I turned as Albert began speaking.

"As I was saying, my man in Yorkshire has been very busy in the short time he has been there. Unfortunately, we still have nothing concrete. Mr. Peter Clairmont Senior was a widower. Lived alone and was a very private man. Kept himself to himself and rarely ventured out, except to go to church. He had no live-in staff, just a daily who was a maid-of-all-work. Consequently my man's finding it difficult to track down anyone who knew him."

"So we're no further forward. We can't say for certain that our man was even there except for the identification card in his wallet, which he could have got from a third party," sighed Jerry.

"Well, certainly at the moment that's the lie of the land. However, my man is still digging up there, so all is not lost," Albert added.

"But without definitive proof it still means Ella will have to go and see Peter tomorrow, won't it?" asked Ginny.

"Only if she's comfortable doing so, Ginny, as I said before," answered Albert. "We're on the case and if there's something to find then we'll find it. My gut feeling is that our man was involved. But if you want to expedite matters then this is currently the best option we have, yes."

Albert rose and stood in front of the mantel.

"There is one interesting piece of information he found though. One woman witness, a member of the same church as the deceased, remembers him mentioning a niece who died as a child."

"Mary!" gasped Ginny.

"That was my first thought," said Albert. "She also said he mentioned that the sister was a 'bad lot.'"

I frowned. "That doesn't make sense. How would he know that if she died at the orphanage?"

"To be honest, Ella, my man was of the opinion that this woman was confused and probably thinking of someone else. She's very old and not the most reliable of witnesses sadly. 'Losing her marbles' was the way he described her."

I nodded. That seemed the most logical explanation.

"DI Wilkes is trying to find photographic evidence of our Peter Clairmont. We can show it around up there and see if anyone recognises him," Albert continued.

"Well, I can help with that," said Jerry. "There was a reporter from the Times at the fundraiser. It was a rather large society event, you know, so quite a lot of well-known faces. There was a spot in the paper about it. I daresay the photographer that was with him got several shots."

"Excellent thinking, Jerry. I'll call Wilkes back and let him know," said Albert, who was once again scribbling in his little black book.

I stood up, smoothing down my skirt.

"Well, if everyone is ready, I think the best thing is to head up to London now. There's still a lot to do before tomorrow."

Fifteen minutes later the car was packed and we were heading over the bridge to the mainland. This time tomorrow, I thought, I'd be entering the lion's den.

CHAPTER THIRTEEN

E
n route back to London in Albert's car, the conversation naturally continued where we had left off.

More than once I was asked if I still wanted to go through with the plan. And if I were being honest with myself, I was beginning to have second thoughts. Mainly because, like Albert, I too had a gut feeling that Peter Clairmont was involved in the death of the man in Yorkshire.

But then my meditations turned to Milly and her need for justice. I had to continue on my path for her sake, otherwise she would never find peace. And aside from that, if I didn't, I would have a ghost in my house forever. Terrific fun at gatherings, I'll admit, but hardly fair.

No. I'd been chosen for a reason and I had to believe that reason would also mean a positive outcome.

"I think Milly found out, you know." I said.

"What do you mean?" said Jerry, turning to face Ginny and me in the back seat.

"I've no doubt now that Milly brought that wallet to me in the hopes I'd realise what the card inside meant. I believe she found out Peter Clairmont was an impostor. And he had to silence her."

"That poor child," said Ginny. "She must have been terrified."

"There's something else too. I can't make sense of why he told us he'd once lived at the orphanage," I said, perplexed.

"Did he not explain that? Because his parents died?" Ginny asked. "Also the reason he was working there was because of the girl that died."

"That's what he said Ginny, yes. But why say it? The man he is supposed to be impersonating wasn't an orphan."

Ginny continued to look confused, but Jerry latched on right away.

"Of course! You think he let it slip by accident?"

I nodded. "I think he must have. I think he let his guard down when he was with us all for lunch and it slipped out. At that point it was too late to retract the information. So he told a little more and then I suspect he hoped we'd think it unimportant and forget about it."

"Which we would have done had it not been for Milly," said Jerry. "But, of course, he doesn't know about her."

"Exactly," I said.

"I'm not sure I follow," said Ginny. "Are you saying he was an orphan, or he wasn't?"

"Oh, I'm sure he was. But we know it wasn't under the name Peter Clairmont. He told us by accident, Ginny. And by doing so he blew his cover."

"Good heavens!" Ginny cried. "I understand now. I've always said that if you lie you'll get found out. It's so easy to lose track and trip yourself up. I wonder if the other staff realise he's not who he says he is?"

That startled me. I'd never given a thought to the other staff, so focused was I on Milly and our suspect.

"That's an angle my men and I are pursuing, Ginny. Ella, that was a fine piece of detective work. You too, Jerry."

"Thank you, old boy. It just goes to show that Peter isn't as clever as he thinks he is. He's already made one crucial mistake. What's the betting he'll make another?"

"I agree," Albert nodded. "And I'll even stick my neck out and say I do believe we're one step ahead of our quarry."

We were soon to find out just how wrong Albert was.

Once back at the apartment, Jerry disappeared to work on his latest manuscript. Apparently, this 'Clairmont Caper' as he'd dubbed it, had given him a wealth of new ideas.

An hour later he popped his head round the door of Ginny's dressing room, where he found us practically buried beneath huge mounds of linens and clothing.

"Good grief, Ginny, are we moving out?" he asked.

"Of course not, Jerry. Ella and I are sorting out things for the orphanage."

I actually wasn't doing much sorting at all. So far all I'd done was barely catch the various items Ginny had thrown from drawers and cupboards. I was amazed at just how much these seemingly small items of furniture could hold. It was like an optical illusion.

Jerry eyed a silk and sequinned evening gown. "I'm not sure that frock would be appropriate."

"Don't be silly, Jerry. That's for Ella," Ginny's muffled voice said from the depths of the wardrobe.

"Ah, of course. Well, here's the book. I'll just put it here, shall I?" he said, eying a particularly precarious pile.

"Yes, of course, dear, that's fine," Ginny said, without looking up.

Needless to say, as soon as he put it down the whole lot teetered for a second before toppling and crashing down in a great avalanche, finally coming to rest an inch before my feet.

"Ah. Right. Jolly good. Well, I'll leave you to it then, shall I?" Jerry said and, making a hasty retreat, went back to his writing.

Ginny, having extricated herself from the depths of the closet, turned and looked aghast at the mess.

"Oh, dear. Do you think this is too much?" she asked me.

For a split second, there was absolute silence, then I burst into peals of laughter. I couldn't help it. Collapsing on the nearest soft pile, I gasped, "Ginny, you are a darling, truly. We can barely move in here, I haven't seen the sofa for hours, I'm on the floor and our only exit is blocked."

She came and sat beside me and began to laugh too.

"So you're politely saying there's too much. Well, let's just pack up half that pile over there and call it a day. I'll have Betty sort the rest out later."

That evening, Jerry came into the drawing room where Ginny and I sat talking by the fire.

"I've just seen the collection in the hall. I must say, you girls did a remarkable job getting all that stuff into just three boxes. Well done."

We just looked at each other and smiled. We both loved Jerry dearly but sometimes he seemed to live in a different world.

"So, Ella. How are you feeling about tomorrow?" he asked, handing us both a drink, then sitting in the chair next to mine, while Ginny lounged on the sofa.

"I'm a little nervous. I keep telling myself that Peter doesn't know the real reason I'll be there, but I can't help being affected by what we've uncovered. I also haven't seen Milly or Phantom since dinner last night. I don't quite know what to make of that."

At that moment the telephone rang and Jerry went to answer it.

"That was Uncle Albert," he said when he returned. "Nothing particularly useful to report, I'm afraid. They managed to get an image from the press photographer, but only one. He was in profile in a group of other chaps, so it's not very good. I'm surprised there's not more. My feeling is that he deliberately avoided having his photograph taken. A sign he's hiding something in my opinion. Albert may have some more news on that tomorrow. He also said his man Jimmy would be here with a car around 11:30 in the morning. That gives us time to pack everything up and for Ella to be there by noon."

"Did he say anything about the other orphanage staff?" I asked.

Jerry shook his head. "Not in so many words. He's spoken to those in charge, the ones that hired Peter. But according to their paperwork, references and so on, Peter Clairmont is an upstanding character and above reproach."

"Well, of course he would be, wouldn't he?" I said, exasperated. "But it's not Peter Clairmont they've given the job to."

"No. It sounds as though they don't know he's an impostor. From what Albert said he's digging a little deeper, but doesn't want to scupper your attempts tomorrow. It's important Peter doesn't get wind of what's going on. Albert's primary concern is your safety at this point, Ella."

I doubted I would sleep at all that night but knew I needed to get as much rest as possible. I needed to have my wits about me to meet Peter Clairmont. The man was clever. I just hoped I could match his cleverness.

CHAPTER FOURTEEN

By the time I got down to the car the next morning, Jimmy Smith was just loading up the last of the boxes. He was a slightly rotund man, short, with a shock of unruly brown hair just beginning to grey at the temples.

"Good morning, Miss," he said, whilst dabbing a sweating brow with a handkerchief. He was rather red in the face and I was concerned he'd over-exerted himself.

"Good morning, Mr. Smith. Are you quite all right?"

"Oh, yes, Miss, nothing to worry about. Just getting over a slight cold, that's all. Are you ready to go?"

I turned and gave Ginny and Jerry a quick wave, then got in the car. We'd already said our goodbyes back in the apartment. Ginny was rather tearful so I insisted she stay inside. Jerry gave me a quick hug.

"Now be careful, old girl. No taking any chances."

I assured him I wouldn't.

It wasn't very far to the orphanage but the traffic was particularly heavy, so the journey took a little longer than expected. Mr. Smith and I spent the time going over the details.

"I expect there will be someone to help you unload the boxes at the other end," I said. "Perhaps Peter will offer."

"Well, I daresay that'll be true, miss, but I'd rather do it myself. I'm here as a paid delivery man so I need to keep up the charade."

"Yes, of course, I understand. But you will be inside with me, won't you?"

"Oh, yes. I've been given strict instructions not to let you out of my sight."

I smiled. It seemed as though Albert had thought of everything and it gave me a sense of relief to know I wouldn't be alone.

As we pulled up in front of the orphanage, we found Peter Clairmont standing at the door waiting for us.

"He's a bit keen, isn't he?" Jimmy commented under his breath. "Well, this is it, miss. Keep calm and don't worry. I'll be right there with you."

I nodded, thanked Jimmy and, taking a deep breath, exited the car. I glanced round briefly to see if I could spot Albert's men, but while I knew they were there, they were very well hidden.

"Hello, Peter, I do apologise for being late but the traffic was terrible."

"Not to worry, Ella. I've the rest of the afternoon off actually so it makes no difference."

Jimmy came over, cap in hand and looked at Peter. "Where do you want these boxes then, gov?"

I winced, wondering if Jimmy was over-playing his part, but Peter didn't seem to notice.

"You can put them in the common room. First door on the left," Peter said, pointing. As Jimmy came over, struggling with one of the boxes, I waited for Peter to offer his help. He didn't. But as luck would have it the common room was exactly where I wanted to be.

"I'll show you the way, Mr. Smith." I said. I'd decided I had to be a little more demonstrative. I didn't want Peter to take control. My plan was to be in and out as quickly as possible and if Peter were allowed to take charge it might take far longer. Plus I might not be successful in obtaining the information I sought. No, I had to force his hand.

With new determination, I marched up the steps with Peter at my side and Jimmy huffing and puffing behind me.

"Oh, I've just remembered, Peter. Jerry sent this for you." I handed him a small parcel wrapped in brown paper and tied with string. While he was opening it, I moved into the common room and wandered down to the display case at the end.

"Well, I must say this is very kind of Jerry. A signed copy of his latest novel. I haven't got around to purchasing it yet. I'll look forward to reading it."

"Yes, he thought you'd like it. I'll let him know how pleased you are," I said, gazing in the cabinet.

"Is there something in particular you're looking for in there?" Peter asked, and I wondered if I'd imagined the sharpness in his tone.

"Not really, no. I just wondered why there were no names listed beside the pictures. It seems strange to remember them in this way but have no names."

"Well, there's a perfectly simple explanation for that. I haven't got around to doing it yet," Peter said.

"Oh, I see," I said, nodding. "Well, perhaps you could tell me their names?"

I could see Peter's reflective frown in the glass of the case and realised I'd not been subtle enough.

"Why do you want to know, Ella?"

Oh, dear. This wasn't going to plan at all. I was definitely raising his suspicions. I had to think of something… and fast. I decided an abbreviated version of the truth would be best, even though I had sworn never to mention I'd been married. But I couldn't think of another angle under such pressured circumstances. I made a bit of a show of gathering myself together and then began.

"I'm not sure how much you know about me, Peter, but I'm a widow. John, my husband, died nearly five years ago. We were only married for two years. We had planned on having a family but he was taken from me before …" I sighed and took a handkerchief from my purse. Quickly dabbing my eyes, I replaced it, then looked directly at him.

"I'm sorry. I still find it difficult to talk about. The fact is I've been thinking about these poor children since I first saw them. They seem to have lodged themselves in my heart. Their stories are so sad, especially the poor child that drowned. It seems such a senseless waste of life."

Peter gently laid a hand on my shoulder.

"I'm terribly sorry, Ella. I didn't realise what you'd been through. Of course, I now understand why this would affect you so much. Look, I have all the old records in my office. Come on, we can go through them together."

As we walked back to the other end of the room, we found Jimmy patiently sitting on a chair. He'd moved all the boxes already and was waiting for me.

"Thank you, Mr. Smith, you can go now. I'll see Miss Bridges safely back."

I shot a panicked glance at Jimmy—this wouldn't do at all.

"Oh, well, I can't do that, I'm afraid, sir. The lady has hired me for a full day's work, you see."

Oh well done, Jimmy! I thought. *Very quick thinking.*

"Is that so?" Peter asked, looking at me. I could see immediately that he was terribly annoyed although was trying to hide it.

"Yes, it is. I have several other errands to run, which Mr. Smith is kindly helping me with. You won't mind waiting, Jimmy, while Peter and I go through some old records?"

"Of course not, miss. You go ahead with the gentleman and I'll wait here for you." He then produced a series of particularly loud sneezes.

"Oh, dear. Are you sure you'll be all right?" I asked. I was becoming increasingly concerned that his cold was a little more serious than he was letting on.

"No need to worry about me, I'll be fine. 'Tis just a bit of a cold, that's all."

"I'll have some tea brought out to you, Mr. Smith. That should warm you up a bit while you wait. Unfortunately the heating isn't working at the moment," Peter said.

"That's very kind of you, sir, thank you."

Peter nodded and then turned on his heel towards the office. I smiled briefly at Jimmy, who returned it with a wink, then set off in Peter's wake. Very soon I would have the information Albert needed and we could leave.

When I got to the office, Peter wasn't there. I was wondering where on earth he'd got to when he came in behind me and I nearly jumped out of my skin. "I've just ordered some tea for us and your man. Shouldn't be long. Please have a seat."

He gestured to the only comfortable piece of furniture in the room—a club chair, upholstered in soft, green damask. It looked incredibly out of place in such an austere setting. The rest of the office by contrast was dark and gloomy. With no window to let in any natural light the only source of illumination was a desk lamp. It was thoroughly depressing. Much like what I'd seen in the rest of the building. I could only suppose this chair had been a recent donation.

As Peter was rifling through an oak filing cabinet, the door opened and a tray of tea was brought in by the maid.

"Ah, Maude, thank you. Would you be so kind as to take a cup to Mr. Smith? He's in the common room."

"Of course, sir." She picked up an already filled cup and, with a brief glance at me, left, closing the door behind her.

Peter filled the other two cups from the teapot and left me to add my own milk and sugar. He returned to the cabinet, periodically taking a folder and placing it on a small pile.

Just as he was turning several minutes later, files in hand, a breathless and panicked Maude crashed into the room.

"Oh, Mr. Clairmont sir, you better come quick. That gentleman wot was in the common room 'as collapsed!"

"What?" I ran out with Peter, who was yelling for Maude to fetch the Matron.

I found Jimmy on the floor, unconscious, but breathing.

The Matron must have been nearby because she was suddenly at my side, examining him.

"He'll be all right. He's just fainted. But he's running a slight temperature. Maude and I will take him to the infirmary and get him settled. Do you know if he's been ill?" This directed at me.

"He mentioned that he was just getting over a cold, but that's all I know."

She nodded. "Well, that would do it. He's obviously done too much. Ah, look, he's coming round."

I glanced down and Jimmy's eyes were fluttering.

"Maude, help me get him in the chair."

I hadn't heard Maude come back, but she moved into view, wheeling a wicker chair.

Jimmy focused on my face. "Sorry about this, miss. I'll be all right in a couple of minutes."

"It doesn't matter in the slightest, Mr. Smith. Matron's going to take you to the infirmary ... "

Jimmy began to protest, which resulted in a coughing fit.

"I'll have no argument now. You need to rest and it's only for a short while. Matron will take care of you until you're feeling better. I'd be much happier knowing you are all right. I'll be along shortly."

He nodded, looking highly embarrassed, but resigned to his fate.

As I watched Matron and Maude wheel Jimmy away, I felt a hand on my elbow. I jumped, having forgotten Peter was there in my worry.

"He'll be all right, Ella, he's in good hands. Let's go back to the office and finish our tea. By then Matron will have Mr. Smith settled and I'll take you to him."

CHAPTER FIFTEEN

ack at the office, having hurriedly finished my tea, I grabbed my bag. Turning, I noticed Peter was putting back the files.

"Perhaps we could take those along with us?" I suggested. Although Jimmy was at the forefront of my concerns, I hadn't lost sight of the real reason I had come. I needed to see those files.

"That won't be possible, I'm afraid. It's policy the files don't leave the office. However, we'll come back after we've been to the infirmary and go through them. I'm sure by the time we get there, Mr. Smith will have recovered."

"Yes, of course, I'm sure you're right," I said, smiling.

As Peter locked the office door, I turned to go in the direction Matron had gone, but Peter turned the opposite way.

"We'll go this way. It's the staff entrance and much quicker."

He strode down the corridor, turned left and opened a door at the end of another hallway, gesturing me to go through first. We entered what looked like a schoolroom, with a chalkboard on the wall and twenty small desks and chairs. All were empty. Peter locked the door and then proceeded to another at the far end of the room.

"Are there no classes today?" I asked.

"No, the children and staff are all out on a trip to the museum."

As I exited the classroom, I found myself in yet another corridor.

"This building is much larger than I thought," I said nervously. I didn't like how things were progressing. It felt very much like the lion's den Jerry had mentioned.

Peter smiled. "Yes, it's a veritable maze and very easy to get lost if you don't know where you're going."

"How far is it? We seemed to have been walking rather a long time," I asked. It wasn't the short cut Peter had intimated.

"Just through that door in front."

At that moment a streak of black shot past me and stopped at the door, hissing at us. Phantom! This was definitely a warning.

I stopped. "Actually, Peter, I think I'd like to go back now. I've just remembered I was supposed to meet Ginny. She'll worry if I'm not there."

He stopped with his hands on his hips, looking at the floor. He was shaking his head and laughing in a sarcastic way. Looking up, he came towards me and grabbed my upper arm in a vice-like grip.

"Did anyone ever tell you, Ella, you are an appalling liar?"

"Peter, that hurts, and what do you mean I'm lying? I can assure you I'm not. Please let go of my arm this instant."

"I think not, dear Ella. You're coming with me," and he dragged me to the door. I fought as hard as I could but he was too strong. As he pushed me through the doorway I heard a click and a light came on. In front were a series of steps heading down. It was a basement. I took a step back and felt something sharp dig into my lower back.

"One single word and I will shoot. Do you understand?"

Oh, my God, he had a gun! What an idiot I'd been. I couldn't believe how badly Jerry, Ginny, Albert and I had underestimated Peter.

"Please," I whimpered, barely recognising my own voice.

I felt him grab my hair and wrench my head back. I let out an involuntary cry of pain.

"This is your last warning, Ella. One more peep out of you and I will kill you. Now move!" He jabbed the gun into my spine.

I took a faltering step forward and slowly began to descend the stairs, tears trickling down my face. It was like descending an abyss into hell and I'd never been more scared in my entire life.

At the bottom of the stairs, Peter pushed me roughly to the right and turned on another light. We were in the boiler room. There were huge pipes running along the walls and disappearing up through the ceiling. To the left was an old sink and on the right a huge unlit furnace. Stacked against the walls were a myriad of broken items; several bedsteads and mattresses, chairs missing legs and wicker baskets with gaping holes. Everywhere had a layer of black soot. It was dark, cold and filthy.

But what frightened me more than anything was the single, solitary chair set in the middle of the room.

It was an old dentist's chair. A black and chrome monstrosity that spoke of untold pain, but horrifically it had been adapted. It now looked like an instrument of torture.

"No," I whispered and backed away. The barrel of the gun was once more cruelly shoved into my back.

"Yes," Peter whispered malevolently in my ear.

The chair was made from metal but had a worn black leather seat, back, arms and headrest. Attached to the arms and the head were thick restraints. He meant to strap me down! I couldn't let him do it, for as soon as I was strapped in I would never escape. I would be at the mercy of a killer. But what could I do? I had to think, and quickly.

As I was about to speak I heard a voice calling from above—salvation!

"Help! Down here! Please help me," I cried.

I felt sudden pain as Peter backhanded me across the face and I fell to the floor. I could taste blood in my mouth and I felt sick and dizzy. The pain was excruciating and I prayed I wouldn't pass out.

I felt myself lifted bodily and thrown in the chair. Before I could recover my senses my worst fears came true and I was crudely restrained.

I thought my shouts had been in vain, but then I heard someone coming down the steps. *Thank goodness.*

"Look out, he's got a gun," I shouted in warning to whoever was coming to my rescue. I didn't want them to get hurt too.

"For god's sake, can't you keep her quiet?" said a voice. As she rounded the corner I saw it was the Matron.

"Why aren't you with Mr. Smith?" demanded Peter.

"Calm down, I've given him another sedative. Combined with the one I slipped into his tea he'll be out for hours, and I've sent Maude home. It's just you and me, dear brother."

Brother?

"Ah, look, the light has dawned. Yes, this is my sister," Peter said with a twisted smile.

Suddenly it began to make sense. The woman from the church in Yorkshire saying the sister was 'a bad lot.' She was no more senile than I was, but no one had taken her seriously.

I realised then just how hopeless my situation was. There was no way to escape with the two of them against me. But I wasn't going to die not knowing the truth.

"I thought Mary was your sister?"

Matron stared at Peter. "You told her?"

"No, of course not. She must have guessed. Didn't I tell you she was poking around asking too many questions? It would seem our dear Ella here has pieced together more than we thought."

"Peter, I really don't understand. I hardly know anything. You're right when you say I guessed Mary was your sister, but that was only because you seemed more upset about her than the others. It was a tragic accident. But what does that have to do with me?"

Peter cocked his head to one side and I could see he was deciding whether or not to believe me. Perhaps I was getting through.

"Well, unfortunately, Ella, even if I did believe you had simply made a clever guess, the fact now is you do know too much."

I stared at him, my heart beating a wild staccato in my throat. He had no idea how much I had pieced together but he would find out soon enough. I did know too much and I realised what he said was true. He couldn't possibly let me go now. There and then I resolved to get some answers. To do what I had set out to do: learn the truth for Milly's sake.

"Is that why you killed Millicent? Because she found out you were an impostor? That the real Peter Clairmont died in a fire eighteen months ago?"

Two single strides and he had caught me by the throat. His eyes bored into mine as though he were trying to see my very thoughts. Spittle caught at the corners of his mouth as he roared in my face.

"How do you know about that?"

I shook my head. I couldn't breathe, let alone speak.

"You're choking her. How is she supposed to answer you?"

Peter glanced back at his sister, then released my throat. I coughed and tried to catch my breath.

"I'll ask you again. How do you know so much, Ella?"

I heard a click as Peter cocked the hammer on the gun and levelled it at my heart.

"I'll tell you if you put the gun away and answer one question."

"I hardly think you're in a position to bargain," he said.

"I have nothing to lose, Peter," I replied. "You're the one holding the gun and I'm the one strapped to a chair. You're going to kill me anyway. I'd just like to know if I was right before I die."

He laughed. It was almost maniacal. Not like the quietly reserved Peter I had thought he was. I felt revulsion that I had ever liked him at all.

"Of course, you are right. I do in fact hold all the cards." He lowered the gun. "And I suppose I could grant your last wish, seeing as though you so cleverly put it all together.

However, I need to know who else you told. It makes no difference obviously because they'll never find your body, and we'll be long gone by the time anyone realises you are missing. However, I find it's always good to know who your enemies are. Just in case. It helps me sleep at night. So, who else knows?"

"No one," I said. I would not risk my family.

He leaned against a pipe with his arms folded, the gun casually resting on his forearm, one leg crossed over the other. He looked, to all intents and purposes, as though he were having a casual conversation in a club, rather than kidnapping me and planning a murder.

"Now, you see, I can tell you are lying with that statement, Ella. But no matter. It's obvious you would have discussed this with your brother and his wife. I know how close you are."

"Don't you dare hurt them," I shouted. "They don't know anything. They believe I came here to donate for the children and that's all. Do you think Jerry would have given you his book if he had any inclination who you really are?"

I was scared out of my wits. But now I was also angry, and this seemed to make my story ring true.

"Well, well, well. I do believe you're telling the truth this time. Good girl."

"Now it's your turn," I said. "Did you kill Millicent because she discovered the truth?"

"That child was as irritating as you. Always sticking her nose in where it didn't belong, and one day she went too far. She found out all right and I couldn't risk her blabbing, I had to shut her up. Of course I killed her, but what I want to know is how you found out?"

I'd done it. He'd confessed and now I knew the truth. I exhaled and smiled.

"You'd never believe it."

"Try me," he said.

"Milly told me."

As soon as I spoke those words utter chaos broke out.

Milly appeared right in front of me. Matron screamed and took a step back, right under a shelf where Phantom was waiting. With one swipe of his paw he dislodged a heavy can, which landed on her head, knocking her out instantly. As she crumpled to the floor, Peter took a step back, utter shock registering on his face. He tripped over an abandoned case, banging his head on the pipe behind and slid to the ground, unconscious.

The gun clattered to the floor and discharged a bullet, which ricocheted off the sink and embedded itself in a water pipe, which promptly burst, spraying foul-smelling brown liquid everywhere. Then a voice shouted from the stairs.

"This is the police! Stay where you are!"

As several men, led by Jimmy, came rushing down into the room, I caught sight of Milly. She smiled, nodded and then, giving me a small wave, slowly faded from view.

CHAPTER SIXTEEN

A few hours later, the four of us were back where we started. Snug in front of the fire in the drawing room of my cottage. It was so very good to be home again.

"So tell me again how Jimmy escaped," I asked Albert.

"Well, of course, he realised at once that his tea had been drugged. He'd only drunk a small amount at that point, and with a spot of quick thinking he poured the remainder away. Once he heard Maude returning, he quickly lay as though passed out."

"He looked terrible when I found him there," I said. "I was so worried."

"Well, it wasn't as bad as it could have been. He was dizzy and disoriented of course, but he did a remarkable job under those circumstances."

"So what happened in the infirmary?" Jerry asked.

Albert continued. "Well, as you know, Matron told Peter she had given him another sedative. She also mentioned that she'd sent Maude home."

I nodded.

"Jimmy knew the likelihood of being drugged again. He realised you were the one they wanted, Ella, and they were making sure he was out of the way. This time the drug was in hot milk, which Matron prepared. She told Jimmy to drink it up whilst she walked Maude to the door, having given her the rest of the afternoon off. During that time, Jimmy poured away the milk and then pretended to be in a deep sleep, which is exactly what Matron saw when she returned. She had no reason to think Jimmy suspected anything."

"So was Maude involved in these shenanigans?" Ginny asked.

Albert shook his head. "Not at all. The tea had already been prepared by Matron. Maude was just following instructions."

"So how did Jimmy find out where I had been taken?"

"He followed Matron, right, Albert?" Jerry asked.

"He did indeed," confirmed Albert. "Once he knew where you were being kept, he came and warned the men I'd posted outside. DI Wilkes then came and got me."

"Goodness. He did very well finding his way around the place. I was hopelessly lost within a couple of minutes," I said.

"Well, as I said, Ella, I gave you my best man. Jimmy spent a number of years as a beat officer and knows the London streets like the back of his hand. A few corridors in the orphanage, if you'll forgive the pun, were like child's play."

I rose and went to the liquor cabinet where I refreshed everyone's drinks.

"So did you hear Peter's confession? How he murdered poor Milly?" I asked.

Albert shook his head. "Not at the time. We'd arrived too late for that, I'm afraid. All we heard was a loud crash and a gunshot. That's when we rushed in."

"Oh, no," cried Ginny. "Do you mean to say that Ella's heroic actions have all been in vain?"

"Not at all, Ginny. Both Peter and his sister have been singing like songbirds since we picked them up. We know much more than we ever did. Peter not only confessed to killing Milly, but also to killing the real Peter Clairmont, who it turns out was actually their uncle."

"But I thought he was in Ireland," I said.

"He was. It's where Peter and his sister grew up. That much was true. However, they moved back to Yorkshire a couple of years ago, after Mr. Clairmont's wife died. It was *her* family that was Irish. Once she'd passed away, the old man decided to spend the remainder of his years where he grew up, in Yorkshire."

"But how is it possible that the neighbours didn't know Peter or his sister?" Ginny asked.

This was something that was troubling me too. Surely, if they'd all come over together then they would have been seen, and then I realised the truth.

"They didn't come back with the old man, did they?"

"No, they didn't," said Albert. "There had been a huge disagreement among them all. The old man didn't want anything more to do with them. Called his niece 'a bad lot' and warned his nephew that they'd both get into serious trouble one day. But I think he underestimated how close they were, and how inherently bad."

"So when did they come back, and to where?" Jerry asked.

"Not long after their uncle actually. But they moved into the next village some miles away. There they made plans to kill him. In their minds he had done them a grave wrong, even though he and his wife had brought them both up as their own."

"But I don't understand how they could have financed all of this," said Ginny.

"Actually, that's what I was going on to tell you. There's much more to this pair than we thought. Initially, they used the inheritance they received from their parents, but that was quite meagre and ran out quickly. After that they took to robbery."

"What?" we all exclaimed.

"Oh, yes," Albert said with a huge grin. "It turns out, Ella, that you are responsible for catching two of the most-wanted criminals this country has ever seen."

CHAPTER SEVENTEEN

A few days later, I was sitting having my breakfast and perusing the paper. Albert's news had taken us all by complete surprise. It turned out that Peter and Matron were really Arthur and Mildred Stone, the heads of the notorious Semaphore Gang, so dubbed as the police believed this was their main method of communication. They were responsible for a number of violent robberies up and down the country and a huge manhunt had been underway for months. But it had brought little in the way of clues and the authorities were fast losing hope that they'd ever be caught. That, of course, was before Milly came on the scene.

Jerry, Ginny, and Albert had all said they would never have put me in harm's way like that had they known with whom we were dealing. I very much appreciated their love and concern, but also knew in my heart that it had played out exactly as it was meant to. Milly and Phantom were there all along to see that no harm would befall me.

I glanced at the vase in the centre of the table. It held a single flower—one that was impossible to get at this time of year—a beautiful red poppy. It had been waiting on the table for me after I'd said goodbye to Albert, Ginny, and Jerry. I think it was Milly's way of saying thank you and I knew I would probably never see her again. She was at peace now.

A loud crash from the downstairs pantry shook me back to reality. Phantom, on the other hand, was still around. I went to investigate.

"Oh! Look at the mess, Phantom. What on earth did you do this for?" He was crouched on the top shelf looking down at the smashed eggs and spilled cocoa with glee. He gave a silent meow and disappeared. I sighed and went to look for something to clean it up.

As I was crouched under the sink the telephone rang. It was Ginny.

"Ella, darling, how are you? I hope you don't mind me calling, but Jerry and I went to dinner with some friends last night. And Lady Davenport, I'm sure I've mentioned her to you—told me about a little problem she's been having."

Oh, dear, I didn't like the sound of this at all.

"Well, of course I mentioned you, and … "

"What sort of problem, Ginny?" I interrupted.

"Well, the ghostly kind of course, silly."

"Oh, Ginny, you didn't!"

"Well, of course I did."

I sighed.

"The fact is you have an incredible gift, courtesy of Mrs. Rose, and I have friends who are willing to pay a lot of money for your services."

"Really?" I asked, surprised, then realised I sounded like I was encouraging her and frowned.

"Of course, you'll be highly sought after once word gets around, you know…" She paused, and my heart sank to my stomach. "…Lady Davenport wants to have a séance."

"No, Ginny. Absolutely not."

"Oh, don't be a spoilsport, darling. It'll be fun."

"Ginny, I'm not being a spoilsport. This is not something I would feel comfortable doing. Firstly, I have no doubt that the experience with Milly was a one-off. She's gone now, at peace, thank goodness. But I doubt very much I have a 'gift' as you call it. Secondly, what do you suppose would happen at a séance if I did have a gift? Have you thought of that?"

"Whatever do you mean, darling?"

"I mean, if I am a 'conduit' or whatever you call it for ghosts, how many do you think would appear? It could be hundreds. And what if they are unfriendly, like poltergeists or something? Not only would it be chaos, it could very well be dangerous."

"Oh, dear. Yes, I suppose you're right. What a shame. But what shall I tell Lady Davenport? She'll be so disappointed. She's already talking to the caterers."

"Well, Ginny, really!" I said, exasperated. She'd obviously told Lady Davenport I'd do it. "Just tell her I'm still recovering. But under no circumstances will I ever consider a séance. And please, Ginny, don't promise her, or anyone else for that matter, that I'll be able to deal with their ghosts. I am quite certain it was a one-time incident."

Suitably mollified, Ginny agreed. We spoke for a little while longer and with promises to meet for lunch later in the week, we said goodbye.

I set to cleaning up the mess that Phantom had made in the pantry.

Whilst it was called a pantry, it was more like a small corridor set off from the kitchen with floor to ceiling shelves on either side. These were very deep and it wasn't until a short while later I understood why. Directly in front was another set of shelves, again floor to ceiling, but these were much narrower in depth. Rather like a bookshelf.

As I was on my hands and knees cleaning up the last of the spillage, I noticed a small hole to the side of the narrower shelves. It was perfectly round and at first I thought it must have been made by a mouse. But on closer inspection it was obviously too small and too perfect.

I pondered it for a while then did what anyone would do in the same circumstances. I stuck my finger inside. There was a gentle click as I depressed a lever and the whole shelving unit moved sideways by an inch.

I stood up in shock, staring at the gap that had appeared on the right. A cool draught was blowing through that smelled of old dust and stale air.

Gingerly, I reached out and slid the shelving sideways, and as it slid back it fitted neatly down the edge like a sliding door. So this was why the shelving on either side was so deep. The door was perfectly hidden if you didn't know it was there.

I took a tentative step forward and found myself in a secret room. It was reminiscent of an old banqueting hall, with dark wood-panelled walls, dark oak parquet floor and an iron candelabra hanging from the ceiling. I noticed there were also matching wall sconces, although the candles had long since melted.

In the middle of the room were a large table and chairs that could have seated forty people, and it was fully set for a grand dinner, right down to the floral centre-pieces. These, of course, had long since perished and everything was coated in a thick layer of dust. I couldn't begin to wonder how long it had all been there, nor why the room had been closed off.

Glancing to my right, at the far end of the room I noticed a large dresser, replete with serving dishes, and in the corner two high-backed red velvet upholstered chairs beside a small occasional table in front of a fireplace.

Whilst I was in shock at discovering such a secret in my cottage, what happened next nearly made my heart stop.

A figure leaned forward in one of the chairs and slowly rose to face me.

It looked as though Ginny was right. I did have a gift after all.

THE
CURSE OF
ARUNDEL HALL

ABOUT THE BOOK

ONE GHOST, ONE MURDER, ONE HUNDRED YEARS APART.
BUT ARE THEY CONNECTED?

Ella has discovered a secret room in The Yellow Cottage, but
with it comes a ghost. Who was she? And how did she die?
Ella needs to find the answers before either of them can find
peace. But suddenly things take a nasty turn for the worse.

Ella Bridges has been living on Linhay Island for several
months but still hasn't discovered the identity of her ghostly
guest. Deciding to research the history of her cottage for
clues she finds it is connected to Arundel Hall, the large
Manor House on the bluff, and when an invitation to dinner
arrives realises it is the perfect opportunity to discover more.

However the evening takes a shocking turn when one of
their party is murdered. Is The Curse of Arundel Hall once
again rearing its ugly head or is there a simpler explanation?

Ella suddenly finds herself involved in two mysteries at
once, and again joins forces with Scotland Yard's Police
Commissioner to try and catch a killer. But will they succeed?

FOR WENDY.

CHAPTER ONE

I t was never my intention to begin what can now only be described as a career in detective work. I fell into the role of amateur sleuth quite by accident.

My younger brother Jerry and I had grown up in an exceptionally happy and carefree environment. Father owned a textile mill and was the main employer in the area, so as befitted a man of his standing in the community, our house was large. I remember us vividly racing up and down the halls on our bicycles with Patch, our little Jack Russell terrier, snapping at the back wheels.

For afternoon tea on Sundays, unless we'd been invited out, we always toasted our own crumpets on the fire in the small sitting room at the back of the house, then played games as a family until supper, after which we children went to bed.

Christmas had always been a magical time and, in my childish memory, every one of them was white. Large fluffy flakes had drifted lazily down from the sky to cover our lawns and trees in a blanket of snow, and there was always a robin redbreast bobbing up and down on the frozen bird-bath, usually stalked by our tom cat Moses. Although being old and rickety of joint, he was never quite fast enough to catch the little bird.

While Christmas Eve and Christmas Day were for the family, for as long as I could remember, Boxing Day was set aside for the workers. After the church service, everybody would trudge back up the snow-filled lane to our house. Invariably, Mother and Father would lead the procession, alongside Jack Scotton, my father's foreman, with his wife and Mr. Pearson the accountant. After that would come the rest of the adult workers, leaving Jerry and me to run back and forth playing with the other children. To me it seemed as though the whole town had been invited.

Once we'd reached the house, the large oak front door would be flung open to welcome our guests and the party would begin. Gifts were given from my family to each of the workers to say thank you for all their hard work that year, and then we'd move to the large dining hall where cook had laid out a sumptuous cold buffet. She'd been preparing it all for days beforehand and for much of that time Jerry and I were camped in the kitchen, where we helped to clean out the bowls and relieve her of any extras. When it was all done, she too took some well-deserved time off and joined in the festivities.

My parents were well-liked and respected by those who worked for them, and this was never more apparent than one day, when I was almost seventeen and Jerry was fifteen, and our lives would forever be changed.

Mother had sheltered us from a lot of what went on, but even then both of us were aware something wasn't quite right. Father was closeted in his study more often and no longer joined us for Sunday tea. There were many times he didn't arise from his bed until after lunch and, as he'd always been an earlier riser, this was particularly unusual. When he did get up, he'd spend his time staring into the fire in the sitting room, morose and silent. What food Mother managed to tempt him with he either barely nibbled at or left completely, and as a result he lost a considerable amount of weight. Eventually, Mother sat us down and explained he'd lost the factory. Even then, with the shock of those words, Jerry and I still didn't fully comprehend the far-reaching implications.

Father, it had turned out, had been caught up in an investment opportunity for which he'd put up the factory as collateral. The investment, while genuine, had failed and as a result he'd lost everything. With the loss of the factory came the loss of our income and as a result we'd had to sell the house and move. But that wasn't the worst of it. Two weeks later, my father, suffering from pneumonia and with his will to live eroded by the guilt of what had happened, passed away.

The funeral was held in the local church and the entire factory workforce came to pay their last respects. For the last time we trudged up the lane to our house and threw open the door to receive our guests. Many wonderful stories were told of Father that day, most of which my brother and I had never heard, and many tears were shed. My father was loved and would be missed by many, but by none more than the three of us.

Later that evening, when everyone else had departed, Jack Scotton and Mr. Pearson remained with Mother, each assuring her they would do all they could to help. Word had obviously spread about our straitened circumstances. True to their word, the very next day both men reappeared to inform her they had negotiated a very favourable deal for us for the sale of the house.

Less than a month later, with the house packed up and everything that hadn't been sold safely in storage, the three of us left our home for the last time. We were to spend the next two and a half years with Aunt Margaret over seventy miles away in Sheffield.

Life with Aunt Margaret more often than not ran smoothly and in the main we all rubbed along quite amicably, but the underlying worry for both of them was of course me and Jerry. Without a paternal figure in his life (Aunt Margaret had never married) and with no business to inherit, Jerry's future was of constant concern to my mother and her sister. However they need not have worried, as Jerry won a scholarship to study "modern greats" at Oxford, and a promising future was assured.

This of course left me, and on that subject the sisters were divided.

My aunt, even with numerous suitors of good pedigree competing for her hand, was a spinster by choice and lived life to its fullest. She had a sharp mind and a rapier wit and was an avid people watcher, as well as a fan of puzzles, having had several of her own published in The Times.

I learned many invaluable lessons at her side and owe much of my success as a detective to her. She was of the opinion I should be left to follow in her footsteps if I wished, and take control of my own life. My mother, on the other hand, was of the opinion a 'suitable match' for me should be found at the earliest opportunity, and no matter how much I pleaded with her on this, she would not budge.

So followed a mind-numbing round of dinner parties and afternoon teas, where I would find myself thrust in front of bored, patronising or over-excitable young men, with whom I had nothing in common and no interest whatsoever. My mother had all but lost hope when I met John, not at one of her interminable soirées, but at a small local bookshop.

We hit it off immediately and after several clandestine meetings, I eventually brought him home to meet the family. Needless to say my mother was ecstatic, my aunt less so, although I paid it little heed at the time. Love is blind as they say, and I was certainly in love. After a courtship and engagement lasting just over a year, John and I were married in the local parish church. I was twenty-one-years-old.

At twenty-three I would become a widow.

After the reported death of my husband, I was advised by his employer to move away from the North of England, take back my maiden name and, aged twenty-three, begin my life again.

"It's for your own safety, Ella," the Home Secretary had said, as we sat in front of a crackling fire, in the parlour of the house John and I had called home for just two short years.

"But I don't understand, Lord Carrick," I choked out over the walnut-sized lump in my throat. "John was just a junior minister for trade. He told me he was helping rebuild our foreign exports to offset the cost of the war. How can that be dangerous to either him or me?"

I'll never forget the withering look on Lord Carrick's face. It was only there fleetingly before he carefully masked his features, but I knew what I'd seen. Pity, tinged with a little guilt perhaps, but it was the scorn and superciliousness that imprinted themselves on my brain. I'd been a naive fool, and at that precise moment, I knew my husband and the life we'd shared together was as artificial as the vase of flowers on the windowsill.

Cast adrift from my home for the second time, I spent the following year with my aunt and my mother while I grieved and contemplated my future.

Often I took the train down to Oxford, booked into a small hotel and spent a few days catching up with my brother. It was during one of these visits that the subject of Linhay came up, which completely changed the course of my life.

It was a glorious summer day, the sky was blue and a warm breeze rustled gently through the foliage. We were enjoying a rather impressive afternoon tea in the gardens of the Trout Inn at Godstow. An impeccably dressed waiter hovered in the background waiting to replenish our cups at a discreet nod. I watched as a punting party came into view under the bridge, and a hand rose, waving at Jerry who returned it with a lazy salute.

"Bickerstaff," he informed me. "His father has a place on Linhay. Invited me down a couple of times, but haven't had a chance to take him up on it yet. Do you remember it?"

"Of course, the yellow cottage," I whispered. I felt my heartbeat increase and a bubble of excitement begin in the pit of my stomach. I knew events thus far had stacked together perfectly to bring me to this pivotal moment. After a year of searching, I realised the island was where I needed to go.

Without knowing it, I was about to embark on a life of murder and mystery.

CHAPTER TWO

The promise of a lovely spring morning had me up and at my desk by seven-thirty. The desk had been my father's, and with her sudden move to the south of France, my mother had had it sent on to me.

"Your father would be pleased to know you had it, darling," she'd said. "He knew how much you loved it."

She was right. The desk was a beautiful oak roll-top with one slim drawer above the knee-hole and three deeper ones down either side. The interior had several cubbyholes, doors and drawers, and the legs were brass capped, culminating in casters that made manoeuvrability simple. Jolly useful when one lived alone.

My original idea when moving to the cottage five months ago was to have a small study area under the stairs. However, with the delivery of the desk, which was far too big for the space, I had moved to the sitting room at the back of the house next to the picture window. There,

I could gaze at the garden and the lawns which sloped gently to the river below.

As I was finishing off some last minute correspondence, there was a gentle tap at the door.

"Come in, Mrs. Shaw."

"Apologies for disturbing you, Miss Bridges, but here's this morning's post." She handed me a small bundle held together with a rubber band.

A quick glance at the writing showed me one was from my mother and the other from my aunt, who sent me a new puzzle to solve once a month.

"The postman is waiting to see if you have anything for him to take back?"

"Well, that's very kind of him, but I'm going to the village later, so I will take them myself. Please do pass on my thanks though, Mrs. Shaw."

"Of course, Miss Bridges," she replied, then left, closing the door gently behind her.

Esther Shaw was a tall stocky woman with short iron-grey hair, an almost military bearing in both stance and attitude, and had been in my employ as housekeeper-cum-cook for just over a fortnight. I'd thought it wise to advertise away from the island, small village gossip being what it was, and had placed an advertisement in The Lady Magazine. Surprisingly, hers was the only application I had received. She came directly from employment as housekeeper in a large London home, and said she was used to a busy household where guests dropped in unannounced expecting to be accommodated, and large dinner parties were held on a regular basis. I questioned the fact she might find life in my employ too quiet and rather dull, becoming disillusioned, but she assured me that was what had appealed most about the job. Even though the advert had disappointingly only garnered one applicant, I came to the conclusion Mrs. Shaw was eminently suited to the position. So after a telephone call to her employers, in which they informed me of her excellent credentials and business-like approach to work, along with the fact she was both discreet and honest, I offered her the position and she accepted immediately.

The last two weeks had proved my decision to take her on had been a good one. She was trustworthy and extremely efficient, and although basic, she cooked more than adequate fare for my needs. She had a rather old-fashioned outlook on life and position. I had on a couple of occasions asked her to call me Ella, but she'd refused.

"Oh, I couldn't possibly. There's a place for everything and everything in its place, as my mother always said. You are my employer, Miss Bridges, and it's only right I respect that," she'd insisted, so I'd let it be. Although it was an emotional wrench to be again addressed as 'Miss' when I had once been a wife.

Unfortunately there was one complication. She would not set foot in the pantry, and considering this was where the food was stored, it posed a bit of a dilemma. Of course it wasn't the pantry per se that was the problem; it was the secret dining room beyond and the spirit of a young woman currently stranded there that was the real issue.

A temporary solution had been to remove all the goods and store them in a large cupboard in the kitchen proper, which I'd done last Sunday on Mrs. Shaw's day off. I'd enlisted the help of my brother Jerry, who alongside his wife Ginny and her Godfather Sir Albert Montesford, Scotland Yard's current Police Commissioner, were the only people to know of my special gift.

While this solution pleased Mrs. Shaw, it didn't bring me any closer to solving the real mystery. Just who was the ghost in my dining room? How had she died? And more importantly, where were her remains? I was hoping the visit to the village later would shed more light on the matter. I was going to visit my friend Harriet Dinworthy, a published local historian and founder of the village library. I needed to find out more about my home.

CHAPTER THREE

A
s I crossed the hall to the breakfast room in search of the coffee I knew Mrs. Shaw would have waiting, the telephone rang.

"Hello, Linhay 546."

"'Ello, do you get rid o' dogs?"

"I beg your pardon?" I said, taken aback. The accent was pure cockney and I had no idea who it was.

"I said, do you get rid o' dogs? I 'ave a problem. The missus finks I'm losin' me marbles, but I'm not, you know. Damn thing keeps movin' me slippers. Found 'em 'arf buried in the yard last night."

"I'm terribly sorry, but I think you have the wrong number."

"Ain't you the Paranormal Investigator then? Dog's bin dead for three months."

I knew then exactly who it was.

"Jerry, you absolute rotter!"

I waited patiently for Jerry to stop laughing. He had one of those almost silent laughs when highly amused, just a constant hiccupping wheeze that started in his chest and set his shoulders shaking. I could almost see him wiping his eyes with his handkerchief as the mirth took hold.

"Sorry, Ella, I couldn't resist. I've waited months to do that."

I knew to what he was referring. The previous Christmas holidays had been a lovely time spent with Ginny and Jerry in London. Jerry had gifted me with an exquisite brooch in the shape of a cat, made from black onyx with two small sapphires for eyes. But Ginny, with a flourish and a great deal of excitement, had presented me with a fine silver box of gilt-edged calling cards proclaiming me to be a Physic Investigator. I still didn't know if it had been a joke or not. They were now safely locked up in my writing desk drawer, never again to see the light of day.

"Do you forgive me?" Jerry said, catching his breath.

"I'll think about it," I replied, although I knew he'd hear the smile in my voice.

"Actually, I was hoping to come down and see you, if that's all right? I'm meeting with a chap on the island in a couple of hours. He has a motorcycle I might buy."

"Of course. I had thought I'd visit the library later, but it can wait until tomorrow."

"Jolly good. I'll see you about one o' clock then. Cheerio."

I replaced the receiver and rang for Mrs. Shaw, telling her my brother would be joining me for lunch.

Jerry's imminent arrival was announced by the tremendous roar of an engine coming up the lane. I hurriedly donned my coat and shoes and rushed out to meet him.

"Well, what do you think, Ella? She's a stunner, isn't she?" he enthused, dismounting and removing his goggles.

"Oh, she's terrific, Jerry!" I agreed as I circled the sleek-lined machine with its open-top sidecar, and admired the shiny black and silver paintwork.

"She's a 1930 BSA, so only five years old, and I got her for a song. And look here..." Jerry crouched down, so I followed suit. "This is a Watsonian sidecar fitted on the company's quick-fit chassis, and with a simple flick of this lever here, the whole thing can be detached and stored until needed."

"How clever." I dutifully enthused. I knew nothing about motorcycles, but Jerry was obviously thrilled with his acquisition and I was very happy for him. "Where are you going to keep her?"

"Actually, I was wondering if I could keep her here until I can sort something out back in the city?"

"Absolutely. You can put her in the garage, seeing as though it's empty." One of the things I hadn't yet managed to do was learn to drive, although I planned on remedying that as soon as possible. Driving had been John's domain and I'd sold his car along with the house.

"So what's this?" I asked, pointing to a large curiously-shaped object precariously balanced in the sidecar.

"Oh, yes, I nearly forgot about that. It's a gift for you."

I watched as Jerry lifted the item out and stood it up. With a quick flick of his wrist worthy of a professional magician, the canvas was slung aside and there, resplendent in matching shiny black paint with a silver bell and a basket on the front, was a bicycle.

"Oh, Jerry, you bought me a bicycle, how wonderful."

"I thought it ideal for you to ride about the island on. There must be much of it you haven't seen yet and what better way than this?"

I smiled inwardly at Jerry's hope that I could explore the entire island on a bicycle. At its longest point it was eighteen miles, rather too much to do in one go, especially considering I hadn't ridden one since I was a child. But cycling to the village or the beach was wonderful idea.

"It's perfect, Jerry, thank you."

"So do you want to try her out then?"

"I'll say. But I'm a bit rusty."

"No need to worry, I'll be right behind you. Once you get back into it, you'll be racing along in no time. I say, do you have a matching pair of shoes inside just like those?"

I looked down and burst out laughing. In my haste I had inadvertently put on one black and one brown shoe. "As a matter of fact, I do. You never know, perhaps I'll start a new fashion craze."

Still laughing at my idiocy, I grasped the handle bars, perched myself on the seat and set off down the track lane at a snail's pace, and with a not inconsiderable wobble. I could hear Jerry jogging alongside shouting encouraging words, but before long I'd left him behind as I gained in confidence and it all came back to me.

It was exhilarating with the wind in my hair and the hedgerows rushing past. I felt I could go for miles. Unfortunately, Phantom had other ideas and suddenly materialised right before me in the road. I should have ridden through him, but in that split second the thought never entered my head and I swerved to avoid him. Of course the inevitable happened, I hit the grass bank, fell off and rolled down the slight incline into the ditch below, where Jerry found me sitting in an inch of dirty water and clutching my right wrist.

"Good god, Ella, are you all right? What on earth happened? You were doing so well."

"Phantom," I said, with no further explanation necessary.

"Come on, we need to get you home and the doctor called to take a look at that wrist."

So with Jerry wheeling my luckily undamaged bicycle back with one hand, and holding me up with the other, I limped back home. Mrs. Shaw immediately called Doctor Brookes, settled me in the drawing room with hot sweet tea, a roaring fire and instructions to ring the little bell she had placed on the side table should I require anything at all.

By the time the doctor arrived, I was feeling much better, although a little sore and my wrist was throbbing terribly. I'd managed a couple of bites of lunch, but couldn't stomach more without feeling nauseous. Luckily, Jerry had no such appetite loss and managed both to polish off his own in short order, and finish mine.

Jerry was putting his motorcycle in the garage when Mrs. Shaw announced, "Doctor Brookes, Miss Bridges," and showed him in.

The doctor made an entrance that day which was rather shocking on two counts. Firstly, I had assumed him to be old, somewhat stooped and rather frail, so the exceptionally tall and handsome man with startling green eyes and dark red hair, which fell foppishly over his forehead, was unexpected to say the least and I was momentarily lost for words. However, my power of speech deserted me completely when he took a large stride into the room, tripped over nothing at all and ended up sprawled across the rug.

Mrs. Shaw, who was still hovering in the background, rushed forward in aid. "Good heavens, Doctor Brookes, are you all right?"

"Oh, I really am most awfully sorry," he said, staggering to his feet and revealing a bloody nose. "I was trying to avoid the cat."

"Cat?" said Mrs. Shaw in a confused tone. "We have no cat here, Doctor. You must have hit your head when you fell. Here, sit down and I'll bring you some hot sweet tea." And with that she rushed out.

She must have passed Jerry on the way as he entered not a moment later. "Good afternoon, Doctor, so what's the prognosis... oh, I say, what happened here then?"

At that point the doctor and I had not spoken a word to each other. I had yet to find my voice and with a handkerchief over half his face and watering eyes, Doctor Brookes was in no fit state. But Jerry's entrance broke the spell.

I rose. "The doctor has had a slight accident, Jerry. He tripped on his way in and as you can see has bloodied his nose. Perhaps you could show him to the cloakroom where he can clean himself up?" I suggested.

As they left, I frowned at the realisation the doctor had probably seen Phantom, but glancing around, could see no sign of him. Sitting back down, my foot connected with a small bottle of pills and I noticed Doctor Brookes' Gladstone bag lay open, partially disgorging its contents over my rug. I knelt and began to replace the various items, marvelling at the paraphernalia a medical man needed to lug around daily. Bandages, pills and powders lay alongside a prescription pad and a note. "PM police." I imagined a doctor would need to work closely with the police for all sorts of reasons, and resolved not to take up too much of his time if he had an appointment with them this evening. I'd finished tidying up when he and Jerry reappeared.

He looked much better. Gone were the streaming eyes and the blood, although a slight swelling and the beginnings of a bruise across the bridge of his nose were apparent. He sat opposite with a rueful smile. "Miss Bridges, I wonder if you'll allow me to start again. As you can see, I am more than capable of entering a room in a dignified manner. I am Nathaniel Brookes, the doctor on the island. I've recently taken over the practice from my father who has retired. Now, I understand that you have an injury to your wrist. Let's take a look, shall we?"

As he carefully and gently inspected my wrist, I took in the long tapered fingers with their short clean fingernails, and unbidden, the absence of a wedding ring. I frowned, cross with myself for being so ridiculous. Unfortunately, Doctor Brookes mistook my meaning.

"I'm sorry, am I hurting you?"

"No, not at all. I was thinking of something else entirely. Please continue."

"Well, the good news is it isn't broken. But it is badly sprained. I'll strap it up for you and give you something for the pain, but use it sparingly for a few days to allow it to heal. I'll come back in a week to see how you're getting on, but do call the surgery if you are having any problems and I'll come back sooner."

I thanked him, and as Mrs. Shaw showed him out, Jerry came to say goodbye.

"Are you sure you'll be all right, Ella? I feel pretty wretched about the whole thing."

"Of course I will, Jerry, it's only a sprain. I'll be right as rain in no time. And don't blame yourself. It was hardly your fault."

Accepting my reassurances, he gave me a quick peck on the cheek and, having elicited a promise that I'd call him if needed, he left to catch the train back to London.

Once again alone and having eaten very little at lunch, I ravenously ate the supper Mrs. Shaw had made and retired early. My plan for the next day was to go to the post office with the letters I had written that morning, and to visit the library. I still had some research to do.

CHAPTER FOUR

The next morning, I awoke to find the throbbing pain in my wrist had lessened to a dull ache, which thankfully became barely noticeable once I had taken the prescribed pain relief. After a breakfast of porridge followed by toast and fruit jam, all consumed with a splendid Assam tea courtesy of Ginny, I informed Mrs. Shaw I would be out for most of the morning, so to dispense with elevenses.

"Will you be requiring lunch, Miss Bridges?"

"Well, that rather depends on how long my visit to the library takes. If I find something of interest I could be gone some time."

"Well, in that case I will prepare a cold buffet lunch which won't spoil and will be ready upon your return. Would that suit?"

"A splendid idea, Mrs. Shaw, well done." And with that sorted out I set off for the village.

All small villages, regardless of their size or geographical location, are subject to gossip and hearsay. No one quite knows where the tales originate, but sooner or later the story has been passed along so many times it barely resembles the original at all. The village of Meadham on Linhay Island was no different, and the most recent rumour concerned the new-found love of Sir Robert Harlow. He was a retired city financier and current owner of Arundel Hall, the large manor house atop the bluff overlooking Smuggler's Cove. Apparently, after just one glance, he had become utterly smitten with American actress Patty-Mae Ludere, whom he had met at a ball at The Dorchester. Without further ado, he'd gone down on one knee in the middle of a packed dance floor and proposed marriage.

While I didn't know Sir Robert particularly well, the whole thing sounded preposterous. Our paths had crossed several times in the months I'd been living there and he'd always struck me as a highly intelligent, quietly spoken and mild-mannered gentleman. He was of middling years with hair more salt than pepper, and sported a full, but neatly trimmed beard and moustache a shade or two lighter than his hair. He was of average height, trim and fit, and habitually wore Harris Tweed.

It was therefore a complete shock when I reached the post office, saw what I thought was a stranger alight from his Rolls Royce dressed like a dandy, and realised it was Robert himself.

"Good morning, Miss Bridges, I trust you are well?" It was at that moment he spied the sling. "Oh, forgive me, I didn't realise you were injured. Nothing too serious, I hope?"

I shook my head. "No, just a silly sprain, that's all."

I was trying not to stare. Gone was the grey hair and beard which had given him a sophisticated air. Now he sported a slicked back hairstyle and a pencil-thin moustache, both of which had been poorly dyed to a rather patchy black. The Harris Tweed was nowhere in sight, in its place white flannel trousers and a powder-blue jacket topped by a navy and white polka dot cravat, and a matching handkerchief just visible in his top pocket. It was ludicrous attire for any man at this time of year, let alone one who lived here and should know better, giving no consideration to our inclement weather. It may have been early spring, but there was a cold snap in the air exacerbated by the wind coming off the sea. He must have been chilled to his marrow. I was trying to imagine what had wrought such an incongruous change when the passenger door of the Rolls opened and I had my answer.

A pair of silken-clad legs shod in the highest red heels I had ever seen emerged first, slowly followed by a mass of white fur crowned by a shock of platinum blonde hair. Calculating blue eyes beneath finely arched brows and thick black lashes appraised me, and dismissed me as no threat in an instant. She tottered quickly to Robert and linking a proprietary arm through his, simpered through lips as scarlet as her shoes, "Bobby, honey, aren't you going to introduce me?"

I flinched, as what I had expected to be dulcet tones rang out as a high-pitched, childish and exaggerated drawl.

"Of course, my dear. Miss Bridges, may I introduce Miss Ludere?"

"Oh, call me Patty-Mae, sugar, everyone does." She giggled, holding out her left hand as if expecting me to kiss it. But more probably to show off the ring on her engagement finger. Though I could hardly miss it, the diamond being of similar size to a sparrow's egg. So the rumour was true.

I smiled. "Of course, and I'm Ella. I'm sorry, I'm afraid I can't shake hands," I said, lifting my sling.

"Oh, now, don't you worry about that none. Where I come from friends hug, and I just know we're going to be friends."

And with that I was suddenly engulfed in a powdery perfumed embrace, and the air above each ear kissed melodramatically.

As she leaned back and let me go, I could see fine lines around her eyes and mouth, which the thick make-up couldn't quite disguise. I had initially thought us of similar age, but she was at least ten years my senior and probably more. Almost half Robert's age.

A polite clearing of the throat interrupted us.

"Patty-Mae, shouldn't we let Ella get on?"

"Oh, of course, silly me. But dear Ella, you must come up to The Hall and have dinner with us. Please do say you will."

Really what could I say? "Dinner sounds wonderful, thank you."

Then, as if the thought had suddenly occurred to her, she gushed, "I know, we'll have a proper dinner party to celebrate our engagement. What do you say, Bobby, isn't that the most wonderful idea?"

"If a small dinner party is what you want, Patty-Mae, then that is what you shall have. Now..."

"Oh, goody," she said, clapping her hands and bouncing on her heels. "I'll get on with it right away. Come on, Bobby. Goodbye, Miss Bridges, look out for the invitation." And with that she carefully sashayed her way to the car.

"Patty-Mae, I still need to pick up my letters."

"What? Oh, go ahead without me, honey, you know I can't stomach that nauseating little man," she said, casting a vicious look at the post office where I was sure the Post Master was spying on us. "I'll wait for you in the Rolls."

Robert turned to me and smiled. "I do hope we've not kept you, Ella."

"Not at all, Robert, I'm heading to the post office myself actually and then up to the library."

"Well, in that case, let me accompany you."

As we crossed the street I congratulated him on his engagement.

"Thank you, my dear. I'm a little long in the tooth, I know, but one rarely gets a second chance at love, especially with such a vibrant young creature as Patty-Mae. I thought it wise to grab her with both hands. Metaphorically speaking of course."

"Well, I wish you both much happiness," I said as he opened the door and we entered the post office.

There was only one post office on the island, and it was run by a tall, thin man with a weasel-like face. Cedric Tipping was a confirmed bachelor of middling years and, although he was always polite to the point of obsequiousness, perhaps uncharitably, I had never really taken to him. Perchance it was his small coal-black eyes, set unnaturally close together, that stared at you for a moment longer than was comfortable. Or the beak-like nose, which he constantly sniffed and wiped at with a crumpled and yellowing handkerchief, coupled with his stertorous breathing. Possibly it was the way he shook your hand in greeting, hanging on to it a little longer than necessary. Or perhaps it was his penchant for idle gossip.

"Good morning, good morning," said the Post Master. "Miss Bridges, I do hope you are on the mend after your bicycle accident yesterday?"

How had he found out so quickly?

"I hope this is a lesson you've learned. I always say if God had wanted us to ride bicycles, we would have been born with wheels." He chuckled, clearing his throat noisily and sniffing. "I was just saying to Mr. Phipps the greengrocer how I hoped the young doctor had prescribed plenty of bed-rest."

Well, the cheek of the man!

"It was nothing, Mr. Tipping, I assure you. A simple sprained wrist, that's all. I've done worse damage pruning my roses."

"And what did you think of the young doctor, my dear? I'm surprised he let you out and about after a nasty shock like that. I was saying to Mr. Wellington the chemist only last week how qualified doctors are getting younger and younger nowadays."

My retort died in my throat as he turned to address Robert.

"And how are you this fine morning, Sir Robert? You certainly have a spring in your step. New love must suit you." He tapped the side of his nose and winked a rheumy eye salaciously. Although to give him his due, he managed to cover his shock at Robert's new look admirably. "And may I be the first to congratulate you on your up-coming nuptials. Now here is your mail. I've bundled it up all neatly for you and taken the liberty of separating it into the many tradesman's bills, which of course are to be expected considering the work you've had done on The Hall, and general correspondence. Mostly quite ordinary, but two from the Americas, which I have put at the top. There's no need to thank me, Sir Robert, it's all part of the service."

I think I was the only one who noticed the tightening of Sir Robert's jaw as he took the proffered letters, but of course he was far too well-mannered to react. Although I had the feeling he'd like to bash Cedric over the head with his umbrella for his impertinence.

"Thank you, Tipping, most kind."

I smiled at the tactful way he'd taken the Post Master down a notch.

"Can I give you a lift, Ella? I'd like to discuss the dinner party with you," he said, turning to me.

"That would be most welcome, Robert, thank you." And with that, we abandoned Mr. Tipping, no doubt already devising ways to pass on the latest gossip.

We continued our discussion outside, both of us studiously ignoring Mr. Tipping, who all but had his ear pressed to the window.

"About this dinner party of Patty-Mae's, it will only be small, nothing too lavish you understand, but still I think it might be too much for my elderly housekeeper to deal with on her own and I wonder, do you know of anyone who might help until I can reorganise my staff?"

"Actually, Robert, I may know of someone," I said. I was of course thinking of my own Mrs. Shaw who I felt would not only be more than up to the task, considering her experience, but would welcome the opportunity to do more than serve simple meals for me. "However, I would have to ask her first."

"Of course. Here, let me give you my card. My telephone number is on there. Perhaps you could call and let me know? Now, let me drop you at the library."

My reason for visiting the library was to find out as much about my new home as I could. The discovery of the secret room had piqued my curiosity. However, I didn't expect to learn that Robert and I had more in common than I had thought, nor that there was a centuries-old curse attached to Arundel Hall. A curse which was about to make itself known in the most insidious of ways.

CHAPTER FIVE

The library was a new and very welcome addition to island life, and was housed in a large anteroom off the foyer of The Royal Norfolk Hotel on the seafront. An exceptionally grandiose arc-shaped building with magnificent views across the water. It was originally built in the reign of King George IV to cater to the wealthy elite and fashionable, who came to the island for its clean air, temperate summer climate, and to partake of the restorative salt baths. The interior of the hotel was still in its original, flamboyant Regency style, with the public rooms and private bedchambers decorated with Chinoiserie wallpaper of numerous colours. The foyer had a magnificent domed ceiling and everywhere you looked were elaborate chandeliers, decorative friezes and gilded furniture. It was opulence at its best and spoke of wealth and pleasures of a bygone era. It still attracted the well-heeled and affluent all year round, which did much to help the island's economy.

Harriet was the dearest old soul who, although in her early sixties, had a mind as sharp as a tack and the energy of someone half her age. Both an islander and a retired historian, she was ideally placed to help me in my quest. For what Harriet didn't know about the island really wasn't worth knowing. Jerry, Ginny, and I had been present at the grand opening of the library a few months ago, as had Robert, and once Harriet realised I was not only new to the island, but living alone, she had practically adopted me. She insisted on addressing me by my given name as persons of that generation are wont to do, and greeted me like the granddaughter she had never had.

"Isobella, my dear child, how lovely to see you," she said, giving me a hug and a light, powdery kiss on my cheek. Then she spied my companion and her face turned pale.

"Good god, Robert, is that you?"

Robert spluttered and I watched a crimson blush suffuse his neck and tinge his face. "Of course it's me, Hettie, who else did you think it was?" he said gruffly, while I frowned at the name 'Hettie'. I'd never heard Harriet addressed as such before.

Heels beat a staccato over the marble floor to join us "Well, I declare! Would you look at this place," Patty-Mae said with eyes as big as saucers. "If that don't beat all. Bobby honey, we should decorate the hall just like this, don't you think?"

Robert sighed and patted her hand. "We'll see, Patty-Mae, we'll see. Now let me introduce Harriet Dinworthy, author and local historian, and of course the founder of this wonderful library. Harriet, this is Patty-Mae Ludere."

"His fiancée," Patty-Mae added, holding out her hand to show off the ring. "It's just so lovely to meet Robert's old friends."

I cringed as Harriet blanched. Had she emphasised the word old? Surely not.

"And you simply must come to our supper party, Harriet. Shouldn't she, Robert?"

"Dinner, Patty-Mae. We have dinner here, remember?"

Patty-Mae giggled. "Bless your heart, Bobby, why I do believe I'd forget my own head if it wasn't fastened on."

Robert turned back to Harriet. "It's just a small gathering of close friends. You'd be most welcome."

However, before Harriet could answer, Patty-Mae clapped in delight. "That's settled then. How excitin'. We'll see you both very soon and don't forget to dress up. Come along, honey." And with that she took Robert's arm and practically dragged him to the car.

Harriet and I stood silently in the foyer of the hotel and watched them leave. I think we were both at a loss for words. Patty-Mae Ludere was a force of nature, garrulous, loud, over the top and obviously used to getting her own way, but there was something else I couldn't put my finger on. Perhaps it was simply the fact we weren't used to such flamboyance and over-familiarity in our quiet English village.

"Have you known Robert long, Harriet?" I asked eventually.

"All my life, dear," she said sadly, turning away. But not before I had seen the shimmering in her eyes.

"Silly old fool," she muttered.

I wasn't sure if she meant Robert or herself.

As we entered the library proper, Harriet seemed to mentally shrug off her previous mood and was back to being the friend I knew.

"I've been helping with some of the history of The Hall recently and I've found some interesting connections to your cottage. Oh, good heavens, what on Earth happened to your arm, Isobella?"

"Actually, I'm surprised you don't already know," I said. "Cedric Tipping knew almost every detail and it only happened yesterday afternoon. Jerry brought me a bicycle as a gift and I fell off. It's just a sprain, nothing to worry about."

"Oh, take no notice of Cedric Tipping, Isobella. That man is enough to try the patience of a saint. He has nothing better to do than gossip. He lives a very small life and is of the opinion he is a large fish in a small pond when nothing could be further from the truth. Personally I have very little time for the Cedric Tippings of this world. You'll find, when you reach my age, my dear, you have less and less tolerance of imbeciles and the fatuous. Now, let us not waste any more time talking about the asinine, we have far more interesting things to discuss."

I was rather taken aback at Harriet's rancorous tone. It was most unlike her, I thought, as I trailed on her heels.

She steered me to one of the many snug seating areas that were dotted around the library. As expected, the style was Regency with gold and green-striped fabric adorning the rosewood armchairs, and oriental rugs on the floor. The mahogany bookshelves rose to the ceiling on all walls, with some set perpendicular to provide intimate corners for reading or research and a large chandelier dominating the ceiling, its crystal teardrops glittering as they caught the light from outside. Dotted throughout were gilt and porcelain table lamps casting cosy glows over objets d'art, and it reminded me of one of the exclusive London clubs of which Jerry spoke.

Tea had already been laid by one of the hotel staff, along with roast beef sandwiches and a rather sumptuous watercress salad.

"One of the perks of being part of the hotel," Harriet said, with an uncharacteristic wink, her previous outburst forgotten.

Later, as a waitress cleared away the remaining detritus, Harriet spread out a large old map of the island.

"This is one of the maps I hunted down and procured whilst doing research for Robert. It dates from the latter half of the 1700s and as you can see, it clearly shows The Hall, and both St. Peter's and St. Mary's churches, both of which pre-date The Hall by several centuries. The island in its entirety at that time was owned by the Duke of Norfolk, who commissioned the building of Arundel Hall as a gift to his new young wife. But what's most interesting for you is this building here."

Harriet pointed out a block denoting a building on a very familiar part of the island.

"That's the cottage," I said.

"Indeed it is, but more importantly it was the Dower House."

"You mean it was the home of the Duke's mother?" I asked, astonished.

"Precisely, my dear. As you are no doubt aware, tradition dictated the widowed dowager moved out of the larger family residence once her son married, and I believe your cottage was specifically built for that purpose."

"Goodness, I had no idea my home had such a stately provenance. Although I am at a loss as to why it's known as a cottage. Isn't it a bit large?"

"I think we can safely assume it was a term of affection used to describe the smaller of the two properties. The Hall has eighteen bedrooms, two libraries, a saloon, a smoking room, a dining room and several others. Not to mention the servants' quarters and the kitchens. So anything with only the four bedchambers, a dining room and two reception rooms, plus of course the kitchen and staff quarters such as yours, would almost certainly be looked upon as a cottage."

"Harriet, this is absolutely fascinating. I can't thank you enough for your help."

"Oh, my dear girl, it's an absolute pleasure. But did I say I had finished?"

I laughed. "You mean there's more?"

"Of course there's more. I never leave a job unfinished, Isobella," she said, reaching for another map. "Now this map is nearly one hundred years later, a mere sixty years ago, and you'll see the landscape has changed considerably."

As she was pointing out some of the differences, several of the hotel guests wandered in to peruse the books.

"Do excuse me, my dear, duty calls. But when I return I'll tell you about the curse of The Hall."

A curse? Gosh, that sounded ominous.

As Harriet attended to her customers, I studied the map in more detail. The most obvious change was that the land belonging to the Arundel estate had diminished considerably and I made a note to ask Harriet about it. I saw the fishermen's cottages and the hotel, which I was currently sitting in, had both been added, along with numerous farmhouses and their lands and other larger residences. The village had grown considerably and was now easily recognisable. Both of the churches remained and were in fact still in use today.

I decided I must visit them as soon as time allowed. The oyster beds and the brick field were likewise shown. I also noticed something much more interesting to me personally, the marking of a large area to the south of the cottage. So intent was I on my study that I didn't notice Harriet had returned.

"How are you getting on, my dear?"

"Oh, Harriet, you made me jump. I was completely lost in the map."

"We'll make an historian of you yet, Isobella." She laughed. "Do you have any questions?"

"Yes, a couple. I was intrigued about the acreage belonging to the Arundel estate. There have been some significant changes and I wondered why they would have had to sell off the land?"

"You're very observant, well spotted. Actually, that's partly to do with the curse I mentioned earlier. Here, let me ring for more tea then I'll close for a while so we're not interrupted."

Once the tea had arrived and the doors were locked, I settled back while Harriet told me about the curse.

"You see, Arundel Hall has been plagued with ill luck for the male owners and their spouses since the last stone was laid. The commissioning owner, the Eleventh Duke of Norfolk, built the hall for his first wife Marion. Sadly she died in childbirth not a year later. It was reported they were very much in love and the Duke never really got over her death."

"How very sad. What happened to the child?"

"Well, historical accounts are rather vague about the babe, but it's widely believed he was still-born, a double tragedy for the Duke. Then not quite four years later, he married a young woman called Frances, the daughter of the Duchess of Beaufort, who herself was a woman of questionable repute. Not many years into the childless marriage, Frances, who was described as being both delicate and irrational, became insane and was locked away for the rest of her life."

"Oh, how awful, Harriet! So he lost two wives?"

"Actually it was three, my dear. After a string of mistresses, the Duke, who was now into middle age, decided it was time to marry again. Frances had died several months earlier so he was free to take another spouse, and although he had a string of illegitimate offspring, he had yet to provide a legitimate heir. So for the final time the Duke got married. His third wife, Mary Ann, was much younger than he ... " Harriet stopped and flashed a frown at the door.

"Harriet, what is it?" I asked, laying my hand on her arm when she failed to reply.

"Mmmm? Oh nothing, my dear. Something just occurred to me. Now where was I? Ah yes, Mary Ann was very popular and attractive and within a year had borne him a son. But not all was harmonious behind closed doors. The Duke, constantly usurped by his pretty and highly regarded wife, became surly and withdrawn. He forbade visitors and by the same token prohibited her from visiting friends. By all accounts, he had also restricted her time with her son. He spent much time with the boy himself and I posit he was sowing seeds of ill in the boy's mind against his mother. For a young woman in the prime of life who loved her child, relished company and was a gay and congenial hostess, this was a terrible hardship and before long the inevitable happened. She found solace in the arms of another."

My hands involuntarily flew to my mouth. "Oh no, who? What happened? Did the Duke find out?"

"I'm afraid he did. Her lover was his own stable master. Although accounts at the time differ slightly, the general consensus was that he was enraged beyond belief. So much so that he immediately went to his gun cabinet, took out the largest shotgun he could find and threatened to blow them both to kingdom come where they stood."

I gasped. "He killed them?"

"I don't think so. He may have been a bitter, selfish old man, but I find it hard to believe he was a cold-blooded murderer. Besides the ruckus had brought every available servant out to gawk and I doubt he wanted quite so many witnesses." She smiled wryly.

"So what happened?"

"No one knows. Mary Ann and her lover simply disappeared and were never seen nor heard from again. It's thought he banished them both, had the marriage annulled and cut her out of his will. He left everything to their son."

"So, do you think she lived a long and happy life together with her lover?" I asked.

Harriet shook her head. "I sincerely doubt it. The Eleventh Duke wasn't given to acts of benevolence as far as his last wife was concerned, and certainly not after such a public indignity. They didn't treat wifely infidelity lightly in those days and he would have been perfectly within his rights to have had her flogged. If it were a simple banishment then I would say they got away with it. But of course we'll never really know."

"But what of the curse?" I asked.

"Well, within days of his wife disappearing, the Duke sold Arundel Hall to one of his contemporaries. The only thing he took was his son. Everything else, right down to the silver buckles on his shoes, was left. The language of the time was rather convoluted so I'll take a few liberties with the translation, but in essence he was heard to yell as he mounted his horse," Harriet closed her eyes and recited from memory … "Beware all ye masters with mistresses who reside in this damnable place, for I curse it with my every breath. Never will the light of joy penetrate these accursed walls for here shall only live despondency and despair. Tragedy and misfortune will plague your days and your wives will be as harlots and she-devils. Until the last stone remains …"

"Harriet, that's truly appalling. What a horrible old man."

"Indeed he was. Never having been happy there himself and with far more than his share of tragedy and ill-luck, he was determined no other would be at peace within its walls."

"But do you believe it to be true?" I asked. "What happened to the owners who followed, were they struck down as the Duke said?"

Harriet laughed. "It's rather a conundrum, Isobella, and one I've mulled over for years. On the one hand I'm an historian, and as such look at the facts before me and the findings I unearth in my research to form a basis of truth as to what happened. Naturally not every question is answerable. We can only take educated guesses in some instances, but again they are based on the evidence before us. With regard to the curse, I can't honestly say whether I believe it or not. It all sounds too far-fetched to be real, but I find I can't dismiss so lightly what happened to the hall's subsequent owners."

"Oh, Harriet, do tell," I begged. I'd become enraptured with the whole tale and simply had to know what happened next.

Harriet removed her pince-nez and rubbed her eyes. Glancing at the ormolu clock above the fireplace, I realised I'd taken up far more of her time than I'd intended.

I began to rise. "Harriet, I'm so sorry. I didn't realise the time."

She waved her hand dismissively. "Oh, do sit down, Isobella, I'm not ready to be put out to pasture yet. There's not much more to tell anyway, just a rather potted history of ownership." She replaced her glasses and continued.

"The Eleventh Duke sold The Hall in 1807 to Baron Shelley who had coveted the place since its inception. He and his wife were of similar age, with children grown and gone. Elizabeth Shelley was reluctant to inhabit such a large property when they were both in their dotage and alone, but the Baron insisted, it was a contentious issue and caused much antagonism between them. As the years passed, they grew more and more distant, eventually living separate lives albeit in the same residence. Seven years after moving in, Elizabeth Shelley died in misery and unhappiness, and the Baron, riddled with guilt, took his own life."

"So the curse continued," I said, more to myself than Harriet. "Who came next?"

"Baron Shelley left The Hall to his eldest son Timothy, who took up residence with his wife Helen and two teenage daughters. At first they were happy at The Hall and two months later, to their utter surprise, they found out Helen was with child. This was extremely unusual considering Helen was almost thirty-five years of age at the time, but they both took it as a good omen, especially when seven months later she gave birth to a boy, Algernon."

I put my head in my hands. "Something awful happened to him, didn't it?"

Harriet sighed and patted my knee. "Isobella, dear, are you sure you want to hear this?"

I nodded. "Of course. I'm fine, Harriet, really. It all happened so many years ago and there's nothing I can do about it. It just grieves me when it's children, I suppose."

Harriet looked at me for a little while longer then, apparently happy I wasn't going to break down, carried on.

"Well, of course you're quite right. Poor little Algernon died at just eight months old. There was nothing to indicate foul play and a cause was never found. The doctor who was summoned put it down as an accidental death. The loss of the boy tore the family apart and Helen eventually ran with her daughters in tow back to her parental home. But she was never the same after that, prone to long periods of melancholy and with no interest in life. She passed away a couple of years later. Timothy, with the loss of everything he held dear, remained at The Hall, but drowned his sorrows in a bottle. By all accounts, the times he was sober were rare and one evening, three or four years after the death of his son, a gang of armed robbers infiltrated his home intent on stealing the valuables. In a drunken rage he tried to defend himself, but obviously he was not in full control and was killed by a shotgun blast through the heart. During the years of his insobriety, he had lost all interest in his business and the running of the estate, so when it came to sorting out his affairs, it was found he died in extreme debt and was declared bankrupt. To pay off his debtors The Hall was put on the market, but it failed to find a buyer at first."

"Perhaps word of the curse had spread?" I said.

"Perhaps," Harriet agreed. "But in order to alleviate the demands of those Timothy Shelley was indebted to, some of the land was sold to raise money."

"Oh, so that's why there's such a change in the two maps you showed me."

"Precisely, and it also happened again with the penultimate owner. However, there was one more who came first. In 1830, ten years after Timothy Shelley died, with much of the place shut up and the remainder looked after by a skeleton staff of three, The Hall changed hands once again. Now this is the one I find most interesting. See if you come to the same conclusion I did."

"Heavens, that sounds intriguing. I hope I can live up to your expectation, Harriet."

She laughed. "George Barnstaple was a naturalist and ornithologist. As you know, the bird life here is remarkable. Even today, in fact, in the spring, you can barely move without bumping into a twitcher. I've found them picnicking on my lawns and sat in my apple trees before now. But I digress. Back to George. He already had several published works under his belt which he'd also illustrated beautifully—I have copies here if you're interested—and The Hall was the most natural place for him to live and continue his work. He lived a quiet and solitary life and for almost four decades lived happily at The Hall until his death in 1871 at the grand old age of eighty-four."

"So the curse had been broken?" I paused and frowned. "No, that can't be right. Why would it have been? Wait a minute, you didn't mention his family. He was a bachelor, wasn't he, so the curse wouldn't have affected him?"

Harriet peered over her pince-nez, eyes shining as though I were a recalcitrant child who'd suddenly learned obedience.

"I knew you wouldn't fail me, Isobella. Sharp as a tack. You're quite correct."

"Well, surely that lends credibility to the authenticity of the curse?"

Harriet nodded. "It does seem that way, doesn't it? But as I said before, Isobella, I'm in two minds about it. It just seems too fantastical."

"I suppose you're right," I said, although I suspected if she knew I could see ghosts and had a phantom cat as a companion, she might have changed her mind. "So what happened next?"

"Well, with no family to bequeath The Hall to, Barnstaple stated in his will it should be sold to raise funds for the newly-founded Royal Society for the Protection of Birds. So once again it was on the market."

"Did it sell quite quickly this time?" I asked. "I would imagine the tales of the curse had somewhat diminished over the forty years George Barnstaple was the owner."

"I think you're most likely correct," Harriet agreed, "for The Hall was snapped up almost immediately. Although the difference this time was the new proprietor didn't reside in it full time. In fact he barely set foot in the place for years as he already owned a Georgian Manor house in London's Clapham Common and an apartment in Mayfair."

"He must have been wealthy. Was he a peer of the realm too?" I asked.

"Good heavens no! Far from it. Adam Worthington was a thoroughly nasty piece of work and had made his vast wealth through illicit gambling, robberies and prostitution. He practically ran London in those days, but he would get his just deserts when he moved to Arundel Hall."

"And this is the man Robert bought it from?"

"Not exactly. Robert and I aren't *that* ancient, you know. Robert was the next owner of course, but by then The Hall had once again remained empty for some time and needed finance to make it habitable."

I nodded. Most of the island knew Robert had been refurbishing Arundel for his retirement.

"So what happened to this villain?"

"Worthington was a wanted man, not just here, but in America. Scotland Yard and the Pinkerton Detective Agency had corresponded and determined the man was suspected of numerous crimes in both countries. But he remained elusive and he was very clever. None of the evidence gathered pointed to him directly, but they were sure he was the mastermind. When word reached him that they were getting close, he did a midnight flit and absconded to The Hall. He'd bought the place under another name, Henry Raymond. He changed his appearance and lived the life of a wealthy country gentleman for some time while the danger passed. But of course the lure of his former world was eventually too strong to resist. He missed the danger and excitement, the wheeling and dealing of his corrupt existence, but most of all he missed the company."

"Oh, so he'd moved to The Hall on his own? How long was he there?"

"Alone, you mean?" Harriet asked.

I nodded.

"Just shy of two years. Ah, I see what you're getting at. Well thought out, Isobella, I must admit the significance had eluded me. Well, it all changed when he moved not only his wife and children in, but his mistress and her youngsters too."

I cringed in disgust. How could anyone live like that?

"I know. Shocking, isn't it?" said Harriet, reading my mind. "But that wasn't all. Over a short period of time, so as not to raise the alarm in London, he moved in most of his gang and their partners and a life of drunken debauchery began. Gambling parties were rife in those days and of course women of dubious morals were already in residence. It was only a matter of time before the curse made itself known.

"The first body, that of a young prostitute, was found hanging from the chandelier in the foyer; the second, a minor henchman of Worthington's, was found drowned in an upstairs bathtub with his wrists cut. They were both thought to be suicide, but of course no one really knows. The only eye-witness was a young street girl who confessed to the goings-on at The Hall on her deathbed many years later. The bodies were disposed of and the remains never found. As the months went on, the body count rose, fights broke out among the inhabitants, many of which ended in death. The costs were also spiralling out of control and Worthington was forced to sell off considerable chunks of the estate to raise funds."

"Harriet, this is absolutely ghastly. It must have been harrowing for the children."

"And thereby hangs the sorriest tale of all, I'm afraid. The wife and mistress, who incidentally had lived quite happily in the knowledge of each other in the city, became incensed with jealousy and rage. The theory is they both simply went insane simultaneously and killed the other's children before turning the guns on themselves."

I found I couldn't speak. I couldn't imagine this horror, but Harriet hadn't finished.

"In abject despair and mad with grief, Adam Worthington ran from the house, screaming, and threw himself off the bluff onto the rocks of Smuggler's Cove below. He died instantly. The remaining members of his household fled and were never seen nor heard from again. The body known as that of Henry Raymond was taken to London and there his true identity as Adam Worthington was discovered. His will stipulated his estate was to be left to his children, but as they were all dead, the responsibility of disposal reverted to the state.

"By now, of course, the whole of the country had heard the tale. There wasn't a newspaper in circulation that wasn't running the story on its front page. Consequently, no one wanted anything to do with the place. Of course there were the usual thrill seekers and ghouls who came on day trips by the coach load to stand and peer through the iron gates, but there were no offers to purchase, even at a considerably reduced market value. So the place was once more closed and languished in decay until Robert came along.

"So there you have it, my dear, the rather insalubrious history of Arundel Hall and its dreadful curse."

I thanked Harriet for her time.

"Not quite what you were expecting, my dear?"

I shook my head. No doubt I would be plagued by nightmares later.

CHAPTER SIX

I awoke the next morning to a light tap on my door.
"Come in," I said, groggily sitting up and reaching for my bed jacket.

My eyes were gritty and my head pounded horribly. I had been right about the nightmares. On my return home I'd found the promised cold buffet laid out and had taken a tray to the cosy sitting room in front of the fire. I'd sat long into the night, nursing my second medicinal brandy while I pondered the tale of the curse. Eventually, in the small hours, I'd wearily climbed the stairs and fallen into a disturbed sleep. Now it was apparently morning and I felt as though I hadn't slept at all.

Mrs. Shaw came in, balancing my breakfast tray, and deftly set it up on the counterpane. A glance to the pillow next to me showed Phantom curled in a ball, fast asleep.

"Thank you, Mrs. Shaw. What time is it?"

"A quarter after nine. I thought it was unusually late for you, so took the liberty of making your breakfast."

"Of course, that's fine, Mrs. Shaw. I had rather a disturbed sleep. Tell me, have you heard of the curse of Arundel Hall?" I asked while I buttered my toast and took the top off my egg.

"A curse on the big house on the bluff? No, I can't say I have. What's it all about then?"

I proceeded to tell her, very briefly, of the first owner cursing The Hall for its subsequent inhabitants.

"Oh, a Romany, was he?"

I started. "No, I don't think so, why?"

"Well, I'd imagine you'd have to have some knowledge and skill. I doubt any Tom, Dick, or Harry could do something like that, not that I believe such nonsense, of course. Will there be anything else?"

"There is one other thing, Mrs. Shaw. Sir Robert approached me yesterday about some additional help for his housekeeper for a small dinner party. I naturally thought of you, but said I would have to ask you first."

"A dinner party? Me? Oh well, I'm not sure I'm the one to ask, I … "

Good heavens, was the woman flustered?

"Oh, come now, Mrs. Shaw. I'm led to believe it will be a very modest group, myself included, so nothing too complicated."

"Well, I'm a little out of practice so … "

Out of practice? She'd only been with me a short time. I couldn't fathom her reticence.

I smiled to take the command from my next words.

"Mrs. Shaw, this is no time for false modesty. with your excellent credentials and experience, I'm sure this will prove to be effortless for you. You would in fact be doing me a favour as well as Sir Robert. I'd like you to help."

I watched as her back straightened and her chin rose. Her eyes fixed on a position above my head. "Well, if you put it like that. I know Mrs. Butterworth marginally. We attend the same church. I'll see to it. Is that all?" she asked stiffly.

"It is, Mrs. Shaw, and thank you."

Well, what on Earth was that all about? I thought as she left. Admittedly, I hadn't known Mrs. Shaw long, but flustered was not a state I'd thought her capable of. Brusque, no nonsense, and decisive perhaps, but flustered? Never. I'd obviously caught her by surprise. I shrugged, dismissing the incident, and continued with my breakfast while I pondered on how a Duke would have the skills to put such a strong curse on a building. *I must ask Harriet about it,* I thought. Then realised I'd forgotten to ask her my second question while at the library. I felt I really must start writing things down and vowed to purchase a small notebook at the earliest opportunity.

Once dressed, I ventured downstairs and was just passing the hall telephone when it rang. Expecting Jerry and another of his practical jokes, I was surprised when I heard Harriet's voice.

"Good morning, dear, how did you sleep?"

I confessed I'd had a disturbed night and was still feeling a little sluggish.

"Well, I'm sure it won't last, dear, but I have several recipes for aiding sleep. I'll send Giles over with them."

The elderly Giles was Harriet's titular butler and chauffeur, and although I had never spoken with him, I knew him by sight.

"That's very kind of you, Harriet. Incidentally, I asked Mrs. Shaw earlier if she'd heard about the curse. She said she hadn't, but made rather a good point. Wouldn't the

Duke have had to have some sort of training in order to cast such a curse? She wondered if there were Romany involved. Do you know?"

"I certainly don't know about any training, but the Romany had camps all over the island in those days, so he may very well have come into contact with them. Or he may have sought them out with the purpose of learning such a skill. It's not something I can verify of course."

"No, of course not, but it does answer the question. Now is there something I can help you with?"

"Actually, I remembered you wanted to ask me something else yesterday. Was it about the boundary marking near your cottage by any chance?"

"Yes, it was. I only remembered myself this morning. Do you know what it is?"

"I believe you'll find it's a walled garden. They were very popular in Victoria's time and I suspect yours was added then."

"Harriet, why that's simply marvellous news. I do so love my garden and it's been in the back of my mind to add a produce section. But if one's already in place, it will save a huge amount of work."

"I'm so glad I've cheered you, Isobella. I was feeling rather guilty about the horrors I inflicted on you yesterday. I take it there's no sign of the wall then?"

"No, none at all. I don't think the garden has been seen to in a long time. There's a veritable forest of briars, hawthorn and weeds over that side, most of it way over my head. It will probably take an army to clear it all."

"Well, I don't have an army to hand, but I do know of a strong young man looking for work. He's not what you'd expect, but he's surprisingly knowledgeable about plants and a hard worker to boot."

"Send him over, Harriet, by all means. A gardener is exactly what I need."

Mrs. Shaw appeared just as I was replacing the receiver. Dressed in her coat and hat and with her handbag over one arm, she put on her gloves and asked, "I'm just popping down to the village, Miss Bridges. Is there anything you need?"

"Yes, a small notebook if you'd be so kind, Mrs. Shaw."

"Of course. I'll pick one up at the stationer's on my way past. Which reminds me, the post arrived earlier. I've left it on the hall table for you."

While Mrs. Shaw was out, I intended once again to visit the secret room, which I'd found behind the pantry. "Oh, Ella!" I chided myself in exasperation. I'd forgotten to tell Harriet about it. It had been my one reason for seeking her out in the first place, but with all the excitement of the curse it had slipped my mind. Thank goodness I'd remembered to ask for a notebook.

The postman had only delivered one item. The envelope was of impeccable quality with a gilt trim and I knew what it was before I even opened it: the invitation to dinner at Arundel Hall. I sighed and put it on the mantelshelf in the sitting room and, crossing to my desk, made a note to purchase a suitable engagement present. Absently, I noticed I had yet to look at the recent puzzle from Aunt Margaret, but before I could there was a knock at the door.

"Doctor Brookes, what a pleasant surprise."

"Good morning, Miss Bridges. I had a couple of home visits nearby and thought I'd come and check how your wrist is. I hope I'm not intruding?"

"No, not at all, do come in."

"I see you've dispensed with the sling," he said as I showed him into the sitting room.

I sat as he unwrapped the bandage.

"Well, it seems to be healing nicely. I'd advise keeping the support on for a few days, but no more than that. Try not to overuse it for a week or so afterward and it should be back to full strength in no time."

As he rose, his eye caught sight of the invitation. "Ah, I see you've been invited up to The Hall. We received our invitation this morning too."

We? I thought dismally. I'd been under the impression the doctor was single. Had rather hoped he was, I admitted to myself with some surprise.

"Do you know Robert and Patty-Mae well?" I asked.

"Him well enough. Her I don't know at all," he added sharply. "Robert's more my father's friend than mine. He's been the family physician for years. Unfortunately, father's a bit under the weather at the moment so I'll have to attend alone. Unless…" Bright green eyes looked at me from under a fringe of dark red hair. "Would it be awfully improper of me to ask to be your escort for the evening?"

I stood and couldn't help the huge smile. "Not at all. I'd like that very much, Doctor Brookes."

His smile mirrored my own. "Well, in that case I'm sure we can dispense with the formalities. Nathaniel," he said, holding out his left hand in deference to my injured right one.

"Ella," I replied, and shook it.

"I'll pick you up at seven then?"

I nodded. Perhaps the evening would turn out to be pleasant after all.

CHAPTER SEVEN

The knocking of my heels on the bare stone treads echoed as I descended the servants' stairs to the kitchen, and I thought what a ludicrous position it was for a dining room. How could guests be expected to traverse this gloom, then proceed through the staff kitchen and then through the pantry to eat? I could just imagine titled ladies in their finery having to negotiate this narrow space, their gowns catching on the rough plaster, ruining cloth and stitching. No, that would never work. The door I had found must be for staff access only, which meant there must be another way leading from the main house which I hadn't yet found. As I mentally went through the positions of the rooms on the primary floor and the likelihood of another secret panel, I reached the pantry where Phantom was already waiting for me.

"Phantom, if it's not too much trouble, I really could do with some help."

He pinned me with a disdainful look for an instant, then disappeared through the solid door to the room beyond.

I sighed and, crouching down, clicked the latch to release the door, then followed him in.

Once I'd lit the new candles in the wall sconces, I sat in the carver at the top end of the large rectangular table and looked around. This room never failed to take my breath away. It was simply stunning. My first impression upon discovery had been one of austerity and gloom, particularly as there was no natural light. Ginny had found the place quite chilling, but the more I ventured down here, the more I appreciated the detail and workmanship. I'd spent a lot of time in the interim period cleaning the place up, prior to hiring Mrs. Shaw.

The artistry of the oak wall panels was exquisite, and it was obvious master craftsmen had been employed to produce them. From the ceiling down to the middle was quite plain, but the lower half was sculpted into something that looked like draped cloth, which I had subsequently found out was called linenfold. Along the wide rail, which split the two halves, a row of acorns chased each other around the room, but it was the highly decorated ceiling I found most enchanting. Each panel was intricately carved with vines and interspersed throughout were rosebuds and roses, not stylised ones like the Tudor version, but realistic replicas in various stages of bloom. It was like a garden. I couldn't wait to hold my first dinner party here and had already imagined how festive it would look at Christmas. But first there was the matter of the unfortunate resident to deal with.

As though she'd heard my thoughts, the woman rose from her place in the fireside chair and began to float gently back and forth. Unlike Phantom, she hadn't acquired any form of solidity, and I could clearly see the fireplace through her elaborate gown. It was aqua in colour with a full length hooped skirt and adorned with lace and bows at her cleavage, and the end of the elbow length sleeves. Her dark hair was piled high and topped off with an elaborate feather ensemble. At her throat were three strings of pearls, which matched the bracelet and earrings, and on the third finger of her left hand was a ring with a large central pearl, surrounded by garnets. Whoever she was, she'd obviously had wealth.

I don't know how long I sat there contemplating my next move, but I was suddenly shaken back to the present by the slam of a motorcar door. Mrs. Shaw! I quickly ran to the pantry and saw her wave at Harriet's driver Giles. I don't know what possessed me to do what I did next, I ran back into the dining room clicked the door in place and leaned back against it with a sigh. Then it struck me: I was trapped.

I could faintly hear Mrs. Shaw bustling about in the kitchen unpacking groceries and humming to herself. It looked as though I would be stuck for a while. I glanced at the far end of the room and saw Phantom's tail disappear through the wall.

"I'm sure you do that on purpose knowing I can't follow," I hissed.

To my surprise he came back through and sat down.

Well, I suppose it was as good a time as any to explore, so taking a candle I began to study the panel where Phantom had once again vanished. As I moved to the far corner I gasped as the flame began to flicker. There was a draft coming through, so there must be a space behind. The panel was so snug against its neighbours there wasn't even the tiniest join to signal a disguised door. I worked my way around it, carefully applying pressure, but there was nothing. Thinking it may work in the same way as the pantry door I rested the candle on the parquet floor, and on hands and knees looked for a hidden latch, but again was disappointed. There was absolutely nothing there. So whatever triggered the opening had to be somewhere else in the room, but where to start?

I tried to think about it logically. Phantom disappeared through a panel which, upon further investigation, due to the flickering candle flame, indicated a likely cavity behind, but there was no apparent way of opening it. The only other unusual aspect to the room was the ghost. I stopped to think. Since I'd first discovered her here, the woman had never ventured away from the fireplace, "Could it really be that simple?" I said aloud.

Approaching, I began to study the ornate marble. The design mirrored that of the ceiling with vines and roses across the frontage, but the sides were made up of statuary in the form of animals. Small birds sat in branches above while a fox sat at floor level on the left side and a hare at the right. After what seemed like hours of pushing and pulling every little carving, on the top left, I discovered a rosebud raised slightly higher than others. With a deep breath I pushed and was rewarded by a click behind me. Turning, I saw the panel had swung forward an inch. I'd found the secret door.

I slowly approached and, holding the candle aloft, carefully pulled the panel toward me. I let out an involuntary cry and stumbled back in shock for there, at the foot of a stone staircase, was a broken skeleton.

CHAPTER EIGHT

"Hello, who's there?" I heard Mrs. Shaw shout faintly from the kitchen.

Ignoring her for the moment, I took a step forward and looked in more detail at the pile of bones. Loosely wrapped around the top vertebrae were three strands of pearls, one had broken and a few loose gems were scattered about. The wrist was likewise adorned, and laying on the stone flags were a pair of pearl earrings. The pearl and garnet ring lay loosely encircled on the third finger of the left hand and tatty scraps of once blue fabric, rotted with time, clung to the bones like moss on damp rocks. I'd finally found the body of my spectral guest. Now all I had to do was identify her.

I strode over to the door and let myself out through the pantry, where I was saved by my quick instincts from being knocked senseless by Mrs. Shaw brandishing a frying pan.

"Now, Mrs. Shaw, please calm yourself. There's nothing to panic about."

"Miss Bridges, really! You frightened me to death. Where on Earth did you come from?"

"From the pantry, Mrs. Shaw. There's a room behind there and I'm afraid I've made a rather gruesome discovery. It's ... "

"I knew there was something wrong in there, didn't I tell you? What have you found?"

There really wasn't a delicate way of telling her. "I'm afraid it's a body. Well, a skeleton to be exact. It's obviously been there a long time."

I'd expected her to fall apart, but the opposite happened. She took control immediately. What an enigma this woman was.

"You'll need to call the police, Miss Bridges. I'll put the kettle on and make some sandwiches. I daresay it's going to be a long night. Let's just hope it was a tragic accident."

It wasn't. My scrutiny had discovered the back half of the skull had been bashed in, it was definitely murder.

I decided to circumvent our local constabulary in favour of calling Uncle Albert. Not because our resident policeman was incapable, he wasn't, but because I knew this particular case would need a specialist.

Albert was the current Police Commissioner with Scotland Yard. He was actually Ginny's Godfather, but insisted we all call him uncle. Luckily he was available when I called.

"Ella, what a pleasant surprise. How are you? Settling in well at the cottage and no more ghostly goings on, I hope?" he finished in a whisper.

Albert had been instrumental in helping me solve the case of a murdered young orphan girl not long after I'd moved in. He'd also met Phantom and ruined a perfectly good shirt in the process. I'm not sure he'd fully got over the shock.

"Actually, Uncle Albert, there are more ghostly goings on as you put it, and I'm afraid it's in your professional capacity I'm calling. I've found a body. Well, a skeleton actually, hidden behind one of the panels in the downstairs dining room."

"Good lord, have you really? What a shock for you. Are you all right?"

"Yes, I'm fine, but wondered if you could help. I'm not sure what to do next."

"Of course I'll help, Ella. That goes without saying. Now if you'll give me all the details, I'll make some notes and get the ball rolling at this end."

I could hear the scratching of Albert's pen while he scribbled extensively, stopping a couple of times to confirm what I'd said.

"And you think it's murder, do you?"

"Well, the back of the skull is extremely damaged, much more so than if she'd simply fallen down the stairs. It looks deliberate to me, very nasty." I looked around to make sure Mrs. Shaw wasn't hovering about and lowered my voice. "Plus, of course, the ghost of a woman has been in residence since I discovered the room, and judging from the jewellery, the body's definitely hers."

"Ah I see, yes. Well, leave it with me. I'll start things moving here. I'll also see to it word gets to your local chap. Not that we're likely to need him, of course, more a matter of courtesy. I should be with you in a couple of hours at most."

"I'll have the guest room made up for you. Thank you, Uncle Albert," I said and rang off.

Back in the kitchen Mrs. Shaw was buttering bread and slicing luncheon meat as though the entire greater London constabulary would descend at any moment.

"I think that will do actually, Mrs. Shaw. I'm not sure how many will be coming, but Albert Montesford will be staying overnight so will require dinner. Also, could you make up the front guest room for him, please?"

"Certainly, Miss Bridges. Oh, and while I remember, there's a package for you there," she nodded to the dresser, "from Miss Dinworthy. Giles was on his way over when he saw me in the village, so he kindly dropped me off. He also said to expect the gardener at nine in the morning. Oh, and here's your notebook."

"Thank you, Mrs. Shaw." I made a note about the gardener, put the notebook and pen in my pocket next to the matches and went to the dresser.

I opened the package to find a small wicker basket full of items. Dried lemon balm and chamomile in paper packets, recipes for the teas as she'd promised and several packets of vegetable seeds, so I could grow my own once I had my garden up and running, the accompanying note said. *Dear Harriet, how thoughtful.* Plus three large red onions. I scanned the note again, wondering what they were for: stewed onion syrup, soup, or eat them raw. I grimaced. Better stick to the tea. Putting them to one side, I informed Mrs. Shaw I would be in the room behind the pantry if she wanted me, and set off to explore the newly-found staircase. I needed to know where it went.

I took a candle, much quicker than trying to hunt for the torch I wasn't sure I'd brought with me when I'd moved, and gingerly stepped over the remains, being careful not to disturb anything. I began to ascend into the gloom. It was much wider than the staff stairs and would easily accommodate guests with the full skirts of a long-ago era. It was clear by the amount of dust and thick cobwebs, this staircase had not been used for aeons. The walls were panelled in a similar fashion to the main room, with a handrail affixed to one side, but the steps themselves were bare stone and uneven from use. The light from the candle was poor, so I had to take my time, but my feet still kicked up many years' worth of dust, causing me to cough and sneeze.

I shivered as thick cobwebs stuck to my hair, and stifled a scream as I felt something drop on the back of my neck. Slapping wildly at my unseen assailant, I dropped the candle and watched as it bounced down a couple of steps and the flame died. With shaking hands, I took the matchbox from my pocket and striking the head produced a flame. Lowering it in search of the candle, I came face to face with a pair of green eyes. I fell back on the step, heart pounding and gasping with fright. The match flame guttered for a second, then went out.

"Phantom! That was not funny," I hissed, as I shakily produced another flame and managed to relight my errant candle. Phantom sat on the step with a smug look on his face. I turned, ignoring him, and continued my journey upwards.

The tickling of another multi-legged creature crawling up my calf induced a strange dance, as I stomped my feet trying to dislodge it. Which, of course, raised more dust and set me to sneezing again. With eyes streaming, I eventually came to a dogleg and with one hand guiding me around the wall, turned left and continued. Surely it couldn't be much further. Several steps more and I finally reached a small landing and what looked like a solid door. I leant my head against it in relief. I felt as though I'd climbed a mountain.

"Well, this is it," I said to myself. "Let's see where you lead to." I put my shoulder against the door, pushed, and nothing happened. I frowned. Of course there must be a hidden catch of some sort released from the other side, but this side it should be easy to spot. It was, about halfway down the left side. I lifted it and the door swung outward about an inch, letting in a much welcome shaft of light and clean air.

After so many years of disuse, I had expected it to be stiff, but with a gentle push, it swung easily and I found myself in the formal reception room. Turning, I saw the secret panel was in fact the left side of a pair of bookshelves, which encompassed the fireplace. I pushed it shut again and stood back to gaze at the clever concealment. I doubted I would ever have found it from this side. Now I knew what to look for I found the mechanism easily. Once again it was a small piece of ornate carving in the fire surround, which when depressed freed the catch with a barely perceptible click.

Nodding at a job well done, I found myself in a cloud of dust and cobwebs. Dashing to the mirror in the hall, I laughed at the stranger staring back at me. I looked like the Ghost of Christmas Past. *I'd better get cleaned up before Albert arrives. It wouldn't do to give him any more frights.*

I'd donned a pair of dark green twill trousers with a leather belt, and teamed them with a matching sweater and brown and white Oxford saddle shoes. Considering my work for the day, my tweed skirt, stockings and heels were an impractical choice. Plus I secretly felt far more comfortable in this attire than the former. It was quite liberating.

By the time I reached the kitchen, Albert was already there, a delicate cup of tea in one meaty hand and a sandwich in the other. Mrs. Shaw frowned briefly at my choice of clothing, but wisely kept her own counsel.

With Albert were two other gentlemen I didn't know, each with their own victuals.

"Ella, may I introduce the police surgeon Doctor Mortimer Smythe?"

"Miss Bridges," the doctor said in a reedy tone, and with a serious look, shook my proffered hand. Wearing a sombre grey suit he was excessively tall and thin, with a bald pate and a grey toothbrush moustache. He was also extremely pale. He obviously spent many hours working indoors. I noticed in him the tell-tale signs of an habitual pipe smoker and didn't want him to feel awkward.

"Do feel free to smoke your pipe indoors, Doctor Smythe. I don't mind in the slightest."

He raised an eyebrow, shot a glance at Albert, but said nothing.

"And this is Sergeant Baxter."

The sergeant raised his sandwich in embarrassed response, and mumbled through a mouthful, "Miss." In contrast he was of ruddy complexion and had a short stocky build. Mid-brown hair, beginning to grey at the temples, was swept back from a wide forehead, but the crinkling around the bright intelligent eyes spoke of an easy humour.

"Well, gentlemen, I see my housekeeper has been looking after you. Thank you, Mrs. Shaw. Now if you've all finished, I'll take you through."

I unfastened the hidden catch, slid the shelf sideways, and the three gentlemen followed me.

Albert held me back momentarily and said in a low voice, "Well done, Ella, regarding the pipe, and what did you notice about the sergeant?"

I whispered back. "I do believe he had eggs for breakfast."

Albert let out a guffaw, then proceeded to the far end of the room where the panel was still open.

"It's a bit dark in 'ere," Sergeant Baxter said. "Is it only candlelight you've got, Miss?"

"The rest of the house has electricity, but I'm afraid it's all we have in here until I can sort out the wiring."

"Sergeant, if you'll assist the doctor," Albert said.

"Yes, sir. I'll start by bringing in the portables," he said and left.

"Portables?" I asked Albert.

"Lanterns. They're a standard part of the field kit. You never know what you're going to find or where you're going to find it."

Albert looked at the skeleton with a sad shake of his head, peered up the staircase and examined the panel. Then came across to where I was waiting. "Ella, we'll stay out of the way for the moment, let Mortimer do his job. Perhaps you can show me where the staircase emerges?"

I nodded and led him upstairs.

"I thought it best we spoke privately, considering the nature of your, er … unusual ability," Albert said when we'd reached the safety of the reception room.

"Oh, quite," I said. "Wouldn't want to upset the natives."

"It's a remarkable room you've discovered there. Must have been quite a surprise?"

"Absolutely, but terribly exciting too. I'm looking forward to using it."

"I'm not sure Ginny will be too keen. I telephoned and told her I was on my way here and why. She likened it to a medieval banqueting hall, full of Vikings with appalling manners," Albert said with a smirk.

I laughed; that was just like Ginny. My sister-in-law had a penchant for drama.

"And you've no idea whose remains they are?" he asked.

I did have a possible idea, but until I was sure I didn't want to say anything. "Not at the moment, but I'm in the process of doing some research. I'll let you know what I find out."

Albert nodded in acceptance. "Well, the doctor should be able to give an approximate age of the bones which should help. I'll pass on what information he gleans. So show me how this door works. I must say I'm intrigued. I've been looking, but can't spot it."

I rose and went to the fireplace. "Keep your eye on the left bookcase," I said and depressed the catch. The bookcase swung forward about an inch revealing the dark space beyond.

Albert went to study it in more detail. "Remarkable. And what craftsmanship. I'll get Baxter to add some lights down there. It will make the job easier."

He called down and the sergeant responded with a, "Yes, sir."

"Will they be staying overnight too? If so, I'll need to let Mrs. Shaw know."

"No, I've arranged for rooms at the Dog and Gun in the village for tonight. With any luck we'll be able to move the deceased tomorrow. She'll be taken to the morgue and Mortimer will continue the examination there."

A few minutes later, Sergeant Baxter appeared with several lanterns and we left him to it.

CHAPTER NINE

A couple of hours later, Albert and I were seated at the large table downstairs, listening to Doctor Smythe's findings.

"I've confirmed it was a female, although with the presence of the jewellery it was rather a moot point. I've bagged those here for you, Miss Bridges." He slid a buff-coloured envelope across the table to me. I must have looked surprised for he continued, "I believe they will be safer in your keeping until a next of kin is found, assuming there is one. It's always difficult with cases as old as this."

"And what happens if there is no next of kin?"

Albert answered, "Unless they're of particular importance to the nation or the crown, then they're yours to do with as you wish. In essence, you bought them along with the contents of the property."

"Good heavens, I had no idea."

"What else did you discover, Doctor?" asked Albert.

"You're quite right about it being murder. The trauma to the back of the skull is considerable. She was repeatedly hit over the head with a blunt, heavy instrument and in my opinion this was excessive. A vicious attack. Whoever did it was extremely angry."

"Yes, I thought so too," I said. "The first blow would have killed her outright, wouldn't it? Then why continue to lash out unless whoever did it was in a blind rage about something she had done."

"You ought to offer her a job, Albert," Doctor Smythe said in all seriousness.

Albert eyed me with interest as the doctor continued.

"Her neck is also broken, as are her left wrist and ankle, but they happened post-mortem, most likely when she was thrown down the stairs."

"It's definite she went down the stairs then and wasn't shoved behind the panel from this room?" asked Albert.

To his surprise, I answered."Yes, it is. I noticed some scuffs down the panelling when I went up the stairs. There are also some old stains which could be blood, and a couple of the pearls from the broken necklace in the corner of the upper treads." I rattled the contents of the envelope for emphasis.

"Is there any way to tell her age? I don't mean how old the bones are, but what age she was when she died?" I asked.

The doctor's lips were twitching in a half smile as he answered. "Well, I'll have a better idea when I get back to London, but there are no obvious signs of age related deformity. That, together with the fact the bones are fully matured leads me to make an educated guess at somewhere between twenty-five and thirty."

She'd been the same age as me.

"It's purely guesswork, you understand," said the doctor, "and not something I do under normal circumstances. It also depends on a number of external factors, you see, such as diet and living conditions, which I won't know until we can put a more definite age to the bones themselves."

I nodded. "Of course. One other thing, is it possible to know whether she'd given birth?"

"While we've made great strides in this area of science, Miss Bridges, I can't help with that particular question. But there is one other point of note. She was missing the last joint of the little finger on her right hand. It could have been a birth defect or a prior accident, difficult to tell now of course, but it may help identify her. Now if you'll excuse me," he said rising, "there's nothing more we can do today. Baxter and I will get on with the photographs and suchlike in the morning, then we can move her to London."

"I'll see you out, Mortimer," said Albert, heaving his great bulk from the chair.

Doctor Smythe turned to me and held out a hand. "It's been a pleasure, Miss Bridges. I seldom meet a mind as bright as yours."

"Well, you've certainly impressed Mortimer. I've rarely heard him speak so highly of anyone at a first meeting," Albert said when he returned. "Now what do you say I take you out for dinner this evening?"

I agreed that was a lovely idea, and after I'd informed Mrs. Shaw, who assured me there was nothing she had prepared that wouldn't be perfectly fine for the next day's lunch, we went to dress.

I woke with a start the next day and dashed out of bed to the phone. The dinner party was the following day and

I still hadn't organised a suitable gift. With the police in my house, the gardener due, no suitable boutique in the village in which to purchase something and no time to go to London myself, I called Ginny.

"Of course I'll help, Ella. Since when have I ever refused a shopping trip? I'll pop along to Harrods later and have them deliver something to you today. But do let me wake up first. I know you rise earlier in the country, but it's still the middle of the night here. Goodbye, darling, talk soon," she said with a yawn and put the telephone down.

I laughed and replaced the receiver. Ginny already treated my island home as though it were a different country with its own weather system, and now it would appear, a different time zone as well.

I reached the dining room and found Albert helping himself to breakfast. The various covered dishes on the sideboard contained bacon, eggs both scrambled and fried, sausages and fried bread. Not to mention several rounds of toast with preserves as well as tea and coffee.

"Good morning, Ella."

"Goodness, Mrs. Shaw has been busy this morning. She must have been up before dawn," I said in amazement. I helped myself, then sat across from Albert and poured us both tea.

"What time will Doctor Smythe and Sergeant Baxter arrive, do you think?" I asked Albert.

He removed the napkin from his knee, wiped his mouth and, glancing at his wristwatch, said, "In about half an hour, I should think. Mortimer is an early riser and there's a lot to do before we set off back to London. I'd imagine you'll find the next bit interesting. Are you staying to watch?"

"I'd certainly like to, yes. I'm expecting a young man to interview for a gardener's position, but that shouldn't take too long. I need to see she's taken care of. That probably sounds silly, doesn't it? But I feel responsible for her and I'm wondering if her spirit will move along with her remains."

"Do you think it will?"

"I'm not sure. I haven't solved everything yet. I mean, we don't even know who she is, so perhaps not. But we do know she was murdered, which is something, I suppose. Ultimately, she's here seeking justice."

"In my experience, once we identify her it should make finding the murderer easier. It's all about those with a motive and the means to commit the act," Albert said.

"Yes, you're right. Well, all we can do is wait and see. If she stays, then I know I have more to do."

Albert put his napkin on the table and sat back, his breakfast finished.

"You know, I was reading a piece in The Times the other day about that Conan-Doyle chap."

"The writer? I believe Jerry met him a couple of times before he died. Only briefly, you understand, and more as an admirer, as it was before Jerry really became known. Have you read any of his Holmes books?"

Albert raised an eyebrow. "The violin playing, opium smoking, master of disguise detective and his greenhorn sidekick? No, not a word," he said with a twinkle in his eye.

I smiled. "Not quite true to life then?"

He shook his head. "Not quite, no. But they are written from a refreshing angle with some astute observations. I find them very entertaining. But that's not why I mentioned it. Did you know he was a spiritualist? He's written much about his beliefs and used to lecture on the subject."

"No, I didn't know that." I frowned as I tried to re-call a fleeting memory. "Wasn't there something about him and the Cottingley fairies? Jerry and I grew up near there."

"That's right, he was a true believer. He published a book about them, all part and parcel of his belief in the spirit world. His children's nanny had psychic abilities as it turned out. I'll try and dig out the article for you. It's fascinating stuff."

"Thank you, Uncle Albert, I'd be most interested to read it. I'll make a note to see if Harriet can obtain some of his spiritualist books for me." I took my notebook from my pocket and had just finished scribbling when Mrs. Shaw came in to announce the arrival of Albert's colleagues.

"They're busy unloading a lot of equipment in the yard, sir," she informed him, beginning to clear the table.

"I'll come and unlock the pantry door for them," I said.

"There's also a young man loitering at the gate, Miss Bridges, the gardener most likely. I think he's a bit nervous of coming in, what with the police being here and everything."

Heavens, I hoped he wasn't a criminal. No, Harriet wouldn't have suggested him if that were the case. In a very unladylike way, thanks to my trousers, I took the stairs at a canter while Albert made steadier progress behind me. I unlocked the pantry door, then went out to the yard.

Shouting a "Good morning," to the policemen, I walked down the drive to the gate.

There, a tall, thin young man stood shivering in a much patched jacket and worn boots, twisting a flat cap in his hands. His face was pink with both the cool morning air and undoubtedly a good scrub of a flannel by the same person who had lovingly repaired his jacket. His pale blond hair had been flattened to within an inch of its life by what looked suspiciously like lard, and he also seemed to have brought a wheelbarrow with him. I doubted he'd need it though. The old barn had every conceivable tool a gardener required. It was one of the first things I'd checked.

"Hello, I'm Isobella Bridges. Did Harriet, Miss Dinworthy, send you?"

In response, he pulled an envelope from his pocket and handed it to me with a shy smile. It was a note from Harriet.

Isobella dear,

This is Tom Parsons, the young man I mentioned to you. He is a dear sweet boy and an innocent, if you comprehend my meaning. He speaks very little, but understands everything you say. I must mention he has an aversion to being touched. It distresses him greatly, even something as simple as shaking hands. He and his parents live in one of the fishermen's cottages and his mother cleans at the hotel, which is how I came to know him. He has been my gardener for the past year and has worked absolute wonders here. Do visit when you get a chance and I'll show you around. Unfortunately there just isn't the amount of work needed as there once was, more a case of keeping on top of things really. I'd gladly keep him on full time, but I can see he's frustrated and eager for a challenge, something to stretch his mind and his talent. Your walled garden, for example. Let me know how you get on.

With best wishes,
Harriet.

P.S. I hope the tea did its job.

"Thank you, Tom. Harriet speaks very highly of you and the work you've done for her. Come in and wait while I get my coat, then we can take a walk around the gardens and I'll show you what needs doing. I do believe Mrs. Shaw has some breakfast going spare."

CHAPTER TEN

While Tom was devouring the remainder of the breakfast in the kitchen, I wrote a letter to his mother. I wanted to introduce myself as Tom's potential employer and to allay any fears she might have. I suspected they were having difficulty making ends meet, but she would be protective of her son and wouldn't let him work for just anyone, he'd be far too easy to take advantage of. I'd said I would be at her cottage at three that afternoon, but if it wasn't convenient to telephone me. I doubted they had a telephone, but knew there was a call box not far away.

That done, I put it in an envelope for Tom to give to his mother when he returned home and went back to the kitchen.

Tom and I had a leisurely stroll around the gardens for almost an hour. I pointed out the lawns which were in dire need of mowing. Trees and bushes needing pruning, hedges needing cutting and various beds and borders which needed bringing back to life. A lot of it was more akin to an archaeological dig than gardening, but I sensed Tom's excitement as we explored. Finally, we came to the immense barricade of weed and briars I had mentioned to Harriet.

"I realise this is a huge undertaking, Tom, and it will take a considerable amount of time to clear. But Harriet and I believe at the back of this lot somewhere there is a walled garden."

He looked at me in amazement, eyes wide and a huge grin on his cherubic face.

"I know, that was my initial reaction too. I'd dearly love to start it up again, produce vegetables and fruit and whatnot. Do you think you'd be up for that?"

He took off his cap and began to twist it. Finally, looking up, he stammered, "Y-yes, Miss. Please."

I was thrilled, not just because he'd spoken, which I hadn't expected after Harriet's note, but because he'd said please. That simple little word spoke volumes.

"Then I would be very pleased to offer you a position here as head gardener, Tom. Here, I've written to your mother. Could you give it to her when you go home? I'd like to visit and introduce myself this afternoon if it's convenient."

He nodded and taking it, carefully put it in his pocket. Then replacing his cap, he ambled off in the direction of the gate. Halfway there he turned round and waved cheerfully before picking up his wheelbarrow and disappearing.

I smiled and went back indoors to telephone Harriet.

Harriet was tremendously pleased I'd taken Tom on and even happier when I'd said I was going to meet his mother.

I also thanked her for the basket of goodies she sent, which she said was no trouble at all.

I rang off, saying I'd see her at The Hall for dinner the next evening, to which she replied with a strange non-committal grunt, and I set off back to the dining room and the police.

Mrs. Shaw caught me in the kitchen to say she'd be leaving at noon sharp to go up to Arundel. "There's a lot to prepare for the dinner tomorrow night and I said I'd help."

I assured her that would be fine.

The ghost of the lady was still hovering around the fireplace when I entered, visible to no one but me, and I also spied Phantom asleep in one of the chairs, one green eye opening to fix me with a stare as I entered, then closing again, disinterested.

Albert was at the table concentrating deeply on paperwork and Doctor Smythe was peering through the lens of a camera, so I wandered over to see what Baxter was doing.

"Why, Sergeant Baxter, what an incredible talent you have." I peered over his shoulder and watched mesmerised as, bent over a drawing pad he drew sections of the skeleton in meticulous detail.

"It's incredible how you make the bones come alive."

He snorted and I giggled, realising what I'd said. I wondered what his reaction would be if he knew the woman's shade was in the room with us.

"You make it look so easy. Did you have training?"

"No, self-taught. Art was hardly a job for a man. Not when I was a lad and probably not now. No money in it unless you're in the business end, buying and selling and so forth. I was expected to follow in my father's footsteps and join the police force, so that's what I did. Mind you, I always carried a sketch book with me, even during the war."

"It must be gratifying to be able to combine both skills now then?"

He nodded over to Albert. "Your uncle's a good man. Recognises the strength of his men and positions them accordingly."

I glanced over at Albert, who was giving an excellent impression of being perfectly oblivious, but I wondered.

Leaving Baxter, I went to watch the doctor.

"Ah, Ella, come to learn? Good, good. You can be my assistant. Now, if you could hold this light and illuminate that area there, a little higher, perfect. Stay still ... got it. Now up a couple of steps, that's it. Hold the light lower. I want to get the angle of the head."

We went along in this vein for some time, me holding lights and the doctor taking photographs. Then he asked if I wanted a try with the camera.

"I'd love to, although I'm not sure what's left to photograph."

He remained silent, waiting. I began to walk around the skeleton, talking to myself as I did so. "You've covered the position of the body in relation to her surroundings. The breakages, such as the neck and the traumatised skull and the missing digit. Have you done the scuffs up the panelling?"

He nodded.

"The possible blood stains and the broken pearls on the stairs?"

Again he nodded.

I frowned, what was I missing?

"Ah, the jewellery!" I said triumphantly.

He smiled and shook his head. "I did those quickly yesterday before I removed them. They needed to be photographed insitu."

I shrugged. "I'll admit I'm stumped."

He took the camera from me and handed me a lantern. "Take that and have a closer look. A much closer look," he added enigmatically.

Dutifully, I got down on my hands and knees and proceeded to scrutinise. Then suddenly I saw it and gasped. "You've already taken some close-up photographs of this, I presume?" I said, turning toward him.

"Yes, several."

"Then we should be able to move her. Do you think it's—"

"The murder weapon? I shouldn't be at all surprised."

I left to make drinks and laid out the lunch Mrs. Shaw had organised before she'd left for The Hall. Glancing at the kitchen clock, I noticed I had just under two hours before I needed to set off to see Mrs. Parsons.

Carrying the tray back to the dining table, I saw the doctor and Sergeant Baxter carefully removing the bones and placing them in a large wooden box, lined with rough cloth. It was no wonder I'd missed the crucial clue initially as it was only a fraction that showed. The rest was underneath the body and obscured by the rotted remains of the gown.

Looking up, Doctor Smythe beckoned me over. I stared at what had been revealed.

"Is that a Griffin?" I asked.

"It is indeed. Cast Iron by the looks of it. No wonder it did so much damage. It's a bookend, undoubtedly one of a pair. You haven't seen its partner here by any chance?"

I shook my head. "There's nothing here like that, I'm afraid."

The doctor rose from his crouched position and stretched his back. "Let's have a spot of lunch, then we can take the remainder of the photographs. I need to get back to London shortly."

"Yes, I have an appointment in the village soon too."

Lunch was a rather subdued affair. We ate quickly and mostly in silence, each with our own thoughts. I assisted the doctor with lighting and took some photographs, while Baxter continued with his drawings of the murder weapon and Albert remained at the table, scribbling notes.

"You see here, Ella?"

I looked to where Doctor Smythe was pointing with the end of his pen.

"Blood and … oh dear, that looks like hair. Well, there's no doubt this was used to kill her. How awful. What do you think happened exactly?"

"Taking an educated guess, I would say her assailant lured her to the top of the steps under some guise or other, then as she turned to descend, he hit her from behind with the bookend. I would imagine she fell on the top landing where he continued to attack her in a blind frenzy. Once she was dead, I think he threw the weapon to the bottom then pushed the body down the stairs, which broke her neck in the process. She landed on top of the bookend, which is why it wasn't noticeable immediately."

"Then he simply locked the secret doors, covered his tracks and left her here to rot," I said.

"That's about the sum of it, yes. Ghastly business."

I silently agreed. To think I'd been living here all this time with the skeleton of a murdered woman hidden in the walls. *I must find out who she was.*

The cars were packed in record time and I stood at the kitchen door and waved until they were out of sight. Doctor Smythe had shaken my hand and said what a pleasure it had been to meet me, and extended an invitation to visit and see his work in more detail, should I ever be in London.

Albert had enfolded me in a bear-hug saying he'd see me soon. Of course, neither of us expected it to be as soon as it was.

I cleared away the dishes, locked the hidden doors and went to Change for my appointment with Tom's mother.

CHAPTER ELEVEN

As I set out to walk to the fisherman's cottages, I was pleasantly surprised to feel a warmer southerly breeze. I had the distinct feeling spring was just around the corner, which lifted my spirits no end. On foot and therefore with no need to take a circuitous route through the village, I halved my journey by taking a shortcut through a less salubrious part of Linhay, past The Kings Head. It was the rougher of two public houses which served the island, and there was always trouble of some sort or other there. The Dog and Gun, where Albert had arranged accommodation for his colleagues, was much nicer and attracted a better clientele altogether. Not least because I believed the quality of beer, while more expensive, was far superior.

As I reached the corner of the pub's tall boundary wall, I glanced up and saw Phantom keeping pace with me, skipping nimbly from stone to stone.

There was a huge commotion and noise coming from beyond the wall with whinnying horses and men shouting.

Wafts of manure and spilled beer drifted on the air to be joined by the sweat of the drays as they rested, ready for the return journey. It was obviously the day for the ale to be delivered from the brewery as I could hear the thunderous roar as unloaded barrels were rolled down the chutes to the cellars. The sheer pandemonium beyond meant it was impossible to pick out individual conversations, but as I neared the end of the wall where the cacophony lessened considerably, I found myself inadvertently being privy to a rather heated argument.

"I tell you I don't have it!"

"Then you'd better find it, boy, and quick before I'm forced to break something. Rumour has it you're racking up debts all over. Not surprising, the stuff's not cheap, but my boss gets paid first or else."

I involuntarily shuddered at the sheer menace and hatred in the voice of the older man. This was no idle threat.

"Take your hands off me! Don't you know who I am?"

"I don't care if you're Bonnie Prince Charlie himself. The boss wants his money and it's my job to make sure you pay … one way or another."

"Yes, well he won't get it if you kill me now, will he? Have you thought of that?"

"Now, now, boy, did I say anything about killing? No, no, no, my instructions are to get it 'by any means necessary short of slitting his throat'. Now, how does two broken legs sound?"

"Don't be so ridiculous, man. You can't just go around breaking a chap's legs. I've told you I will have the money soon. In a week, ten days at the most. Now kindly unhand me and let me go about my business, and you can tell your boss I will only deal with him directly in future. I don't take kindly to threats."

It seemed to me that this young man was either extraordinarily brave, particularly stupid or just plain arrogant. I don't believe he realised how serious his situation was. He was obviously highly educated and his speech and accent marked him as belonging to the upper classes, but I didn't recognise his voice. I just hoped he found a way to extricate himself from the predicament before it was too late.

I continued on with the malevolent laughter of the thuggish man ringing in my ears.

I reached Tom's home a few minutes before the arranged time, but Mrs. Parsons must have been watching out for me as the door opened before I could even raise my hand to knock.

"Good afternoon, Miss Bridges, do come in. It's such a pleasure to finally meet you and thank you for your letter. I'm so happy our Tom has a job with you. Thank you for taking him on. It means so much, what with his father being so ill and his older brothers away doing their own work. Here, let me take your coat. Do go through to the parlour. I've lit a fire so it should be warm for you and the kettle's just set to boiling."

Goodness, when would she pause for breath?

As I had originally surmised, they were in straitened circumstances, partially due to Mr. Parsons being an invalid and of poor health, and Tom's wage would be a much needed addition to the family funds. Mrs. Parsons had gone to a great deal of trouble for me. Over tea, served in what was obviously the best china and a delicious Victoria sponge she'd made herself, I learned Tom had been what was termed 'an accident', coming several years after Patrick, who his parents had thought their third and final son, and when Mrs. Parsons herself was getting on in years. The birth had been a difficult one and it was touch and go whether mother and son would survive the ordeal. As it was, Tom had been starved of oxygen for the first crucial minutes of his life, and as a result was slow and found difficulty in learning, but he had always shown a particular love for nature, his mother had said. This was much apparent in the small square patch of land at the rear of the two-up-two-down fisherman's cottage, where Tom had transformed a once ugly and barren piece of bare earth into a tiny cottage garden of their own.

For the duration of my visit to the Parsons house a small gray scruffy little mongrel, with an endearing face and a happy countenance, made himself at home on my feet.

"That's Digger, Tom's dog," Mrs. Parsons informed me. "Tom rescued him from a trap when he was a pup and they've been inseparable ever since. He'll miss Tom when he's working up at your place."

"Well, Mrs. Parsons, I see no reason why Tom and Digger need be separated at all," I said. "Please, let Tom know I am more than happy for Digger to accompany him to work."

I spent an hour and a half with Mrs. Parsons and the conversation ranged from the walled garden and Tom's duties, to his elder brothers and the scrapes they got into as children. She had raised a fine family on little means and most probably with much sacrifice to herself, and I could see she wouldn't accept handouts or help without doing something of value in return. It was a trait I admired and the more I got to know Mrs. Parsons, the more I liked her.

Finally, I took my leave with promises to call again. I also extended an invitation for her to visit the cottage and have lunch with Tom on occasion.

By the time I left, the air had turned cooler and the sky had darkened considerably. It was as though someone had turned the light-switch off. There was no mistaking the imminence of rain, so I walked to the telephone box on the corner and summoned a taxi to take me home. There was no sign of Phantom although that wasn't unusual, but in fact I wouldn't see him again until I sat down to dinner at The Hall.

CHAPTER TWELVE

'd purchased the dress on a whim the last time I'd been shopping in London with Ginny. It was a deep raspberry satin silk, full length, sleeveless, and to my dismay, backless. I'd balked at the idea initially, but Ginny, along with the owner of the exclusive boutique, had assured me it was the epitome of style and grace. "The perfect combination of risqué and modesty, madam," she'd assured me.

This was the first time I had worn it and standing in front of the mirror in my dressing room, I barely recognised the sleek Grecian Goddess staring back at me. The fabric was cut on the bias, the design hugging my body, creating the ultimate feminine silhouette. I'd never looked nor felt as beautiful. Small groups of beaded flowers adorned the neckline, each one with a tiny pearl in the centre, and at the insistence of Ginny I'd had an evening bag and pair of shoes made to match.

I'd swept back my hair and affixed it with a silver and pearl hair-comb, which showed off the pearl drop earrings my mother had given me and I was just fastening the matching cuff bracelet when the doorbell rang. Mrs. Shaw was already up at The Hall, so I grabbed my black velvet cloak and carefully descended the stairs to answer it.

As expected it was Nathaniel.

He let out a low appreciative whistle. "Ella, you look absolutely stunning," he said as he bent low to kiss my cheek.

"Thank you, Nathaniel." I smiled, blushing a little as my heart pounded.

He looked very dapper in his black tie ensemble, tall and slim; it was the perfect outfit to show off his physique."Shall we go?" he said, extending his arm for me to take.

I took the gift from the hall table and we set off.

Ginny had done awfully well with the gift. It was a beautiful globe lamp on a marble base. A vine with leaves in wrought iron entwined the base and rose above on one side to where two love birds were perched nuzzling together. I was sure Robert and Patty-Mae would appreciate it.

"Are you looking forward to this evening?" Nathaniel asked as he drove down the village high street and took a left at the end, to climb the hill to the bluff.

Was I? I found I wasn't altogether sure. I must have hesitated a little too long for Nathaniel suddenly burst out laughing.

"Yes, they're my sentiments as well."

"Oh, no, I didn't mean I wasn't, that sounds terribly ungrateful. This is my first dinner party since I moved to Linhay and I am determined to enjoy myself."

"Your first? Well, we'll have to make amends for that appalling oversight. So what's the trouble?"

"It just seems rather an odd group of people and I'm not sure how well we'll all get on."

"I confess, apart from us and our hosts, I don't know who else will be there."

"The only other I know of is Harriet, but that would mean an odd number so there must be at least one other, I think there's only going to be six of us."

"Harriet? Heavens, you do surprise me. Well, that might liven things up a bit."

"Whatever do you mean, Nathaniel? I understood Robert and she are old friends. It seems only natural he would ask her to celebrate his engagement, wouldn't he?"

"Of course, you're absolutely right, Ella. Forgive me. I spoke out of turn, water under the bridge and all that. I'm sure we'll have a perfectly pleasant evening." And he refused to say another word on the matter.

I'd never been up to The Hall before and as we passed through the huge wrought-iron gates guarded by giant stone Griffins, and began our slow commute down the long gravel drive I felt as though I'd been transported to an enchanted land.

Torches lined either side of the drive, their flickering flames sheltered by the row of beech running parallel to their rear. Entwined within their branches were hundreds of tiny little lights sparkling like stardust.

"Goodness, Robert's certainly pushing the boat out tonight," said Nathaniel.

"I half expect Pan to trot across the drive playing his flute, followed by half a dozen nymphs."

Nathaniel cast me a sidelong glance. "Uncanny you should say that."

"Why?"

"Look ahead," he said, nodding through the windscreen.

We were just coming to the end of the avenue of trees and in the centre of the circular drive was a huge fountain. Up-lit from the base, it cast the enormous central statuary into relief giving it an eerie realism. It was the God Pan sitting on a tumulus of rocks, flute lifted to his mouth, while sitting at his cloven hoofs bare-breasted nymphs gazed in magically-induced adoration, mesmerised by the sweet piercing music.

"It's a shame the water isn't switched on," Nathaniel said as he opened my door. "It would look spectacular in this evening's setting."

Personally I was glad it was dry. Cascading water would give an illusion of animation and it already looked too real for my liking. It was both sinister and evocative, and knowing the history of The Hall as I did, more than a little ominous.

"Good evening, sir, Miss. Welcome to Arundel Hall." It was Sir Robert's butler Hobbes. He took our coats, handing them to a hovering maid, placed our gifts on a side table commandeered for the purpose, then announced, "Sir Robert and ... her Ladyship are in the drawing room if you'll follow me."

"Ladyship, Hobbes?" questioned Nathaniel. "Goodness, have they married already?"

Hobbes cleared his throat and continued walking. "Not yet, sir, no. Those are my orders. Here we are. I'll have your car moved to the garages at the rear of the house." He opened the drawing room doors and standing to one side, announced, "Doctor Brookes and Miss Bridges." Then he removed himself quickly shutting the door behind him. I saw no sign of Patty-Mae, but Robert was there to greet us.

"Ella, lovely to see you, my dear, and how splendid you look."

"Thank you, Robert."

I saw Nathaniel's face momentarily blanch in shock at Robert's transformation. He obviously hadn't seen him since the bizarre metamorphosis. Luckily Robert was oblivious.

"Nathaniel, welcome, good of you to come. Pity about your father, do send him my regards."

While Robert and Nathaniel chatted, I glanced into the long gallery style room and spied Harriet sitting alone by the fire, a large sherry in her hand. Dressed in an austere black gown heavily beaded with jet, she reminded me of a mourning Queen Victoria. Oh, dear.

"Hello Harriet," I greeted her.

"Isobella, at last. Sit, sit do."

I hurriedly sat in the red velvet and gold brocade chair next to her, only recently vacated if the warm seat and squashed cushion was anything to go by.

"What an exquisite gown. You look simply delightful, my dear."

"Thank you, Harriet. I wondered if it might be a little too risqué?"

"Nonsense, it's chic and very stylish. You are the embodiment of English elegance, Isobella, and don't let anyone tell you otherwise. Now what's this I hear about you finding a body in your basement?"

I sighed. "Cedric?"

"Of course Cedric. So is it true?"

"Isobella, what can I get you to drink? A sherry perhaps?" interrupted Robert.

Before I could answer, a discordant voice rang out. "Sherry? Oh, that will never do, Bobby. Sherry is for old folk."

I cringed inwardly.

"Oh, silly me. Harriet, of course I didn't mean you," she continued, which just compounded the insult. "Mix Ella a cocktail, honey, she'll just love it."

Our hostess had returned.

"And Doctor Brookes, what a shame your father couldn't come," she said over her shoulder, tottering across to Harriet and me in her ubiquitous heels, a tight, blood-red gown which looked as though it had been painted on, and twirling a gold slim woven tasselled belt.

"Goodness, are all Americans this rude?" I whispered to Harriet.

"No, my dear, they are not," Harriet answered in a shrewd whisper.

I puzzled at Patty-Mae's impoliteness to Nathaniel, a comparative stranger and her guest, but he just shrugged and gave me a wink.

"Ella, honey, so lovely to see you. And what a cute little dress. We could be sisters." She giggled, kissing my cheeks.

Nathaniel momentarily choked in the background, while Harriet snorted in a most unladylike manner, but Patty-Mae was oblivious.

I noticed under the thick, but expertly applied maquillage, pitted scars and the fine redness of dilated blood vessels. A childhood illness perhaps? It surely couldn't be drink?

"Bobby, where are those cocktails? A lady could die of thirst over here."

"Please, don't go to any trouble for me. A sherry will be perfectly fine," I said, but she disregarded my comment with a wave and an irritated glance at Robert.

"I'm afraid I'm rather hopeless at cocktails, Patty-Mae. Perhaps Hobbes could assist?" Robert said, dejectedly eying the mystifying variety of bottles and assorted paraphernalia on the bar top.

I felt a little sorry for him.

"Oh, never mind, Edgar will see to them when he gets here," she said as she affixed a cigarette to a black and diamante holder, lit it and taking a long drag proceeded to blow out plumes of smoke above her head.

"Edgar?" I inquired, for I didn't recognise the name.

"Rutherford," said Robert. "It was rather a last minute decision to make up the numbers, you know, as your father couldn't make it, Nathaniel."

"Now, Bobby, you know that's not true," Patty-Mae said. "I invited Edgar before we knew about that. How could we not have him here? He introduced us, remember?" She leaned over and patted my knee. "If it hadn't been for Edgar, dear Bobby and me wouldn't have met. The least we can do is have him here to celebrate. We owe him our happiness."

"Well, let's hope he doesn't want to make good the debt," Harriet said sweetly, but the comment went over Patty-Mae's head.

Suddenly the double doors banged opened and a young man strutted in. He was devastatingly handsome, thick blond hair with a side parting swept back from astonishingly blue eyes framed with long lashes. His evening suit was of impeccable quality and the cut showed off his broad shoulders, narrow waist and long legs.

Hobbes hovering in the background announced, "Mr. Rutherford."

"Call this a party?" the newcomer asked, laughing. "Where's the music and the dancing?"

I didn't know Edgar Rutherford, had never seen him before, but his voice was unmistakable. It was the young man I'd heard arguing behind the wall of The Kings Head public house.

Patty-Mae rose giggling. "Now, Edgar, behave yourself. I told you it was a quiet get-together. You can make yourself useful by mixing us some cocktails. Robert doesn't know how and Ella and me are just gasping for a decent drink."

Well, really enough was enough, I thought. "Actually, I would much prefer a sherry, if you wouldn't mind, Robert."

"Of course, my dear. Now that I can do," he said gratefully.

Patty-Mae gave me a brittle smile and shrugged. "Suit yourself, sugar."

"Well done, Isobella," Harriet said quietly.

After brief introductions, Hobbes came and announced dinner was served and we all trooped through to the dining room.

"It's all rather ghastly so far, isn't it?" whispered Nathaniel as he escorted me to dinner. "But I suppose it can't get any worse."

Unfortunately he couldn't have been more wrong.

CHAPTER THIRTEEN

The dining table was beautifully laid out with sparkling glassware, highly polished silver and a wonderfully artistic central silver epergne. Filled to overflowing with white calla lilies and delicate pink carnations, the scent was subtle and evocative of spring. Candelabra at either end cast delicate cosy glows over the linen cloth and subtly highlighted the place names.

As expected, our host and hostess were seated at either end and I found myself sitting next to Patty-Mae on my left, with Nathaniel to my right. Edgar was opposite with Harriet on his right next to Robert.

The hors d'oeuvres arrived and, to my delight, six oysters on the half shell nestled on a bed of crushed ice, was placed before me.

Robert smiled at my obvious pleasure. "Well, we could hardly have a dinner party on Linhay without oysters now, could we?"

"Goodness me, no," I replied. "It would be a terrible dishonour to our little island."

"And why would that be?" drawled Patty-Mae, gesturing to Hobbes to refill her glass.

"Linhay is famous for its oysters," Harriet told her. "They have been fished here since the time of the Romans and are transported to London and further afield by the railway. They were a favourite of Victoria, I believe."

"Fascinating," said Patty-Mae, in a tone which suggested it wasn't.

As the first course was whipped away by an efficient waitress and the Consommé Olga arrived, I tried to engage Edgar in conversation. I'd noticed he was sulking rather after being treated like a cocktail waiter by Patty-Mae.

"Patty-Mae tells us you were the one that introduced her to Robert, Edgar. How did you both meet?"

"Oh, you know how it is in the city. I'm always being invited to aristocratic parties, the most popular nightclubs, and opening nights at the theatre. It was at one of those, I can't remember which one now, where we met," he replied. As we delighted over the food he regaled us with humorous stories and anecdotes.

After several minutes, I found my mind drifting. The food was an utter delight, and I could not help but think what a huge help Mrs. Shaw must have been to Robert's housekeeper.

Over the third course of poached salmon with mousseline sauce and cucumbers, as Edgar continued with more of his tales, I thought, *it's little wonder he has so much debt. Gadding about as he described must leave little time for running his parents' wine business and actually earning his money.*

"The wine trade must be doing better than I thought," said Nathaniel, eerily echoing my thoughts, as Edgar paused for breath.

Edgar glared at him. "And what would a small village doctor know about wine?" he sneered, definitely a little worse for wear as he took another large gulp from his glass.

Nathaniel smiled. "Nothing at all, dear chap, just an observation. So Patty-Mae, you've retired from the silver screen, I believe? Such a shame now that the talkies have taken off. Are you not tempted to go back?"

She shrugged, eying him distastefully. "Of course the studios begged me, just wouldn't take no for an answer. They wined and dined me, sent flowers and gifts and I very nearly gave in, I did. For my fans, you know? How could I let them down? But then I met Bobby and my mind was made up. I am going to be a proper wife to my husband. I thought, what does fame and fortune mean when you have the love of a good man? So that was that," she slurred, and giggled in a way that set my teeth on edge.

Harriet caught my eye. It was inconceivable with a voice like Patty-Mae's she would be considered for a talking film. Everything she had said was pure deception and sadly we all knew it, though no one said a word. Perhaps this was her way of coping with the inevitable, pretend the decision to leave was hers. Even though I hadn't heard of her myself, it appeared she had been successful. It can't have been easy to suddenly find herself cast aside.

"I'm sure your admirers will miss you terribly, Patty-Mae," I consoled her, "but as you say, you're about to embark on a new life, one in which I'm sure you'll be very happy. I'm sure your fans would understand."

"Here, here," said Robert, raising his glass and unfortunately giving Patty-Mae an excuse to refill hers.

Over the lamb, fillet mignon, and chicken, with a wonderful array of side dishes, Harriet asked about the goings on at the cottage recently.

"Yes, I had heard the police had been. Joe, the landlord at the Dog and Gun mentioned he had a distinguished guest, Scotland Yard's police surgeon no less, and an officer staying," said Robert.

My goodness, word does travel fast on this island.

"Yes, that's right. A few months ago, quite by chance I found a hidden room at the back of the pantry ... "

"Oh, my, did you really? How excitin'," gushed Patty-Mae.

"Up until a few days ago I hadn't managed to find the access from the main floor of the house, but knew there must be one. I came across the secret door in a panel near the fireplace. I subsequently discovered this led up a staircase to the formal reception room. However, at the bottom of the staircase when I opened the panel, I discovered a female skeleton."

There was a collective intake of breath. "A murder then," stated Harriet, as sharp as ever.

I nodded.

"But how do you know it was murder?" slurred Edgar. "Couldn't she have fallen down the stairs?"

"If it had been an accident I'm sure someone would have missed her, Rutherford. But I think there must be more to the tale. Is that right, Ella?" Nathaniel asked.

"Yes, it is. On further examination, it was obvious her skull had been bashed repeatedly. She was then pushed down the stairs and left there. It was a heinous crime, but it happened over one hundred years ago." I flashed a quick look at Harriet who, with a barely perceptible raised eyebrow, confirmed she understood what I meant. "I'll know more when the police have finished their examination."

The desserts arrived then: sumptuous chocolate and vanilla éclairs, peaches in chartreuse jelly and a divine French ice cream.

"Do you know who she could be?" asked Robert, tucking into his peaches.

"Not really, no, but Harriet mentioned my cottage used to be the Dower House so there is a connection to The Hall. I wondered if perhaps she used to live here or possibly was a relation of some sort?"

"It's possible, I suppose, but I wouldn't know where to start. That's more Harriet's thing. There were various papers and whatnot when I bought the place. I put them all in the attics, but you're welcome to go through them. What do you think, Harriet?"

"I'd certainly be happy to help and the papers are the best place to begin. Ella, let's get together one day this week and make a plan."

"Yes, all right, Harriet, thank you."

"There were some paintings, of course," Robert continued. "Portraits mostly, large heavy gilt frames, subjects looking austere and quite terrifying in one or two, you know the sort. Had a chap in London value them and they're worth a bob or two, quite old he said. Perhaps your lady is one of those? I hung them in the library if you want to take a look. I thought we'd dispense with tradition anyway and all take coffee there."

"If you'll excuse me, I just need to visit the powder room. Do start without me," said Patty-Mae, rising with a wobble and gingerly making her way from the room.

"Feel free to start without me too, old boy. Need a bit of air." And Edgar too lurched his way out of the door.

Harriet and Nathaniel also made their excuses and left, so Robert and I adjourned to the library alone where I hoped I would be able to shed more light on my ghostly lodger.

The library was breath-taking. "What a splendid room, Robert," I said gazing around. The floor to ceiling panels with their intricately designed bookshelves were the colour of rich dark honey and shone with the patina of age.

The hard wooden floor was softened by large hand-woven Aubusson rugs in deep reds, creams and golds.

Row after row of books, with their gold and richly-coloured leather spines adorned the shelves, interspersed with curious objects from around the world. African masks sat alongside inlaid boxes from Asia. A set of mouth pipes from the Andes snuggled next to an eighteenth century French musical box, inlaid with gold in the Rococo style. When the lid was lifted, a delightful singing bird rose up, its beak opening in time with the notes and a fluttering of wings.

In between each of the bookshelves, highlighted by individual gold picture lights, were the various portraits Robert had mentioned at dinner. I perused each one, interested in the names, some of whom I recognised from Harriet's tale of the curse. Most were men and of the three that were female, none of them matched the spirit of the dead woman. I still had to find her, but I felt sure I was getting close.

"Oh, this is interesting," I said.

"What's that, Ella?" asked Robert, sauntering to my side. "Ah yes, the bookend. Unusual I thought, and I rather liked it. Griffins of course are everywhere here. You probably noticed the guards at the gate? They're also on the coat of arms worked into the fireplace over there, and numerous other places. A shame I couldn't find the other. It would have been nice to have the matching pair."

"Actually, Robert, I recently found its twin at the cottage."

"Did you really? Heavens, what a stroke of luck, would you consider selling it?"

"It's no longer in my possession. The police have it. I'm afraid it was the murder weapon, you see."

"Well, that certainly proves there's a connection between the victim and The Hall, Isobella. The sooner we start on those papers, the better," said Harriet brusquely as she joined us. She was flushed and looked upset.

What on Earth has happened?

"Excuse me, Sir Robert, there is a gentleman here to see you." Hobbes had entered in his usual silent manner.

"Gentleman? What gentleman?"

"He wouldn't say, sir. Just that he wished to see you as a matter of urgency and that it was a private matter."

"I see. Do excuse me, ladies," he said, addressing Harriet and me.

When Robert had left I asked Harriet what was wrong.

"What a despicable woman. She's just accused me of having designs on her fiancé. What preposterous nonsense. Robert and I have been friends all our lives, but she threatened me in no uncertain terms to stay away. How dare she? What on Earth was Robert thinking, getting involved with such an abominable creature? I could quite happily throttle the ignorant, ill-mannered hussy."

"Oh, Harriet, how appalling. Would you like me to have a discreet word with her?"

"Absolutely not. I'm perfectly capable of fighting my own battles, thank you very much. Besides she's taking a walk around the garden. I'm afraid I gave her a piece of my mind and she didn't take kindly to the truth." She paused and took a deep breath. "I do apologise, Isobella. I didn't mean for you to bear the brunt of my wrath, but I'm absolutely livid."

I needed to pay a visit to the powder room myself, but I couldn't possibly leave Harriet in such a state. Luckily Nathaniel returned.

"Can I get you ladies coffee?" he asked, moving to the sideboard.

"Please, Nathaniel," Harriet said, lowering herself into one of the plush fireside sofas.

"Not for me at the moment, thank you. I'll help myself when I come back." I moved towards Nathaniel and whispered, "Could you add a splash of Brandy to Harriet's coffee? I'm afraid she's rather upset." He glanced over at her and raised a questioning eyebrow at me. I shook my head and went in search of the powder room.

CHAPTER FOURTEEN

The Hall was a warren of corridors and rooms which seemed to lead nowhere and within minutes I was hopelessly lost. I should have asked for directions, or better still a map. As I rounded a corner and entered yet another hallway, I heard voices. Robert and another gentleman. Not wanting to intrude, I ducked behind a large jardinière housing an enormous palm, and waited for them to leave.

"It's as you thought, sir. I'm sorry to say, a fraud."

"Dear god, what a fool I've been," Robert said quietly. "And the other matter?"

The other man let out a sigh. "I'm terribly sorry, sir, you were quite right, there is someone else involved. It's all in my report."

"You'd better come into the office, Entwhistle. I have guests and this needs to be kept between us, you understand?"

"Of course, sir. Discretion is my middle ..."

A door clicked softly and the final words were lost.

I frowned. *What an Earth was that about?* I peeked between the fronds of the palm to ensure they'd gone …

"Ahem," cleared a throat behind me.

I only just held back a scream and spun round. "Hobbes, you frightened me to death."

"I do apologise, Miss Bridges. Are you looking for something in particular?" Neither his voice nor his face gave away any surprise at seeing me hiding behind a large plant and spying on an empty corridor.

"Actually, I was looking for the powder room and became hopelessly lost."

"It's this way, Miss, if you'd like to follow me." And he turned on his heel and went back the way he'd come. Taking a right, then a left, he pointed to a door.

"There you are, Miss. And the library is just there," he said, pointing to another door just a little further along.

I blushed. If I'd just gone right instead of left, I would have found it immediately. Hobbes must think I'm either dim-witted or up to no good, I thought. I found I didn't like either option, but it was too late now.

"Thank you, Hobbes," I said, mustering as much dignity as I could.

He nodded, then left as silently as he'd arrived.

Back in the Library I found Edgar had returned and was lounging insolently in one of the armchairs, long legs stretched out in front of him, staring morosely into yet another glass, this one containing a deep amber liquid. There was no sign of Robert. He must still be with his visitor, but Nathaniel and Harriet were in quiet conversation by the warm fire. I helped myself to coffee and joined them.

"How are you feeling now, Harriet?" I asked.

"I'll be fine, Isobella. I'm sure the worst of it is over."

"It's all rather horrible, isn't it?" I said in a whisper.

"Well, I certainly won't be attending the wedding," laughed Nathaniel.

"Oh, I rather doubt there'll be a wedding," said Harriet. "Not after tonight."

Before I could ask what made her so sure, she changed the subject.

"Now do tell us about your secret room, Isobella. The staircase went up to the main reception room, you said?"

"Yes, it was behind one of the bookshelves. It's opened by this ingenious little catch on the … Oh, I say." I put my coffee cup down and stood up. "Harriet, do you know if Robert has found any secret rooms here at The Hall?"

"Not to my knowledge. But of course we've lost touch recently. I doubt he'd tell me even if he had. I wouldn't be surprised though. The place is old, so there's bound to be some hidden passages."

"Here's Robert now, Ella. You can ask him yourself," said Nathaniel.

"Apologies everyone; a little problem with the boundary wall on the north east side. Sheep all over the paddocks."

I frowned. I didn't think that was what I'd overheard, and why would escaped sheep, as per Hobbes's announcement, be considered a private matter?

Robert cast a disgusted look at Edgar, then helped himself to coffee. "Anyone need a top up? No? Jolly good."

He brought his coffee over and sat with us. "Has anyone seen Patty-Mae?"

"Garden last time I saw," slurred Edgar in the background. "Told me in no uncertain terms to sod off. Charming, after all I've done. Well, we'll see about that ..." he tapered off quietly.

"I see. Well, I'll get Hobbes to look for her if she hasn't come back soon."

"Isobella has a question for you, Robert," Harriet said, giving him a sad smile.

"What is it, my dear?"

"I was wondering if you'd found any secret passages here?"

"Do you know, I haven't. Of course I've never really looked. It wasn't something that crossed my mind, but in light of your findings, I suppose I should. Why? Do you have an idea?"

I got up and went to the fireplace.

"Your fireplace, although the designs are different, is incredibly similar to mine and I posit the same craftsmen were used for both our houses."

"What exactly are we looking for?" asked Nathaniel, joining me and peering at the carvings.

"A slightly raised piece of moulding in the design. It will be barely noticeable and out of the way, so it's not knocked accidentally or apparent to strangers."

Harriet rooted around in her handbag and came up with her pince-nez, while Robert slipped on his spectacles from their place in his top pocket. The four of us studied the ornate surround, reaching out to touch a likely candidate every now and then.

"I think I've found something," said Nathaniel eventually, moving a large brass coal scuttle and the heavy iron and brass companion set.

I crouched behind him looking at the place he was pointing to at the bottom right. Unlike my fireplaces, which were carved with intricate aspects of nature, this one consisted of decorative scroll-work with a cherub at the base on either side. One had a drum and the other, which Nathaniel was studying, had a harp. It was the last string of the harp he was pointing to.

"Yes, I should think that's it," I agreed.

"What an extraordinary piece of work," Robert said. "I would never have discovered it."

"Press it and see what happens," I said to Nathaniel. "We'll keep an eye on the walls. The panel should click and open slightly."

Nathaniel took a deep breath and depressed the harp's string. There was a soft click, and to the left the bottom half of a bookshelf swung forward a few inches, revealing the void behind.

"Well done, Isobella," Harriet said. "An excellent piece of deduction and what a find."

Robert rang the bell-pull in the corner.

"You rang, sir?" inquired Hobbes a second later, who had as usual appeared from nowhere.

"Hobbes," said Robert, "we've found a secret passageway."

"So it would appear, sir. Will you be requiring light?"

"We will. And perhaps you could rouse that fool while we are gone?" he said, nodding to a hebetudinous Edgar, who seemed to have slept through all the excitement.

"It will be my pleasure, sir," Hobbes said with some relish and left.

I looked back at the open panel just in time to see a black tail disappear into the darkness. Phantom had joined us.

Robert pulled the hidden door open, took a few steps forward and peered into the gloom, "There's a staircase leading down," he informed us.

Harriet approached and using a lace handkerchief, brushed away cob-webs and dust from his shoulder. It was an instinctive intimate gesture, yet one Robert accepted as natural. I sighed. I should have realised. No wonder she'd been so upset.

"It's obviously filthy down there," she said, returning her handkerchief to her handbag. "We're hardly dressed to go exploring the bowels of The Hall."

I looked at my beautiful gown in dismay. I certainly didn't want to ruin it, but I desperately wanted to see where the steps led to.

Hobbes returned at that moment, armed with several torches, a pitcher of iced water and several items of clothing.

"I took the liberty of gathering together some more suitable attire for you all, sir." He placed the torches on the table, handed us all various items of clothing, then, throwing the water in Edgar's face, turned and left with absolute decorum.

Edgar shot up out of his chair, looking around wildly. "What the … ?"

I stared, shocked for an instant, then burst out laughing. I couldn't help myself. It was the funniest thing I had ever seen, and done with such aplomb. My estimation of Hobbes had risen considerably. I turned to the others who were likewise in hysterics. Nathaniel was bent double, gasping and clutching his stomach. Robert had his head thrown back and was guffawing loudly. While dear Harriet was wiping her eyes with her lace handkerchief and transferring dust and cobwebs to her face, which set me to laughing all the more.

"It's just not cricket, you know, Harlow, treating your guests in such an abominable way," sputtered Edgar.

"Oh, stop being such a wet blanket," said Nathaniel.

Which of course sent us into fits again.

"And what are you staring at?" Edgar snarled at Hobbes who had returned.

"I thought you might require a towel, sir."

Edgar snatched the towel, giving Hobbes a filthy look.

"Come, Isobella, we need to change," said Harriet, taking my arm.

As we made our way to the powder room, I heard Robert say, "Come on, buck up, Rutherford, you're like a wet weekend."

Harriet and I shared a look and stifled giggles.

Ensconced in the powder room, Harriet said, "Good heavens, where on Earth did Hobbes dredge these up from?" She was holding up a pair of sludge brown dungarees and a bottle green jumper.

Mine were identical, although the jumper was an iron grey. He'd also thoughtfully provided head-scarves and wellington boots. As we changed, I asked Harriet about Hobbes.

"Not the sort of behaviour I'd expect from a butler, although it was hilarious and done with such panache," I said.

"Hobbes is more than a mere servant, Isobella. He was Robert's batman in the war and when Robert was decommissioned Hobbes came with him. As for Rutherford, Hobbes was quite right. That boy is a spoiled brat who doesn't know the meaning of hard work. He's had everything handed to him on a plate since birth and it's done him no favours. When you've lived through such atrocities as Robert and Hobbes, when you've seen friends killed and wounded and driven mad with grief and fear, it's no wonder he has little time for such shallow, selfish people. He got what he deserved in my opinion. Now, how on Earth am I going to squeeze into these?"

After a lot of pushing and shoving and tightening of Harriet's corsets, we were eventually dressed and joined the men in the library.

"What ho! It's the land girls," exclaimed Robert. "That takes me back a bit."

"It's been years since I wore something like this," said Harriet. "I must say I remember it being far more comfortable then, at least I could breathe. I feel like a goose trussed up for Christmas dinner."

"Well, I for one think you look very fetching, Hettie," Robert said, a little flustered.

I glanced at Harriet who tutted, "Nonsense, Robert." Although I could tell she was flattered.

"Are you coming with us, Rutherford?" asked Nathaniel.

"Of course, but I refuse to dress like a farmer," he said, eying the men's rough spun trousers and shirts with immense distaste. Removing his jacket and tie, he rolled up his sleeves. "Right, let's see what treasure's been hiding down there. Finder's keeper's, eh Harlow?" he said with a laugh.

CHAPTER FIFTEEN

The steps were wider and much longer than the ones I'd navigated at the cottage, but just as sepulchral and I was very grateful for the torches. Robert went first, followed by Harriet. I was behind her with Nathaniel to my back and a disgruntled Edgar bringing up the rear.

Years' worth of dust and cobwebs lined this space too and I rather wished I'd had the foresight to tie the scarf around my mouth rather than my hair, as breathing without choking was proving a challenge.

Twenty or so steps down, we reached a dogleg to the right and continued to descend, then about the same distance further on we turned right again.

"I think we just went around the chimney," said Nathaniel.

"Not much further now," said Robert, "I think I can see the bottom."

A few minutes later we were stood side by side in a cavernous space, where even our powerful lights couldn't penetrate the darkness much more than a few feet in front of us. It was damp and musty smelling, but at least the floor was dry. By unspoken agreement we began to move forward as one, shining our torches into obscure corners and lighting up partial objects not seen for decades. The space as far as I could see was packed to the gills with disused furniture and goodness knows what else, all stored in such a way as to leave walkways amongst the towering objects. It was like a labyrinth.

"Do you think these cellars run the whole width of the Hall?" asked Nathaniel.

"I wouldn't be surprised," said Harriet. "We're at a subterranean level below the kitchens and staff quarters, I think. I doubt it's a continuous space, more a series of inter-joining rooms with the load-bearing walls probably mirroring those upstairs. But it will cover a huge area."

"There's access to some of the cellars from the kitchen. But I suspect these have been walled off somewhere with this stairway as the only access now. I certainly never knew about it," said Robert.

"We need to be careful," I said. "It will be easy to get lost down here."

"Ella's right. It's dangerous too. Half this stuff looks as though it could topple at any moment. I think we should go back upstairs," said Robert.

"Good god, this stuff's priceless. You've really hit the jackpot here, Robert."

I wasn't the only one who'd noticed how solicitous Edgar had suddenly become.

"I bet it's wine and Edgar wants to make a deal," whispered Nathaniel in my ear.

He was right. A tall set of shelves against the left wall was stacked with wine bottles, each with a layer of grime so thick it obscured the label. Edgar had already taken one down and was carefully removing the dust.

He held it reverently as though it were a child. "Chateau Lafitte Rothschild, 1787. The rarest of the rare," he breathed in awe.

Nathaniel whistled. "I'm no oenophile, but wasn't that Jefferson's tipple?"

Edgar looked at him with interest, a small smile crossing his lips. "Not just a simple doctor then. Yes, you're quite right. Jefferson spent a lot of time in France during that time. Robert, this is a superlative find. You simply can't leave them languishing down here forgotten, they need to be out in the world. I can deal with all of that for you, of course. Find the best buyers and organise the auction and so forth. There'll be world interest once the discovery is made known."

"Superlative or not, I haven't got time to deal with all of this now. Just put it back where you found it for the moment, we'll talk about it another time."

"Look Robert, really ... "

"Edgar", Harriet interrupted with a warning, "there must be at least two hundred bottles here, all quite possibly of superior vintage, if the first is anything to go by. They need to be handled properly, catalogued and suchlike. I'm sure I don't need to tell you that. These things take time, as you know, which Robert has told you he doesn't have at the moment. He's not dismissing your assistance, just delaying it. Might I suggest you practice a bit of patience for once?"

"Yes, all right, but I want first dibs on them, agreed?"

I didn't wait to see what Robert's response was, for I had spied Phantom disappearing behind a stack of chairs. Following carefully to the right and then to the left I found him sitting in front of a huge object shrouded in velvet dust cloths. Lifting a corner I shone my torch and discovered a large swept frame, somewhat dusty, but still giving off that lustre which only genuine gilt can do.

Resting my torch on a large dresser angled to give me some light, I carefully removed the cloth and found a stack of paintings leaning against a wardrobe. There were six in total, the largest a head taller than I was and heavy. I didn't want to risk moving them by myself so went back for Harriet and Nathaniel.

"I tell you something, Isobella, I didn't expect this Aladdin's cave when we ventured down here. It's an historian's dream. I only hope I live long enough to go through it all. Now what have you found?"

"Portraits by the look of it, old ones too, I would imagine. Looking for the owner of your skeleton, Ella?" Nathaniel said.

"Yes. I feel sure there must be something here to mark her life, connected as she was to The Hall. Could you help me move them?"

"Of course. You take that end. Now carefully, let's stack them one at a time over here."

As Nathaniel and I moved the paintings, Harriet called out the names from the brass plaques attached to the frames. After the fourth one I was beginning to doubt my confidence, and then we unveiled the fifth.

"That's her," I said. "Oh, Harriet, we've found her."

"How do you know?" asked Nathaniel, who hadn't been privy to either the tale of the curse or the discovery of the bones.

"I recognise the jewellery. She was murdered wearing exactly the same items. Harriet, is it who I think it is ...?"

Harriet wiped the plaque, then peered through her pince-nez. "Who do you think it is, Isobella?"

"Mary-Ann, the Eleventh Duke's missing wife."

"Then, yes, you're quite correct. It looks as though she was murdered after all."

I was thrilled I had solved the mystery of my ghostly guest, although I couldn't help also wondering what had happened to her lover. Mary-Ann had been restless for nearly one hundred and thirty years, waiting for someone to discover she'd been murdered, and what remained of her body. Now I could arrange a suitable interment and allow her to rest in peace.

However, my elation was short-lived and our own peace shattered with the panicked arrival of Hobbes.

"That's most unlike Hobbes, I wonder what's happened," said Harriet. "Come on."

We hurried back to the main steps to find Hobbes, in an extreme state of agitation.

Hobbes was just shaking his head repeating, "I'm sorry, sir. I'm so sorry, sir."

Robert looked at Harriet in despair. "I can't get a word out of him, Hettie. Damned unusual."

I approached Hobbes and laid my hand on his shoulder. "Can you show us what's troubling you, Hobbes?" I asked gently.

He looked at me with blank eyes. I didn't think he had understood me at first, but then he focused, gave a sharp nod and headed back up the steps. The rest of us followed in puzzled silence.

We all piled back into the library, the light coming as a bit of a shock after being in the gloom for so long, but Hobbes didn't stop. We went after him as he marched from the library, down the hall and back into the foyer. Across the foyer he opened the large front door and went down the steps to the drive. On the lawns I saw a figure, and was about to speak when I realised who it was.

"Oh, no," I whispered.

Nathaniel glanced at me, a concerned look on his face. "Hobbes is in shock, I recognise the symptoms. Whatever has happened has shaken him to his core."

I nodded. I wasn't surprised. I now knew what had happened.

We continued around to the side of the house where a large evergreen Azalea bush was showing signs of bud. Here Hobbes stopped.

"It was the dogs that found her, sir," he said shakily.

I moved forward and saw the body of Patty-Mae squashed under the bush at an unnatural angle. Her blank eyes staring, no longer seeing anything, and around her throat her gold tasselled belt. She'd been strangled. Glancing back across the lawn I saw her ethereal figure watching me.

Nathaniel checked for a pulse. Rising, he shook his head. "I'm sorry. I'm afraid she's dead."

"Oh, dear god," said Robert, staggering forward.

I grabbed his arm to stop him. I'd learned a lot over the last couple of days. "No, Robert, you mustn't. The police will need to look for evidence, I'm so sorry." I gently pulled him back and spoke to Hobbes. "Hobbes, go and get Mrs. Shaw, please. You'll find her in the kitchen."

He looked at me blankly.

"Hobbes," I shouted. "Go and get Mrs. Shaw. Now, please."

"Yes, Miss Bridges."

I looked at Harriet. She was as still and pale as a marble statue.

"Harriet?"

She looked up.

"Can you take Robert inside and get him some hot sweet tea?" I asked her. "Ask Mrs. Butterworth to make a pot. I think we'll all need it"

She nodded and moved toward Robert.

"Nathaniel, where's Edgar?" I asked.

"By the fountain."

We both looked over to see Edgar being violently sick.

"Can you take him inside and make sure everyone is settled and warm and has something for the shock?"

"Of course. I have my bag in the car in case they need something a little stronger than tea. But I won't use it until absolutely necessary. I daresay we'll all need our wits about us when the police arrive. Shall I call them?"

I shook my head. "No, I'd rather do it if you don't mind. I'll speak to Albert Montesford."

As Nathaniel half carried, half dragged Edgar back to the house, Mrs. Shaw came rushing over.

"Dear God, is it true? Hobbes said Miss Ludere's been killed?"

"Yes, I'm afraid it is. Mrs. Shaw, I need you to stay here and make sure nobody touches anything. The police will need to investigate the area. I'm sorry. I know it's not a pleasant task, but I'm afraid there's no one else I can ask."

"I understand. Of course I'll stay. You get on with calling the police. The sooner they arrive the better, I think," she said, glancing at the body and crossing herself.

I made my way back to the house in a state of shock. Patty-Mae was difficult, uncouth and outrageous, and she'd been terribly rude to most of us during the evening, but no one deserved to die in this awful way. I stopped halfway up the steps and leaned against the balustrade, my heart pounding enough to burst out of my chest as a horrifying thought struck. One of the people I had dined with this evening was a murderer.

CHAPTER SIXTEEN

lbert had been suffering through a bureaucratic dinner when I'd called and his relief at my interruption was palpable.

"Ella, thank goodness. I believe you've just thwarted some dastardly deeds over desserts," he chuckled. "What a tiresome lot they are. Now what can I do for you?"

I explained what had happened and after a short silence he apologised for his flippancy and said, "I'll depart now. I'll arrange for the local bobby to be with you shortly, and whatever you do, don't let anyone leave."

I assured him I wouldn't.

"And make sure the gates are locked at all times. Once the press gets wind of what's happened, and they will, believe me, they'll be camped outside."

Just over an hour later, Albert and I were ensconced in Robert's office.

"Let's start at the beginning, shall we?" Albert said. "It was some sort of fancy dress do, was it?"

"Sorry?"

He waved a hand at my clothing. "Not the normal sort of thing you'd wear to a dinner party is it, Ella?"

"Oh, this? Hardly," I said and explained how we'd found and explored the cellars. "I found out who the bones belonged to, Albert. Her name was Mary-Ann and she was the young wife of the Eleventh Duke of Arundel. According to the curse she disappeared some time in 1807."

"Well, that's one mystery solved at least. Mortimer's outside at the scene with Baxter. Not much they can do tonight of course, too dark. But you can let him know, he'll certainly be interested. Now what's this about a curse?"

So I went through everything Harriet had told me about The Hall's history, while Albert made notes in his ubiquitous black book.

"And who else, among the people here I mean, knew about this curse?"

"I really couldn't say. Harriet and myself of course. I can't remember if we discussed it at dinner, but I don't think so. Of course those who've lived here a while most probably do know the story. It's part of the fabric of the island. Why? Do you think it's important?"

"Everything is important at the beginning of an inquiry, Ella. Now I'd like to sit down and get your opinion on certain matters, but before I do, I need to address the guests and the staff. I've asked them all to gather in the library. Shall we go through?"

"You realise of course, Ella, no one is going to be able to leave The Hall until the perpetrator is caught?" Albert said as we made our way back to the others. "I've already asked the housekeeper to make up the necessary beds."

"Oh dear, no, I didn't. It's fine for Robert, he lives here. Harriet and I will also be fine, although we'll need changes of clothes, but Nathaniel is a doctor and the only one on the island. What if there's an emergency?"

"He'll have to arrange for a locum to take over in his absence. I'm sure his father can arrange that."

"What about Edgar? He has a business in the city."

"From what I've heard about that boy I doubt he'll be missed."

"Here we are," I said, opening the library doors. Albert strode in while I hovered in the background taking in the scene.

Harriet was sitting on the sofa staring blankly into the fire. I noticed she'd removed her headscarf and was absentmindedly twisting it in her lap. Robert sat opposite, an untouched snifter of whiskey in a cut crystal glass balanced precariously on one knee. He too was lost in the flames. Edgar was back in his chair, working his way through a bottle of brandy. He looked wretched with his tear streaked face, unruly hair, and splashes across the front of his shirt where he'd vomited. Nathaniel was leaning against a bookshelf, hands in his pockets. He was the only one of the four who moved when we entered.

The staff: Hobbes, Mrs. Shaw, Mrs. Butterworth and the serving girl, whose name I didn't know, were huddled together in the corner next to the door. Mrs. Shaw looked her usual stoical self, and Hobbes, although still pale, had come round. The housekeeper was silently dabbing her eyes and sniffing, with her arm around the girl's shoulders making comforting noises as the youngster sobbed into her apron.

"Thank you all for waiting patiently. I realise the hour is late and you'll be wanting to retire," began Albert.

I glanced at the grandfather clock in the corner. It showed three in the morning. No wonder I felt so exhausted.

"However," Albert continued, "until the murderer of Miss Ludere is caught, you will all have to remain here."

I had expected a clamouring of objection at this announcement, but the only one who moved was Nathaniel. The housekeeper had obviously imparted the news prior to our arrival.

"Commissioner, I certainly appreciate the gravity of the situation, but I'm a doctor and as such need to be available for my patients. I will of course ... "

Albert stopped him with a raised hand. "I'm sorry for the inconvenience, Doctor Brookes, but this isn't a request. I suggest you telephone your father in the morning and ask him to arrange a locum in your absence. Now if you'll all see Mrs. Butterworth about your sleeping arrangements, we'll convene again in the morning."

I awoke the next morning to a light tap at the door and Mrs. Shaw entered, carrying a breakfast tray. I looked at the room in confusion wondering where I was. Then it all came flooding back.

"What time is it, Mrs. Shaw?" I asked, stifling a yawn.

"Ten-fifteen."

I groaned. "Half the morning gone already. Is there anyone else up and about?"

"Only the police and the staff. Sir Albert felt it was best everyone had breakfast served in their rooms. I expect he wants to keep people from talking and getting their stories straight."

"Possibly."

"I was allowed back to the cottage this morning. A constable drove me to pick up the things you need and I also telephoned Giles and picked up things for Miss Dinworthy. Her housekeeper had everything ready for me."

"Have you seen Harriet this morning?" I asked.

"No, but Mrs. Butterworth's niece is assisting her. She served you last night, her name's Alice."

I nodded while refreshing my tea.

"Well, if there's nothing else, I'll go down and help in the kitchen. Sir Albert said he'd like to see you as soon as you're ready."

"Thank you, Mrs. Shaw, please tell him I won't be long. Oh, and by the way, the meal was excellent last night. You must have worked very hard. Thank you for helping out. I'm sure Mrs. Butterworth appreciated your help and experience."

She gave a curt nod. "It's a pity it all ended in such tragedy."

I found Albert had set up a sort of command centre in a small drawing room to the south of the house, overlooking the terraces and lawns.

"You've moved from the office," I said.

He nodded, pouring me a coffee from a large silver urn. "I have. Sir Robert said he would prefer it. A lot of private papers and whatnot in the office apparently, although he'll soon find out there's no such thing as privacy in a murder investigation. How did you sleep, Ella?"

"Actually very well considering. I feel quite guilty about it."

"Emotions, Ella. No room for emotions if you want to be a detective."

"Who said I wanted to be a detective?"

He pinned me with a stare.

"Mortimer's right, you know, you have a brain and a knack for this type of work. You shouldn't let it go to waste. Now tell me about the dinner, how did the guests seem? Did they get on or was there some tension?"

"To be honest, it was all quite frightful from the start."

I went on to explain how Nathaniel and I had arrived and been escorted through to the drawing room by Hobbes.

"Patty-Mae wasn't there, but Robert greeted us effusively, and seemed genuinely pleased to see us. I noticed Harriet sitting alone by the fire and left Nathaniel and Robert talking while I went over. She was very relieved to see me, Albert, and urged me to sit down quickly. I did notice the cushion was squashed and the seat was warm, not from the fire, but as though someone had been sitting there a moment earlier. I got the feeling she didn't want whoever it was to come back."

"Go on," said Albert.

"I thought at the time how unusual Harriet's choice of clothing was. It was very austere, black and unforgiving. More suitable for a funeral than an engagement party. I think it was deliberate, a statement of some kind."

"What sort of statement?"

I sighed and went to the window. I felt quite sick. It was easy for Albert to say set aside your emotions, but Harriet was my friend and I was gossiping about her. It wasn't just light-hearted nonsense either, no, this was information that could get her into serious trouble. *But could dear Harriet be a cold-hearted killer?* I found I couldn't reconcile that possibility with what I knew of her. Surely it wasn't possible? But then I remembered her words the night before and a cold shiver ran down my spine and my stomach roiled with fear. What was I to do?

Albert had been patient while I wrestled with my internal conscience, but now he spoke.

"Ella, I know this is difficult for you. These are people you know, consider friends even. But the fact of the matter is Miss Ludere has been murdered and one of these people here is responsible. We owe it to her to see her killer caught and punished."

I turned and slumped into the window seat, my back against the cold pane. At that moment Phantom appeared and jumped into my lap, nudging my hand with his head. He was solid for a change. I scooped him up and buried my face in his fur. It was just what I needed and I think he knew.

"Harriet was far from happy about the engagement," I continued, stroking Phantom as I spoke. "And I think her choice of clothing reflected that. When Robert dropped me off at the library that day, Patty-Mae was with us. Harriet barely recognised Robert..."

"Why was that? Had she not seen him for some time?"

"I'm not sure when she saw him last. She intimated they had drifted apart recently, possibly because Patty-Mae was now on the scene, but he's changed considerably. His clothes are vastly different for one thing. Gone are his tweeds. Now he's wearing pastel sweaters and jackets, white linen trousers and gaily spotted cravats. He's coloured his hair as well."

"Mmmm, trying to keep up with a much younger fiancée, do you think?"

I shook my head. "Actually, I don't think Robert had much say in the matter. He looked uncomfortable when I met him in the village and positively embarrassed when he saw Harriet. I think it was all Patty-Mae's doing personally."

"And how did Harriet react?"

"When they left, I noticed her eyes filled with tears," I said sadly. "I heard her whisper 'silly old fool' and wondered at the time if she meant herself or Robert. Could have been both, I suppose. Harriet and Robert have been friends all their lives."

"And how was she with Miss Ludere?"

"Actually we hardly got a word in edgeways. I think we were both a little shell-shocked. Patty-Mae is ... " I gulped, "was, a force of nature. Loud and over the top and used to getting her own way. She quite simply ploughed over the people she met. However, I think she was a shrewd operator and recognised something in Harriet, because she emphasised the word 'old' when she said it was lovely meeting Robert's old friends. She was speaking to Harriet at the time. Then of course she threatened her last night."

Albert looked up sharply. "Threatened?"

"Albert, before I tell you what was said, I want you to know I don't think Harriet killed Patty-Mae. I can't see her as a murderer, she's my friend, and while she can be a bit brusque at times and doesn't suffer fools gladly, she is at heart very kind and considerate."

"Duly noted, Ella. So if you don't think it was Harriet, who do you think it was?"

"I don't know," I said quietly. "I can't believe anyone here did it."

"Well, somebody did and in my experience in cases like this it usually boils down to one of two reasons, love or money. Or both."

"A crime of passion, do you mean?"

"Possibly. Now what of this threat?"

"Harriet told me Patty-Mae threatened her in the powder room after dinner last night. She told her in no uncertain terms to 'lay off her fiancé and stay out of the way or else'."

"And how did Harriet react?"

"She was livid, as you can imagine, but also extremely upset and shaken. It distressed her no end." I took a deep breath. "Harriet's words to me were, 'I could quite happily throttle the ignorant, ill-mannered hussy'."

Albert leant back in his chair and took in the view behind me, brow furrowed as he thought.

"Oh, dear, she's in terrible trouble, isn't she?" I said.

"No more than anybody else at this stage, Ella. Now I think you need a break. Take a walk round the grounds and get some fresh air. It will clear your head. I saw the glistening of water down there." He nodded outside. "Could be a lake. Go and feed the ducks and we'll reconvene here in an hour. I realise while we're all under the same roof, it will be difficult to avoid one another, but if you do happen to speak to anyone, please do not discuss the case or what you and I have talked about today."

"No, of course I won't. I'll see you later," I said, and left to find my coat with Phantom on my heels.

CHAPTER SEVENTEEN

lbert was right. Down the terrace steps through the formal knot garden, down the large sweep of verdant lawn and through a small copse, sat a lake. It was man-made and while not large, I could probably walk around it in less than an hour. It was beautifully proportioned and well established. In the centre sat an island with a weeping willow just beginning to bud, and beneath it a dozen ducks waddled. So comical on land, but once they entered the water with a flutter of wings and a little splash, they glided elegantly and colourfully as the sun glinted off their plumage.

I sauntered along the lakeside path breathing in the fresh air and letting my mind go blank. I stopped to watch as a pair of mallards squabbled in the tall reeds, and looked up to see a raptor of indeterminate breed circling overhead, eyes keenly watching for signs of prey scurrying in the undergrowth.

Dotted here and there were clumps of crocus leaves, their delicate flowers waiting for the warmer weather before pushing up and opening in a riot of colour. A few yards ahead, I spied a bench set back slightly from the water's edge and decided to sit awhile.

I had to agree with Albert. There was no room for emotions in a murder case. I was appalled that one of us could be capable of killing another, but the evidence was there in the form of Patty-Mae's strangled and lifeless body. What was the reason though? Who had a motive?

I hated to admit it, but Harriet was the strongest contender. She'd argued with Patty-Mae, been insulted and threatened by her, and had admitted she'd like to throttle her.

Robert. Would there be any reason for him to want to kill the woman he was going to marry? I couldn't see it. There had been a little tension between them last night, but mostly due to Patty-Mae being a little impatient with him. He had been quite gracious throughout, but she had made him look silly and slow, and old. Of course she'd been instrumental in making him dress like a dandy, but surely he wouldn't have agreed to that nonsense if he hadn't wanted to please her? Then again she had been rude to his guests, which would have chafed against his old world gentlemanly disposition, and she was drinking heavily, which I knew he would disapprove of. But were those reasons enough to kill her?

Edgar Rutherford, as far as I was concerned, was an unknown quantity. I hadn't met him until last night, but he was friends with Patty-Mae and had introduced her to Robert. Had something happened last night to turn him from friend to killer? Patty-Mae had treated him rather shabbily, more as a servant than a friend, and he did mention they had had a bit of a tiff in the garden, which he seemed very upset and angry about. I also knew he was in financial trouble. Had the argument escalated and ended in tragedy?

Then there was Nathaniel. When I'd asked him if he knew Patty-Mae he'd said no, but when we'd arrived last night and she'd seen him, she had been very rude. Would you treat a stranger that way? No, they must have known each other somehow, in which case he had lied to me. And if he'd lied, then there must be more to the relationship than I knew. Enough to kill her? Possibly. Albert and I needed to know more.

I found myself feeling depressed at the thought that Nathaniel had lied to me. *Emotions, Ella!* I admonished myself silently. I was also a little angry. Once again I had taken a person at face value, not looking beneath the surface veneer to what lay below. I'd done that with my husband and look where that had got me.

Deep in thought, I nearly shot out of my skin when two black Labradors appeared out of nowhere, and in a flurry of excited yips and wagging tails tried to get on my knee.

"Goodness, what a rambunctious pair you are," I exclaimed, as I tried in vain to stop them licking my face.

"Colt. Bess. To me. Heel!" shouted a voice behind me.

The dogs clambered down and, ignoring the command completely, ran up the path a little way and promptly launched themselves into the lake.

"I do apologise, Miss," said a breathless Hobbes, coming to stand beside me. "I didn't realise anyone was here. As you can see I've got them under perfect control."

I laughed at Hobbes' unexpected show of humour.

"Don't worry, Hobbes, no harm done. I take it walking duties don't normally fall to you?"

He gave a heavy sigh. "No Miss, they don't."

We watched the dogs in silence for a while. Black shiny heads just visible above the water, they were as sleek as otters and having the time of their lives.

"Well, Miss, I'd better get on. Luncheon will be served shortly in the breakfast room."

I watched him walk down the path, hunched over as though the weight of the world were on his shoulders, and mentally added him to the list of suspects.

I thought lunch would be a very subdued affair, a world away from the dinner we had enjoyed together the previous evening, even though it had been somewhat strained. I was wrong.

Of Edgar and Robert there was no sign, but Harriet was sitting at the table picking at her food, her face drawn and tight.

Nathaniel was at the buffet, helping himself to ham and eggs, so I joined him. Surprisingly, even after all that had happened I was feeling hungry.

"Ella, thank god. I was beginning to worry about you. How are you feeling?"

"Much the same as everyone else I expect, Nathaniel, shocked and upset. It all seems quite unreal."

"Yes, it's a dreadful business. Quite dreadful. Here let me," he said, taking my plate to the table.

"Harriet, can I get you some tea?" I asked, noticing she had nothing to drink.

"Please, dear."

As I gave Harriet her tea and sat opposite next to Nathaniel, she reached across and gripped my hand.

"Isobella, please believe me when I say I had nothing to do with this heinous crime. What I said to you last night was in the heat of the moment. It was a stupid thing to say. I was angry and upset, but I wouldn't have even wished ill on Miss Ludere, let alone killed her."

"Oh, Harriet," I said, squeezing her hand in comfort. "I know it was all said in anger and not like you at all. We'll find out who did it. I promise."

She nodded and gave me a tentative smile, then drawing back her hand began to eat. She must have been awake all night worrying and waiting to speak with me. The three of us ate in silence for a while, each with our own thoughts.

"Are you working with the police then?" asked Nathaniel a few minutes later. "I thought we were all suspects?"

"It's rather a long story, Nathaniel. I've helped the Commissioner with two previous cases, both now solved, and he seems to think I'm in an ideal position to help with this one. I suppose he's right. I was here after all."

"So we've got a spy in the camp, have we?" Edgar said as he stormed in and began to heap his plate with food. "Just what we need. You running back and telling tales of our every thought to the police."

"Oh, for god's sake lay off, Rutherford, you're being ridiculous," said Nathaniel. "Not to mention rude. Although come to think of it, you seem incapable of acting any other way."

Edgar let out a vicious laugh. "Got the hots for our little snoop, have you, Doctor? Well, you're welcome to her."

"Now see here, you impudent ... " Nathaniel began, rising somewhat aggressively.

"Stop it, both of you," I shouted, standing so abruptly my chair fell with a crash. "Have you any idea how foolish you both look? Do you really think this is the time or the place? Mr. Rutherford, I don't give a hoot what you either think of me or call me, the fact of the matter is there was a brutal murder here last night, and like it or not someone in this house is responsible. If being a spy is what it takes to catch the killer, then that's exactly what I'll be. Now if you'll excuse me, I have things to do." And with that I marched out of the room and bumped straight into Albert.

"Interesting tactics, Ella," he said with a wry smile.

"Oh, dear, that was stupid, wasn't it?"

"Not at all, keeps them on their toes. Now do you have time to continue our discussion?"

"Of course."

"Tell me what you need to know, Albert," I said, sitting myself in the window seat of the drawing room and taking out my notebook, which Mrs. Shaw had thoughtfully brought with my clothes. I noticed the crossword puzzle from Aunt Margaret tucked in the back. Well, I hardly had time to do that now. I had a bigger puzzle to solve.

"The murderer needed to have both the motive and the opportunity to do what he did," Albert began. "We need to establish those who had alibis at the time of the murder. I've already questioned the staff and all of them, apart from the butler Hobbes, are accounted for. Of those that are left, we need to know what their motive for killing Miss Ludere would be. When was the last time you saw her?"

"When we'd all finished dinner. She left first to go to the powder room and I never saw her again. Edgar followed within minutes saying he needed air, which I think he probably did as he'd drunk an awful lot. Nathaniel and

Harriet also excused themselves, which left Robert and me. We both went to the library and were there for a short while together before Harriet returned. Robert was then called away by Hobbes as he had a visitor, and he'd just left when Nathaniel returned, which gave me a chance to pay a visit to the powder room myself without leaving Harriet alone. She was upset due to the confrontation with Patty-Mae I told you about earlier. Unfortunately, I got hopelessly lost. Hobbes found me and showed me the way back, then left me at the powder room door. When I got back to the library, Edgar had returned and was drinking heavily again, and not long after that Robert came back too."

"And how much time had passed between Harriet returning and you all being back in the library?"

"You think Harriet was the last one to see her alive?" I asked.

"Either her or the killer, and at the moment they could both be one and the same. There's nothing to indicate how long it took for Harriet to come back after the argument. Was it straight away? Or did she follow Miss Ludere into the garden, strangle her and return to the library with a fabricated story of an argument? Or did the argument take place, but earlier than she indicated to you?"

"I can't help with the time, Albert, I was out of the library as well and was gone for a good fifteen minutes. Edgar had already returned by the time I did and any one of them could have left and returned a second time before I got back."

"Well, we'll ask them all during the interview stage. I needed to get your information first."

"There is something else. When I got lost ... " I had no time to finish what I was going to say as there was an abrupt knock at the door and Mortimer came in, holding up an envelope.

"Ella." He nodded to me then spoke to Albert, "We've just found this in the hand of the deceased, Albert. Casts rather a different light on things I think."

I stood up and approached as Albert tipped out the contents onto a small side table. It was a shirt button, a monogrammed shirt button to be precise.

"We'll need the shirt."

"Baxter's already on it," said Mortimer. "Gone to check both gentlemen's closets and the laundry room. He'll find it."

I looked again at the small button and the subtle letter R engraved in the centre, and wondered which of the two men it belonged to.

We didn't have long to wait as with a short rat-a-tat at the door Baxter entered, with not only the shirt, but its owner.

Mortimer left while Baxter took up position by the door so I remained quietly on the window seat while Albert spoke.

"Please take a seat," Albert said.

"I'd rather stand. What's the meaning of this?"

"It's not a request, Mr. Rutherford. Sit down."

Edgar shot a nervous glance at me, all bravado vanishing in an instant at Albert's tone and did as he was told.

"Look, Commissioner—"

Albert held up a hand. "Mr. Rutherford, let me explain how this interview is going to progress. I will ask the questions and you will provide the answers. Understood? At no time while I am speaking are you to interrupt me. You will be given an opportunity to give me your side of the story and to defend yourself afterward."

"Defend?" Edgar said in a hoarse whisper.

Albert ignored him."Mr. Rutherford, take a good look at this shirt. Is it yours?"

Edgar looked at the shirt on the table and nodded. "Yes."

"You're quite sure?"

"Yes, of course, my buttons are monogrammed."

"And is this the shirt you were wearing last night?"

"It is."

Albert made a great show of writing in his note book, taking his time while Edgar sat nervously shaking his leg and running his hand through his hair.

"Tell me about the argument you and Miss Ludere had in the garden last night, please."

"What? What argument?"

"I would advise you to not take me for an idiot, Mr. Rutherford," Albert said sternly.

Edgar waved his hand in the air and leant back in the chair.

"It was nothing. I went to see if she was all right, that's all. She'd had a bit to drink at dinner and looked a little worse for wear."

"And was she pleased to see you?"

"No, actually she wasn't. But you obviously know all this otherwise you wouldn't be asking."

"I'd like to hear it in your own words, Mr. Rutherford. Please continue."

"She was on her way to the powder room when I met up with her. I was going for some fresh air and asked her to join me."

"And how did she seem, apart from a little drunk?"

"Annoyed actually, though I didn't know why then. Anyway I left and walked along the front of the house trying to clear my head. I'd almost reached the corner when I heard her behind me. I could tell she was angry immediately. She'd had some row with that librarian, put her in a god-awful mood."

I let out a shaky breath as I realised Edgar's words had not only confirmed Harriet's story, but had possibly put her in the clear.

"And what was the argument about?"

"Patty-Mae seemed to think she was trying to steal Robert away from her." Edgar let out a humourless laugh. "As if she could. I mean, why the hell would Robert be interested in some dowdy, frumpy, antiquated fossil when he was going to marry her? She was being a stupid little fool and I told her so."

I clenched my fists and bit my tongue so I wouldn't give him a piece of my mind. Goodness, how I disliked this horrible shallow man.

There was silence. Albert looked up from his scribblings, but Edgar remained mute.

"What happened then, Mr. Rutherford?"

"Nothing."

"Nothing? You mean to tell me the victim, not only drunk, but furious after a row with Miss Dinworthy, came to you only to be told she was a stupid little fool, and nothing else happened? Perhaps you're assuming I'm also a fool, Mr. Rutherford?" Albert said coldly.

"No. No, of course not. Look, if I tell you, it's not what it sounds like. It was just—I'm sorry, I can't." Edgar jumped up from his chair in a state of agitation.

"Sit down, Mr. Rutherford. Do you recognise this?"

Albert took the envelope containing the button and emptied it onto the table. Edgar peered at it, a frown marring his face.

"Yes, it's one of my buttons. But where …?"

"Is there a button missing from this shirt, the one you have stated is yours and which you were wearing last night?"

Edgar cautiously lifted the shirt and examined it carefully.

"Yes, the right cuff button is missing. I didn't realise I'd lost it."

"Would you like to know where that button was found, Mr. Rutherford?"

Edgar looked up and gulped audibly, but didn't answer.

"It was found in the hand of the victim."

Edgar moaned and began to sob.

"I didn't kill her. Please, you have to believe me. I would never hurt Patty-Mae."

"Then how did the button of your shirt end up in her hand?"

"She hit me. Slapped me across the face when I insulted her. She was furious, like a wild animal. She kept hitting me over and over, pulling my shirt and calling me names. I had to hold her wrists to stop her, but then she started kicking. It was like she was possessed or something. I couldn't stop her. I must have lost the button then."

He was sobbing like a child, furiously wiping his nose and eyes on his sleeve. It was pitiful to watch and I honestly didn't know how much more I could take.

"You did nothing to defend yourself? Come now, this woman was hitting you, kicking you and calling you names as though possessed, you said. I could see easily how you would be provoked to anger. Is that what happened, Edgar?

Did you hit her harder than you meant to? Was it an accident which, when you realised what you'd done, you made look like a murder?"

Albert's voice had softened. Gone was the harsh Police Commissioner and in his place a sympathetic friend.

"No!" Edgar wailed. "Please, that's not how it happened. Eventually her anger fizzled out," he hiccupped through sobs. "She told me to bugger off, so I did. I left and went back inside, but she was alive when I left her, I swear she was."

"You mean you let her get away with it? You didn't hit her once? I find that very hard to believe, Edgar. Are you sure? Just think back to last night and tell me what really happened. I'm here to help you, Edgar."

Albert's voice was hypnotic as he tried to coax the truth from an increasingly hysterical Edgar.

"Dammit! Just once. I slapped her, but only once. She was hysterical! It was the only thing I could do to calm her down, shock her back to reality. But I didn't kill her."

I hadn't seen Albert signal Baxter, but he came over, handcuffs at the ready.

"Edgar Rutherford, I am arresting you for the murder of Miss Patty-Mae Ludere," said Albert, standing.

"What? No! Please, I didn't do it! You have the wrong man. Whoever did it has set me up."

He wrestled himself away from Baxter and was heading for the door, but Baxter was too quick for him. Tackling him to the ground, Baxter placed one knee on his back, grabbed his arms up behind him and in a flash had him trussed up like a turkey.

"On your feet, lad, don't make it worse for yourself," Baxter said gruffly, hauling Edgar upright.

Edgar took a step toward me. "Ella, please, I didn't do it. Please keep snooping. Find out who did kill her because he's still around. Please, Ella, please help me. I didn't kill Patty-Mae. I couldn't."

He then broke down in sobs as Baxter led him out of the room and to the waiting police car.

Mortimer came to stand with us and watched as Edgar was taken away.

"Looks like you got your man then, Albert?" he said.

Albert nodded thoughtfully.

But I wasn't so sure.

CHAPTER EIGHTEEN

Albert and I walked back into the foyer of Arundel Hall, both deep in thought.

"Ella, I want you to do as Mr. Rutherford suggested and keep snooping," he said quietly.

I looked at him in astonishment.

"You don't think he killed her?"

"I'm reserving judgment at this stage, but my gut says not. However, there's certainly more to all this than meets the eye and that young man knows more than he's saying."

"But why arrest him if you don't think he's guilty?"

"I didn't say he wasn't guilty. He most certainly is guilty of something. If not the murder, then something associated with it. Let him stew for a while. This way he'll have time to consider his actions and his character. I expect he'll find himself wanting on both scores. And it may very well flush the real culprit out into the open."

"Albert, how did you know Edgar had slapped Patty-Mae?"

"Apart from the reasons I mentioned when questioning him, you mean?"

I nodded.

"Mortimer informed me there was the marking of a hand print across her left cheek. She died not long afterward, so it was still visible."

"Is it true, Commissioner? You've arrested that young scoundrel for the murder of my poor Patty-Mae?"

Sir Robert came shuffling up the hall looking years older than he had when I'd first arrived. The dandy had gone and he was once more an old country gentleman dressed in his tweeds. But his pallor was sallow and the lines in his face accentuated. He looked wretched. Behind him stood Harriet and Nathaniel, eyes unnaturally bright and restless with the expectation of news.

"Mr. Rutherford has just been taken into custody, Sir Robert, yes."

"Thank god. I hope he hangs," he said vehemently. "I suppose I should sort out the funeral arrangements."

Albert stepped forward and laying a hand on Robert's shoulder, spoke quietly. "Sir Robert, might I suggest you wait a few days? There are still some loose ends we need to tie up, and until those are concluded, Patty-Mae will need to remain with my colleagues in London. I'm sure you understand. I'll telephone you as soon as I know when she can be released."

"Yes, all right, Commissioner. But don't drag it out. I don't think I could bear it."

As Robert slowly departed, Nathaniel approached. "Does this mean we're allowed to leave, Commissioner?"

"Not just yet, Doctor Brookes. I'd still like to speak to you and Miss Dinworthy. Come to the drawing room in ten minutes please. Miss Dinworthy, we'll call for you shortly."

Harriet nodded in response.

Ten minutes later, Doctor Brookes entered the drawing room, holding the door for Mrs. Shaw who had thoughtfully provided afternoon tea for us.

"So what's all this about, Commissioner? I thought the perpetrator had been caught and the case closed."

"As I said to Sir Robert, there are a number of loose ends I wish to tie up to my satisfaction before I close the case. Can you tell me your movements after you left the dinner table last night?"

"I left with Harriet. We had a brief chat in the hall about the library and her published works, then we went our separate ways. It took me a short while to find the gentleman's facilities. I used them, then went back to the library for coffee, where I found Ella with a rather upset Harriet. When Ella left, Harriet asked if I had something to soothe her nerves, so I went to the car to pick up my bag. When I got back, Harriet was still seated by the fire, so we waited together until everyone returned. Edgar came back first and promptly grabbed a bottle of brandy, then Ella and finally Robert. After that we searched for a hidden door and found the cellars."

"Did you hear the argument between Miss Ludere and Harriet?"

"Ah, so that's why she was upset? I didn't realise. No, I never heard a thing."

"And when you went to get your bag, did you see Miss Ludere at all?"

"No. The car had been taken around the back to the stable block. It's at the opposite side of the building to where she was found, so I wouldn't have seen her. I used the door at that side to leave and return."

"Nathaniel," I said, gathering my courage, "When I asked if you knew Patty-Mae you said no."

"I don't. Sorry, didn't."

"But when we arrived she was exceptionally rude to you. I don't think she liked you very much, but how could that be? It's hardly the way you'd treat a stranger."

Nathaniel rose and sauntered to look out of the window, hands in his pockets. Albert and I shared a glance and waited for him to speak. He was obviously wrestling with his conscience and I was intrigued as to what he was going to say. Eventually he made up his mind and turned to face us, leaning against the wall with his arms folded.

"As a doctor I'm bound by certain laws and ethics when it comes to confidentiality."

"Was Miss Ludere a patient of yours?" asked Albert.

"Not as such no, but I don't suppose it matters if I tell you now she's dead. In all honesty I was planning on going to the police anyway. I wanted to do a little detective work of my own first though."

"Of course, the note in your bag," I exclaimed. "PM Police. I thought you had an evening visit with the police, but I see now PM stood for Patty-Mae, not post meridiem."

"Ella, you searched my doctor's bag?" Nathaniel was surprised, but seemed to be more amused than angry.

"No, of course I didn't. When you came to see me about my wrist and fell that day, all the contents scattered everywhere. I put everything back, but I couldn't help but notice the note. I certainly wasn't snooping."

Nathaniel laughed. "Not one of my finer moments."

Albert cleared his throat. "Please, go on with your story, Doctor Brookes."

"Patty-Mae came to see me a few days ago, accosted me actually on my doorstep one night. It was pitch black and well after hours and I was returning home from an emergency house visit. I was just putting my key in the lock and suddenly there she was. Practically jumped out of the privet and gave me a terrible start, I can tell you."

"What did she want?" I asked.

"Drugs," Nathaniel said simply. "She had an addiction to opiates and had run out. Apparently the chap who usually supplied her, and don't ask me who it was because I don't know, was in a bit of trouble, got himself into debt and no one was prepared to give him any more credit. I of course refused point blank. Even if I could have helped her, it's not something I would have done. Unfortunately she turned quite nasty when I refused. She'd been drinking and became belligerent and abusive, but I stuck to my guns and eventually she left. That was the one and only time I had met her until last night. Of course, I was aware of who she was. You can't live in a small village like this and not hear the rumours."

"Was she wearing heels?" I asked.

Both men stared at me as though I'd gone quite potty.

"Bear with me. Well?"

"Yes, she was actually. I remember because she damn near broke her ankle in her rush to leave."

"And this was at your surgery?" asked Albert.

Nathaniel shook his head. "No, actually, it was at my home. Surgery hours were over."

I knew roughly where Nathaniel lived and it wasn't easy to get to. It was off an obscure little road, which unless you knew it was there you would miss entirely. It would take the knowledge of a local to find it, which Patty-Mae was not.

"Gentlemen, if you'll excuse me just one minute," I said and dashed out the door.

"Hobbes?" I called.

"Yes, Miss?" a voice inquired from behind my left shoulder.

How did he do that?

"Hobbes, do you know if Miss Ludere drove a motor car?"

"I do, and she didn't. She preferred to be chauffeur driven and had never sat behind a wheel herself."

"Thank you, Hobbes, you've been very helpful," I said, returning to the drawing room. "I've just spoken with Hobbes and Patty-Mae didn't know how to drive. She was in high heels when she came to see you, Nathaniel, and it was at your house not the surgery, which is difficult enough to get to by car, let alone walk."

"So she must have had a friend with her," Nathaniel said. "Someone who drove and knew where to find me. I can't see Robert doing it, so it must have been someone else."

"Exactly. And her main friend on the island, one who would know where you live, Nathaniel, is … "

"Mr. Rutherford," finished Albert. "Very interesting."

"And something else interesting, Albert. I overheard an argument the other day between an insalubrious gentleman, most definitely a thug, and another younger, well-spoken man at the rear of the King's Head. The young man was being quite seriously threatened due to a significant debt. I thought nothing more of it. To tell you the truth, it was none of my business. But when Edgar arrived here, I recognised his voice straight away. He was the one in trouble."

"Well, it seems I have a lot of questions to ask Mr. Rutherford," said Albert. "Doctor Brookes, is there anything more? No? Well, if you'd be so kind as to ask Miss

Dinworthy to come in, you're also free to go home. However, I may need to speak with you again."

"Of course, Commissioner, you know where to find me. Ella, I'll telephone you tomorrow," Nathaniel said and left.

CHAPTER NINETEEN

arriet entered, looking very smart. She'd changed into a tweed skirt and jacket the colour of moorland heathers, and the soft lilacs and purples suited her tremendously. A small gold filigree brooch in the shape of a rose was pinned at the throat of her soft cream blouse and she'd done her hair. But most surprisingly, she was wearing lipstick. It was a soft pink colour, very delicate and barely noticeable, but I had never seen her wearing cosmetics of any kind.

"Ah, Miss Dinworthy, please do take a seat," Albert said graciously.

"Now, as you have no doubt heard, there are some details I would like to go over in order to tie up some loose ends. Could you tell me what you did after dinner last night?"

Harriet nodded. Settling back in the chair, she crossed her feet at the ankles and clasped her hands neatly in her lap.

"I left the dining room with Doctor Brookes. After a little conversation we parted company and I went to the powder room. When I entered, I found Miss Ludere was there. She was reapplying her lipstick, rather unsteadily I might add, and gave me such a venomous look I was quite taken aback. I had met the woman precisely once before and couldn't understand initially why she would obviously hate me so much. It was craven, I know, but I deliberately took my time using the facilities in the hope she would leave, but unfortunately she had waited for me."

"I hardly think wanting to avoid a confrontation is a sign of cowardice, Harriet," I said.

"Well, perhaps you're right, Isobella. However, I'm afraid when cornered I come out fighting, and regrettably that's just what I did last night. Not physically, you understand, but verbally, and by the time I had finished she was furious. A few unvarnished truths and having a mirror held up to you will do that. It's not something I'm proud of and I was quite shaken and upset afterward, but I wasn't prepared to stand by and be spoken to like that."

"And what exactly did Miss Ludere say to you?" asked Albert.

"I'm sure Isobella has brought you up to date, Commissioner, but if you insist. She quite simply told me to stay away from Robert. That after the party was over I was to sever all contact with him. She said with my feelings for him I was a threat to her marriage and her happy life. All nonsense of course and I refused. Robert and I have been friends all our lives and I wasn't going to be dictated to by the likes of Miss Ludere, who in my opinion was in this relationship for one thing and one thing only, money."

"But Patty-Mae's accusations and concerns weren't all nonsense were they, Harriet?" I asked softly.

"My dear Isobella, as sharp as always. Well, I don't suppose there's any point in denying it. I loved Robert, I still do. When we were young, it was assumed we would marry. Of course life conspired against us. Robert left when war broke out and when he returned, he was married. I was shocked and heartbroken of course. I'd waited, you see, and for me there was no other. But the atrocities of war change people and Robert had seen much in his service.

"But life goes on and I slowly mended by throwing myself into studying, then teaching, then writing. My work was and still is a lifeline, and I've been lucky enough to be successful in my chosen field. I have no regrets apart from the obvious one, but I couldn't stand aside and watch while Robert was hoodwinked by a gold-digger. I told her in no uncertain terms what I thought of her, but I didn't kill her as you now know, nor could I have done. But I can't say I'm sorry she no longer has her claws set into Robert."

"You've been very candid, Miss Dinworthy, in what was obviously a difficult and emotional telling and I appreciate your honesty. I think I have all I need from you, but will call again if questions crop up. You are of course free to return home," said Albert.

"Actually, Robert has asked me to stay on and I have agreed. It's a difficult time for him to be alone and he needs a friend."

Ah, I thought, *that explains the lipstick and the extra care she's taken with her appearance.* I was happy for her. After several decades apart, perhaps they could find love and companionship together in their twilight years. I also fervently hoped the curse wouldn't rear its ugly head and thwart their chances.

••‹‹◈››••

"Oh, isn't it wonderful to be home, Mrs. Shaw?" I said as we entered the cottage and laid our cases in the hall. "I know it's only been a short while, but it has felt like a lifetime with all that's gone on."

"It is indeed, Miss Bridges. I for one shall be glad to get to my own bed. Not that the accommodation at Arundel Hall wasn't good, but I won't miss the snores of Mrs. Butterworth, God bless her heart. I was amazed the roof was still on this morning. Now, shall I make you a pot of tea and a small supper before I retire?"

"That would be most welcome, Mrs. Shaw, thank you. I'll light the fire in the sitting room and eat in there," I told her. But first I wanted to check something.

I followed her downstairs and while she put away her bags, I slipped into the pantry. Taking the torch from a shelf, I opened the secret door and moving down to the far end I shone the torch at the chair.

"Oh, no. I thought you would have left by now," I said to the apparition in front of me.

I was sure I had solved her mystery, but perhaps I was wrong and there was something else I needed to do. However, if that was the case, I didn't know what it could be. More disturbingly though, she carried a black cat in her arms, the one I'd come to think of as my own. Dear Phantom. Had he belonged to her so many years ago? Had he appeared to me purely seeking justice for his mistress?

She gave me a small bow of her head and raised her hand. I watched as she gradually faded, then disappeared completely, taking my feline friend with her.

It was a bittersweet moment. She was free and had obviously waited to say goodbye. I had solved the mystery, after all, but she'd taken Phantom with her and I found a lump in my throat at the thought I would never see him again. For a ghost cat, who appeared at will and was rarely solid, he had certainly wormed his way into my heart.

I left and climbed the steps back to the sitting room, sniffing and blinking tears from my eyes.

"Not catching a cold I hope, Miss Bridges?" Mrs. Shaw said as she laid out my supper tray.

"Nothing like that, just a bit of dust from the downstairs dining room. I think the pantry can be restocked now. Tom Parsons is due to start work in the morning. Perhaps you could ask him to help? Also I think he could be trusted to lay the fires too, it will save you a job."

"Very well. Good night, Miss Bridges."

"Good night, Mrs. Shaw."

As I sat and stared into the flames, my mind went over the events of the last twenty-four hours. The fire was more of an extravagance than a necessity as it wasn't particularly cold, but I found it both comforting and relaxing.

I'd felt considerably put out when Albert had informed me I wouldn't be there to help interview Robert.

"Sir Robert doesn't want you to be present, I'm afraid, Ella, and I will respect his wishes. I believe he'll be more forthcoming with me alone," he'd said.

"But that's ridiculous, Albert. I can sit in the background and not speak if you'd prefer. He won't even know I'm there."

But Albert wouldn't budge. Robert was old fashioned in his beliefs and didn't think it was the place for a woman, let alone a 'young chit of a girl'. Albert had said he would make copious notes. "And I'll come and see you at the cottage tomorrow to let you know what was said," he'd promised.

"Well, don't forget to ask him about his visitor," and I went on to confirm how Hobbes had called Robert out from the library, how I'd got lost and inadvertently overheard a partial conversation, then Robert's account when he'd returned.

"There might very well be a perfectly reasonable explanation, but it struck me as odd at the time, and I think it's worth investigating a little more."

Now, a few hours later, and sat alone in my cottage, I wondered how the conversation between Robert and Albert was playing out up at The Hall. I suspected it was all very genial over a brandy and a cigar or two in front of the library fire. Two men chatting as though at their club. No wonder there was no place for me.

Sighing, I spent a little time on Aunt Margaret's latest puzzle to take my mind off them. It was a particularly ingenious one and without my trusted little dictionary to hand and my eyes blurring with fatigue, I barely managed to complete half of it. Too tired to concentrate, I tamped down the fire and went up to bed. Tomorrow was going to be a busy day.

CHAPTER TWENTY

Several things happened at once the next morning. I'd just finished breakfast when Mrs. Shaw came to inform me Tom Parsons was at the door. "With his dog," she said with a disapproving sniff.

I was halfway down the back stairs when the telephone rang, then just before I picked up the receiver the front door bell chimed.

"My word, it's like Piccadilly Circus here this morning," said Mrs. Shaw as she went to answer the door.

"Hello, Linhay..."

"Ella, good morning, it's Nathaniel," the deep voice said before I could finish. "I just wanted to make sure you got home all right."

"I did, yes, thank you, Nathaniel. Sorry, could you excuse me one moment?"

I looked at my housekeeper who was hovering behind me.

"Sorry to interrupt, Miss Bridges, but Sir Arthur Montesford is here. Shall I show him to the drawing room?"

"Put him in the small sitting room please, Mrs. Shaw, I'll not be long."

Turning back to the telephone, I said, "Nathaniel, I'm sorry, but Albert has just arrived. Could I call you back?"

"Yes, of course, although I'll be out and about most of the day, so the evening will be best."

After hanging up, I went to see Albert to explain I needed to see Tom, but I'd not be a moment. "In the meantime, help yourself to coffee," I said, indicating the tray Mrs. Shaw had deposited in front of him.

Down in the kitchen, I greeted Tom warmly, patted Digger on the head and explained Mrs. Shaw would be looking after him, but I would be back down to see him if I could before he left for the day.

Back upstairs I went to the sitting room and joined Albert in a cup of coffee and asked him how it had gone at The Hall.

"It was as you suspected, Ella," Albert said, adding cream and four heaped teaspoons of sugar to his coffee as well as another inch to his ever-expanding girth.

"It was nothing to do with escaped sheep, rather a painting he wished to purchase as a wedding present for Miss Ludere. She'd seen it in London apparently and fallen for it. He'd got this fellow Entwhistle to investigate it for him, check the provenance and so forth and it turned out to be a fake."

"And what about the other man I heard them mention?"

"Another buyer who was interested. Robert wanted to make sure he was successful in the purchase, didn't want any competition. But as it was a fake it was a moot point."

"But why make up some silly story about sheep?"

"He didn't want to let the cat out of the bag. It was to be a surprise gift and he didn't want anyone to accidentally spill the beans. Remember, he also didn't know where Miss Ludere was at the time and didn't want her to overhear. As simple as that really."

"But, Albert," I said, not willing to let it go, "does it not strike you as rather an odd time for this Entwhistle man to be calling? It was late, we'd just finished dinner."

"Robert is a wealthy man, Ella. I daresay he can demand people work all hours if he pays them enough. He wanted to know as soon as possible and told Entwhistle so. Entwhistle took him literally and so turned up as soon as he'd garnered the information."

"It would have been much easier to telephone," I muttered, sipping my coffee.

"Of course it would, but Robert's the sort of man who doesn't trust telephones. Ears listening in and all that. No, he asked for a report in person and that's what he got."

"So you're just taking what he said at face value?" I asked.

Albert gave me a combined stern and semi-amused look over the rim of his coffee cup. "You should know me better than that, Ella. I have a man checking his story at the gallery where the painting is located."

"Of course, I apologise, Albert. I felt rather peeved when I wasn't included last night and I'm being a bit crotchety about it. Just ignore me. I'm over it now. Are you going back to London today?"

"I am. I need to speak with young Rutherford again. Why? Do you want to tag along?"

"May I?"

"You may. I'd like you present when I speak to Edgar actually. He seems to trust you."

I chuckled. "I doubt that very much, but he considers me a snoop of the first order, and if he is telling the truth when he says he had nothing to do with the death of Patty-Mae, then I think he'll be more forthcoming in his answers if I'm there."

"Well, shall we say half an hour then?"

I'll go and tell Mrs. Shaw I'll be out for the day and to look after Tom and his dog."

Thirty minutes later, I was seated in Albert's splendid motor car leaving the island behind for the hustle and bustle of the capital. And the alien world of a prison cell.

I had never before set foot in Scotland Yard, although I had seen the building many times, located as it was upon Victoria Embankment. An imposing Victorian Romanesque style structure, built in banded red brick and white Portland stone on a base of granite, it was built on land reclaimed from the River Thames. Ironically during construction, the dismembered torso of a woman was found by workers, and the case was never solved.

Albert drove to the rear of the building and we entered through a small unobtrusive door painted bottle green, beyond which a set of stone steps led down to a basement.

"Apologies for using the 'tradesman's entrance', Ella. I find it preferable to come in unannounced on occasion."

At the foot of the stairs a wood panel door with a round glass window showed a corridor beyond bustling with life, and this was where Albert led me.

A couple of men in white coats jostled against others in suits and ties, who in turn rubbed shoulders and shouted jocular greetings to uniformed officers. All spoke or nodded to Albert with the deference awarded to him by rank, but gave me openly puzzled looks or surreptitious glances, not quite able to label me one thing or another. Was I a suspect, a witness or something more? And what was I doing in such exalted company? I doubt anyone would have believed I was consulting on a murder case.

"Good morning, Commissioner, and Miss Bridges, what a pleasant surprise. What brings you to the bowels of the yard?"

"Hello, Mortimer," Albert said. "Ella's helping me out with the Arundel Hall case. We're here to have another talk with young Rutherford."

"Well, if you have time, please do call up to the laboratory, Ella. I'd like to show you around our latest forensic techniques. I'm sure you'll find it interesting."

"Thank you. Certainly, if time allows, I'd very much like to visit," I said.

"And, Albert, I finished my report with regard to Miss Ludere. You'll find it on your desk."

Albert and I took our leave of Mortimer and descended another staircase, this one leading to the holding cells where prisoners were kept prior to being sentenced, or drunks picked up in the night lay sleeping it off. Through the door, a uniformed constable sat at a scarred table reading the paper. He jumped up sharpish when Albert pushed open the door and thrust a clipboard out for him to sign.

"Thank you, sir. Will you be needing an interview room, sir?"

"Not this time, constable. Has Mr. Rutherford contacted a solicitor, do you know?"

"He has, sir. According to the docket," the constable checked one of numerous official looking forms on the board, "he should be here in about an hour, sir."

"Well, that should give us enough time, thank you, constable. Oh, and please bring two chairs to cell twelve."

The atmosphere as we walked on was dismal in the extreme, with an overpowering smell of human waste and unwashed bodies, mixed with cleaning fluid and lye soap. It took all of my willpower, and a handkerchief over my nose and mouth, to prevent me from gagging. It was also very cold. The narrow corridor was stone underfoot with a brick arched ceiling and brick walls, and every step echoed around our heads and bounced back to assault our ears.

The brick was painted in what originally would have been a soft cream, but now bore dubious stains and the grime of years, which mottled it to a sickly dark yellow. There were twelve cells in total, six to a side and each one no bigger than a broom closet.

They contained identical cots covered in thin grey woollen blankets and a bucket in the opposite corner. The only light came from a small arched window set high in the wall and faced with bars. Only three of the cells were occupied. One held what looked at first glance to be a bunch of rags on the cot, but was in fact a vagrant. Brought in for being drunk and disorderly the night before, according to Albert. He would soon be turned out to begin the cycle again, and no doubt would find himself a bed for tonight in the same place.

The second cell, opposite the beggar, was occupied by a huge, terrifying individual with a mass of dirty black hair and only one eye. A vivid puckered scar running from hairline to chin spoke of how he'd lost the other. His single orb glared at me with black malevolence and I hurried past the gated door to his cell to the accompaniment of jeers and laughter, and the aggressive rattling of bars.

The third cell at the farthest end and well away from the others housed Edgar.

As soon as we came into sight he jumped up, eyes wild and desperate, and clung to the bars. "Thank god. Have you news? Have you caught the killer?"

Albert glanced at me and remained silent.

"Edgar, there's been little progress, but there is something that's come to light, which we need to ask you about," I said.

At that moment the constable came dragging two remarkably uncomfortable-looking wooden chairs behind him. We thanked him, positioned them a few feet from the front of Edgar's cell door and sat.

"Edgar, did you take Patty-Mae to visit Doctor Brookes the other night?"

"Yes."

"Why?"

"Because she asked me to. She didn't drive a motor car."

"Edgar, you know very well that's not what I meant. Why did Patty-Mae need to see the doctor?"

"I don't know, she never said."

And there it was, that little sign Aunt Margaret had told me to watch out for.

"Edgar, you are lying to me. I'm here to try and help you, at your request I might add, but if you're going to lie then there's not much point in my being here."

I stood up to leave.

"No, wait. She needed drugs. She had an addiction. I tried to help her, but it was no good. She just couldn't do without it."

It was at that moment I realised just what I'd heard between Edgar and the man who had threatened him at The King's Head.

"It was you who was procuring the drugs for her, wasn't it? But of course she couldn't pay you for them and now you're in debt and a lot of trouble as a result. Why did you do it, Edgar, out of friendship? No of course not. It was because you loved her, didn't you?"

This was pure guesswork on my part, but I couldn't think what else it could be. I prayed I was right and waited for a response.

Edgar sat on the cot and put his head in his hands and wept.

"Edgar, do you realise how much trouble you're in?" I asked softly. "If you're found guilty then you will hang. Why would you want to hang for a murder you did not commit? I will try to help you, Edgar, but you must tell me what happened."

He sat up, wiping his eyes and nose on the back of his hand and began to speak in a monotone, eyes unfocused and staring ahead as though recalling a visual memory.

"I was getting the drugs from someone in London. I'd sold a few things to get the money and it was all working out fine for a while. But then Patty-Mae wanted more and more and eventually I ran out of things to sell. So I started getting it on credit using different suppliers and paying off bits when I could. Eventually the word got out I couldn't pay and every door was slammed in my face. People came after me, threatening to break my legs, or worse. So I ran back to Linhay and kept my head down. Patty-Mae had enough to last a couple of weeks and then she ran out. She was getting desperate and I didn't know where else to go. I couldn't go back to London, I'd have been killed on the spot and my body thrown in the Thames. So as a last resort I took her to Doctor Brookes. No doubt he's told you he refused to help."

I glanced at Albert who'd been making notes in his little black book from the moment we'd sat down. He made a motion with his hand for me to continue, but didn't interrupt.

"Edgar, you introduced Robert to Patty-Mae. How did you feel when they fell in love and decided to marry? It must have hurt a great deal."

"Have you ever been on the wrong end of unrequited love, Ella? Well, that was how it was with Patty-Mae. She never loved me, barely knew I existed except to provide her with her drug."

I sighed and got up, moving closer to the bars.

"How am I supposed to help you if you won't tell me the truth? Perhaps I should tell you some truths to make you see how serious this is."

I began to count the points on my fingers.

"Number one, so far you are the only one in the frame for the murder. Number two, you knew the victim well, you were friends. Number three, you've said you were in love with her, yet she didn't look upon you in the same way. Frankly, I believe that's a lie. However, all it does is add more ammunition to the case against you. Number four, you supplied her with drugs and got into debt and danger because of it. Number five, by your own admission you had a violent argument on the night she was killed. Number six, your shirt button was found in her dead hand, and number seven, because thus far there is no evidence to the contrary, you were the last person to see her alive. Do you see what this means, Edgar? You had both the opportunity and more than one motive to murder Patty-Mae."

"But I didn't do it," he shouted.

"Then why are you lying?" I shouted back. "What are you hiding?"

I couldn't believe I'd raised my voice, but I was frustrated beyond belief. I couldn't understand why Edgar was being such an obstinate fool when his life was hanging in the balance. But If I'd thought my shouting and laying out of the facts would shock him into telling me the truth, I was sadly wrong.

"I can't, Ella," he said in a quiet shaky voice. "Please, just keep looking, I beg of you. I didn't kill Patty-Mae, I couldn't. I truly did love her. But I've told you all I can."

Turning away, he curled up on the cot facing the wall and would speak no more.

"Edgar, I can't begin to understand your reluctance to speak," I said to his back, "but if you change your mind, you can get word to me through the commissioner and I'll return."

On my way out I called in briefly to let Mortimer know I wouldn't be able to join him, and he assured me the invitation was always open. To be honest I felt wrung out after my visit to Edgar. It had been far more emotionally tiring, confrontational and disheartening than I'd imagined and all I wanted to do was curl up in front of the fire at home and sleep.

Albert, ever gracious, had offered to drive me back to Linhay, but I'd refused. I wanted to be alone for a while, and the perfect place for me to restore my wits and my equilibrium would be on the train. He insisted on driving me to the station, which I gladly accepted. Being jostled in the crowded city streets held no appeal at all. In my exhausted state I could very well find myself under a bus.

"That was an excellent interview, Ella. I doubt very much I could have done better myself. I'm intrigued as to how you knew he was lying? That sort of skill would be deuced useful to The Yard."

"It was my Aunt Margaret who taught me. I spent some time living with her and she showed me what to look for. She is a puzzle expert and an avid people watcher. Over the years she put together a lot of clues and the result was various signs to look for when people are being less than truthful."

"So it's a teachable skill?"

"Yes. I said to her once she should write a book about it, but she said she was too long in the tooth to start such a project, that sort of thing was for the younger generation, plus she thought it would take all the fun out of it."

"And have you thought of taking up that particular mantle? Not for the public market, of course, otherwise every criminal in the country will have the advantage, but perhaps for law enforcement officers. It could work very well in conjunction with some classroom type training."

"Dear Albert," I laughed. "That was far from subtle, even for you. Perhaps you'll give me time to think about it? I'm barely coherent at present, but I'm not discounting the idea of a manual to help with training your policemen. It is rather a good idea actually, and one I'll give some serious thought to. But later."

"And that's all I can ask, my dear. Although there is another thing I would like you to consider. I'd like to take you on in an official capacity, as a consultant, you understand. There will be remuneration involved for your time and expenses of course. You've shown immense intuition in the cases we've been involved in together, but in this one in particular and I'd like you to be part of my team. Will you think about it?"

In all honesty I didn't need to think about it. Never before had I felt so worthwhile, so alive, as though I were contributing to something that mattered while doing something I was actually good at.

"My answer is yes, Albert. I would very much like to be part of your team, and thank you for not only asking me, but for having the faith in me to do the job."

"Well, that's excellent news. I'll get the ball rolling when I get back to the office. I'm due to see the Home Secretary this evening anyway, so I'll discuss it with him then."

"Lord Carrick?" I asked in shock. This was most unexpected. I hadn't spoken with him since his awful visit when John had died and he'd told me I needed to move out of my home and start life again under my maiden name.

"Of course. The department falls under the jurisdiction of the Home Office so naturally he'll need to be informed. Why? Is there a problem?"

I thought about it, then smiled inwardly. I would love to be a fly on the wall when Albert informed Lord Carrick I was to be taken on as a consultant detective, and in the murder division no less. How far I had come from the naive little woman he'd patronised, pitied and lied to a few years before.

"Actually I see no problem, Albert. No problem at all."

We'd reached the train station and Albert parked the car, then walked with me into the building.

"Is there anything you'd like to add to the case, Ella, now you're officially on the payroll as it were?"

"I was thinking that perhaps we need to find out more about Patty-Mae. I for one haven't heard of her, but that means nothing. I'm neither a theatre nor movie goer, but it strikes me, and please don't take this as me telling you how to do your job, that as the victim she must have done something to warrant being killed in the first place. It seems as though we have been privy to the secrets of the others, but we still know next to nothing about the victim."

"A very good point, Ella," Albert said in such a way that I knew he'd already considered this avenue of investigation, and most probably was already in pursuit of answers. "I'll oversee those inquiries myself and will keep you updated."

I said goodbye and went to board my train, sinking into the seat with great relief. Within minutes of it setting off I was fast asleep and didn't wake again until I was back on the island.

CHAPTER TWENTY-ONE

The following morning passed quickly. Tom arrived at eight on the dot with his excitable and thoroughly enjoyable little dog, and we spent a few hours together working in the garden. The sky was a pale misty blue tinged with creamy yellow, and the sun, still low, looked like a ball of lemon sherbet, its mild warmth suffusing and loosening my limbs and boosting my sense of well-being.

Tom had already made progress through the wild thicket and brush we believed led to the walled garden, but there was still much to do. I left him to it and spent the morning trimming the roses and shrubs, cleaning and preparing tubs for spring planting, and generally pottering about. But all the while the murder case rattled around in my head, the fragmented information attempting to weld itself into some coherent whole, while the front part of my mind concentrated on more mundane matters such as compost.

At noon Tom disappeared to the kitchen for his lunch, Digger to his basket by the warm range, which I'd put there for just that purpose, and I took myself to the sitting room with a tray.

I'd barely sat down when a black shape launched itself through the window glass with barely a ripple, and landed on my desk, scattering papers hither and thither. My cat was back.

"Well, what a theatrical entrance, Phantom. I'm so glad to see you, my little feline friend. I thought you had gone for good."

Phantom gave me a haughty stare as if to say, 'you won't get rid of me that easily,' and then stretching, proceeded to curl up in the chair by the fire and fall asleep. I laughed and bent to pick up my scattered papers. As I did so, my eye caught the puzzle I'd been doing two nights before and my heart missed a beat. One word was glaring at me, not one I had filled in, but one that had automatically revealed itself as I'd filled in the other clues. In my fatigue the other night I had missed it completely. I picked it up and stared, but I had no idea what it meant, was it even English?

I dashed to the bookshelf and grabbed my little dictionary. Quickly finding the correct letter, I scanned through the entire list, but it wasn't there. Oh, why was I wasting time? A telephone call to Aunt Margaret would solve the mystery.

"Aunt Margaret, it's Ella. How are you?"

"Well, hello, my dear, I was wondering when you would call. You've solved it then?"

I always called her when I'd solved her puzzles.

"Actually no, I haven't just yet, but it is the reason I'm calling. Aunt Margaret, this is terribly important. Do you have a copy to hand?"

"Of course, but I don't need it. Whatever is the problem, Ella? You sound quite flustered."

"Can you recall seven down? What does it mean?"

"Seven down ... oh yes, one of my more ingenious clues, I thought. It's Latin, an unusual word, not much heard of nowadays of course. Unless you've studied the language you wouldn't know of it."

"So what does it mean?"

"It means bogus, Ella. Ludere is Latin for fake. Does that help, dear?"

"More than you know, Aunt Margaret."

"Can you tell me what this is all about or is it a little hush-hush?"

Astute as ever, I thought with a proud smile. "Actually, it is a little hush-hush for now, but I'll let you know as soon as I can. Thank you, Aunt Margaret, you may have helped me to solve more than just a puzzle."

"Glad to be of help, my dear, and even more so to hear you're using that brain of yours at last. Much love, darling." And she hung up.

So Patty-Mae Ludere was a fraud. I knew a puzzle clue was rather tenuous reasoning, but in my heart I knew I was right. And another thing I was almost sure of was that Edgar Rutherford knew all about it. With his education, he would be well versed in Latin. I believed this was what he refused to tell us yesterday and he'd lied about this unrequited love nonsense. Patty-Mae Ludere and Edgar Rutherford were in this together. I needed to find out why they had created such an elaborate ruse. Time to telephone Albert.

"Albert, it's Ella. Have you found out any more about Patty-Mae?"

"Nothing definitive yet, I'm sorry to say. I wired Pinkerton's Detective Agency the day following the murder, but thus far all avenues of inquiry have hit a brick wall. According to Sir Robert, she hailed from a wealthy plantation owner family in the south, but nobody down there has heard of her. It's all rather suspect."

"They won't find anything, Albert. Patty-Mae Ludere is a fake. I don't even know if she was American."

There was a lengthy pause while Albert chewed over my startling pronouncement. "How did you find out? And how sure are you, Ella?"

"As sure as I can be, and what's more, I believe Edgar knew about it. In fact, I'd be willing to bet they worked together. Although what their plan was, I don't know, but we need to talk to him again."

"I agree. How soon can you get here?"

I checked the clock in the hall. "Expect me within two hours, and Albert, could you please arrange an interview room this time. I don't think I could bear another trip to the cells."

"He's through here," Albert said, opening a door to a small gloomy room, not dissimilar to the holding cells below. Naturally there was no cot, but in the centre of the room was a scarred wooden table, with two empty chairs one side and another, occupied, opposite. A constable stood to attention next to the wall behind the prisoner.

Edgar sat with his hands on the surface, forced there by the manacles enfolding his wrists being chained through a loop in the table. He glanced up when we entered and I saw him visibly blanch at the obvious fury he saw in my face.

"So Patty-Mae was a fraud. A fake. A completely bogus persona you and she dreamed up together," I said, slapping my gloves down on the table.

Edgar was shocked. He hadn't been expecting this at all. "How … ?"

"How did I find out? I'm a snoop, remember, and a good one, as it turns out. Now you had better start talking, Edgar. Otherwise I'm going to leave you to rot here until it's time for the hangman to slip his noose over your neck. I'm sick to my stomach of your lying, and your misplaced martyrdom and erroneous loyalty. If it's Patty-Mae you're trying to protect, it's too late. She's dead, Edgar, and you'll be next unless you tell us everything you know. Now, who was she really and where did you meet her?"

I saw the moment in Edgar's eyes when he finally decided to tell us the truth. He was beaten and he knew it. Now all he could do was salvage what he could from the mess he had made.

"Her name was Martha Brown and I met her at a seedy little club a couple of years ago. She was … she was one of the hostesses and also did some of the song and dance numbers. The stage was her life, it was all she'd ever wanted and if being on the stage meant she had to do a little hostess work too, then she'd do it. Her dream was to be a famous actress and singer and she was good, really good, but she just never got her break. She started in some of the better clubs and was beginning to make a name for herself when she got involved with Lucas Stamp. He'd seen her at the club and taken a fancy to her, and when Lucas wants something, he gets it," Edgar said bitterly.

Albert looked up. "Lucas Stamp, you say?"

Edgar nodded.

"Who is Lucas Stamp?" I asked.

"He is the head of organised crime in London's seedier underground. The British equivalent of a mafia crime boss with his hands in every sordid racket imaginable. From gambling to prostitution and everything in-between, including drugs," said Albert, his dark eyes like flint. "I assume he was responsible for Miss Brown's addiction?"

Again Edgar nodded. "It was his way of making her toe the line, to possess her completely and he was ruthless. Eventually, he grew tired of her and cast her aside. She lost her job at the club and with her addiction, it grew more and more difficult to find employment. She worked in eight different clubs in as many months, each one worse than the last, but she could barely function enough to do the job. Eventually she ended up in the lowest of the low, which is where I found her."

"And you became friends?" I asked, barely keeping the scepticism from my voice.

"Not at first, no. I went back several times and we started to talk. The more I got to know her, the more I realised how scared and vulnerable she was, everything else was an act. Hidden beneath the thick, poorly applied makeup, the scanty outfits and the coquettish manner, was a scared little girl and I wanted to help her, to protect her."

"So how did Martha Brown, opiate addict, hostess and dancer in a seedy London nightclub, morph into Miss Patty-Mae Ludere, celebrated American star of the silver screen?" asked Albert. "And to what purpose?"

"To be honest, I can barely remember whose idea it was. I'd taken Martha away from London. I couldn't stand the thought of her being there any longer. I took her to Linhay and put her in The Lodge. It stands empty most of the time anyway with my parents being away, and I prefer the London flat. One night I took her to see a new flick at the Granada in Tooting. I forget the star, Lombard or Garbo I think, but Martha was transfixed. At the end she said it should have been her up there on the screen, she could have done it so much better, she said, and I believed her. In the motor on the way back she recited most of the film word for word, and if I hadn't known better I could have sworn it was Garbo or Lombard sitting next to me. She was a terrific mimic. I suppose that's where the seed of the idea was planted."

"I think we will take a break there, Edgar," Albert said. "I'll have some refreshments brought in to you. Do you smoke?"

Edgar shook his head.

Albert and I left and went to his office for our own refreshments.

"So what do you think, Ella? Is he telling the truth this time?"

"Undoubtedly. It's a very raw and painful telling for him too. I wonder if Robert is aware of the deception?"

"Yes, I wonder also. It would be a first-rate motive for murder if he was. I think once we've finished here, you and I should pay another visit to Arundel Hall."

Back in the interview room, Edgar looked much better after having something to eat and a cup of tea. I also suspected sharing the weighty secret he had harboured for so long had been a huge relief.

"Please continue, Edgar. What happened next?"

"It started as a bit of fun at first. Martha wanted to put the past behind her, reinvent herself so she could appear in public, see if she could fool people. I bought her clothes and jewellery, paid for a day or two at a beauty salon and by the time she left she was barely recognisable. She practiced her make-up, copying the styles of the starlets and she practiced her accent. Before long it was second nature and Patty-Mae Ludere was born."

I asked the question I'd been pondering for a while. "Did you deliberately target Sir Robert Harlow?"

He nodded.

"Yes. What I told you before was true. Patty-Mae's addiction was costing more money than I had and I was in trouble. We both were, we needed money. She joked that if she could find herself a sugar daddy then both our troubles would be over. A few days later, I was in Robert's old bank when I overheard a couple of the ladies talking about how sad it was he'd never remarried after his wife had died. And that was that."

"But how did you know he would be attracted to her?"

He shrugged. "I didn't for sure, but Linhay is a small island and my parents and Robert became friends years ago and often attended the same London functions. It didn't take long to find a photograph of him and his wife with my mother and father. With a few tweaks … "

"Patty-Mae modelled her look on his deceased wife," I finished for him.

Dear god, it was quite ingenious, I thought. Sly, calculating and underhand, but clever nonetheless.

"Thank you for being so candid, Edgar," Albert said. "You'll have to remain here of course, until our inquiries are complete."

"I'm probably safer here than out there anyway. Although it hardly matters. Martha is dead. I may as well be too."

"Don't be so ridiculous," I said. "Martha wouldn't want you to stop living. Besides, if what you're saying is true, her murderer is still out there and she'd want you to see justice done, I'm sure of it."

Albert and I left, but not before he'd taken the constable to one side and urged him to remove everything from Edgar's cell with which he could harm himself.

At my request, Albert escorted me to Mortimer then left to go to his office. He had rather a backlog of reports and paperwork as a result of choosing to be in the thick of this case. Under normal circumstances, it would have been assigned to a senior officer, but due to the violence and rarity of the crime, Albert had decided to become directly involved.

Mortimer was unnaturally effusive in his greeting, obviously eager to show off the department's forensic science."Now this is the area I particularly wanted to show you," said Mortimer, "The Dactyloscopy Department."

I looked at him blankly. I had no idea what he was talking about.

"Fingerprints, my dear. Fingerprints. The most significant discovery for law enforcement this century. Did you know no two fingerprints are the same? And more importantly in our field, everyone can be identified by their own?"

"Mortimer, this is astonishing," I said in genuine awe. "I had no idea things had become so advanced." Then something else occurred to me. "Mortimer, is it possible to see if there is such a print on the button from Patty-Mae's hand?"

He glanced at me quizzically. "I assume you feel Mr. Rutherford is no longer the prime suspect then? I rather thought with the button coming from his shirt, the fight he admitted to between himself and Miss Ludere, and said button being found in her hand, it was all cut and dried, so to speak?"

"I'd rather not assume anything at this stage," I said. "Personally, I feel it's all a little too obvious. I've spent several hours speaking with Edgar Rutherford and I'm now almost convinced he didn't commit the murder. If you remove him as the perpetrator then you begin to see how he could have been set up to take the blame, which is what he has maintained all along. What if someone else, the murderer, had overheard the confrontation? Say the button from his shirt had fallen to the ground during their argument, then after Patty-Mae was killed our culprit could have spied the button on the ground, picked it up and placed it in her hand. It was the perfect opportunity to throw the scent in Edgar's direction."

He nodded and smiled at me as though I were a clever pupil. I was almost surprised when he didn't pat me on the head.

"Then I shall do as you ask, my dear. However, it's a delicate procedure and as I'm sure you'll understand we only have one attempt at it. If we get it wrong during any part of the process, then this particular piece of evidence will be lost. But if we're successful then you'll need the fingerprints of the suspects in order to make a match. Let me show you how."

There followed an hour of training where Mortimer showed me how to take Exemplar prints and put them on an evidence card. It was a tricky business, and particularly messy. There were several times I smudged the card so the resulting print was useless, but eventually, after much trial and error, and blackened fingers, I got the hang of it.

"Did you take Edgar's prints or do I need to do those?"

"We already have Mr. Rutherford's prints on file. It's a mandatory procedure when bringing in a suspect. It's the others you need to obtain now. I'll get together a sampling kit to take with you."

Five minutes later, armed with my first detective kit, I went in search of Albert to tell him my plans.

"I believe this could be the break we need, Ella. Did Mortimer say how long it would take to obtain the print from the button?"

"He should have something for us tomorrow if it works. He's put it to the head of the queue."

"Then let's be on our way to Linhay. I'll telephone Doctor Brookes and we can obtain his prints first, then we can go on to Arundel Hall."

Albert drove at a much more sedate pace than was his norm on the return journey. The wind had risen during the time we were cosseted in Scotland Yard, not so apparent in the built up city streets, but once we'd hit the open road and the countryside, it buffeted the motorcar considerably.

It was already quite late and the sun was setting, its pale orb disappearing below the horizon as I watched. It would be dark by the time we arrived at Arundel Hall. Albert had decided not to call ahead. He wanted the element of surprise this time, and I wondered what sort of reception I would get. Robert had been adamant I be excluded from the initial interview. However, Albert would insist I be present this time. No more 'chit of a girl', on this occasion I was an employee of Scotland Yard.

The plan was to inform Sir Robert that through the course of our inquiries we'd discovered Patty-Mae was a fraud. Our objective was to determine whether he already knew or not and I felt sure I would be able to tell if he was lying.

"I spoke with the Home Secretary, by the way," Albert said, jarring me from my thoughts.

"And?"

"You're officially on the staff," he said, taking his eyes off the road for a minute to favour me with a smile. "However, he did take a little more persuading than I had thought."

"Because I'm a woman, you mean?"

"Not at all. Carrick's quite a progressive thinker in his way. No, it was more that I got the impression he knew your name. It was a momentary shock when I mentioned you, which he covered well, but I was intrigued."

I leant back in my seat and closed my eyes. Did I really want to open this particular Pandora's Box? Lord Carrick had insisted I would be in danger if I let slip I'd once been married to John, and so far, discounting my momentary slip on a previous case which no longer mattered as the culprits had been caught, I'd not breathed a word. The only living souls who knew were my brother Jerry, my sister-in-law Ginny, my mother and my aunt, and they also hadn't said anything. Nor had they in fact asked any questions apart from the initial ones borne of curiosity, which I'd refused to answer. But if I spoke now who knew how many complicated problems it would generate? Then again, Albert was the Commissioner of Scotland Yard, and as Ginny's godfather was almost family. If I couldn't trust him, then who could I trust? There was also a little voice in my head telling me with his connections and my new found access to Scotland Yard, I could discover more about who John really was, and that was extremely tempting.

I decided to trust my intuition and for the first time in two years spoke about my marriage, the death of my husband and the resulting visit from the Home Secretary.

"Good lord, Ella. I am sorry, I had no idea."

"Of course you didn't, there's no need to apologise. What I found most difficult was the knowledge that I had been lied to, both by John and by Lord Carrick. You must remember this was before I went to live with Aunt Margaret so she hadn't yet passed on her knowledge. But I must have had some skill even then; it was intuitive I suppose. I still don't know what sort of danger I could possibly have been in. However, that will be determined when I find out exactly who, or what, John was."

"And is your intuition telling you anything now?"

"As a matter of fact, it is. I think John may have been a spy."

CHAPTER TWENTY-TWO

Nathaniel was waiting for us in the surgery. It was well after closing time, but he'd suggested we meet him there as it was more convenient.

"So you're a detective now, Ella?" Nathaniel asked with a grin as I inked each finger and carefully transferred the prints to the two cards, one for each hand.

I smiled. "On a consultancy basis, yes."

"And you need my prints to eliminate me as a suspect, I suppose?"

"That's right, although I also need the practice. You're my first," I said, then felt myself blush at the look he gave me.

He looked down and cleared his throat. "So what of Rutherford? I thought he was your man?"

I hesitated. I didn't for one minute think Nathaniel had murdered Patty-Mae, but he was still a suspect and I needed to be circumspect regarding the information I imparted. And regardless of Albert's warning, where Nathaniel was concerned I was letting my emotions get in the way. However, before I'd had chance to think of a suitable reply, Albert answered.

"Rutherford is still in custody, Doctor Brookes. However, we need to ensure we've crossed all our 'T's' and dotted all our 'i's', as it were. There is such a thing as the 'chain of evidence', which we need to strictly adhere to."

"Of course, I understand," Nathaniel said, reaching for a small brown bottle of swabbing alcohol to remove the ink stains from his hands.

"The ink is dry now," I said. "Could you add your signature at the bottom to confirm these are your prints. And date it here, please."

Nathaniel did as I asked and I put the cards away safely in my evidence kit.

As we were leaving, Nathaniel put his hand on my arm, holding me back.

"Ella, when all this is over, would you like to go out to dinner with me? Perhaps take in a show beforehand?"

I glanced up into his handsome face and his clear, seductive eyes. "When this is over, there's nothing I'd like more, Nathaniel," I said.

The approach to The Hall was very different than the last time I had come this way, remarkably only a few short days ago. Gone were the torches and the twinkling fairy lights in the trees that cast a glow of magic and enchanted expectation; now dark and foreboding, its length seemed interminable. The statuary in the fountain was thankfully unchanged. Still no sign of the water that would add to its ghoulishness, but it looked more malevolent than ever.

Albert pulled up at the door and once again Hobbes was there to greet us.

"Commissioner, Miss Bridges. Are you expected?"

"We're not, Hobbes. If you'd like to tell Sir Robert we are here on official police business."

"Of course, sir. If you'd like to take a seat in the drawing room."

Albert and I didn't have long to wait before both Robert and Harriet entered.

"Commissioner, this is most unexpected. What can I do for you? Hobbes said it was a police matter. I thought the case had all but been solved? And, Miss Bridges, while it's always a pleasure to see you, in what capacity are you here? Not as a policeman obviously."

"As a matter of fact, Sir Robert, Miss Bridges is indeed here in an official capacity. She is now in the employ of Scotland Yard as a consultant detective," Albert said.

"My dear Isobella, I'm astonished," said Harriet, coming over to greet me. "Although I really shouldn't be, should I? I always said you were sharp enough to cut yourself."

"Good god," muttered Robert. "Women detectives, whatever next?"

"Sir Robert, we would like to talk to you privately in a moment, just a few points needing clarification. But first, purely for elimination purposes, Miss Bridges will need to take both your and Miss Dinworthy's fingerprints."

As I readied my cards and ink, Robert spoke harshly to Albert.

"No, I'm afraid this won't do at all, Commissioner. I refuse to be treated as a suspect, especially in my own home."

"I'm afraid you are a suspect, Sir Robert," Albert said succinctly. "And if you'd prefer, we can always do this at

Scotland Yard, although I admit the surroundings will be far less comfortable."

"How dare you come in here and treat Harriet and me like this? Neither of us had anything to do with Patty-Mae's murder. It's preposterous and I shan't have anything to do with it."

"It's not a request, Sir Robert," said Albert, and for the second time I saw his eyes turn to hard cold flint.

Harriet gently laid a hand on Robert's arm. "It will be perfectly all right, Robert, you'll see. And I'm afraid we really have no say in the matter. It's to eliminate us, my dear, not to accuse us. Look, I'll go first. Isobella, are you ready?"

I nodded and watched as Robert resigned himself. Harriet certainly had a calming effect on him and I thought again what a shame it had been the two hadn't married.

Once Harriet had witnessed her fingerprint cards with signature and date, I called for Robert.

He grudgingly gave me his left hand and I began the inking process. "Just how am I supposed to remove this infernal stuff?" he muttered. Even though Harriet had made him see sense, he was still incredibly annoyed. He was an old man, set in his ways and chary in his acceptance of change, especially when it came to women in the workplace. I mistakenly tried to appease him.

"It's rather like clerical work, Sir Robert. Just think of me as a secretary of sorts."

"Please don't patronise me, Miss Bridges."

I straightened and looked him squarely in the eye. "Then I would appreciate it if you would award me the same respect, Sir Robert."

He met my gaze for a moment, then gave a curt nod and looked away. Hardly a resounding success, but I'd take what little victory I could.

With the fingerprint cards completed and safely stored in my case, Harriet left the room and Albert and I continued our questioning of Robert. Albert didn't hold back as I'd expected him to, but launched straight to the heart of the matter.

"Sir Robert, were you aware Patty-Mae Ludere was a fraud? That the woman to whom you were engaged was a made up caricature by someone entirely different?"

I held my breath, waiting for vehement denials and protestations, but they never came. Instead Robert sat calmly and gave first Albert, then myself, a shrewd look. The silence seemed eternal and he was obviously not intending to speak. I surmised he was waiting to see exactly how much we knew before imparting his own knowledge.

"So how did you find out?" I asked. "Was it in the letters the postmaster gave you from America? I suppose a man of your wealth and position would need to make sure of your future wife's credentials. Did you hire a firm of detectives over there?"

Robert bristled visibly. "You've obviously done your homework, Miss Bridges," he said in a sour tone. "Yes, I did employ someone to do a little research. However, every lead resulted in a blind alley. It was as though she didn't exist."

"So you employed someone at this end to find out more," said Albert. "One Mr. Entwhistle."

"I've already told you about Entwhistle, Commissioner."

"So you did, Sir Robert, but I've been doing a little research of my own and I'm afraid your version doesn't quite match my findings. Mr. Entwhistle is a Private Investigator specialising in, among other things, spousal infidelities."

Once again the conversation I'd overheard began to make more sense.

"When he arrived here the night of the dinner party, I distinctly heard the word fraud. He meant Patty-Mae, didn't he?" I said.

Robert shot from his seat, his face filled with fury. "My god, you were spying on me? A guest in my own home and you were snooping and sneaking about? Just who do you think you are?"

"Please do calm down. It was purely an accident. I got lost on my way to the powder room. Hobbes found me eventually, but not before I'd unwittingly heard part of your conversation. It most certainly wasn't deliberate. Nor would I have thought twice about it. It was no concern of mine. However, the murder of Patty-Mae changes all that, Sir Robert, and casts a different light on your conversation with Mr. Entwhistle, given the new context. How did you feel when you found out that Patty-Mae Ludere was a fraud?"

"For heaven's sake, woman, have you lost your wits? How do you think I felt? I was shocked and upset. At first I thought there must have been some sort of mistake. How could my dear sweet Patty-Mae be anything other than she claimed? And why would she go to all that trouble? But then Entwhistle confirmed the findings. I had every intention of ending the engagement quietly and privately after you had all left. But by then it was too late."

He resumed his seat, slumping dejectedly as though all the fight had left him, but I knew it was an act.

"But that wasn't all Entwhistle found out, was it? The 'other matter' was his discovering she was seeing someone else. Patty-Mae had a long-term lover, Sir Robert, one that in all likelihood she wouldn't give up even after you were wed. Surely that must have made you angry?"

I held my breath, heart hammering wildly. Had I pushed him too far? Out of the corner of my eye I saw Albert lean forward slightly ready to intervene in case Robert turned fierce.

"Good god, you never give up, do you?" he roared, standing and taking a step toward me.

Albert was silently hovering at his elbow in an instant.

"Yes, I found out she had a lover and yes, I was furious. She'd lied to me and schemed behind my back to marry me for my money so that she and her inamorato could live in luxury. I've already found several items missing, which I assume she's sold to feather their nest."

I realised he didn't know Patty-Mae was an addict and in all probability had stolen the items to purchase drugs.

"She'd made me look like a pathetic fool in front of my peers and a laughing stock in the village. Even my staff were giving me pitying looks. Oh yes, don't think I didn't see them. Her actions were unforgivable."

"So you killed her?" I ventured.

He leaned toward me, fists and teeth clenched, spittle collecting at the corner of his mouth and eyes consumed with rage.

"And what if I did?" he hissed.

Albert and I looked at each other. Was this a confession? Before we could ask, Harriet rushed through the door to Robert's side.

"No, don't listen to him. Robert didn't kill Patty-Mae. I did."

Robert looked at Harriet in shock. "No, Hettie." Turning back to us he said, "Don't listen to her. She's trying to protect me."

"Ahem." We all glanced at the door where Hobbes was standing.

"I'm afraid neither Sir Robert nor Miss Dinworthy could have killed Miss Ludere," he said.

"And why is that, Hobbes?" asked Albert.

"Because it was, in fact, I who carried out the murder."

CHAPTER
TWENTY-THREE

lbert threw up his hands in despair.

"What on Earth do you people think this is, some sort of parlour game?"

Nobody said a word.

"You do all realise we will find the true culprit eventually? No matter who you think you are protecting, the truth will come out."

Still, they all remained stubbornly silent. What a ridiculously tangled web this was turning out to be. At that moment Phantom chose to make an appearance, weaving his way in a figure eight around the legs of Harriet, then Robert and finally Hobbes. Was this supposed to be some kind of message? If so, it was far too cryptic for me to understand.

"That's not in the least bit helpful, you know," I admonished him, then looked up to see everyone staring.

"I mean all this nonsense, everybody confessing. It's not helping matters," I concluded, abashed.

"Right, everybody take a seat. No one is allowed to leave this room until I say so," Albert said. "Ella, remain with them please. I have a phone call to make. Oh, and get Hobbes' fingerprints."

I did as he asked, then took in the scene. Robert and Harriet sat opposite each other near the fire, while Hobbes, uncomfortable at being made to sit, perched on a hard chair by the door. I looked at Harriet, but she refused to meet my eye. *Guilt?* Could my dear friend really have it in her to kill another person? I glanced at Robert staring furiously into the flickering flames. Did he really kill Patty-Mae? And Hobbes loyal to a fault, was he simply protecting his master and friend or were those the hands of a man capable of strangling a woman? I found I didn't know the answer to any of my questions and by the time Albert returned, I was feeling quite dizzy.

"Your attention, please. I have arranged for round the clock police presence. They will be here shortly. Each man is under strict instructions not to allow anyone to leave or enter the premises without my or Miss Bridges' permission. As of this moment, you are all under house arrest."

Robert looked up as though to argue, but Albert cut him off. "Just be thankful I'm not dragging you all back to the city cells for wasting police time."

Once Albert's men had arrived and been fully briefed, we took our leave and returned to the cottage. It was late and we were exhausted, but neither of us could contemplate sleep at that moment. So with a fire crackling in the hearth, I poured us both a nightcap.

"I have to admit in all my years dealing with the law, Ella, I have never come across a case where almost every suspect confesses to the crime. It's sheer lunacy."

"I can't understand what they all hope to achieve? We have Harriet protecting Robert, Robert protecting Harriet, and Hobbes protecting them both. Surely they realise it's only a matter of time before we find out who was really responsible?"

"Unfortunately, we are now reliant on one thing and one thing only. That Mortimer is successful in determining the owner of the print from the button. If he fails, and if our suspects continue with this folly, then I'll have no choice but to arrest and charge them all."

Bright and early the next morning, I was awoken by the ringing of the telephone. Grabbing my gown, I rushed down the stairs to answer it.

"Ella, it's Mortimer. Good news, I have the print from the button."

"That's marvellous. Albert and I will be there shortly. Thank you."

I replaced the receiver and called up the stairs. "Albert?"

"Here, Ella," he said, coming out of the dining room with a slice of toast in his hand. Mrs. Shaw must have already laid breakfast. "What is it?"

"That was Mortimer. He's managed to extract the print from the button. I said we'd be there shortly."

"Excellent. We'll leave within the hour."

An hour and a half later we were outside Mortimer's laboratory at Scotland Yard.

"Well, the time has finally arrived, Ella. Now we'll find out who our murderer is."

I nodded and took a deep breath as Albert opened the door.

"Ah, Commissioner, Ella. Right on time," Mortimer said. "Ella, I trust you've brought the fingerprint cards?"

I nodded and handed over my kit.

"Good, good. If you'll follow me."

We accompanied him through a door to the rear of the laboratory, where inside we found racks of shelving with small white cards in various slots, and a number of officers examining them through magnifying glasses. From a box marked 'Arundel Hall Murder: Evidence', he extracted two envelopes: one containing the button with its singular monogram, and the other a piece of white card with a fingerprint on it.

"We were very lucky to be able to lift this print. We found it on the reverse of the button and although it's only a partial of the whole, I believe it to be the mark of the perpetrator's right thumb."

I peered closely at the card and saw the familiar mass of ridges and whorls. Mortimer laid the card with the singular print at the top of the desk and placed the four cards of the suspects below. It would be impossible to discern a match with the naked eye, but Mortimer was already clutching a single magnifying lens in his right hand.

"It will take some time to identify the correct print. You're welcome to stay and wait, of course, but feel free to help yourselves to coffee or take a walk while I work."

I glanced at Albert. I didn't want to leave. My stomach was in knots and I was impatient for the results, but there seemed little sense in my loitering around and getting underfoot. Albert was of the same opinion. We could be of no practical help, so we adjourned to a small tea-room around the corner to await the runner Mortimer had promised to send as soon as he had news.

Several cups of tea, a toasted tea-cake and a small iced fancy later, a breathless boy, no older than fourteen, rushed to our table.

"Begging your pardon, sir, Miss. Doctor Smythe says he's ready for you now."

Albert thanked him and gave him tuppence.

"Run back and tell Doctor Smythe we're on our way, there's a good lad."

A few minutes later we were back at The Yard.

"So what do you have for us, Mortimer?" asked Albert.

"Here's your murderer," he replied, gesturing to the solitary card which remained with the print from the button.

"You're quite sure?"

"Absolutely certain. There's no doubt it's the same print."

I slowly walked toward the table, my heart beating frantically. Half of me wanted to know, the other half was afraid of what I would see.

Taking a deep breath, I glanced at the name and all the air whooshed out of my lungs.

"Oh, dear god," I whispered, groping behind me for the chair as my legs buckled. Albert put a comforting hand on my shoulder.

"Are you all right, Ella?"

"How could I have been so wrong about a friend?" I whispered.

"It happens to the best of us, my dear. But the first time is a terrible shock. I am truly sorry."

I nodded, the stirrings of anger beginning in my chest. There was no point becoming lachrymose. That would have to wait. Nor would second guessing myself help. We had a murderer to catch. I looked up.

"Albert, we need to finish this once and for all, and I have a plan."

We thanked Mortimer, took the evidence and retired to Albert's office for a meeting to fine tune the details. Albert made several phone calls to arrange for his men to tie up the loose ends and retrieve the additional information we would need. Finally, after three fraught hours in which I must have paced the equivalent of several miles, one of his men returned with a report confirming our suspicions, and I made a telephone call.

"Nathaniel, it's Ella. I'm calling to ask you a favour."

"I'll try, but I'm rather tied up with appointments at present. What did you need?"

"Could you find someone else to cover your appointments, do you think? We've found the murderer of Patty-Mae and we could do with a doctor at The Hall when we make the arrest. I rather think it's going to be a shock and we may need medical assistance."

There was a slight pause before he answered. "Yes, I think I can re-arrange a few things. I take it I'm no longer a suspect?"

"No, you're not a suspect, Nathaniel. Shall we say outside the gates in a couple of hours? I'd rather we all arrived together so as not to forewarn those inside?"

"Of course, I'll see you then."

"Thank you, Nathaniel," I said and replaced the receiver.

Albert rose and gathered the reports and evidence we'd need, and we stopped to release Edgar Rutherford on our way out. He'd also accompany us to The Hall for what I hoped would be the last time.

CHAPTER TWENTY-FOUR

Nathaniel was already parked at the gates of Arundel Hall when the three of us arrived, and followed in his own car as we made our way up the drive to the front door. Albert told Hobbes we would be in the library and to ask Sir Robert and Harriet to join us.

Once we were all present, the doors to the library closed and guarded outside by two constables, Albert urged everyone to take a seat, Hobbes included, and standing with his back to the fire, addressed his audience.

"There has been in my experience several cases where there was more than one viable suspect for a crime, but never have I come across a group of people so intent on muddying the waters that half of them confessed to murder. A more ludicrous state of affairs, I can't imagine. I warned you then I would find the perpetrator and I have gathered you all here this evening to inform you I have been successful. I now know who murdered Miss Patty-Mae Ludere."

As Albert spoke, I glanced at the faces of those present. Edgar, seated alone by the window, over which the heavy red velvet curtains were drawn, looked pale and exhausted. The time spent in the city cells had knocked every ounce of arrogance from his demeanour. No longer was he filled with blustering bravado; now he appeared small and tired, and very young. We'd given him no indication in the car as to the reason he'd been released and brought to The Hall, and his eyes flicked toward Albert with interest at the pronouncement the murderer had been identified.

The eyes of both Harriet and Robert had never left Albert from the moment he'd begun to speak. They were sat together on the sofa to his right, hands clasped and eyes wary. Robert's face indicated bubbling anger just below the surface and I felt he could erupt at any moment. Harriet, on the other hand, was wound as tight as a bowstring and looked as though she might bolt at the earliest opportunity.

In complete contrast, Nathaniel sat opposite them, the epitome of relaxation, long legs stretched out in front of him and one arm strewn across the back of the sofa. He rewarded my glance with a wink and a small smile.

As was his custom as a servant, Hobbes had chosen to remain seated by the door. Stoical as ever, the only indication of his discomfort was the tightening of his jaw and the narrowing of his eyes at the mention of the murderer.

"Sir Robert and Miss Ludere," Albert continued, "met at a ball held at The Dorchester several months ago. However, during the course of this inquiry, it has come to light this was no chance meeting. It was in fact instigated deliberately by Miss Ludere herself and Mr. Rutherford."

All eyes swung to Edgar as he visibly shrank in his chair, refusing to meet anyone's gaze. Robert's eyes were murderous as he glared at Edgar.

"Why, you despicable ... " he began, but was stayed by Harriet's hand.

"A man in Sir Robert's position would naturally need to know more about his future wife, so prior to the engagement he enlisted the help of a detective agency in America. A short time later he received word that no trace of her could be found. Miss Patty-Mae Ludere did not in fact exist."

Edgar put his head in his hands and groaned softly, realising no doubt that the scheme he and Martha had painstakingly put together would never have worked. This was most definitely news to Nathaniel, Harriet, and Hobbes, however, as I noticed their surprise at the revelation.

Albert continued, "Thus, perturbed at the news, Sir Robert went on to hire the services of a Private Investigator in London. He followed Miss Ludere on several occasions and subsequently discovered not only was she a fraud, but she was also in a long-term relationship with another man." Albert paused and looked at Sir Robert. "I assume your man Entwhistle, while describing her lover to you, was unable to give you his name?"

Robert nodded curtly. "It was a generic description and could have been any one of a dozen dandies. I know damn well who it was now though. It was you, Rutherford!" he bellowed, a shaky hand pointing in Edgar's direction.

"Indeed," said Albert. "But if there was no such person as Patty-Mae Ludere, then just who was she?"

All eyes, bar Edgar's, turned back to Albert.

"Her true name was Martha Brown and she was formerly a singer, dancer and hostess at a notoriously bawdy club in London."

Robert went white with shock. Harriet's sharp in-take of breath was audible as she clutched her breast, and

Nathaniel blurted out, "I don't believe it." Even the news had shocked Hobbes enough for him to momentarily lose his mannequin-like pose.

"But I'm afraid that's not all. Martha, or Patty-Mae as you knew her, was an opiate addict."

Robert rose suddenly and shakily made his way to the drinks tray, where he poured himself a stiff whiskey, downed it in one gulp, and then immediately poured another.

"I can tell from your reaction you were unaware of these additional facts, Sir Robert. Regardless, you had both the motive and the opportunity to commit the murder. You had already discovered Miss Ludere was not the American heiress and well-known actress she claimed to be. Moreover, you had noticed several small and expensive items had gone missing since her arrival. The final straw came on the evening of the dinner when your investigator came to give his report, and informed you that not only was she a fraud, but she was involved with another. In your own words," and here Albert took out his black notebook, "'She'd made me look like a pathetic fool in front of my peers and a laughing stock in the village. Even my staff were giving me pitying looks. Her actions were unforgivable.' A huge loss of face, I agree, Sir Robert, but enough to commit murder? You had plenty of time on the night of the dinner, after Entwhistle had left, to enter the garden, find Miss Ludere and strangle her, then appear back in the library. Then later on, of course, you confessed.

"But let us move on for a moment because you were not the only one to admit to the murder. Nor, in fact, were you the only one to have the motive and opportunity to commit the crime."

Here Albert glanced at me to continue, but I shook my head. Perhaps it was cowardly of me, but I didn't want to be the one to air Harriet's secrets in public. She'd been my friend. So Albert continued.

"Miss Dinworthy, you have known Sir Robert since you were children and recently admitted you've been in love with him for most of your life. In fact, you said yourself your families expected you to marry. It must have been difficult for you when he returned from the war with a wife on his arm? Surely, however, when she passed away your chance had finally come? But no, once again you were cast aside when it was announced Sir Robert had become betrothed to Miss Ludere. But of course that's not the whole story, is it? On the night of the dinner, Miss Ludere approached you in the powder room and told you in no uncertain terms to leave Sir Robert alone. Even she could see how obvious your true feelings were. Naturally, when cornered you came out fighting, you said, and gave her a piece of your mind, a few home-truths as it were. But I posit you could have taken it one step further and killed her in a jealous rage. Returning to the library, you found Miss Bridges and Doctor Brookes already there, but Miss Bridges left shortly afterward, leaving you alone with the doctor. At your request he went to his car to retrieve a mild sedative for your nerves, which gave you plenty of time to seek out Miss Ludere in the garden, strangle her and return with no one the wiser. Let's not forget Miss Ludere had consumed a lot of alcohol that evening and was already unsteady. It would have been quite easy for you to subdue her. And then, as with Sir Robert, you also confessed to the crime."

Albert once again glanced at me, and this time I was happy to take up the reins.

"Not long before the dinner here, Doctor Brookes visited me in a professional capacity. During that visit, I found a note in his bag saying 'PM police'. Initially, I thought it indicated an evening appointment he had, but upon questioning, Doctor Brookes informed us the PM did in fact pertain to Patty-Mae. As you've already been informed, she was addicted to opiates, and as her supplier was no longer available to her, she sought out Doctor Brookes in the hope he would be able to give her the drug she craved. Doctor Brookes categorically refused, but told us he intended to seek out the police once he'd done a little investigation of his own. But is that simply the end of the matter or was there something more sinister happening? Perhaps Patty-Mae pestered him so much he could no longer stand it. Or could she have threatened him in some way? Or perhaps her propositions were more amorous in nature? Whatever the reasons, Doctor Brookes also had the opportunity to rid himself of the victim when he left to retrieve the sedative for Harriet. His car was parked at the back and it would only have been a matter of minutes for him to reach Patty-Mae at the side of the house, kill her and return to the library. But while the opportunity was there, is this really a strong enough motive to take a life? And wouldn't it also go against everything a doctor is supposed to stand for?"

I turned to Hobbes.

"Hobbes, you've been with Sir Robert for a long time now. Originally as his batman, you then came here to act as his butler and valet. I also surmise you were a much-needed friend and companion, particularly during the years after the death of his first wife. Your loyalty to him is without question, which is why, I believe, you also confessed to the murder. Rather than allow Robert to be convicted for a crime to which he'd confessed, you would quite happily take his place as a final act of friendship, not least because

Robert saved your life during the war. But did you in fact kill Miss Ludere? You certainly had the opportunity, knowing the house and its short-cuts as well as you do, and of course a good servant goes about his business silently and unobtrusively, hardly noticed by those in the house. But what could be your motive? Well, of course, that's simple. Patty-Mae had used Robert in the most horrible of ways and I suspect you also overheard the report from Entwhistle, but being privy to Robert's life in a way I was not, you knew immediately whom they were talking about. Deciding to save Robert from the future anguish of having such a wife, you took it upon yourself to get rid of her. So you had both the motive and the opportunity. But are you really the one we are looking for, or is it someone else?"

I looked back to Albert who nodded and once again took up the narrative.

"Mr. Rutherford has already spent time in the city cells for this crime. He admitted to arguing with and striking Miss Ludere, and the missing button from his shirt was found in her dead hand. Compelling evidence, as I'm sure you'll agree. But from the start, he has maintained his innocence and while he may be guilty of many other crimes, he is in fact wholly innocent of this one. Edgar Rutherford did not murder the woman known as Patty-Mae Ludere. But one of you sitting before me here tonight, did."

CHAPTER TWENTY-FIVE

A ll eyes turned toward Albert, the change in the atmosphere palpable, charged with a crackling of expectation, tinged with fear. It lifted the hairs on the back of my neck and despite the heat from the fire, I shivered. We all knew the time had finally come to unveil the murderer.

"Doctor Brookes, your explanation of the note Miss Bridges saw was that you were going to speak to the police about Patty-Mae, correct?"

Nathaniel frowned. "Yes."

"But it didn't mean that at all, did it?" I asked.

Nathaniel turned to face me.

"What do you mean, Ella?"

"I mean you lied. What the note actually meant was completely the opposite. Patty-Mae was going to the police about you! She'd stumbled upon your secret, Nathaniel, and I suspect she tried to blackmail you into supplying her drugs in return for her silence."

"What? Of course not, that's ridiculous. What on Earth could she blackmail me about? I'm a simple village doctor." He stood up and took a step toward me.

I took an involuntary step back.

"No, you're not. You failed to qualify and fraudulently took over your father's practice. Who would know, considering you shared the same name? And why would people not believe you? You are the son of an honest and respected man and expected to follow in his footsteps. But that's not all. You've been selling drugs in the city. Patty-Mae found out, as Martha Brown it was her real world, after all. You killed her, Nathaniel. You are the murderer we have been looking for."

I heard the gasps of shock behind me, but my eyes never left Nathaniel's.

He held out his hands placatingly, "Ella, this is nonsense. You have no proof ... "

Albert interrupted before he could finish.

"That's where you're wrong, Doctor Brookes. Do you really think we would make these accusations without proof?" Albert lifted from his case the report his officers had given him earlier.

"We have here sworn statements from a number of people to whom you sold drugs. Each one of them has formally identified you from a photograph."

"And you'd take the word of prostitutes and drug addicts over mine, a well-respected doctor? They are lying," Nathaniel scoffed.

"We also have statements from the head of your college and several tutors stating you failed the final examinations. You are not in fact a registered doctor, you are a cheat."

"There were extenuating circumstances, which are none of your business. I fully intend to re-sit my examinations in due course. It's purely a formality. However, none of this means I killed Miss Ludere."

"No, it doesn't," I said. "But it was your motive for doing so."

"But, Ella, surely you don't believe all this. I thought we had something between us. You said yourself on the telephone I was no longer a suspect."

"But don't you understand, Nathaniel? You are no longer a suspect because you are the murderer, and here is the proof." I held up the two fingerprint cards.

"These are your fingerprints, the ones I took, remember? And this ..." I held up the second card, "is the print from the back of the shirt button taken from Patty-Mae's hand. They are a perfect match, Nathaniel, and only her murderer could have placed that button after her death."

I should have seen the intention in his eyes then, but I missed it. Suddenly, he lunged forward, knocking me to the floor and sprinting for the door. Wrenching it open, he came face to face with the two constables, but before they could act, Edgar had sprung from his chair, tackled him to the floor and punched him in the face.

"That's for Martha, you murdering bas ... "

"Enough!" bellowed Albert. "Constables, place Doctor Brookes under arrest and take him back to The Yard."

Albert grabbed Edgar by his collar and hauled him to his feet.

"Take a seat, Edgar. It's over."

Hobbes had come to my assistance the moment I was knocked to the ground and helped me stand on shaking legs. I could already feel the beginnings of a bruise on my cheek.

Harriet and Robert clung to each other, struck dumb by the revelations and the subsequent violence. It was difficult to see who was holding up whom.

After Nathaniel had been unceremoniously thrust into the rear of the police vehicle and was on his way back to Scotland Yard, the rest of us gathered together in the library once more.

"Nathaniel Brookes. I can't believe it," said Harriet. "It will be the death of his poor father. He's already in precarious health, so I understand."

"So Brookes was supplying Patty-Mae drugs?" asked Robert.

I shook my head. "No, I don't think he was. I'm sure that part of his story was true. It was too close to home to risk it. He wouldn't want to soil his own patch, as it were. He would have been caught. No, he preferred the anonymity of the city; I hate to think how long it's been going on. Certainly over a year, if the statements are anything to go by."

"He must have been planning to kill her that night," said Edgar.

"I don't believe so, Edgar," said Albert. "This was not a premeditated murder. He saw an opportunity that night and took it. But if it hadn't been that night then I'm sure it would have been another. Martha's threat was very real and he needed to stop her once and for all. Overhearing the two of you arguing was convenient, and finding your button to throw us off the scent was a stroke of good fortune as far as he was concerned."

"Oh, god, it's all my fault. If we hadn't argued ... "

"If you hadn't dreamed up this diabolical scheme in the first place, none of it would have happened," snapped Robert.

"Edgar," I said, "if you hadn't argued and lost your button, then we wouldn't have caught him at all. All the other evidence was circumstantial. The only thing we caught him on was the fingerprint. He would have killed her eventually and while it's no solace to you, at least this way he will be tried and punished for the crime."

Edgar didn't speak, but nodded dejectedly. I doubted he would ever get over his loss, but I hoped he would find a better way of living his life in the future.

"I think it's time we left, Ella," Albert said, rising. "I'll drop you at your cottage as I intend to go straight back to London."

I nodded and also rose to gather my belongings.

"Edgar, will you be staying on at Linhay or at your London Apartment? I'll drop you either way."

"I'll come to London. Thanks."

At the door, Robert held out his hand to Albert. "Thank you, Commissioner."

"Goodbye, Sir Robert," he said, shaking the proffered hand. "Miss Dinworthy."

Harriet smiled and said goodbye, then turned to me."Isobella, perhaps we could have tea together soon?" she asked in a tentative tone.

I smiled. "I'd like that, Harriet, thank you."

"Splendid. I'll telephone you."

Albert dropped me at my cottage and within moments of my head hitting the pillow, I was fast asleep.

CHAPTER TWENTY-SIX

arriet's call to tea came several days later and as Hobbes drove closer to The Hall, I saw there were several moving vehicles being packed with boxes.

"Good heavens, Harriet, is Robert moving?" I asked as she came to greet me.

"Actually, Isobella, we both are."

It was then I noticed how well she looked. Happy and glowing and …

"Harriet, you got married?" I asked, spying the rings.

She nodded. "Yes, we did, yesterday. Just a small registry office affair. It was all we wanted."

"Oh, that's wonderful news, Harriet, congratulations. I really am so very happy for you."

"Thank you, my dear. Come inside and I'll tell you all about it over tea."

Harriet took us to a small, bright and cheerful sitting room at the back of the house with a splendid view of the gardens. The sun was dazzling and I could just make out the glint of the lake in the distance along with the small figure of Robert walking his dogs. After Harriet had told me about the wedding, I asked her where they were moving to.

"Everywhere. We've decided to travel the world, starting in Europe and then moving where the fates decide. Certainly to Africa, we both have a desire to visit Kenya and Egypt. The world is a huge place, Isobella, and we're not getting any younger."

"So what about The Hall? Is it to be sold?"

"It is, although it will be some time before it's ready to be put on the market. Hobbes has agreed to stay and oversee the sale of the contents, particularly the rare wines and the other items in the hidden cellars. They're all worth rather a lot of money as it turns out. He'll also look after the dogs and whatnot, then when he's ready, he's free to join us if he wishes, wherever that may be. In all honesty, I don't feel I would ever be comfortable living here and Robert feels the same."

"Because of Patty-Mae?" I asked.

"Partly yes, but the house has an ominous history, as you well know, and now we've finally found each other, I don't want to put our marriage at risk in any way."

"You mean the curse? I didn't think you really believed in it."

"Well, as I said before, as an historian I work with facts and figures, but considering all that happened previously and of course the most recent tragedy, I find I can't simply dismiss it."

"So when are you leaving? And what about your home?"

"Actually, this is goodbye, Isobella, we are heading up to London this evening and we leave England the day after tomorrow. As for my home, it's already occupied. I needed someone to live there long term and look after it in my absence, so I've given it to Mrs. Parsons and her husband. Tom will live there with them of course. They rented their little fisherman's cottage and it was just too dark and damp for them all, but particularly for Mr. Parsons whose health is deteriorating rapidly. At least this way he can live out the remainder of his days in comfort. I've also bequeathed both it and an annual income to them in my will, so if anything happens to me, they will still be looked after and have a roof over their heads."

I found I was inordinately pleased Harriet had been so generous to the Parsons. They were a good family and deserved some good fortune.

"And what about Mrs. Butterworth? I daresay she'll be at a bit of a loose end with only herself and Hobbes to cook for," I said.

"Oh, she intends to retire when Hobbes leaves. Robert has given her enough money to purchase a small cottage on Linhay. She's been a faithful member of staff, it's the least he could do. To be honest I think she found catering for the dinner party by herself a bit too much."

"Whatever do you mean, Harriet? I sent Mrs. Shaw up to assist. Was she of no help at all?"

"Oh, dear, forgive me for speaking out of turn, Isobella. It completely slipped my mind Mrs. Shaw is your housekeeper."

"Harriet, you must tell me what happened."

Harriet sighed deeply. "Well, between you and me, Mrs. Butterworth informed me Mrs. Shaw was completely ignorant of catering such a specialised menu. Her exact words were, 'if she used to cater for posh dinner parties in London, then I'll eat my apron so I will'. I am sorry, Isobella."

I forced a smile, but my mind was a whirl. "Don't worry, Harriet. I'm sure there's a simple explanation. I'll talk to her when I get back."

Harriet patted my hand and we continued to talk for a while about how Robert had given Edgar enough money to organise the funeral of Martha Brown and other, more inconsequential things until it was my time to depart.

As Hobbes was bringing the motorcar round to the front, Harriet hugged me and gave me a powdery kiss on both cheeks.

"Goodbye, Isobella, it really has been such a pleasure to know you. I'll write and send you postcards from our travels and do keep up your detective work. You really are very good at it."

I assured her I would, then with final farewells I left to go home.

When I arrived, with the intention of immediately speaking to Mrs. Shaw regarding Harriet's revelation, I found Albert sitting in the drawing room with a snifter of whiskey.

"Albert, how lovely to see you. I wasn't expecting a visit today or I would have made sure I was at home."

Albert waved a dismissive hand. "Don't worry, Ella, I've not been here long. I had an appointment with Doctor Brookes Senior to bring him up to date, so thought I'd take the opportunity to see you while I was here."

At that moment the telephone rang.

"Sorry, Albert, do excuse me a moment."

I went to the hall and picked up the receiver just as Mrs. Shaw came to answer it.

"Hello?"

"Ella? Is that you? Ella, can you hear me?"

I was instantly weak and my legs began to give way as though my bones had liquefied and could no longer support me. A cold rush of sweat ran up my back and across my shoulders, and I clutched the edge of the table as my peripheral vision began to turn black.

In the far off distance I heard a voice call out, "Commissioner, come quick!"

My last thought before my world went dark was, 'impossible'. For the voice on the other end of the phone was unmistakably John's, my husband who had been dead for the last two years.

A
CLERICAL
ERROR

A Clerical Error

ABOUT THE BOOK

WHEN THE CRIME SCENE IS PURE COINCIDENCE AND THERE'S
NO EVIDENCE, HOW DO YOU PROVE IT WAS MURDER?

Ella Bridges faces her most challenging investigation so
far when the vicar dies suddenly at the May Day Fete. But
with evidence scarce and her personal life unravelling in
ways she could never have imagined, she misses vital clues
in the investigation.

Working alongside Sergeant Baxter of Scotland Yard, will
Ella manage to unearth the clues needed to catch the killer
before another life is lost? Or will personal shock cloud her
mind and result in another tragedy?

FOR MY FAMILY

CHAPTER ONE

The May Day celebrations on Linhay were as much a part of island life as the tides themselves, and the undercurrent of excitement as arrangements were made was almost palpable. However, my first attendance at the festivities, in nineteen thirty-six, was memorable for all the wrong reasons; for that was the year a particularly nasty murder occurred.

To make matters worse my own life was unravelling in ways I could never have envisaged, and my worry would begin to overshadow the investigation when it came. With the luxury of hindsight it took me longer than normal to realise the importance of certain clues.

Starting with a telephone call from my husband John, whom I had been told had died, it had become apparent that everything I had believed for the last two years was a lie, including the role of my housekeeper Mrs Shaw.

Just over a week after the call, still smarting from a combination of embarrassment and fury at what had come to light since, and with the feeling of claustrophobia threatening to overwhelm, I decided a change of scenery was needed and made plans to spend the week with Aunt Margaret.

I said goodbye to my gardener Tom, who was hard at work unearthing the Victorian walled garden we had discovered some weeks earlier, and took a taxi to the station. Mrs Shaw was under strict instructions to telephone me at my aunt's immediately if there was news. I had been seated in my train carriage for only a few minutes when suddenly there was a shrill whistle, and a loud hiss of steam came billowing along the platform and past my window moments later, then with a jolt we started slowly forward and gradually picked up speed. Within minutes the station was left behind, then the city suburbs rushed past and before long we were moving into open country. I settled back in my seat and replayed the conversation I'd had a few days ago with the Home Secretary...

"Are you telling me John is in fact still alive?" I asked with barely suppressed fury and the threatening sting of tears behind my eyes.

He paused looking extremely uncomfortable. Eventually he leaned back and sighed.

"We're not sure, I'm afraid he's gone missing. This telephone call you received is the first indication we've had in months he may still be alive."

"What do you mean he's gone missing? He was supposed to be dead. I don't understand anything you're saying."

"I think you'd better tell her everything from the beginning, old chap. She deserves to know the truth," said Uncle Albert, who had accompanied Lord Carrick.

Albert wasn't strictly my uncle, but was Godfather to my sister-in-law Ginny. He was also the Police Commissioner at Scotland Yard, and I had worked closely with him on two previous murder inquiries. It was at his recommendation I had been employed as a consultant detective.

"Yes, you're right of course, I apologise, Miss Bridges. The fact of the matter is John was recruited to MI5 directly upon graduating from Oxford. This was prior to his meeting and marrying you of course. He turned out to be an exceptional operative, one of our best in fact."

"So he was a spy all along?" I asked.

Lord Carrick gave a curt nod.

"He was fluent in several languages, which of course made him a valuable asset."

I was astonished at that news.

"I had no idea. It looks as though I didn't know my husband at all," I said lamely.

I clasped my hands until my knuckles turned white, as a wave of cold spread through my body and I began to shiver. I felt quite sick and fought to suppress the feeling of nausea as Lord Carrick continued.

"You saw what you expected to see. John was a trained undercover operative and there was no reason for you to suspect he was anything other than what he claimed. But if it's any consolation I think you knew the real him better than anyone."

"I'm sorry, but I don't find it in the least bit consoling, the man I thought was my husband was in fact a total stranger. I can't think why he married me in the first place."

"He married you because he fell in love with you, it's as simple as that. We tried to talk him out of it of course; the type of work he was doing was dangerous and having a family makes it all the more difficult. We encourage our men to remain single in fact but, John was insistent and rather than lose him we relented."

"So what happened to him?"

"Please understand I am bound by the Official Secrets Act so am not at liberty to divulge everything. However, I will tell you what I can. John was one of the best under-cover men we had as I said, and he was used extensively to infiltrate organisations abroad and send back information we needed."

"What sort of information?"

"I'm afraid I can't tell you that. But suffice to say he was very successful. During his last mission … "

"Where exactly was his last mission?"

"Germany. And just so you understand, it was indeed to be his last assignment. He'd formally put in for retirement from active overseas duties as he wanted to spend more time at home. With you. Unfortunately things didn't go according to plan and we lost communication with him. He missed several rendezvous then disappeared from the radar completely. It's thought his cover had been blown."

"You mean he was taken prisoner?"

"We're not sure. I'm afraid the intelligence is somewhat lacking, but it's assumed so, yes."

I was simply stunned and was finding it difficult to formulate simple questions, as though my head were stuffed with cotton. I felt the prick of tears as I realised John had intended to retire and come home so we could begin a normal life together. I'd had no idea, yet his plans were derailed at the last moment by some dastardly quirk of fate. I swallowed past the lump in my throat and the rising bile; it was all so unfair.

"So you assumed whoever took him had him killed? You told me at the time he was shot accidentally on a farm in

India and that he didn't suffer at all. I take it this was not actually the case considering what I know now?"

"Well the body ... "

"What about the body? Two years ago you identified it as my husband. You came to my home and told me he was dead and gave me his wedding ring. If my husband is dead, Lord Carrick, then just how is it he telephoned me last evening?"

Lord Carrick rose and approached the fire. Leaning on the mantel he stared into the flames and began to talk softly, almost to himself.

"The news came in that a body had been found in the early hours. One of our chaps happened to be in the area at the time and went to investigate. What he found was the body of a man, charred beyond recognition, in the lower level of a factory which was still partially burning. We know now it was arson used to cover up a murder; the victim had been shot. Naturally our man quickly searched the body for any means of identification, but the only thing he found was the wedding ring. He removed it, then left the scene. There was nothing more he could do; he was putting himself at great risk as it was. Because the ring was engraved it was naturally assumed the body belonged to your husband, it was his ring after all."

"But now you don't think it was?" I asked.

He glanced at me quickly but didn't answer my question.

"A couple of months ago we received a report citing the possibility John had been spotted in the company of some high level German officials, but before it could be confirmed he disappeared. Naturally we've been searching for him ever since but to no avail."

I shot out of my chair before I had a chance to think about what I was doing.

"You mean to say you knew my husband was alive two months ago and didn't tell me? How dare you keep this from me? Dear God, what sort of people are you?"

"Miss Bridges, please understand we couldn't confirm anything. We didn't know whether it was your husband or someone who simply bore a striking resemblance to him. Remember, in these situations John would be in disguise. It would have been remiss, no, it would have been cruel of me to come to you then only to find out it wasn't him."

I sat down at the end of this little speech and put my head in my hands, all the fight had left me. My skin felt cold and clammy, and along with the shakes, which were getting worse, my heart was beating wildly. I felt a hand on my shoulder and looked up to see the blurry shape of Albert hovering over me, a large brandy in his hand. So mired was I in my own thoughts I hadn't even heard him move.

"Drink this, Ella, you've had a nasty shock."

I nodded, and taking a large gulp immediately felt the warmth of the liquid suffuse my body, and the anxiousness abate somewhat, though not entirely. John was alive. It was almost too much to believe after all this time, but in my heart I knew it was true. I felt a surge of hope course through my veins as I asked Lord Carrick for confirmation. I needed to hear him say it out loud.

"But now you think it was him because he telephoned me?"

"Yes, and we're doing everything within our power to find him."

"And bring him home? You must bring him home, it's much too dangerous for him there."

My emotions were vacillating between elation that John was alive, and abject fear of the peril he was in. The thought I would lose him again forever was simply unbearable.

"We're doing everything we can to find him, Miss Bridges, and as soon as I know anything I will come and speak with you. However, please be aware it may not be a simple job to extract him. If the reports we've received are true then he has managed to infiltrate the highest echelons of the German government, and blowing his cover at this stage would almost certainly result in his death."

"But surely he must be in some sort of jeopardy if he telephoned me? Why would he risk doing so otherwise?"

"God only knows how he managed it, especially considering you have moved away from your shared home. But he's not the best spy we have for nothing. I'm inclined to agree with your analysis, however, and subsequently finding him has been given top priority."

"Who did the body belong to if it wasn't John? And how did he happen to be wearing my husband's wedding ring?"

Lord Carrick shrugged. "Until we find John, I'm afraid we won't know the answers. The fact is he shouldn't have taken any form of identification with him at all. Taking the ring, engraved as it was and in English, was foolhardy and could have exposed him. I can't think what possessed him to risk everything by doing so. But again that question can only be answered by John himself."

"And what about Mrs Shaw? I know she's one of yours."

Lord Carrick eyed me shrewdly for a moment, then nodded.

"Mrs Shaw will remain here for your protection. John may try to contact you again and if he does so, Mrs Shaw will need to speak with him."

But several days had passed and there had been no more news from Lord Carrick and John had not telephoned again.

Approximately half an hour before reaching my station, a black cat wearing a familiar purple collar with a silver bell attached materialised on the seat opposite. It was Phantom, my ghost cat. Luckily I had the carriage to myself, for Phantom was only visible to me and I would have looked decidedly odd holding a conversation with fresh air. I had inherited both him, and the unusual ability of being able to see spirits who needed my help, from Mrs Rose, the former owner of The Yellow Cottage which was now my home. Phantom had saved my life during my first case and it was thanks, in part, to these special gifts that I had been so successful as a detective.

Now Phantom jumped nimbly across the gap and landed on my lap, where he spent the remainder of the journey curled up asleep, then vanished into thin air just as we pulled into Broughton station. He had an uncanny sense of when I needed his company.

Aunt Margaret's driver was already waiting for me and before long we were pulling up outside the house. My aunt engulfed me in a hug as soon as I alighted.

"Darling, how lovely to see you, it's been too long. Now come in and tell me what's bothering you. I've had tea set up in the orangery. Potts will see to your bags."

Divesting myself of coat and hat, I allowed myself to be shepherded through to the back of the house and into the orangery, where the large walls of glass looked out over a magnificent vista of verdant lawns and topiary hedges. Inside, giant ferns, orange trees and rare orchids vied for space with several more exotic varieties for which I had no name, and to the right a comfortable seating area and low table had been set for tea.

I threw myself in a chair and breathed a sigh of relief.

"Now, Ella, I realise you couldn't speak on the telephone but I sensed in your voice something was wrong, and I can see now you've lost some weight. What on earth has happened?"

"Oh, Aunt Margaret, it appears John is still alive," I wailed, and to my absolute horror I promptly burst into tears.

"Good heavens! Well, that's the last thing I expected you to say. You go ahead and have a good cry, dear girl. Personally I feel all this British stiff upper lip malarkey is perfect nonsense. I find one always feels much better when one can let it all out as it were."

As usual Aunt Margaret was correct. Once the sobs had subsided and the pent up emotion released I did feel better.

"Now dry your eyes, dear, and tell me what you know."

I began with the shock of the phone call, then related subsequent events as they had happened, including the conversation with Lord Carrick.

"So John is in Germany?" Aunt Margaret asked.

"As far as is known, yes, but it seems he's vanished."

She sighed and took my hand in hers.

"I'll not beat about the bush, Ella, that's not my way as you know, but there is rumour of another world war, one with Germany at the heart of it."

I gasped. "How do you know?"

"You don't reach my age without knowing a bit about the world, darling. Plus I have friends in high places. However I don't want you to worry too much, it is just a rumour and may never happen."

"But I do worry, Aunt Margaret. How can I not when John is in so much danger?"

"Oh, darling, I feel for you I truly do, but if anyone knows exactly what's going on, far more than my friends I hasten to add, it's John. He's there and knows first-hand their intentions. Whether it comes to war or not it's John's job to ensure our government is kept abreast of what is happening. It's an exceptionally important job he's doing."

I stood up and went to gaze out of the window, my mind in turmoil at my aunt's revelation there may be another war. I wondered where John was and what he was doing at that moment. Was he thinking of me as I was thinking of him?

"Did you know John was a spy? I seem to remember you weren't really taken with him when I brought him home that first time."

"Then you remember incorrectly, Ella. I liked him very much and thought him perfect for you. However, to answer your question, no, I didn't know his job was espionage but I felt he was being a little circumspect with the truth. Not lying, you understand, more holding something back, secretive. Of course it's obvious why now we know the truth."

I sighed and took my seat again.

"Whatever am I to do, Aunt Margaret?"

"Do? Why there's nothing you can do except continue to live your life and wait to see what happens. I'm quite sure John would be appalled to realise he's caused you so much distress, and even more that you've put your life on hold to just sit about and worry. There is an entire organisation behind John and they will be doing their utmost to bring him home safely."

I knew every word she spoke was true, but I was feeling angry and frustrated and more than a little afraid. I was exhausted truth be told, but sleep was difficult and I was perpetually tired. I was also feeling quite sorry for myself, which was childish and not like me at all, which then made me feel guilty and started the whole cycle again.

"I'm sure you're running the gamut of emotions, my dear," Aunt Margaret said, her usual prescient self. "But feeling angry and guilty is both pointless and harmful to your well-being. You'd do much better to concentrate your energies on something more positive."

I frowned and looked at her.

"Are you sure you're not a witch?"

She laughed. "Now that's more like my Ella. No, I'm not a witch, I've just lived longer than you have. Now I have a telephone call to make, I think you need cheering up and I have just the thing. Tomorrow we will visit the old part of the town, do some shopping, have lunch and in the afternoon I'll introduce you to a friend of mine. I'd advise you to get a good night's sleep; you'll need your wits about you."

The next morning I awoke feeling more refreshed than I had for days, the emotional talk I had had with Aunt Margaret obviously being more cathartic than I'd realised, although the knot of anxiety for John still lay like a stone in the pit of my stomach.

After a late leisurely breakfast we bundled ourselves into our warmest coats and set off for town.

"No need for the car I think, a brisk walk will do us good and it's a beautiful day," my aunt said.

My dubious look at the grey louring sky caused her to chuckle.

"Ella, this is the North of England remember, any day where it doesn't rain is considered positively balmy. Besides it's almost summer."

I laughed. "I think I must have been in the south for too long. I'd almost forgotten what it's like."

As we walked down the lane on the outskirts of the town the conversation turned to my housekeeper Mrs Shaw.

"And she was the only applicant you say?"

"Hers was the only application I received," I corrected her.

"Ah, I see."

"Can you believe they intercepted my post?"

"Of course I can, Ella, this is the Government we're talking about, normal rules don't apply."

"Well, they should," I said in a petulant voice and was rewarded with a raised eyebrow. I sighed. "Don't do that Aunt Margaret."

"Do what dear?"

"Make me feel guilty."

"I'm doing no such thing, that's your conscience talking."

"You'd be furious in my position too. My freedom of choice was removed, not to mention my privacy. The sheer audacity of these people astounds me."

"Well, correct me if I'm wrong, but I believe it was all done in order to protect you?"

"But I don't need protection. I've already had to change back to my maiden name and move miles away from our home. I did everything the Home Secretary advised but it still wasn't enough, so they ensconced a charlatan in my home under false pretenses. It's appalling behaviour."

"Goodness me, Ella, if you keep this up I'll have no choice but to send you to bed without any supper."

I glanced at her, spied the smirk and the twinkle in her eye.

"Yes, all right, point taken. But I'm still furious and I don't know what to do about Mrs Shaw, if indeed that's her name."

"What do you mean 'do?'"

"Well I can hardly keep her on as my housekeeper now, I can barely bring myself to talk to her."

"Ella, that's simply dreadful behaviour, rather like shooting the messenger. The poor woman is just doing her job, following orders actually. How would you feel in her position?"

That brought me up short. Remarkably I hadn't considered things from Mrs Shaw's point of view and I was rather ashamed of the fact. Emotion and shock had obviously clouded my normally sound judgment. I resolved to speak with her as soon as I returned home. It would be a difficult conversation but it had to be done.

"Thank you, Aunt Margaret."

"Think nothing of it, my dear. I feel it always helps to speak to someone on the periphery as it were, it brings things into perspective. And there's no need to feel guilty, Ella, you're perfectly entitled to have a tantrum now and again, particularly as the root cause is worry about John. Just so long as you don't make a habit of it."

I smiled. "There's no need to worry on that score, Aunt Margaret. Admittedly it's all a bit of a mare's nest, but there's really very little I can do now except wait, and hope," and worry, I silently added to myself.

"And keep yourself busy," my aunt added. "There's nothing worse than sitting around brooding and worrying. Now, there's been a couple of additions to the town since you were here last, a perfectly lovely milliners and a delightful tea room close to the Guild Hall. My treat."

True to her word, I departed The Lilly Tea Rooms stuffed to the gills, which was an immense change compared to recent days where I pushed food around my plate and barely ate a morsel. My appetite had all but disappeared since I'd heard from John, and I was definitely a few pounds lighter if my loose skirt was anything to go by. But I'd always been a little overweight so could afford the loss.

My aunt took me to the milliner's, where I left with a thoroughly practical and sensible new hat in dove grey with a button detail. Although it would have been quite a different story had I let the shop girl have her way.

"I'm so very relieved you didn't choose that first hat, Ella," Aunt Margaret said, laughing.

"The one with all the feathers you mean? Goodness, while I appreciate the artistry, I would have been too afraid of wearing it lest I be shot at."

Laughing at my near escape we wandered companionably down the High Street through the bustling crowds, and I was pleased to note the clouds I had been worried about earlier had almost disappeared. In their place a hazy sunshine was valiantly attempting to cast its rays down to street level.

We stopped periodically to peer in shop windows if a particular item caught our eye, and it was in front of the newly established delicatessen, where an impressive range of French cheeses were on display, that my aunt remembered her recent correspondence. My mother had moved to the

South of France, and judging from her periodic letters and postcards, was having a perfectly wonderful time.

"I received a letter from your mother a couple of days ago, it seems she's caught the interest of a retired British Colonel out there and he's making gallant attempts to woo her, much to her amusement."

"Really? Is it serious do you think?"

"Oh, I doubt it, well certainly not on your mother's part, although heaven knows how the Colonel feels. He's probably smitten; men usually are around your mother you know."

"Well, I'm sure she knows what she's doing and will let him down gently if needs be."

"I expect you're right, Ella. Now what do you say we enter this fine establishment? I've recently been gifted a rather superior port, which is crying out for a special accompaniment."

Twenty minutes later, my aunt having purchased enough cheese to feed the Foreign Legion and the British Army combined, we exited the shop and continued to the end of the street, where I was expertly steered left in the direction of a small art gallery. I knew the gallery existed, but had never visited during the times I had lived with my aunt.

"Are you of a mind to purchase a painting, Aunt Margaret?" I asked, as we crossed the road.

"Not at present, dear. Although it has been known for me to leave this particular gallery with a piece I didn't know I wanted," she said with a laugh. "Now tell me, what do you think?"

I gazed at the artwork on display in the window.

"Well, art isn't normally my bailiwick, Aunt Margaret, I feel it's quite subjective. I find I like things because of what they are as opposed to what is deemed fashionable."

"Quite right too."

"But he does have an accomplished hand, and a unique style."

I gazed at the pictures in the window, each one a depiction of hard northern life painted in monochrome. Men in large overcoats and flat caps slogged up cobbled roads on their way to work, huge old factories in the background, grey and dull, belched smoke into the atmosphere, the plumes rising to join the miasma of fog overhead.

Urchins playing in the street in boots too big for their feet and rags barely covering their skeletal frames looked out with huge eyes and cheeky grins. While mothers, babes on their hips and toddlers grasping at their skirts, stared defiantly out of the canvas, proud and strangely regal despite their reduced circumstances. They were a peculiar combination of dispiriting and uplifting, and I found I liked them. One, an impish little girl, reminded me of my very first case at an orphanage in London, and unexpectedly I felt a pang at the family John and I had thus far missed out on.

There was one painting, however, tucked into the bottom right hand corner as though it were an afterthought to place it on display, which I disliked immediately. Unlike the others it was bright and colourful, and at first glance it appeared to be an image of a beautiful young woman sitting on a park bench with an old church in the background. On closer inspection however she appeared to be a woman of two halves.

It was remarkably well done, and was testament to the prowess of the artist that I had such a visceral response to it. The left side of her face was perfect in every way, from the rich cornflower blue of her long lashed eye, the finely arched brow and the rosebud pink of her smiling mouth, she appeared happy and carefree. A woman who was selfless, an open book and one you'd be glad to call a friend. But with a few clever strokes of the brush the right side was transformed. The eye became malevolent with a hard glint suggesting an underlying animosity, the mouth a sneer as though full of contempt for the viewer and above the top lip an ugly and exaggerated black mole grew, as though the rottenness of the core were attempting to burst through the skin. I gave an involuntary shiver, as though evil had crossed my path and glanced at the title, 'From Mistress to Wife.'

I straightened and looked at Aunt Margaret with a raised brow.

"Very clever, isn't it?" she said.

"Undoubtedly. But I can't say I like it, and I find I'm hard pushed to believe anyone in their right mind would want to hang it on their wall."

She laughed. "Come along, let's go in."

I followed her into the shop and smiled as I glimpsed a black cat, wearing a purple collar with a silver bell, curled up asleep in the window.

The little bell above the shop door signalled our arrival, and we entered what I can only describe as an Aladdin's Cave. I had expected a light and airy space, with bright walls and strategically placed easels showing off the paintings to their best advantage. Instead we were greeted with an interior more akin to an antique curiosity shop, with the artist's work adorning every imaginable surface. Propped up against large bureaus, on the shelves of a book case, on several occasional tables and even displayed on a velvet chaise-longue. And everywhere I looked there were ladders of all sizes.

To the rear of the room was a floor to ceiling curtain in a heavy rich purple fabric with gold tassels; however, of the proprietor himself there was no sign. But before I could convey my astonishment to my aunt I caught movement out of the corner of my eye. Toward the back of the room, hidden behind a large oak chiffonier, was a wing-back chair upholstered in turquoise satin, and it was from this a man of diminutive stature suddenly moved. I'd failed to notice him previously so perfectly camouflaged was he against the background, but at least it explained the ladders for he must have been no taller than three feet.

He hopped down from the chair dressed in a matching turquoise satin smoking jacket, and a gold and purple brocade fez, replete with a gold tassel which hung jauntily over his right ear.

"Maggie! What a deeelightful surprise, ma chére," he intoned in a heavy French accent and bent to kiss her outstretched hand. "It has simply been toooo long."

I glanced at my aunt waiting for her to scold him; I knew how much she despised the shortening of her name, particularly to Maggie. But to my surprise she remained silent.

"And who might this be?" the dwarf continued.

"No, don't tell me. Mmmm, let me see."

My aunt smirked but still said nothing.

Dragging a small step ladder directly in front of me, he proceeded to climb until we were at eye level, then grasped my chin and tilted my head from side to side.

"Mmmm, not a classic beauty, rather plain at first glance."

Well really, how rude!

"But there is something about her. The bone structure is good, and the face pleasing, if oddly asymmetrical. But it is the eyes that speak to me! Such eyes and such depth.

Ah yes, there is an interesting story behind those eyes. You see the world differently perhaps. Yes?"

I frowned wondering what he meant by that comment. He couldn't possibly have guessed about my special gifts. As he jumped down from the ladder and went to peruse my rear, I hissed at my aunt.

"What on earth is going on? Who is this insufferably rude little man?"

"Don't worry, dear, it means he likes you," she whispered back.

"Oh, my word! Whatever is he like with those he doesn't care for?"

"Terribly flattering," she replied.

Having completed his inspection of my physique and deemed me becoming, but rather on the heavy side to be fashionable, he strode forward to face me.

"So what is it you do, ma chère?"

"Do?" I asked, nonplussed for a moment.

"Yes 'do,'" he repeated in an exasperated tone. "What are your interests, your hobbies? What are your hopes and dreams?"

I frowned. "As a matter of fact I am a consultant detective with Scotland Yard."

The small man clutched his chest and staggered back, eyes wide as though he'd been shot.

"Oh my gawd, you're 'avin a larf, ain't ya?"

I raised an eyebrow in surprise. "Obviously not as much as you are Mr … ?"

"Oh dear, well that's rather let the cat out of the bag," Aunt Margaret said. "Ella, I'd like to introduce you to the world renowned artist, Monsieur Pierre DuPont. Formerly known as Norman Sprout, master forger of Brick Lane, London."

"Maggie, I can't believe you've brought a copper to me door, after all we've been through," said the thoroughly dejected artist. He moved to the chaise-longue and sat with his head in his hands.

"Oh, stop being so melodramatic, Norman, I've done no such thing. Ella happens to be my niece and is currently taking a few days holiday to visit her old aunt."

"What, so you mean you're not the old bill?"

"I'm exactly what I told you, Mr Sprout, I'm not in the habit of lying. However, unless you have an inclination to murder your customers I doubt our paths will cross in a professional capacity."

"Murder! Gordon Bennet, Maggie, what is this? I ain't never murdered anyone in me life! I'm just a simple artist tryin' to earn a crust. All right, I admit I started on the wrong side of the tracks, but I've been straight as an arrow ever since that incident with The Duke of Bainbridge and 'Desdemona with Sheep.'"

I raised a quizzical eyebrow.

"It's a painting, dear," Aunt Margaret explained. "A long story and I won't bore you with the details, but it's how Norman and I met. And, Norman, do you really think after all this time, not to mention the investment, I would do anything to jeopardise our friendship?"

"Oh, Maggie, please forgive me, I wasn't thinkin' straight."

"No matter, I shall put it down to artistic temperament. However if you are as you say, 'on the straight and narrow,' I do believe your reaction was a little over the top, don't you?"

Norman sighed and rose to his feet shaking his head.

"Only I could have gone into partnership with the cleverest woman in Christendom."

Partnership? This was certainly news to me and I glanced at my aunt in wonder. There was obviously a lot I didn't know.

"There's been rumours," continued Norman. "Come on, I'll shut up shop and put the kettle on, we can discuss it over a pot of Rosie Lea. It's a new blend from Carnaby's Emporium which I think you'll appreciate, Maggie."

"That sounds like a splendid idea. Ella, remind me to take you to Carnaby's on the way home, it's a magnificent place and the teas are superlative."

The tea was indeed superlative, the smell and taste conjuring up images of exotic climes under palm trees and the allure of the East, however if I'd thought the conversation would provide me with a wealth of revelatory details about my aunt's life I was sadly disappointed.

"Now, Pierre, tell me about these rumours which were cause for your agitation earlier. And please do dispense with the accent, dear, you're no more a Cockney than I am."

Pierre waved his hand in dismissal and chuckled.

"I overreacted, Maggie, nothing more. It was the shock of finding the law on my doorstep after all this time, I'm afraid I put two and two together and came up with five. I haven't been Norman Sprout for many years. As far as anyone knows he went abroad and hasn't set foot in England since."

I stared at the little man in wonder, for while at my aunt's request the rough Cockney accent had disappeared, so too had the French one. Instead the voice was that of refined gentry and would have been perfectly at home announcing the BBC news on the wireless. Even his movements had been subdued according to character, instead of the flamboyant and over-the-top artist, a calm, tidy and slightly arrogant English aristocrat sat before me. It was quite extraordinary.

"Pierre is a positive chameleon, Ella," my aunt explained. "His acting skills, mimicry and disguises are superlative, and I have no doubt if he hadn't chosen art as a profession he would have been a celebrated actor."

Pierre twinkled at Aunt Margaret with fondness. "You're too kind, Maggie. Officially there is only Pierre DuPont now and I'd like to keep it that way."

This last was directed at me and I nodded.

"I understand, Monsieur DuPont, and rest assured I have no intention of speaking about our discussions today with anyone else. As far as I am concerned my aunt thinks highly of you and considers you a friend. That's enough for me. However there is one thing I would dearly like to know."

Both my aunt and Monsieur DuPont looked at me expectantly.

"How on earth did you two meet?"

And so between them, they told me the story of the summer ball held by the Duke of Bainbridge at his country retreat in Oxfordshire.

"I was dancing with the duke at the time, a rather invigorating Pasadena if I'm not mistaken, when we were quietly interrupted by his butler. He informed us a thief had been caught in the long gallery attempting to steal a painting."

"Desdemona with Sheep?" I hazarded a guess.

"Quite right," confirmed my aunt. "It's a very famous painting by the Dutch master, Johannes Van-der Bleck, and quite priceless. So the duke and I quietly made our way to the gallery so as not to arouse suspicion, and once there we were greeted by the sight of dear Pierre, or Norman as he was then, halfway up a curtain and clinging on for dear life, while one of the duke's dogs stood guard below."

"It was the size of a horse!" said Pierre, shuddering at the memory.

"It was a Pomeranian," corrected my aunt. "Of course I could see immediately he was innocent."

Pierre chuckled and shook his head.

"Only Maggie could have seen my innocence while in that predicament. I'd been caught halfway out of the window, my rope was still in place, my tools were in a bag on the floor and the spoils were at my feet. I'd been caught red-handed and it was only a matter of time before the police arrived and I was thrown in a cell."

"But however did you manage to escape?" I asked.

My Aunt once again took up the narrative.

"Oh, he didn't need to escape. As I said before he was entirely innocent, not that the duke thought so. Of course a discreet word in his ear about certain matters soon had him seeing my point of view."

"You mean to say you blackmailed him?" I asked in astonishment.

"Of course not. I just gently reminded him of the incident between his son, a local tavern maid and Lord Ellesmere's prize race horse. I'd been instrumental in keeping it quiet, you see. But of course that's a story for another time. Back to Desdemona."

Pierre rose at this point and collected the tea things.

"I'll leave your aunt to explain while I make more tea."

"That reminds me, why on earth are you playing housemaid?" asked my Aunt. "Where's that girl of yours?"

"Hilda? It's her day off. Why do you suppose you found me in the shop and not in the studio."

When Pierre had gone I asked Aunt Margaret to explain how she knew immediately he was innocent of the crime when all evidence said otherwise.

"Well you see, Ella, the duke and I had been friends for a long time and I had visited the gallery on many occasions. It was on one such visit that I realised the painting in question was actually a rather masterful forgery. Goodness knows how long it had hung there without anyone noticing, rather a long time I suspect. The duke had grown up in that house, you see, and had passed through the gallery numerous times. It's amazing when you see something every day for years just how little notice you take of it, it becomes nothing more than background."

"So Pierre had actually stolen a forgery?"

"Goodness me, no. Pierre can spot a forgery a mile away, it was his stock-in-trade at the time. No, the original was hanging in its rightful place on the wall. That's how I knew he was innocent."

I sat back in amazement as it all became clearer.

"But why on earth would he go to all the trouble of replacing a forgery with the original, knowing he may be caught? And who painted the forgery? And for that matter who stole the original in the first place?"

"Oh, Isobella, so many questions," my aunt said, patting my knee. "I doubt we'll ever know the answers."

I doubted that was the case but knew better than to pursue it, I would get nothing more from Aunt Margaret.

"So you became his benefactor."

"I did."

"A known art thief, forger and criminal?" I said in wonder.

"In my experience the world is very rarely black and white, but instead various shades of grey. Norman needed my help and I gave it to him. And not once have I ever regretted the decision. Ah now, here's the tea."

"But how did the duke explain it all to his butler?" I asked, rising to take the tray from Pierre.

"Oh, something about a test designed to find any flaws in the security. Everyone went away with a pat on the back and a hefty bonus. Now be an angel and pass me some of that delectable looking cake."

I poured the tea and cut the fruit cake while Pierre explained the rumours he'd mentioned previously.

"As your aunt knows, the professional art world is remarkably small, Miss Bridges, and the underside of that world even more so. I keep my ear to the ground and hear various murmurings, and once in a while I am contacted by a most trusted confidant for information. He contacted me last week to ask if I'd heard anything about a British gang targeting the French. Apparently there are plans afoot to attempt the most audacious of crimes, a theft from the Louvre."

"My goodness!" exclaimed my Aunt. "And what have you heard, Pierre? I can't for one moment imagine how they expect to succeed in such an endeavour; the Louvre is as well guarded as the Crown Jewels."

"I agree, Maggie. It would take an exceptional mind to pull off that particular job and the risks are high. In my opinion it's impossible. As to what I've heard, well that is even more peculiar, for I have heard nothing at all. The grapevine is deathly silent."

"Well, wouldn't that indicate your chap has got it wrong?" I asked.

Pierre stroked his graying goatee absentmindedly and nodded slowly. "That is possibly so. But I shall keep my ear to the ground and make some discreet inquiries nonetheless."

I continued to sip my tea while Pierre and my aunt discussed the art world. I knew little of it myself, which is undoubtedly why I didn't realise how important my meeting with Pierre would turn out to be. Not only with regard to the imminent murder inquiry, but also to a worrying telephone conversation I would soon have with my mother.

In the excitement of the conversation both my aunt and I had lost track of the time, and it was late afternoon when we left.

On the way out Pierre stopped me.

"How do you think of my work, Meez Bridges?" he asked, once again reverting to his impeccable French accent.

"As a matter of fact I said to Aunt Margaret earlier how much I liked it. Well, apart from one that is."

"Oh? And which one is it that you do not care for?"

"I'm afraid the one of the woman in the window isn't much to my liking. It's a personal choice, you understand, the work itself is exceptionally good but the subject matter just doesn't appeal I'm afraid. I hope I haven't offended you?"

"Oh, but of course not. You are the niece of Maggie, no? So all is well. If you had been any other though? Pfft! Who knows? But what is this painting, I cannot place it?"

"The two-faced woman."

"Mon Dieu! Theese should not be in the window! It is the fault of the idiotic Hilda, no doubt. It shall be removed at once."

He hurried to the display, removed the offending painting and deposited it deftly behind the curtain.

"There, order and beauty is once again restored," he said with a smile, which didn't quite mask the panic in his eyes. "Now I shall bestow upon you a gift, Ella."

"Oh, there's really no need."

"I insist. Now stand there and do not move so much as an inch, there is something most perfect here for you. I shall know it when I see it."

My aunt smiled at me, and moving aside a painting of a boy throwing a stick for a small scruffy dog, sat on the chaise-longue to wait.

"You'd better do as he says, dear, there's no talking him out of it."

So I stood patiently while Pierre ran up and down ladders with amazing agility looking for the perfect piece. Every so often Aunt Margaret and I shared a smile as the small man muttered, "No, not this one," and "Oh thees will never do," but eventually it seemed the perfect painting was indeed found.

"Aha! Thees is the one."

He scurried down the ladder, approached me, and with a flourish presented me with a small painting approximately ten inches square in a gilt frame. I gasped when I saw it was a beautiful rendition of a small urchin girl sitting on a stoop with a black cat on her knee. I eyed Monsieur Dupont closely. He couldn't possibly know I could see spirits, yet this was the second time he had intimated he knew of my unusual way of seeing the world. Nor could he know I had a black ghost cat, yet his prescience at choosing such a remarkably apt painting was uncanny, and I wondered if there was more to this diminutive little man than I had first thought.

"Thank you, Pierre, it is perfect, as you knew it would be. It appears I am not the only one who views the world differently."

Pierre inclined his head in agreement, and with eyes twinkling in amusement deftly wrapped the picture for me to take. I already knew the perfect place to hang it once I returned to the cottage.

With promises to meet again soon, my aunt and I left Monsieur DuPont to what remained of his day and continued back up the high street to Carnaby's Tea Emporium, from whence, armed with several dark green and gold boxes emblazoned with the Carnaby name, we caught a taxi back home.

CHAPTER TWO

The few days I spent with Aunt Margaret were exactly what I needed to restore my equilibrium, and prevent my mind from dwelling on matters over which I had no control. She had kept me busy and entertained throughout the week, but all too soon our time together came to an end. However in her usual show of intuition she detected my slight trepidation in returning to the cottage.

"Now, Ella, as you know I have been meaning to visit you on Linhay as soon as time allowed, and as it turns out I have some free time toward the end of the month. Mrs Shipley has informed me her church has cancelled the usual fundraiser this year, therefore my managerial skills are not needed. I never used to attend of course, you know my views on organised religion."

"So why help if you don't believe?" I asked.

"I didn't say I don't believe; however, my housekeeper believes and that's all that matters. Besides the building is old and I do believe for both history and posterity's sake

351

it needs to be maintained for future generations. Now as I was saying, it presents a perfect opportunity for me to come and stay with you, so you can expect me in two weeks' time."

It was exactly what I needed and I agreed immediately, and so it was with a lighter heart I boarded the train to begin my journey home. Of course the plans I had for gentle excursions and exploration of the island together never transpired, because not long after her arrival I was once again embroiled in a murder investigation.

I had telephoned Mrs Shaw the evening before to inform her of my arrival and she had insisted on meeting me at the station.

"It will be dark by the time you arrive, Miss Bridges," she had said. "And I don't think it wise for you to walk along the coastal path alone."

I sighed inwardly but acquiesced. She was right of course and the coastal walk would still be quite pleasant with the two of us. Imagine my surprise then, when she met me off the train, took my bag and proceeded to steer me to a small motor car. She stowed my bag in the boot, settled in the driver's seat and after pulling and pushing on a bewildering array of levers and pedals, expertly manoeuvred the vehicle into the lane which would take us home.

"I had no idea you could drive, Mrs Shaw. Is this your motor car?"

"It comes with the job, Miss Bridges."

"You mean your real job as opposed to the position of lowly housekeeper you have with me?"

"That's the one," she agreed cheerily, completely unperturbed at my slightly sarcastic tone. "My boss considered it wiser to have a vehicle on hand in case of emergencies, and now you know who I really am there was little reason for me to say no."

I glanced out of the window, although there was nothing to see in the dark, giving me time to gather my thoughts.

"Mrs Shaw, I believe I owe you an apology."

"It's really not necessary, Miss Bridges, I understand."

"Oh, but it is. I behaved dreadfully when I found out the truth, and I'm afraid being nearest, you took the brunt of my anger. I realise now you were only following orders but at the time I felt quite deceived and I was furious. I am awfully sorry, Mrs Shaw."

"Apology accepted, Miss Bridges."

I nodded gratefully.

"Could you bring yourself to call me Ella now, do you think?"

She laughed; it would seem she had felt the previously difficult atmosphere between us too.

"If I could be honest for a moment, I would prefer to keep things as they are. It is easier for me to play my role if things are done properly."

"Of course I understand. But I'm afraid I no longer feel comfortable with you in the role of my housekeeper. I'm certain Tom's mother would relish the opportunity to be once again employed, there's little for her to do now she lives in Harriet's house. Especially considering her husband's health has, against all the odds, improved dramatically. Consider yourself promoted to the lofty position of my secretary. I assume you have the required skills?"

"I do. I started out in the typing pool as a matter of fact."

"Excellent. Well, your first job will be to procure a suitable typewriter. Albert Montesford has tasked me with compiling a working document to assist the police. It's to teach them how to identify when a person is lying, and I believe it would be a perfect project for us to work on together."

Mrs Shaw nodded. "I'll speak with Mrs Parsons tomorrow, and I already have a suitable typewriter. Will there be anything else?"

"Yes," I said. "I would like you to teach me how to drive."

The next day with breakfast over and Mrs Shaw already on her way to see Mrs Parsons, I decided to go for a bicycle ride. I set off down the track as fast as I could, my mind blissfully blank and with no idea where I was going.

Half an hour later I found myself at the quiet south beach, where I dismounted and wheeled my bicycle over the tussocks of grass and down onto the sand. It was a wonderfully warm day with summer just around the corner, and watching the sun glint off the water and with a mild, slight breeze on my face I felt peaceful and relaxed.

I was day-dreaming quite happily when I noticed the appearance of small prints in the sand steadily making their way toward me. There was no sign of the owner of course and I smiled.

"Hello, Phantom," I said, and in a shimmering of air he materialised next to me and sat down to watch the waves break on the shore, his feline gaze steady and unblinking.

He'd made himself scarce during the last few days I'd spent with Aunt Margaret, and I found now I was terribly pleased to see him, although it was difficult to tell if the feeling was mutual. I settled down with my notebook and began to organise my thoughts for the project Albert had requested. Unfortunately it was more difficult than

I imagined, either that or I simply wasn't in the mood. Regardless, before long I found the page blurring and my eyelids getting heavy, and I am ashamed to say I fell asleep.

I woke with a start some time later as a shower of pebbles and sand rained down upon my head. Glancing behind me I saw Phantom standing a few yards up the bank, the epitome of innocence. When he was certain I had seen him, he turned and trotted away only to stop and look at me again seconds later.

"I suppose you want me to follow?"

I swear if he'd had the ability to roll his eyes, at that moment he would have done so, instead he pinned me with a stare which spoke volumes as to my stupidity. To be honest, considering how I had had the wool pulled over my eyes recently I couldn't fault his reasoning.

I stood up, dusted the sand from my clothing and retrieving my bicycle, followed my demanding feline friend.

Back upon the coastal path Phantom jumped into the basket mounted on the front of my bicycle and I set off. I had every intention of returning home but as was his wont Phantom had other ideas, and before long I was pedalling up the hill toward St. Mary's Church on the East side of the island.

Before she had left, due to my previous case up at Arundel Hall, Harriet Dinworthy and I had been researching my home and she had shown me various historical maps. One such map showed this area of Linhay and the church, and I had been meaning to explore here but complications in my life had meant I had never found the time until now.

The area was similar to other parts of the island, with rows of stone-built terrace housing with small gardens at the base of the hill, giving way to larger abodes which sat behind private hedges and walls the further up I rode. At the top of School Lane I spied the building which gave the lane its name, a quaint stone structure with a clock tower and a wrought iron fence. I could hear the shouts of children playing in the yard as I cycled past and smiled to see them playing the games I had as a child, hop-scotch, marbles and an energetic game of leap-frog.

At the prow of the hill I stopped to catch my breath.

"Well, Phantom, that's the hard bit done. Now for some fun. I can't remember when I last free-wheeled down a hill like this. Hold on tight," I told him, although he ignored me as usual.

I hopped back on my bicycle and hurtled down the hill at breakneck speed. As I swung around the bend in the lane the wind was in my face and my eyes were beginning to water just as I approached the second bend. I got past the blind spot and was back on the straight, when a few yards ahead I saw a woman armed with several flower baskets, and she was right in my path.

"Look out!" I yelled.

The woman dropped her baskets and froze in shock. I barely had time to register the large owlish eyes behind thick-lensed glasses or the carpet of flowers across the road. Slamming my feet to the ground and pulling on the brakes I swerved to avoid her and careened to the right, where my fall was softened slightly by a well-established yew hedge. Leaving my bike on the ground, I got up and rushed over to the woman who was still staring at me, a wild look on a face which seemed to have been drained of all blood.

"Oh, my goodness, I am most terribly sorry. Are you all right?"

"Oh yes, I'm quite all right. Sorry, you startled me," she said in such a quiet voice as to be little more than a whisper.

"No need for you to apologise, it was entirely my fault. Are you sure you're all right?"

She tittered nervously and wrung her hands. She couldn't be much older than thirty but she was as tiny and nervous as a mouse. Magnified brown eyes peered myopically from beyond her spectacles, frizzy brown hair escaped from beneath her lopsided hat and it was all topped off by a misshapen cardigan in an unflattering shade of green.

"Sorry, yes, I'm fine."

"I'm sorry about your flowers," I said.

"Oh no, the flowers!"

Her shaking hands flew to her mouth and to my shock her lower lip trembled and tears welled.

"Well at least the flowers are the only casualty, it could have been worse," I said trying to reassure her without success.

"But you don't understand," she whispered, her horrified gaze still resting on the blooms. "Jocasta will be furious."

"I don't think it's as bad as it looks, here let me help." I hunched down and began to retrieve the tall stemmed white lilies and pink carnations, gently placing them back in their baskets. "See, a few broken stems and a little bruising, not much damage at all really. Who's Jocasta?"

But she didn't have time to answer before a sharp voice interrupted us.

"Shepherd! What have you done? I trust you to do one simple job for me and you can't even do that properly. Honestly, I can't fathom how you've got on in life so far. Look at my beautiful flowers, they're completely ruined."

This must be Jocasta.

Shepherd stood up, wringing her hands, "I'm so sorry, Jocasta," She whispered.

"Oh, Shep. Whatever am I to do with you?" Jocasta sighed, giving her an exasperated half-smile.

I quickly glanced at Shepherd's ring finger.

"Actually, Miss Shepherd is truly faultless, the blame is entirely mine. I was coming down the hill at a tremendous speed and couldn't stop, faulty brakes as it happens." I could feel the start of a blush at the tarradiddle, but realised this explanation would be received better than admitting I was freewheeling down the hill whooping like a child. "Unfortunately Miss Shepherd was directly in my path, but if it hadn't have been for her quick wits I would have run her over completely. I'm terribly sorry about your flowers, although they are far from ruined if you don't mind me saying so, but at least neither Miss Shepherd nor myself were injured. A blessing, I'm sure you'll agree," I said with a smile.

Jocasta stared at me, nonplussed for a moment.

"Well yes, quite," she said. "Right, well there's nothing for it but to see what we can salvage from the mess. The vicar is due back today and I'll just have to do my best to ensure the arrangements are up to par. I'll be in the Church meeting room when you're ready."

Miss Shepherd and I bent to retrieve the remaining flowers.

"Thank you," she said in her pale voice. "Although there really was no need to make me sound heroic, I froze like a fool as you well know."

"Oh no, that was absolutely the correct thing to do under the circumstances, don't you see? If you'd have moved an inch I wouldn't have been able to avoid you and catastrophe would have been absolute."

She tittered again. "Well, thank you anyway; you may possibly have redeemed my reputation in Jocasta's eyes. She means well but she's just so terribly good at everything and very efficient. I think she genuinely can't see why others aren't like her."

Personally I thought she was giving her too much credit but I kept quiet. However, I agreed with her assessment. Jocasta positively oozed competence from every pore.

"I'm Isobella Bridges by the way; call me Ella," I said, rising with a full basket and offering my hand.

"Agnes Shepherd. But of course I know who you are."

"You do?"

"Oh yes. I saw the story of how you solved the murder up at Arundel Hall in the Parish News. Actually it was in the Island Gazette too along with your photograph, although it wasn't a very good likeness. You're quite the talk of the island, you know."

Oh dear. I hadn't seen either publication but I daresay that had been intentional. However, Mrs Shaw and I had reached a sort of harmony and I preferred not to rock the boat; the interference was probably her following orders anyway. I retrieved my bicycle from the hedge, none the worse for wear, but Phantom had already disappeared. No doubt he would turn up when he was ready, at least as a ghost cat he wouldn't have been hurt.

"It must be terribly exciting being a detective," Agnes continued as we made our way through the lych-gate into the church yard, and continued up the stone-flagged walkway.

"I'm afraid it sounds much grander than it is. I'm only a part time consultant, you see, so a lot of the time I'm not actually detecting anything at all. My life is quite ordinary really."

"Still it must be wonderful to be good at something so important. I'm afraid Jocasta is right, I'm not very good at anything much at all. The meeting room is to the side, we just follow the path this way."

Rounding the corner we came across the largest yew I had ever seen, which quite dominated the setting.

"My goodness," I exclaimed.

"It's beautiful, isn't it? It's believed to be the oldest in the country, nearly two thousand years apparently, with a girth spanning nearly nine yards."

"And was that a sundial I saw carved into the front wall?"

"Well spotted. Oh, but of course you'd need to have good observational skills in your line of work, wouldn't you? Yes, it's actually one of four, they were used for the timings of the services prior to mechanical timepieces. St Mary's has a wonderful history, you know. And talking of the time we had better go in before Jocasta thinks we've abandoned her."

The meeting room was obviously a much later addition to the church, which was the oldest of three on the island and the only one of Catholic denomination, the others being Anglican. I'd read it was built some time during the thirteenth century when a large part of the island on which the previous church had stood was lost to the sea. The meeting room, however, couldn't have been much older than twenty years. It was quite poorly constructed, as well as being utterly bland and lacking in character. It was also frightfully cold.

"Sorry. It's quite awful, isn't it?" whispered Agnes. "Luckily it's only temporary, we're hoping to raise enough funds to build something more in keeping with the original architecture. We're quite close to the target as a matter of fact; a big push at the May Day Fete should see us hit it."

"Oh, there you are at last," Jocasta called from behind a trestle table groaning with the weight of greenery. "I was beginning to think I'd need to send out a search party. Come along then, no lolly-gagging, we've a lot to do and we're already behind."

Agnes and I deposited the baskets on the floor, and as I peered under the table I spied Phantom curled up asleep on an empty Hessian sack.

"I see you've brought a new sheep to the fold, Shepherd. I'm Jocasta Blenkinsop. And you are?"

"Ella Bridges."

"Bridges? Now where have I heard that name before? Mmmm, no I can't think, I'm sure it will come to me eventually. So how are you at flower arranging, Ella?"

"Oh no, Jocasta," said Agnes breathlessly. "Ella's not here to help, we only just met outside."

"Oh, drat it, really? We're short one person. Anne has had to run some errands and can't come."

"Oh, I don't mind. I have nothing planned, and it's the least I can do," I said.

"That's the spirit. Now, Shep, perhaps you can rustle up some warming tea? As you can tell the boiler's on the blink again. You would have thought they'd at least try to organise some heating, it's like Siberia in here."

Agnes disappeared while Jocasta and I set to stripping the greenery, but a moment later she was back.

"Sorry, Jocasta, but it seems we have run out of tea. Would coffee be all right instead?"

"No tea? Honestly, Shep, whatever next? Coffee gives me a dreadful headache as you very well know; it will have to be tea. I tell you what, nip along to the vicarage and get some of the vicar's stash, I'm sure he won't mind this once."

She turned to me and explained.

"He orders it in specially from somewhere or other, goodness knows why, our tea is perfectly fine. One of his little foibles. Shep?"

Agnes was still hovering, wringing her hands.

"Jocasta, I couldn't," she whispered.

Jocasta sighed and dropped the stem she was snipping on the table. Wiping her hands on her apron she strode to the door.

"I'll go, you make coffee for two. I'll be back lickety-split."

"Sorry, Ella. Is coffee all right with you?" Agnes asked, blushing with embarrassment at her friend.

I nodded. "Coffee is fine. Can I help?"

"Oh no, it won't take a moment."

Fortified with warm drinks, the three of us set to with earnest, and before long we were making real headway with the floral arrangements. I learned that Jocasta and Agnes had been friends since early childhood and had attended the school I had passed earlier. The more time I spent with them the more I realised how much their friendship was based on a genuine affection for one another. Jocasta was a sporty type, good at games, head girl and popular among her peers, whereas Agnes was shy and studious, academically inclined and socially inept. It was a pairing born initially of mutual need, with Jocasta preventing Agnes from being bullied and in turn receiving much needed help with academic matters, but somewhere along the line it had morphed into something more, a shared solidarity perhaps. Jocasta was the mother of two boys who were away at boarding school, and had a husband who was something high up in banking in the city. Agnes was unmarried, and had moved back into the familial home to look after her elderly mother after her father had passed away eight months ago.

Half an hour later Jocasta placed the final stem and leaned back to stretch.

"Finished!" she declared. "And a job well done I must say, girls. Now I think we'll have another drink and call it a day."

Agnes was once again dispatched to the small kitchen while Jocasta made a final raid on the vicar's tea, and some moments later we were seated on a bench outside, letting the much needed warmth of the afternoon sun seep into our chilled bones. With the sound of birdsong on the air and the sun warming my skin, my thoughts once again turned to John. In such interesting company and with something to do, I'd pushed the distressing situation to the back of my mind. Now, once again sitting idle, it came rushing back and my stomach fluttered with nerves. I idly wondered if the sun was shining where he was.

"You say the vicar, is due back today. Has he been away?" I asked conversationally, in an attempt to counteract the building anxiety.

"Actually he's hardly been here," Jocasta said. "He first arrived about ten months ago wasn't it, Shep?"

Agnes nodded in agreement and Jocasta continued.

"He was only here for a couple of months or so then went on some sort of sabbatical. We've had a temporary chap here ever since, pleasant enough chap, but ancient and terribly forgetful. But at least Father Michael is back now and we can resume normal services, as it were."

We had chosen a seat beneath the bell tower, and as the chimes struck three each of us jumped in shock.

"Golly, I didn't realise the time, I must be off. Now, Ella, don't forget the May Day Fete meeting on Friday, I'll pop you down for the Bric-a-Brac stall, it's usually our most popular. Shep, I'll catch up with you before then, let's do lunch tomorrow. Thanks for your help, girls. Toodle pip."

Agnes and I went back inside to wash up the crockery, then armed with several bags of discarded greenery set off to the vicarage a short walk away, to deposit them in the compost pile. On our way out she once again apologised.

"I'm awfully sorry, I feel you've been rather steamrollered into volunteering at the fete. Jocasta, has a heart of gold and quite frankly we wouldn't be half as successful without her ability to rally the troops, but she is a tad forceful. If you can't do it just say so."

"Well, I must admit it caught me by surprise, but actually I'm rather looking forward to it," I said.

As we walked back down the path I spied Phantom sitting patiently in my bicycle basket; it was obviously time to go. I was rooting in my bag for a card to give to Agnes when suddenly and without warning I was knocked to one side.

"Terribly sorry," a woman's voice said as she hurried on down the path without a second glance.

We stared open-mouthed at the slim departing figure dressed head to toe in black with a net veil obscuring her face.

"Gosh, I wonder what that was about. Are you all right, Ella?"

I nodded, looked back in the direction the woman had come from and saw the figure of the vicar in the church doorway, a very worried look on his ashen face. And to the right under one of the yews I spied an older man in smart tweeds with a walking cane. The woman's husband,

I supposed. It wasn't until much later I realised I had been both right and wrong about that assessment.

"Well, it looks as though your vicar already has a troubled parishioner to cope with, and he's not been back more than five minutes," I said.

Agnes frowned. "Actually I'm not sure she's one of Father Michael's flock, I've not seen her before. But of course he will help if he can. Anyway I'll see you on Friday at the meeting, and thank you for helping and being such a good sport about everything. Oh, and do take care cycling home."

"I'll try to avoid knocking down any residents," I said, and with a final wave Phantom and I made our way back to the cottage.

CHAPTER THREE

The remainder of the week flew by as Mrs Shaw and I settled down to writing 'The Compendium of Ways it is possible for an officer of the law to tell when a suspect is lying', but it was proving difficult to explain by words alone. I also needed to think of a much snappier title.

"I think it would benefit from having pictures," said Mrs Shaw glumly, after we had attempted to write a particularly stubborn paragraph in three different ways.

"An excellent idea, Mrs Shaw, I don't know why I didn't think of it. I may know of someone who would be perfect for the job too."

After a quick telephone call to leave a message at Scotland Yard I returned to Mrs Shaw.

"I think we'll call it a day. I have the meeting for the Fete Committee shortly and I need to eat something before I go."

"I believe Mrs Parsons has left something in the kitchen for you."

At Mrs Shaw's request, Mrs Parsons had agreed to come in three mornings a week until I found someone permanent.

"What with looking after him indoors and still cleaning up at the hotel, I can't promise more than that, Miss Bridges. I am sorry."

I assured her it was perfectly all right, and I appreciated her help during the interim.

"If you know of anyone who is looking for such work, do let me know," I said.

I ate my dinner at my desk and half an hour later was ready to leave. Mrs Shaw had volunteered to drop me off and wait for me.

"We have a motor car at our disposal, Miss Bridges, we may as well use it."

I was through the lych-gate and had just started to wend my way up the church path when a breathless voice called out behind me. It was Agnes.

"Hello, Ella. Gosh, it's a chilly breeze this evening, isn't it? I do so hope they've managed to fix the boiler otherwise it will be a very short meeting. Actually I'm glad I caught you. I have some news. Do you remember that woman who bumped into you the other day? Well I've found out who she is."

"I didn't realise you were looking for her," I said.

"Oh, I wasn't really, it was purely by chance. I was just entering the post office yesterday when she came rushing out and bumped into me."

"And I daresay Mr Tipping supplied you with a few details?"

Cedric Tipping was the postmaster and a notorious gossip. I'd been on the receiving end of his innuendo during my last case and found the man quite repugnant. Although it still astounded me how quickly he obtained his information.

Agnes giggled like a little girl. "Precisely, you obviously know him well. In fact I didn't ask any questions at all. But surprisingly for him he seemed to know very little."

That was a surprise, normally Cedric Tipping could recite chapter and verse of anyone's life, along with several unfounded details.

"Anyway, her name is Mrs Whittingstall and apparently her husband is very ill, not much time left by all accounts, but she was a nurse so I expect he's getting good care."

We entered the meeting hall behind several others and shed our coats in the small cloakroom. Thankfully the boiler had indeed been fixed, but it would seem the temperature gauge had not. It was positively stifling and I looked down at my thick pullover in dismay.

"I thought I might call upon her," continued Agnes as we took our seats.

My puzzlement must have been apparent as she went on.

"I head 'The Friends of St. Mary's,' we're just a small group who help out those in need by running small errands, shopping, housework and companionship, that sort of thing. I thought Mrs Whittingstall might be in need of a friend."

I nodded in understanding just as Jocasta took to the dais and brought the meeting to order. She was explaining refreshments would be available at the end, when suddenly Agnes gripped my arm and looked at me in mortification, her eyes even wider than normal behind the thick lenses.

"Ella. I've forgotten to replace the tea."

As the meeting drew to a close stall assignments were con-firmed. As promised Jocasta had allotted me the Bric-a-Brac stall; what she had failed to mention initially was alongside the manning of the stall I was also responsible for supplying the items. Luckily several of the more seasoned participants had brought along donations. Thank heavens Mrs Shaw had insisted on the motor car. The meeting concluded with Jocasta saying there was no one currently available to offi-cially open the fete.

"What about the princess?" someone asked.

"She's turned down the invitation the last two years so I'm rather reluctant to ask again," Jocasta replied.

"Who's the princess?" I whispered to Agnes.

"Oh, Princess Katerina is the genuine article. A Russian, the daughter of Tsar Alexander the second, I think it is. She fled with her husband to escape the communist revolution apparently and ended up in London. She was a splendid opera singer by all accounts, although I think she's retired now. She moved to Linhay about three years ago, but is almost a recluse so no one really knows her."

"Well, if anyone can think of a suitable candidate let me know," concluded Jocasta.

Horrifyingly, I noticed several furtive glances in my direction but no one spoke up thankfully. I stared stoically ahead willing them all to keep quiet, the last thing I needed was the attention.

Eventually Jocasta finished and we all made our way to the refreshments table. Already I could see Agnes had taken Jocasta aside to explain there was once again no tea. Luckily out of the twelve of us, only three insisted upon it: Jocasta, Anne and an elderly lady called Prudence Fielding. The rest of us were quite happy with coffee.

At Agnes's beckoning I went through to the small kitchen to help her.

"I take it Jocasta has gone to procure more tea?" I said with a knowing smile.

"Yes, Father Michael is out visiting parishioners this evening. Honestly, Ella, I feel quite wretched about the duplicity; it's tantamount to stealing and my conscience isn't at ease at all."

"If Father Michael were here and realised we were short, do you think he would offer to share his private supply?"

"Oh, I'm sure he would; he's very kind and generous. But that's hardly the point, is it?"

"Well no, it's not, but while I do agree with you it is just a few tealeaves, and if he were here I'm sure Jocasta would have asked him. But we'll make sure it doesn't happen again, and we could always give him a gift of his particular brand sometime to salve your conscience."

"That's such a good idea. I'll make a note to do just that."

Jocasta returned at that moment.

"Right, there should be enough there for a decent pot. He must have had a delivery recently as the caddy was quite full so I'm sure he won't miss it, but I'm not doing it again. Let's remember to stock our own supply, shall we?"

The morning of the fete dawned bright and clear and already wonderfully warm considering the early hour. Aunt Margaret had arrived a few days before, and thanks to a previous telephone call to explain the situation, had been preceded by several boxes of donations for my stall.

"With my housekeeper no longer in need this year, she said you may as well make use of it," my aunt informed me.

I knew my sister-in-law Ginny would also have helped out, but they'd had an invitation to stay at a castle in Scotland, a friend of Ginny's whom she hadn't seen for a while, so they had decided to take advantage of it. Ginny had been feeling a little under the weather recently and my brother Jerry had said the highland air would do her good.

Thankfully I hadn't been called upon to cut the ribbon and declare the fete open, as according to Agnes, Jocasta had managed to secure the services of a suitable personage, although she was keeping tight-lipped as to who it was.

The fete was to be held on the village green, a large open space of well-kept lawns which also doubled as the pitch for Linhay's cricket team. The tented tea pavilion had been erected the day before along with the stalls; all I had to do was furnish it with the goods. Hence being up before the sparrows. As Mrs Shaw, my gardener Tom and I were loading the last of the boxes into the motor car, Aunt Margaret joined us.

"Are you sure you don't mind helping out, Aunt Margaret?"

"Of course not, dear. I daresay it will be an enjoyable day and as you are two people short it makes sense."

We had indeed lost two of our members. Unfortunately the elderly Mrs Fielding had been laid low with a particularly virulent cold and fever, and Anne, who as a member of 'The Friends of St. Mary's' had been visiting daily, had also succumbed.

"That's the last of the boxes, Miss Bridges, I think we can be on our way. I assume you want to drive?"

"Are you learning to drive, Ella?"

"I am, Aunt. Mrs Shaw has been teaching me. It's not as difficult as one would imagine, I should be driving on my own before long."

"Well, good for you, it will give you no end of freedom. I wish I'd learned when I was younger."

"There's news about that actually," said Mrs Shaw. "Would you believe it, today is actually the day when they have made taking a driving test compulsory?"

"Just my luck. Well, I suppose it makes sense, with more people learning a certain level of competence needs to be reached otherwise there would be no end of accidents."

I said goodbye to Tom who would come along when the fete opened officially at ten, then we all settled in as I went through the start-up procedure. I gently steered the vehicle down the track to the road which would take us to the green, turned left and we were off. It was a beautiful day for a drive and I felt quite positive that the day would be a success all round. Unfortunately the feeling was decidedly short-lived.

The village green was already a hive of activity by the time we arrived. The maypole with its glorious red and white ribbons took centre stage, while the stalls had been set up around the perimeter with the tea pavilion at the far end closer to the bandstand. To one side I spied the Morris Dancers practicing their moves and every so often a resounding crack filled the air as they struck sticks.

The skittle game was already proving popular with the children who had come with the volunteers, as was the ice cream vendor from Jacob's Dairy farm. Although he was under strict instructions from the mothers not to be swayed by the pleading of cherubic faces and saucer-like eyes.

I waved at Agnes who was setting up her jams and preserves at the opposite side of the green, and to Jocasta next to her, who had a wonderful display of plants and cut flowers from her greenhouses.

By the time I had set up my table it was positively groaning with the weight, and I still had several full boxes hidden underneath. The assortment and quality of goods was surprisingly good, from candlesticks to pottery ornaments, from bowls and plates to several jelly moulds, and various jugs and vases. I felt sure they would do well toward the target. I had volunteered Aunt Margaret to take over Mrs Fielding's stall which had been placed next to mine, and I wandered over to see what she had.

"Oh, poor Mrs Fielding," I said. "She must have worked all year to get these ready, and they are all so beautiful. What a shame to not be able come after all this work."

"Oh, indeed, and what a talent she has. I've a good mind to purchase that tablecloth myself."

I looked at where my aunt pointed and saw it was an exquisite piece with hand-embroidered daisies around the edge. There were matching napkins too. I gently fingered several crocheted antimacassars as well as a knitted scarf in red and grey stripes with matching mittens. I smiled at the egg and teapot cosies, not quite my thing but lovely just the same.

"There's plenty more, but I haven't the room at the moment. Oh, and look at this," said Aunt Margaret delving beneath the table, and rising with the most beautiful patchwork quilt in shades of pale green and rose pink.

"Oh, I say! Do you know, that would be perfect in the cottage. If you haven't managed to sell it for a decent price then put it aside for me please. Also I'll take that scarf and mittens for Tom, and that knitted hat for Mrs. Shaw."

"Well, in that case I'll take the tablecloth and napkin set, it's perfect for the breakfast room. There's a similar one here I can replace it with."

I laughed, although a sudden lump appeared in my throat as I spied a beautiful waistcoat which John would have loved. I took a deep breath and pushed worrying thoughts to the back of my mind.

"If we carry on like this there will be nothing left for anyone else. We have a few minutes before the opening so I'll go and see how Agnes and Jocasta are getting on. I rather liked the look of the raspberry preserve Agnes was unpacking earlier."

I sauntered across the green, careful to avoid a number of children who had started a raucous game of British Bulldog while waiting for the fete to officially open. It had been a favourite of mine and Jerry's when we were younger, and I watched in delight as the children ran from one end of the designated pitch to the other, while trying to avoid being tagged by one of the 'Bulldogs.' When we had played, I always ended up being caught and turned into a bulldog, which meant I then had to catch the others. The one left free at the end was the winner and more often than not it had been Jerry, as he was fleet of foot and could turn on a sixpence. After a few minutes I left them to play and reached the other side unscathed.

"Good morning, Ella. How are you and your aunt getting on?" asked Agnes.

"Oh, we've finished setting up now, just waiting for the customers."

"Well, there's already a huge crowd outside the gate and several charabancs queuing to drop off their passengers. There's obviously a few work outings been planned for today. You'll need to have your wits about you when the gate opens as there's always a rush for your stall."

"I'm not surprised. There's some lovely pieces, my aunt and I have already purchased some. Is that raspberry preserve I spy there?"

"It is, mother and I make it. And this one is apple and ginger. Would you like some?"

"I would indeed, could you put one of each aside for me? I'd better take some of that red onion chutney too, it's a favourite of my aunt's. Jocasta, are you all right?" I asked, spying her behind the horticulture.

She was sitting in a deck chair behind her stall, fanning herself with a newspaper.

"Truth be told, Ella, I feel quite ghastly. I think I must be running a slight temperature and feel quite nauseous."

"Oh dear, have you caught the same infection Prudence Fielding and Anne have?"

"It certainly looks like it, unfortunately I think Father Michael might be likewise afflicted. He's supposed to be opening the fete today but he looks much worse than I do. He visited Prudence the other day when he heard she was poorly so obviously picked it up then. I do hope he's all right."

"Don't worry, I saw him not five minutes ago heading toward the ribbon. He did look quite flushed and shaky, but he'll not let the side down, especially today," said Agnes.

At that moment we were interrupted by the ringing of the bell.

"That's the signal, it's opening time," announced Jocasta staggering to her feet. "Good luck, girls. Here's to a successful fundraiser."

I most definitely underestimated Agnes's meaning when she said there would be a rush for my stall. Once the gates were open a swarm of humanity surged onto the green and all seemed to be headed in my direction. Before long the table was six deep with everyone jostling for space, grabbing things from the table and thrusting coins into my hands. It was absolute chaos and I can't say I had much control at all in the beginning.

More than once a fight broke out between members of the lower classes who desired the same item and I had to play referee, and twice I caught someone trying to take an item without paying for it. But a stern talking to, a slap on the wrist and the threat of a policeman soon sorted that out. After the third wave of customers had been served and the items replenished, it calmed down to a more manageable pace as people moved on to other vendors and the tea pavilion. I glanced at Aunt Margaret who had been every bit as busy as I had, but seemed much more serene.

"You're very popular today, Miss Bridges, I've been trying to get to see you for the last hour."

"Sergeant Baxter, how lovely to see you. I didn't realise you would be here today."

"I always bring the missus here for the May Day celebrations, take a room at a lovely little boarding house on the front for a couple of days. It's run by the wife's sister, Elsie

Pennyworth. Mrs Baxter deserves a bit of a holiday after putting up with me all year."

The sergeant and I had first met during the case up at Arundel Hall, and I had been very taken with his artistic ability. He was a very nice man and an astute policeman who was highly regarded by his boss, the Chief of Police Sir Albert Montesford, who also happened to be Ginny's Godfather.

"So where is Mrs Baxter?" I asked.

"She's gone to have tea with Elsie. Actually I wanted to have a word about the message you left at The Yard the other day."

"Yes, the illustrations for the compendium? Mrs Shaw and I have agreed it would be far more useful to illustrate the points and of course I immediately thought of you. I wondered if you would be agreeable to providing drawings? You would be paid for your time of course."

"I think that would be right up my street, Miss Bridges, I'd be honoured. Do you have time to have a chat over a cup of tea and a bun?"

"That's a very good idea, I'm quite parched myself."

After Aunt Margaret had agreed to hold the fort at both our stalls, Sergeant Baxter and I made our way to the pavilion. It was lovely and cool inside and it looked very inviting with its crisp white tablecloths and large potted palms. We were guided to a recently vacated table just inside the entrance by a smart waitress, who took our order and informed us it would be along shortly. We were lucky to have found a table as nearly all the others were full. I spied the vicar on the next one over talking to an elderly parishioner. Jocasta was right he didn't look well at all, and I noticed him constantly mopping his sweating brow with his handkerchief.

"I'll just go next door and let Mrs Baxter know where I am."

By 'next door' he meant the section beyond the bank of greenery reserved for the less genteel clientele. It was situated nearer to the bandstand, and while the string quartet behind me were exceptionally good, the lively rendition of 'Knees up Mother Brown' coming from that direction signalled a much more fun time was being had by all.

"She and Elsie are fine, having a lovely catch up and a bit of a sing song as you can no doubt hear," Baxter said with a sheepish smile.

"I was just thinking what fun it must be. You're sure you don't want to join them, it is your holiday after all?"

"I've only ever sung once in my life, Miss Bridges, and that was..."

But I never found out when it was, as a resounding crash from the next table had me jumping from my seat. Father Michael had collapsed, taking the tablecloth and the crockery with him.

CHAPTER FOUR

rushed over and crouching next to the fallen vicar, felt for a pulse. Leaning back I glanced at Baxter and whispered. "I'm afraid your holiday is to be cut short, Sergeant Baxter. Father Michael is quite dead."

Neither Sergeant Baxter nor myself could hazard a guess at what had befallen the vicar, but both of us agreed it was suspicious. Therefore we came to a mutual understanding, we would treat everything as though a crime had taken place until we knew otherwise.

Baxter immediately took charge of the situation, sending a runner to find the doctor and commandeering several constables, who had initially been seconded from the force on the mainland to deal with crowd control, to guard the pavilion and prevent anyone from leaving. He cordoned off the immediate area surrounding the body and saw that the tea paraphernalia was collected properly.

Once order had been somewhat restored, he set two constables to take names and addresses and witness statements, while I spoke with the vicar's tea companion. Unfortunately there was very little she could tell me. The meeting had not been prearranged, it was simply that he had greeted her in passing, and realising he didn't look at all well she had asked him to join her.

"To let the poor man have a rest," she said.

Apparently he had joined her in several cups of tea but hadn't partaken of any of the sandwiches or cakes. They had talked of the day and the success of the fete from the view of the funds raised, and that was all before he had collapsed.

"Of course I suggested he seek a doctor, but he said as it was nothing more than a nasty cold, he wouldn't dream of seeking a medical opinion on a mere trifle. Oh dear, perhaps I should have insisted?"

"I assure you, Mrs Markham, it would have made little difference if you had, considering how quickly he succumbed."

I thanked her and having taken her contact details in case I needed to speak with her further, went to introduce myself to the doctor who'd just arrived.

"Good afternoon Doctor, I'm Ella Bridges, I work as a consultant with Scotland Yard. Is there anything you can tell me about the cause of death?"

"Good afternoon, Miss Bridges, I'm Doctor Wenhope. I've recently taken over the surgery here along with a partner, Doctor Russell. As to cause of death I'm afraid I can't pass an opinion until the post mortem results come in. I'll make arrangements for the body to be taken to London as Scotland Yard's pursuing the case. As you probably know, due to the relatively young age of the deceased and the suddenness of death, it will be treated as suspicious until we have evidence to the contrary. Did you know him?"

"No I didn't, I'm afraid. I've only recently become involved with St. Mary's, and prior to that I understand Father Michael had been away on an extended sabbatical so our paths never crossed."

"Was this sabbatical abroad?"

"I'm afraid I couldn't say. Why, is it important?"

He took my arm and guided me to a spot where we couldn't be overheard.

"Is there any way you can find out quickly? If he's picked up some infectious disease abroad then we may need to activate some sort of quarantine."

"Oh, my word! Yes, of course, just give me a few minutes."

I made my way across the green toward Agnes's stall; if anyone knew of Father Michael's whereabouts during his sabbatical it would be she. I moved through small knots of people each discussing in hushed tones the turn of events, but the further from the pavilion I ventured the less people seemed to know. By the time I reached Agnes there were only a few intermittent whispers.

"Oh, Ella, thank goodness, I've just heard a rumour that someone has collapsed. Do you know anything?" Agnes asked.

"I'll explain in a minute. First, do you know where Father Michael went on his Sabbatical?"

"Well yes, but what does that have to do ... ?"

Her eyes widened as she made the connection.

"Has Father Michael collapsed? Is he all right?"

Seeing the distress of her friend Jocasta came over.

"Ella, what's happened?"

I took Agnes's hands in my own and looked her in the eye.

"Agnes, just answer my question, it's important. Did the father travel abroad recently?"

"Abroad? No. I don't think he's ever been abroad in his life, has he, Jocasta? He gets terribly seasick and doesn't trust aeroplanes. He went to York. The Archbishop is a long-time friend, they went to seminary school together, I believe. Now please, tell us what's happened."

I left a shocked Jocasta comforting a distraught Agnes and took a quick detour to bring my Aunt up to date.

"Well, that is tragic news, and such a shock. I suppose considering his age it must be treated as suspicious but I do hope there is a simple explanation. Let me know if I can help in any way, dear."

"Actually I wondered if you'd start to pack up the stalls? There's barely anything left anyway and in light of what's happened …"

"Consider it done. I spied Mrs Shaw a few minutes ago. I'll commandeer her to assist. What happens to the surplus goods?"

"I've no idea. I assume they'd go back to Jocasta as she's the organiser."

"I'll go and speak with her and Miss Shepherd, I daresay they are at sixes and sevens."

I thanked her, gave her a peck on the cheek and returned to Doctor Wenhope. Having given him the news that a quarantine was unnecessary I met with Sergeant Baxter and brought him up to date.

"I never thought of quarantine. A relief it weren't necessary, it would have been a nightmare to sort out today, what with the crowds and suchlike."

"It would indeed, Sergeant. Can you imagine the riot we'd have had on our hands if we had tried to put some of the upper classes in isolation?"

"I shudder to think of it, Miss Bridges, I really do. Well, I'd better get on overseeing this lot."

"I need to assist with packing up the stalls. I'll meet you back here when I'm finished."

"Righto."

Aunt Margaret, Mrs Shaw and I worked quickly and efficiently, but it still took an hour and a half to pack everything away and carry it all to the motor car. By the time I returned to Baxter I found he'd concluded his investigations and was placing the last of the samples in a box ready for transport.

"Well, I think we've done all we can here, Miss Bridges. Samples of all the victuals have been taken and labeled, witness statements and contact details obtained and the scene gone over with a fine-tooth comb. I've also practically filled my notebook with sketches and observations."

"Apologies for not being on hand to help," I said. "But very well done, Baxter. If it does turn out to be something other than natural causes we're in jolly good shape to investigate. Ah, here come the ambulance men."

We stood aside as the St John's ambulance volunteers covered the body and wheeled him away to an awaiting vehicle.

"Well, Sergeant Baxter, I don't think there is much more we can do here so I'll take my leave. I think it's time I took my aunt home. What are your plans?"

"I'll collect Mrs Baxter and see her and Elsie safely back, then I'll return to London. It's best if I'm on hand for the results then I can pass 'em straight on to you."

"Will you inform Uncle Albert?"

"I will, 'though I doubt there's much he can do. He's away in Oxfordshire at present, so it'll be up to us to pursue matters if needed."

"I see. Well, let us hope nothing criminal has occurred. Goodbye, Sergeant Baxter."

"Goodbye, Miss Bridges. I'll telephone as soon as I have news."

Aunt Margaret had informed me all the surplus items from the stalls needed to go back to the meeting room. She had passed over our funds and obtained a key from Jocasta who told us she would follow on as soon as she could. So with the car packed, Mrs Shaw drove us back up the hill to St. Mary's.

We left Aunt Margaret in the car. She would never admit it but I could see she was tired from the day's exertions. Having safely returned the unsold items to the meeting room, we were making our way back down the churchyard path when I caught a movement out of the corner of my eye. Turning, I saw the same elderly gentleman dressed in tweeds as I had on my first visit. I raised a hand to wave but he turned and walked through the solid perimeter wall. I sighed.

"Is something wrong, Miss Bridges?"

I could hardly tell Mrs Shaw what I had seen, so a watered down version of the truth would have to suffice.

"I have a feeling that not all is as it should be, Mrs Shaw. There's a mystery here which needs solving and I may be the only one who can do it."

Mrs Shaw, used to my odd ways now, said nothing and we continued toward the car. At the lych-gate we found Jocasta and Agnes talking with Aunt Margaret.

"Oh, Ella, I just can't believe it. Poor Father Michael," said Agnes.

I handed the keys back to Jocasta, who ironically was beginning to look a little better.

"I am sorry for your loss. I know I didn't know the father personally but I know how much he meant to the both of you."

"You will tell us as soon as you know anything, won't you?" Jocasta asked.

"We know you're investigating," whispered Agnes.

I looked at them, unsure what to say, but Agnes continued.

"I caught Doctor Wenhope as he was leaving and asked him what his thoughts were. He said he couldn't comment but you should have some information soon. He mentioned Scotland Yard. You will let us know, won't you, Ella?"

"I am sorry to interrupt, dear, but would you mind if we went home? I'm feeling quite weary."

"Yes, of course. I'm sorry, Agnes, Jocasta, but I really must get my aunt back, it's been quite an ordeal for her. I'm sure you understand. Do take care, and once again please accept my condolences."

I took Aunt Margaret's arm, and settled her in the back of the car with a rug over her knees as Mrs Shaw started the engine and pulled away.

"Thank you, Aunt."

"Don't mention it," she said, removing the rug. "I could see what a predicament you were in."

I leant back and closed my eyes.

"I know what you're thinking," she said a moment later.

"I'm not sure you do."

"It must be very difficult to retain friends when one minute you're having afternoon tea and the next you're interrogating them as a suspect."

I opened one eye and looked at her.

"As I thought, definitely part witch."

She laughed. "If you want my advice, Ella, try not to dwell on it too much. The real friends will understand when you explain you cannot discuss an ongoing investigation, and won't press you further. They will also still be around when it's concluded."

"Judicious words indeed," I mumbled, half asleep.

"Of course they are; I'm an old woman who has lived twice as long as you have."

"I'm glad you didn't say wiser."

"I didn't need to, dear."

CHAPTER FIVE

S everal days passed before I heard from Sergeant Baxter.
Life at the cottage had settled into a welcome routine
with the three of us working on the police compendium in the morning. Aunt Margaret, who had taught me
all I knew, was an invaluable help and we were beginning
to make real progress. Then in the afternoon, my aunt and
I would venture out for walks or drives around the island
if the weather was fine, or settle down to a game of Goof
spiel or Mau mau if not. But at the back of my mind always
was the death of Father Michael, alongside the continual
worry about John.

The news when it came was mixed.

"So there were nothing in any of the food or drink served
to Father Michael at the fete to cause his death. In fact
nothing unusual were found in the victuals served from
the pavilion that day at all," Baxter told me.

"I see. I suppose it is good news from the point of view of
the other patrons," I said. "I also had a word with the doctor

before he left the fete, and asked him to inform us if anyone came to his surgery feeling ill who had also taken tea in the pavilion. He's not been in contact so I assume all is well."

"But you're not convinced his death were natural?"

"No I'm not, Sergeant Baxter. There is more to the demise of the vicar than we know, I'm sure of it. But without any evidence there's no proof. Is there anything to report from the post-mortem?"

"I'm sorry to say that news isn't so good. There's a bit of a delay. A combination of staff shortage and a streak of unexplained deaths in the city, which take precedence apparently. The pathologist can't start on our case 'til next week."

"What? But that means it will have been over a week since Father Michael died. Evidence may be lost. Is there nothing you can do to hurry things along?"

"I'm sorry, Miss Bridges, but there isn't. I've already called in a few favours to get the lab to run tests based on nothing but a gut feeling..."

"And not even your own gut. I'm sorry, Sergeant, I should know you're doing all you can."

"Well, I've worked with you for a while now, Miss Bridges, and I trust your intuition. Leave it with me; if I can push our case further up the pile then I will. But I can't make any promises. By the way, my superintendent has informed the Diocese. They'll be sending over another priest to run things for a while."

Having thanked Baxter I rang off and returned to my aunt.

"I take it the news wasn't good?" she said, taking one look at my face.

"I suppose it depends on which side you're on. From my side unfortunately not. Sorry to be such a misery, it's just so frustrating. It's not much of a holiday for you, is it? I am sorry, Aunt Margaret."

"Oh, do stop apologising, Ella, you're beginning to sound like Agnes. I'm having a perfectly lovely time, murder aside."

"So you think it was murder too?"

"It doesn't matter what I think, you think it's suspicious and that's enough for me. What we need to do is set our minds to solving the problem."

"I can hardly investigate when there's no proof a crime has been committed. Until we have the post-mortem results giving us a 'yay' or 'nay' to something beastly having happened, my hands are tied. Unfortunately Baxter has just informed me the results will be delayed."

"Well, remember there is more than one way to skin a cat, Ella."

Phantom, who had up until that moment been asleep on hearth rug, raised his head and glared at my aunt with such indignation, I couldn't help but laugh.

"What do you have in mind?" I asked.

"The police force isn't the only organisation in the land which wields power, you know."

"The Church," I said after a moment's thought.

She nodded. "I understood your vicar had some friends in high places, perhaps that would be a place to start?"

Strictly speaking, having not passed this new test I wasn't supposed to drive alone, but I felt a little uncomfortable having Mrs Shaw with me constantly while I was investigating, so I decided I would plead ignorance if I was stopped.

After my aunt's excellent observation my next port of call was to Agnes, in the hope I could obtain information which would expedite matters.

"Ella, come through to the parlour, I'll have Molly make us some tea and then we can talk. Mother is resting so we should be left alone for a while," Agnes said in her hushed tone.

Once the tea had been served Agnes asked her most pressing question.

"Have you come with news, Ella?"

I took a sip of my tea, giving me time to gather my thoughts. I needed to be careful for if it was proved Father Michael was murdered then Agnes would obviously become a suspect.

"Actually the lack of news is the reason I have come, Agnes."

"I'm sorry, I don't quite understand."

"I'll explain in a moment, but first I need to talk to you. At present there is nothing to suggest the father's death was anything other than natural ... "

"But ... "

"I'm not saying it was, Agnes, and as it stands currently we have no evidence, but if proof were found that it was murder then my role will become official. Consequently our relationship will change. This goes for the other members of the church whom I know also. Do you understand?"

"But of course. You will be investigating on behalf of Scotland Yard. Therefore myself, Jocasta, and the others will automatically become suspects. But I knew this, Ella, and it's how it should be. I have nothing to hide and nor do the others. I trust you to do your job and find the culprit if there is one but it won't change my regard for you, nor our friendship. We just want to find out what happened, Ella, and we know you can help us do that."

"And you understand that if this becomes an official inquiry I will not be able to share any findings with you?"

"I do. Now is there anything I can do to help?"

"As a matter of fact there is. I need to get in contact with the Archbishop of York and thought you would be the best person to ask how it would be possible."

I briefly explained the delays Baxter had informed me of, the fact that direct liaison with the Church was in the hands of the Superintendent rather than us, and the hope that the Archbishop, as both a friend of the deceased and a man of notable position, could perhaps apply a little pressure in the right quarters. I might get in trouble by circumventing the normal protocol, but Baxter and I couldn't wait. We needed to know as soon as possible if this were a case of murder.

"I'm sure he can, in fact I'm positive of it. Daddy always said he was a man to be reckoned with once he had a bee in his bonnet about something, and this is much more important."

"Your father knew him?"

"Of course, Daddy was the Priest at St. Mary's before Father Michael took over. He and my mother married before he took his vows. Sorry I thought I'd mentioned it."

"No, you didn't. Does that mean you know the Archbishop?"

"Yes. Would you like me to telephone and explain the situation? I promise to be circumspect."

"Actually that's a very good idea, Agnes. I have no official capacity as yet, but as both a concerned parishioner and the daughter of the previous vicar, then it would only be natural for you to want to move things along. I believe a representative from Diocese is already on his way but according to Baxter, he didn't know Father Michael, so I doubt he'll be much help to us."

"I'll do it now. Would you like more tea while you wait?"

"Yes, all right, I would."

"I'll send Molly in."

Agnes returned just as Molly set down the new tea tray.

"Gosh, would you believe I just caught him in time, Ella, and he is going to make some calls. He would be here himself but is travelling to Rome tomorrow and won't be back for at least a week. Linhay doesn't fall under his jurisdiction as I'm sure you know, but he was a personal friend as well as Father Michael's spiritual adviser and is greatly perturbed at the delay. It's not only important that we find out what happened you see, but that Father Michael is laid to rest. His spirit is with his God now but his earthly remains need to be interred. There needs to be a funeral, Ella."

She took a handkerchief from her sleeve and dabbed her eyes beneath her glasses. The mention of a funeral had caused my heart to contract and an ice cold shiver to sweep from my head to my toes. The last funeral I had attended had been John's, and I remembered it with a clarity now as though it had been yesterday. I had to remind myself he was actually still alive, but the conversation with Agnes had left me with a terrifying feeling of foreboding.

"Sorry," she said, sniffing.

"There's no need to apologise, Agnes," I said softly, coming back to the present. "I realise this is a terrible ordeal for you and I promise we will do all we can to get a speedy resolution."

She nodded, and wiping her eyes a final time, tucked the handkerchief back into her sleeve.

"Thank you, Ella. There's to be a memorial service for Father Michael on Sunday, will you come?"

I promised I would do my best then took my leave. On the drive home I fervently hoped the Archbishop's telephone calls were yielding positive results.

The next morning sergeant Baxter telephoned bright and early with news.

"I don't know how you managed it, Miss Bridges, but I've just been told the post-mortem 'as been re-scheduled for this afternoon. With a bit of luck we should 'ave the cause of death confirmed by tomorrow at the latest."

"That is excellent news, Sergeant. Telephone as soon as you have the results."

Within four hours he called me back.

"My goodness that was quick," I said.

"I called to see the coroner on the off chance, you were right about it being murder. Father Michael was poisoned. I've squared it with the 'Top Brass,' we're now officially investigating."

"I knew it! What type of poison?"

"Ricin. Nasty stuff but common enough to get hold of if you know what yer doin'."

"Yes, from the beans of the Castor Oil plant, I believe. How was it administered do you know?"

"Let me look at me notes."

There was a rustle of paper as Baxter found the correct page.

"'Ere we are. 'A combination of ingestion and inhalation,' 'though he can't say how much of each."

"So it was in something he ate and breathed in?"

"So the coroner says. And not all at once neither, over a short period of time apparently. He estimates exposure somewhere between three days to a week."

"Well, that may make our job more difficult, but it does suggest it was in something he had regular access to. Did the coroner tell you anything of the symptoms of this type of poison?" I asked.

"He did, and a bit too accurate if you ask me. I was in danger of losing me lunch several times. But I'll make it less grisly for you. Your question about how it were carried out were a good one as symptoms vary according to if it were breathed in, eaten or a needle were used. I'll stick with eaten or breathed in as it's what we know to be fact."

Sergeant Baxter went on to explain early symptoms of inhalation included a fever and a cough. Which we knew was correct in the vicar's case. Excessive thirst was indicative of ingestion.

"According to Mrs Markham, he consumed several cups of tea while with her, so that would certainly fit," I said.

With the use of his notebook, Baxter then went on to describe a litany of symptoms which made my blood run cold. These included pain, inflammation, hemorrhage, severe nausea, skin irritation and tightening of the chest. Eventually it would lead to organ failure and death.

"What an appalling way to die. Father Michael must have suffered a great deal."

"It's a rum do and no mistake, Miss Bridges."

"Well, I think we should keep this information under our hats, Baxter. The last thing his friends and colleagues need is to know of his suffering. Now, what we need to do is to ascertain Father Michael's exact movements in the week or so leading up to his death. How soon can you be here?"

"There's a few things to sort out 'ere so it won't be before this evenin'. Mrs Baxter, is still at Elsie's, so I'll stay there. I'll meet you at the vicarage first thing. Do you know who 'as the keys?"

"I'll ask, Agnes. Can you get the local constable to guard the place until the morning? It's now officially part of a crime."

"Consider it done. I'll see yer tomorrow."

I telephoned Agnes and informed her the death of Father Michael was indeed deliberate and it was now officially a murder inquiry. I made no mention of poison and cautioned her against telling anyone else what I'd told her. It was vitally important she remained quiet, we didn't know who was responsible and we didn't want to tip off the culprit. I told her I would need the keys to the vicarage, and she informed me she still had the spare set which had belonged to her father. I arranged for Mrs Shaw to collect them post-haste.

After ringing off, I went through to the small sitting room where my aunt had organised lunch.

"It seems you have a difficult case, Ella."

"You heard? I'm afraid it won't be as straightforward as I'd hoped. It seems the fete was the place the vicar finally succumbed to the poison, as opposed to where the crime was committed. Now comes the daunting task of verifying Father Michael's movements prior to his death, as well as trying to ascertain who would want to harm him and why. Not to mention how he came to consume enough poison over a period of time to kill him. As murders go this one is near perfect."

"There is no such thing as a perfect crime in my opinion. A murderer will always be punished whether in this life or the next."

"Well, if it's in the next it won't help me or Sergeant Baxter one jot."

"I have every faith in you both, Ella. Now, how about I beat you at a final game of Mau mau? I daresay you will be too busy to play after today."

"Yes, all right. And you can tell me all you know about the Castor Oil plant and their poisonous beans while we play. It appears Father Michael was killed using Ricin."

CHAPTER SIX

T here was no sign of the new priest the Church had sent when I arrived at the vicarage the following morning, but knowing it was now a crime scene, arrangements had been made for him to lodge in the village. Sergeant Baxter was waiting for me however.

"Good morning, Baxter."

"Miss Bridges," He replied with a nod.

"Nothing to report overnight?"

"No, I sent the young constable 'ome as soon as I got 'ere, he were almost asleep on 'is feet. But he said all were quiet, if a little spooky what with the graves being over yonder."

"I can imagine, it must be very different in the middle of the night. Now I think the key is for the door to the side."

The vicarage was everything I'd expected. A single level dwelling built of stone, not as old as the church itself, but still quite ancient. The interior was well appointed but leaned toward comfort and practicality as opposed to the aesthetic, and most obviously was the space of a single cleric living in furnished accommodation, which in essence was not his own.

It was also typical of a property belonging to a religious organisation, saintly paintings on the wall, icons on shelves, a piano in the sitting room and several bibles on tables. The windows were small and let in little light, which gave the space a dark and claustrophobic feel. I daresay in the evenings with lamps lit, a roaring fire and the wireless on, it would be quite cosy, but in the cold light of day it was shabby and depressing.

"What do you say we start in the office, Baxter? That's where his appointment book is most likely to be. Do we know anything about his staff?"

"You go and find the office and I'll see if I can rustle up a housekeeper."

The office when I found it was a decent sized room running the full width of the building to the rear of the property. Its double aspect meant there were windows to either side which should have lightened it, but the dark colours of the rugs and soft furnishings, as well as the almost black wood of the furniture rendered the attempt useless. The room was one of two halves, containing a desk and bookshelves at one end and a lounge area and fireplace, complete with drinks cabinet, at the other.

I sat at the desk and had just begun opening drawers when I heard someone enter.

"I found her waiting outside," said Baxter.

"Agnes, what are you doing here?"

"I thought I might be needed. The sergeant said you wanted to speak with the housekeeper?"

"You were Father Michael's housekeeper?"

"Yes, sorry, didn't I mention it? It was only temporary until he could find someone permanent. Jocasta and I shared the position actually, although she couldn't do it for long as she was so busy with the riding school. I did three mornings per week and she the other three. No work on Sundays of course. It made sense considering I knew the vicarage so well having lived here, and of course Jocasta practically grew up here too. Why, is it important?"

I caught Baxter's eye and he raised an eyebrow. I wondered if Agnes realised what a hole she was digging for herself and her friend.

"Please sit down, Agnes," I said, indicating the chair at the other side of the desk. "We're trying to find out Father Michael's movements over the last few months. Do you know where he was prior to joining St Mary's?"

"Sorry, I don't I'm afraid. The Archbishop of York, once he knew daddy was to retire, suggested Father Michael as a replacement. They both came to visit a few months before daddy passed away, but that's all I can tell you. I suppose Father Michael liked the look of the place and accepted the position, but I obviously wasn't included in the discussions."

"Jocasta said he arrived about ten months ago? So that would have been late July?"

"Early August, I think. Then at the end of September he announced he was to go on a sabbatical and a temporary vicar would take over during the interim. He returned the day you helped with the flowers as you know."

"Is it normal for a priest to leave his position for so long after just arriving?"

"Well, not normal particularly, but it's not unheard of. I suppose it would depend on the reasons he needed to leave."

"What sort of reasons are typical?"

"Illness perhaps or a crisis of faith. Special work for the church maybe, I really couldn't say. None of us knew Father Michael particularly well; he hadn't been here long enough."

"So you wouldn't know if he had any enemies?" asked Baxter.

Agnes looked up at him, wide owlish eyes blinking behind her thick lenses.

"Enemies? No. But of course he must have had one, mustn't he?"

"What about 'is family, do you know anything of them?"

"He has no siblings and his parents are both deceased. I suppose there may be extended family but I know nothing of them."

"And do you know what his appointments were since he returned?" I asked.

"I don't, I'm afraid. He was rather remiss about keeping his appointment book up to date, preferred to keep it all in his head. He had a very good memory."

There was little more Agnes could tell us so I sent her home. Once she'd left, Baxter and I explored the various rooms. The appointment book had told us nothing more than we already knew; unfortunately none of the rooms threw up any useful clues either. No threatening letters, no list of enemies and no convenient bottle marked poison stashed at the back of a cupboard. I sighed and went to look out of the bedroom window. I could see the church from this vantage point just the other side of the lane, and once again I spied the old gent in tweeds. He seemed to be staring in my direction. I had no idea who he was or what he wanted, but considering he was hovering about, I wondered if he was connected to the murder in some way.

"Well, that's the last of the rooms bar the kitchen," Baxter said coming to join me.

"Did you find anything useful?"

"Not a thing. I think we might need a miracle."

"I'm holding out for divine intervention personally."

Baxter laughed. "Well, if ever there were a case more fitting, I don't know of it."

The kitchen was old fashioned and functional at best. A large range, newly blackened, stood in the chimney breast to the right, with an assortment of copper pans and kettles hanging above. A curtain below the large glazed stoneware sink revealed nothing more than a bucket and a few cleaning rags. The central table of well-scrubbed pine was empty, and this is where we stacked the contents of the cupboards.

"Oh," I exclaimed as I opened a cupboard and found a familiar green and gold box. "I know this tea, it's made and sold in the town where my aunt lives and is the best in the land according to her. I remember Jocasta mentioning Father Michael ordered his tea in specially."

"Well, let's box it up with the other foodstuffs for the lab boys to take a butcher's at. If the vicar were being poisoned over a number o' days it makes sense for it to be somewhere in this lot."

"We'll remove the contents of the drinks cabinet in the office too. How are we to get it all to London?"

"I've arranged for one of the local bobbies to take it, the lab is expecting him with some test items. So where to next?"

"I think lunch is in order I can't possibly think on an empty stomach. Then I believe we pay a visit to Mrs Jocasta Blenkinsop."

"The woman from the flower stall?"

"Precisely, Baxter. Let's see if she knows anything about growing Castor Oil plants."

Jocasta had married into money, and a great deal of it if the house were any indication. A Georgian pile of red brick with a plethora of windows and chimneys. The discreet sign at the gate had read, 'Briarlea Stud and Riding School,' and as we proceeded up the gravel drive we glimpsed horses grazing in distant paddocks and others being put through their paces by experienced riders. On the horizon was a large stable block where a group of children were being helped to mount a row of patiently waiting miniature horses.

"How the other half lives, eh?" said Baxter.

As we pulled up at the house a rider broke away and galloped towards us. Jocasta dismounted with practiced ease and handed the reins off to a waiting groom.

"Ella, I saw the car coming up the drive, what a lovely surprise."

She then noticed my companion.

"Ah, an official visit then? Give me a moment to change, I'll have Maud take you through to the drawing room."

Maud was patiently waiting by the front steps and gave a quick curtsy.

"This way, sir, madam."

We followed through the grand pillared portico flanked by large topiary bushes, and entered a hall of gargantuan proportions, with a chequered tile floor and numerous giant vases of eastern origin. Maud escorted us through to a drawing room with stunning views over the surrounding countryside, and informed us tea would be served shortly.

Baxter and I had briefly discussed how we would handle the interview on the drive over; he would wait for a suitable opening in the conversation to elicit the invitation we needed, hopefully without it being too obvious.

Maud arrived with the tea tray moments before Jocasta returned, freshly scrubbed and attired and smelling faintly of Lily of the Valley.

"So you've come about Father Michael's murder I assume? I must admit I was shocked when I heard the news. As awful as it sounds we were all hoping for it to be natural causes. But to think of it being deliberate, and a man of God no less. It's terrifying to think there is a murderer loose in the parish, thank goodness the boys are away at school, none of us will be safe until he's caught. How did he die?"

"I'm afraid we can't say at present. Jocasta, how well did you know Father Michael?" I asked.

"Honestly, hardly at all. He wasn't here long, then went away for an extended period as you know. Getting to know someone takes time and there simply wasn't any."

"I believe you shared his housekeeping duties with Agnes? If you don't mind me asking, why was that? It's not as though you needed ... "

"The money?"

"Actually I was going to say work but money will do," I said, smiling at her bluntness.

"You're quite right. I needed neither the money nor the work. I did it as a favour to Agnes, and purely voluntarily, I wasn't paid. And anyway I gave it up after about six weeks or so as I was needed here. Agnes called me one day and said the new vicar needed someone temporarily, and she needed someone to do the three days she couldn't; she looks after her mother you know. She simply asked me if I'd help out and I said yes."

"And was the father there when you were working?"

"More often than not, yes. I usually arrived about an hour after he'd had breakfast; he got his own, you know, wouldn't hear of being waited on. I dusted and cleaned, stocked the cupboards and if necessary prepared an evening meal for him. There was very little to do if I'm being truthful, Father Michael did much of it himself. Preferred to actually."

"And did you talk much?"

"Sometimes if he wasn't in his office, but nothing of great import, just polite small talk mostly, inconsequential stuff. The weather, as we English are apt to do. He'd ask after the boys and how they were enjoying school, ideas for the Sunday sermons sometimes. As I say, nothing of real substance and nothing about himself."

"And you don't know where he lived prior to coming here?"

"No, and I didn't ask. You have to understand that he was a relative stranger here when all is said and done. He wasn't very forthcoming about personal details, played his cards close to his chest and quite frankly had an air about him that discouraged questions. It wasn't that he was unfriendly, more, how shall I put it, preoccupied."

"Do you think there were something on 'is mind then, something troubling him?" asked Baxter, who up until this point had remained quiet.

Jocasta paused for a moment, deep in thought.

"Yes, now you come to mention it I do."

"Were this something that happened recently?"

"It's difficult to say. Let me think."

She stood up and began to rearrange the flowers in a nearby vase.

"It helps me concentrate," she said.

"It's a beautiful display," said Baxter, jumping on the opening we had discussed previously. "I meant to get something from your stall at the fete the other day for my wife, unfortunately I never got a chance."

"I grow them all myself in the hothouse and the greenhouses. I'll show you around before you go if you like? I'm sure we can find something suitable for you to take to your wife."

"That's very kind of you, Mrs Blenkinsop, I'd like that. And it'll certainly earn me a few brownie points with the missus."

Nicely done, Sergeant Baxter.

Finishing the arrangement Jocasta once again took her seat.

"I would say Father Michael already had something on his mind when he took over at St Mary's. But he was definitely much more worried over the last weeks since his return. Whether or not it was the same problem I can't tell you, but it does rather point to something happening before he arrived here, doesn't it? Perhaps it was the reason he took a sabbatical? The Archbishop of York would be able to tell you more of course, he and Father Michael were friends."

"Unfortunately, the Archbishop is currently in Rome and out of contact, but we will speak with him when he returns. You've been very helpful, Jocasta, however I think that's all we need to know for the moment," I said, rising from my chair.

"Well, you know where I am if you need to speak with me further. Come along, I'll give you both a tour of the greenhouses."

••‹‹◇››••

As we walked through the garden I inquired after Jocasta's health.

"Oh, I'm as right as rain now, thank goodness. We're awash with tourists at the moment, I must have caught a dose of something from one of them."

"And Anne and Prudence?"

"Well on the road to recovery too by all accounts, although Prudence is still a little shaky. Here we are."

She opened a large gate and led us through into a beautiful walled garden.

"Do you know, I've recently discovered a walled garden like this at my cottage? I hope I can do it the same justice you have here, it's quite stunning," I said, gazing around the space with pleasure.

"Well, I'm happy to give you or your gardener any pointers when you have time, planting marigolds in with your tomatoes for example keeps the insects away."

"I'll certainly pass along the tip, however it may be some time before we're at the stage of planting, although I really don't know for sure. Tom, my gardener, has requested I leave the entire project in his hands as he wants it to be a surprise, and I'm quite happy to do so."

I gazed around Jocasta's garden with deep appreciation.

"You certainly 'ave a fine array of produce here," said Baxter.

"The majority of fresh food for the house comes from this garden. The central beds as you can see are for the vegetables and the fruit bushes. The ones along the perimeter walls I use to grow cut flowers, carnations and daffs and whatnot, then we have the larger trained trees, such as apples and pears along the walls. And over here we're even experimenting with hops, my head gardener rather likes the idea of producing his own beer. Of course the staff deal with all of that, this here is my domain."

We entered quite the largest glass house I had ever seen, filled with tables on which stood a vast array of exotic flowering plants.

The temperature outside was extremely warm but inside it rose further by several degrees, and immediately I felt a thin sheen of perspiration form on my face and neck as the humidity hit me.

Above us were various hanging baskets each with a profusion of dangling greenery, and as we moved through the space I saw several beds had been dug into the ground from which large ferns, huge palms and smaller cacti grew. Baxter caught my eye and with a flick of his hand indicated to the left. I glanced over and nodded briefly. It was a Castor Oil plant.

"It's like walking through another world," said Baxter, obviously enchanted with the place.

"Marvellous, isn't it?" said Jocasta, oblivious to our exchange. "I visited The Royal Botanical Gardens at Kew when I was younger and fell in love. I vowed there and then I would have my own version when I grew up, and this is the result."

We meandered along wooden walkways taking in the beauty of the specimens for some time before we reached another door. Jocasta opened it, hurried us through then quickly closed it. We were standing in a small square room with glass walls and ceiling.

"This allows us to preserve the temperature in the main area," she explained.

She opened another door opposite the last, and we stepped into what obviously was a behind-the-scenes work area. Rows of long trestle tables, on which an assortment of terracotta pots stood waiting for a small seed or bulb, greeted us. Hessian sacks full of compost were stacked underneath, a couple of wheelbarrows and various tools were scattered throughout, and above it all rose an earthy smell which reminded me of walking through an autumnal woodland on a bed of wet leaves.

"Through here is where the real work is done. Seed collection, potting out, taking cuttings and whatnot. Almost everything you saw next door started out life as a small cutting or a seed in here," Jocasta informed us as she continued the tour.

I realised one section of the original Victorian walled garden must have been removed in order to accommodate this space, as the back wall of this greenhouse had access to an external working area, where I saw several compost heaps being forked over by a gardener in shirtsleeves and a long jute apron. Beyond were hedgerows over which views of the surrounding fields could be seen.

I spied the broken pane just as Jocasta gave a cry of dismay.

Turning quickly, I saw a scene of utter chaos. A large bank of drawers such as you would find in an apothecary shop, had been well and truly ransacked. Drawers flung onto the floor where their contents had scattered far and wide.

"My seeds!"

Jocasta Blenkinsop had been burgled.

I asked Jocasta to see if she could ascertain what had been stolen, but under no circumstances was she to touch anything. We'd need to bring in a specialist to see if he could find some fingerprints. I took Baxter to one side out of earshot.

"I think we both know what she'll find," I whispered.

"Yes, but we need to be certain. Whoever it were made a right old mess."

"A distraction to conceal what they were really after perhaps? I don't suppose it will do any good to ask who had access?"

"We can ask but I doubt it'll help. The pane was broken from the outside, glass is on the inside you see, 'ere. They just climbed in, pinched what they wanted, wrecked the place to maybe cause confusion like you say, and went out the same way. It can't 'ave taken long. There's no sign of footprints in or out and they could 'ave come from any-where. It's surrounded by open countryside, albeit most of what you can see is the Blenkinsop's land, but somehow I doubt a charge of trespass would bother someone with murder on their mind. No, it would 'ave been easy to get up 'ere unseen at night then return the same way," Baxter said, making notes in his little black book.

"We need to confirm when anyone was last in here. If the Ricin used to poison Father Michael originated as a Castor Oil bean here, then it had to have been over a week ago. I do think it's the case though, I noticed a fine layer of dust on the plundered drawers."

"Well if yer right, it's likely any trail outside will 'ave long since disappeared. I'm afraid our thief's trail is stone cold, but I'll go and 'ave a chat with that gardener out there on the off chance he saw or 'eard something."

As Baxter left to go outside I returned to Jocasta, who was on hands and knees carefully picking up discarded seeds and putting them into paper envelopes. There were hundreds, if not thousands of seeds ranging from those no bigger than a pin head, to some as large as a kidney bean. It would take weeks to sort them out properly.

"Have you found anything missing?" I asked gently.

"Four types so far. These drawers were all full and there's barely any of the seeds on the floor. Shouldn't have been full of course, I should have potted them up long before now but I've not been in here for over a month as my time has been taken up elsewhere. Why on earth would someone break in to steal my seeds? All they had to do was ask and I'd have gladly given them some, and told them how to grow and look after them. It doesn't make sense. Damn it! It's going to take years for me to get the collection back up to what it was."

She pointed to the four drawers and I looked at the labels.

"These are in Latin? Not my strong point I'm afraid," I said.

"Of course, sorry. Look, do you mind if I sit, I'm losing all feeling in my legs?"

She rose and went to a nearby bench where she still had a close view of the drawers, then explained what they had contained.

"Now let's have a look. Ageratina altissima, that's white snakeroot, Ricinus communis is the Castor Oil plant. Nerium oleander is the oleander, and Abrus precatorius is the Rosary ..."

She tailed off and looked at me with wide eyes.

"What is it?"

"Ella, every single one of these is poisonous."

I left Jocasta having elicited a promise from her not to tell anyone about what was missing, and also made a suggestion to keep the seeds under lock and key from now on. Rather a case of shutting the greenhouse door after the thief had already bolted, but there was nothing else for it. I went in search of Baxter. He'd just finished speaking with the gardener and walked over to join me.

"Well, the gardener, Archer's his name, didn't 'ear nor see a thing. Not being able to pinpoint the time of the theft is a bit of a problem of course, but he's never even been inside the greenhouses. Only the head bloke, a man called ... "

Here he consulted his black book.

"Peterson, and Mrs Blenkinsop 'erself ever worked with the exotic stuff. But Archer assures me Peterson hasn't set foot in the place for more'n a month, other duties apparently."

"I think we may have a bigger problem," I said, and proceeded to tell him what Jocasta had discovered.

"Well, that does shed a different light on things. We're obviously looking for someone with specialist knowledge if they could pick out poisonous seeds, not only from that lot but by their Latin names. And so far we only know of one person who fits that particular bill."

We both turned back to look at the greenhouse behind us, and to where Jocasta was back on her hands and knees amongst the scattered seeds.

"She certainly has both means and opportunity but what could her motive be? And why go to the trouble of making it look like a break in? Surely she must realise the evidence is pointing in her direction?" I said.

"Could be like you said earlier, causes confusion and throws the investigation in a different direction. But either she's innocent or 'as been far too clever for 'er own good.

Our job now is to find out what 'er motive could be while also looking for other potential suspects."

"Nothing too complicated then," I said as we made our way back to the greenhouse and asked to use the telephone.

Jocasta accompanied us back the way we'd come, having thrust a delicate looking orchid in Baxter's arms as we'd left the greenhouse.

"I thought you might like to take this for your wife. Keep it indoors in a light warm spot, kitchen would be best as it likes a little humidity, but be careful not to over water it."

"Well that's very kind, Mrs Blenkinsop, I'm sure Mrs Baxter will cherish it. How much do I owe yer."

"Consider it a gift, Sergeant."

"I'm afraid I can't do that, not while on the job yer understand. Plus it's for a good cause, the new meeting room at St Mary's?"

"Well, if you insist. Thank you."

Back at the house she took Baxter to the telephone. He called The Yard and ordered a team to search the scene of the crime for fingerprints, then contacted a local bobby to guard it while they arrived. We then returned to the greenhouse to wait. It wasn't long before the constable arrived and once Baxter had explained the situation we returned to the car.

"Do you think she was trying to bribe you with an orchid?" I asked him.

We were making our way to the guest house where Mrs Baxter was getting ready to accompany her husband back to London. He intended to go to the police laboratory first thing next morning to see if he could chivvy along the tests on the food from the vicarage. We needed to confirm the source of the poison and the vicarage foodstuff was our only clue at this stage.

"I doubt it, but it's best not to muddy the waters."

"I've been thinking. Two points concern me at the moment."

"Only two?" said Baxter wryly.

"The first is we only have Jocasta's word for the fact the seeds are missing. And the second, if they have been stolen, then perhaps Father Michael isn't the only victim. Maybe he was a test of sorts and the thief is planning on using the other seeds on someone else? It could be the vicar wasn't the intended target at all but was in fact killed in order to throw our suspicion that way, guaranteeing our time will be taken up investigating while one or more murders take place elsewhere."

Baxter turned and stared at me, a look of horror on his face.

"What a terrifyin' thought! And 'ere I was worrying about muddying the waters by accepting a plant. I admit it's not an impossible idea, although it's not far off. But we can't investigate 'what ifs' and 'maybes.' No we 'ave to stick to the facts as we know 'em, gather evidence and move the case forward. All things bein' equal we'll find our murderer. But if the evidence points us in more than one direction then we'll just 'ave to follow it. You have an uncanny knack for this type of work, Miss Bridges, and yer mind works in astonishing ways, but I 'ope for all our sakes yer wrong about this."

I dropped him off at the guest-house with a reminder of the memorial service for Father Michael.

"Do you think it would be prudent to go?" I asked.

"I do. It's the one occasion where we could 'ave all the suspects in one place, we'd be fools not to go. Pick me up at the train station and we'll go a little earlier to see who turns up."

As it happened the service itself didn't help in any way, but an incident outside certainly did. Although it would be a while before I realised its significance.

CHAPTER SEVEN

The afternoon of the memorial service found Baxter and I sitting in the car opposite the Church, while the rain beat a noisy staccato on the roof and the windows steamed up so as to be almost opaque. Which, considering our purpose was to arrive early and observe those entering, we found most annoying. Not only that, the rain resulted in all and sundry scurrying inside under umbrellas so it was impossible to tell who was who.

"Oh, this is pointless. King George himself could have entered that church and I wouldn't have recognised him. Of all the days to have a summer storm," I said.

"I don't know, it seems fittin' somehow. It don't seem quite right to 'ave funerals, memorials and the ilk under a blue sky and sunshine."

"I suppose it depends on whether you're celebrating a life well lived or mourning a terrible loss. My Aunt thinks the Irish have got it right when it comes to this sort of thing. A huge celebratory wake, shared stories of the deceased, music, dancing plus lots of alcohol of course. Although I concede the weather today is well suited for the occasion. Shall we go in?"

"We may as well, the last of the stragglers are makin' their way in now, it looks as though the entire village 'as turned up, we'll be 'ard pressed to get a pew. No matter, we'll 'ave a better vantage point if we're stood at the back."

Baxter was right, the church was packed tight and it was standing room only. We squashed in at the rear not far from the door where we had a good view, but although I recognised a few faces, in the main they were unknown to me. Baxter not being a resident was faced with a sea of strangers apart from those he'd met during the investigation, and I was beginning to think this was a foolhardy quest.

Just over an hour later, having listened to Father Michael's replacement, the ancient Father Jacob, speak in both English and Latin, interspersed with several hymns and a few bouts of sobbing, it was over, and we quickly moved outside. Thank goodness the rain had stopped. I was jostled several times and Baxter took my elbow to prevent me from falling. I was trying to move unsuccessfully out of the way when I was bumped into quite roughly, luckily Baxter was once again on hand otherwise I would have found myself face down on the path.

"Sorry Miss," a young girl said as she charged down the path.

I caught nothing more than a pale face covered in freckles and wisps of red hair under a hat, before a hand was laid on my arm and I turned to its owner. It was Agnes.

"Thank you for coming, Ella."

"It was a lovely service and very well patronised," I told her.

"Yes, although he hadn't been here very long, Father Michael was well liked, particularly by the elder parishioners as he visited them quite often. He will be missed by everyone."

I looked around for Baxter whom I seemed to have lost in the crowd, and eventually spied him leaning against the wall not far from the gate. He raised a hand.

"Listen, Agnes, I'm afraid I must go. Will you be all right?"

"Yes, of course I will. I need to go and find mother anyway, I left her with Jocasta. Goodbye, Ella."

"I can't say I learned much at all from that exercise. What about you?" I asked Baxter as I drove him back to the train station.

"Not much at all I'm afraid, although it'll have done our image no 'arm to 'ave been seen."

"Do you think the murderer was there?"

"Hard to say. Possibly, but there were certainly nothing obvious."

"When do you think the lab will have some results for us?"

"Not fer a couple of days yet I shouldn't think, but I'll let you know as soon as I 'ear anything."

I said goodbye to Baxter and drove back to the cottage. With a few days grace before we could do anything more I vowed to spend a bit more time on the compendium and with my aunt, who I felt quite guilty at leaving to her own devices considering she was my guest.

Alighting from the car, I noticed a mark on the hem of my good wool coat. It only ever saw the light of day for funerals or other sombre occasions, but it was my best one and I made a mental note to put it out for Mrs Parsons to clean.

The minute I walked in through the garden gate I knew something was dreadfully wrong, for both Mrs Shaw and Aunt Margaret were waiting at the door, concerned looks on their faces.

"What is it?" I said.

"Ella ... " began my aunt.

"Dear god, there's news. Have they found him? Is he alive?"

"Come inside and Mrs Shaw will explain, dear."

It was with great agitation and impatience I fumbled with my buttons and eventually divested myself of my coat.

"It needs cleaning," I said to no one in particular as I followed Mrs Shaw through to the drawing room. "What is it? What's happened?"

"I received a telephone message not ten minutes ago. There was an accident. John was involved. I'm afraid there were no survivors. I am most dreadfully sorry, Miss Bridges."

"What sort of accident?"

"I'm afraid I can't tell you that."

"Can't or won't?"

"Can't. This is not a secure line and consequently the message I received was in a prearranged code. All I know is what I told you, except the accident happened in Scotland."

"Scotland? John was coming home?" I asked in a strangled voice, and suddenly I began to shiver. "I want to see him, Mrs Shaw."

"I'm sorry but that won't be possible."

"Then make it possible. I took the word of MI5 the last time you said he'd been killed and look what happened. I won't believe you until I see him for myself."

Mrs Shaw paused for a moment then gave a curt nod. "I'll make a call."

Once she'd left the room Aunt Margaret came an enfolded me in a hug.

"Oh, Ella, I'm so sorry, darling."

"It might not be him you know. They made a mistake last time, they could have done so again."

"I'm afraid they are quite sure this time."

"Well, I need to be just as sure. I can't go on living the rest of my life in limbo not knowing."

Mrs Shaw returned at that moment.

"Well?" I asked.

"I've been instructed to take you both to RAF Andover. It's an hour and a half drive so we should go now."

"John's at a military airbase?"

"Yes."

We gathered our belongings and were soon on our way. The journey seemed interminably long and was spent mostly in silence. My aunt and I sat in the back and she gripped my hand the entire time. I was grateful for the contact and the comfort it brought, I'd never felt so alone.

After what seemed like hours we pulled up at a barrier where a guard spoke to Mrs Shaw through the window, peered into the back at us, then saluted. Moving the barrier to one side he stood in position saluting while we drove forward. Five minutes later we were pulling up outside a hangar where an official-looking black car was waiting and a familiar figure alighted.

"Miss Bridges," said the Home Secretary. "Please accept my sincere condolences. I'm terribly sorry for your loss."

Dusk was almost upon us and a dark looming sky threatened rain overhead. Baxter was right, it was fitting.

"What can you tell me?" I asked.

"We received notification that an aircraft of German make had crashed in a farmer's field in Scotland. There were three men aboard, the pilot and two passengers. Both the pilot and one of the passengers have yet to be formally identified but we believe them to be German. The other passenger was your husband. We had no prior intelligence to indicate this aircraft was headed here, nor the reasons why."

"But you believe John was aiding a member of the German government who wished to escape?"

"It's a theory but that's all it is, we have no way of knowing. However we are looking into it. I'm afraid that's all I can tell you, Miss Bridges."

I nodded.

"I'd like to see my husband now, Lord Carrick," I said in a voice I didn't recognise.

The hangar was a cavernous space, cold and mostly empty but all I saw was a casket on a table in the centre, lid raised waiting for me to lay eyes on my husband for the last time. I took a deep breath and clutching Aunt Margaret's arm I walked forward on legs that felt as weak as a new born colt's.

I spent the next two days in bed, listless, lethargic and utterly exhausted having cried a well of tears. I had recognised John straightaway, although he had changed considerably since the last time I had seen him. There was a smattering of grey in his hair, fine lines at his eyes and mouth and he'd lost weight, the stresses and strains of his job I supposed. But in the main he was the husband I had once known and loved, and now I had lost him forever.

I turned as the door opened and Aunt Margaret came in bearing a breakfast tray. She had done the same thing each morning since we'd returned and had taken it away again a few hours later, barely touched. This time she laid the tray as normal but then sat on my bed.

"Ella, you can't go on like this, it's doing you no good at all. You need to get up today. Sergeant Baxter has called and so has Agnes, and I've made your excuses but I shan't do it anymore, you need to speak with them yourself. Now I'm not leaving until you've eaten every last crumb of your breakfast, you need to keep your energy up."

And so she went on, badgering, cajoling and bullying until I sat up and began to nibble at the toast.

"It's not much fun being here alone, you know. Of course I'm quite capable of keeping myself occupied but it's difficult when it's not one's own house."

"Not above a little blackmail, I see?"

"Anything to get you to join the living again, dear. Did it work?"

"Yes, of course it did," I said with a brief smile.

"I'm glad, Ella, we are all missing you downstairs."

"Do you know, Aunt Margaret, I must be the only woman ever to have been widowed twice by the same man."

"Perhaps not the only one, darling, but undoubtedly it's a very exclusive club. Now finish your tea and I'll take your tray."

Half an hour later I was dressed and made my way downstairs feeling more human than I had for a while. The message from Baxter was simply that there was no news from the food tests as yet, but he would let me know as soon as he heard. The one from Agnes said she'd be grateful if I could accompany her to visit Mrs Whittingstall, if my time allowed.

"It will do you good to get out, Ella, and with the case at a standstill you have time on your hands. From what I understand from Agnes, the woman might appreciate some female company, her husband is quite ill."

"Would you like to come, Aunt Margaret?"

"I'm afraid I can't. I met an old friend, Constance Burridge, on the promenade yesterday and we're meeting for tea and canasta later."

"Burridge? Of Burridge's department store?" I asked.

"That's the one. She's here with her sister. Sir Algernon is far too busy running the empire to accompany her."

"I didn't realise you knew Lady Burridge, how did the two of you meet?"

"Oh, I met her husband first. I helped him out of a rather sticky situation regarding a set of counterfeit Ming vases and a high stakes poker game. Constance and I became firm friends after that. Now if there's nothing else, dear, I need to get on." And she departed the drawing room like a ship in full sail.

"Would you like me to drive you to the hotel?" I called to her retreating back.

"No need, darling, Constance is sending a car."

I'd arranged to pick Agnes up at St. Mary's and as I parked she came hurrying out from under the lych-gate, a basket covered in a red and white checked cloth over her arm.

"Hello, Ella," she said breathlessly. "Thank you for coming with me. I do hope you are feeling better now, your aunt said you've been feeling a bit below par?"

"I'm quite well now, Agnes, thank you for asking."

"Is there any news about the investigation?" she whispered, even though there was only the two of us in the car.

"Nothing as yet, inquiries are still ongoing. There's some delicious smells coming from that basket. Is it a gift for Mrs Whittingstall?"

"Yes, mother and I have baked some scones and an apple pie for her, I doubt she has much time to bake, what with nursing her husband."

"She doesn't have a cook?"

"As far as I know it's just the two of them. She prefers it that way I suppose as they aren't short of money for help."

"What time is she expecting us?"

"Um, actually I'm afraid she isn't. Sorry, I had no way of contacting her you see, only directions to the house. Oh dear, do you think it will be all right?"

Taking my eyes off the road for a moment I glanced at her. Her large eyes were filled with worry and an embarrassed hue tinged her cheeks.

"Well, either we will be made welcome or it will be a short-lived visit, either way our intentions are good. But we'll soon find out. I believe this is the place?"

Agnes peered through the windscreen.

"Yes, this is it."

I parked the car outside and we walked up the short drive to the front door. The house was quite large with a small garden to the front laid mostly to lawn, and a few wilted shrubs striving for life on its periphery. From the road the house had looked quite well kept but close to it was apparent it needed work. The paint was beginning to peel from the front door and several of the window frames were rotten. The glass panes themselves were quite clean but behind them were net curtains so thick it was impossible to see inside.

Agnes knocked on the door and almost immediately I saw a slight twitch of a curtain in the right hand side window. But several seconds passed and no one answered, so I knocked again a little louder. This time someone came.

I didn't know what I'd expected but the stunning young woman before us was certainly not it. She was quite beautiful with a flawless complexion, light blue eyes and a discreet beauty mark above the right side of her lip. Her pale blond hair was perfectly set in waves and curled about petite ears, which in turn were set with small diamond and pearl earrings. She looked familiar but I couldn't think where I'd seen her before unless it was at the church. Yes, of course, this was the lady who had knocked into me that first day. With everything that had happened since I'd forgotten all about it.

"Can I help you?" she asked in perfectly modulated tones.

"Mrs Whittingstall?" asked Agnes quietly.

"Yes."

"My name is Agnes, and this is my friend Ella. We're from the 'Friends of St. Mary's.'"

"If you're looking for a donation I'm afraid…"

"Oh, goodness me, no, nothing of the sort. Sorry, we just came to visit to see if there is anything we could do for you. My mother and I…"

While Agnes explained our impromptu visit to the perplexed Mrs Whittingstall I took in what little I could see of the house behind her. Next to the door was an oak hall stand filled with several umbrellas, walking canes, three golf clubs and disconcertingly, a shotgun. The latter of which I fervently hoped wasn't loaded as our visit hadn't been particularly well received. Above were several hooks on which hung a variety of outdoor coats and hats. Beyond was a small sideboard with a framed photograph, which I could barely make out but thought was of an older gentleman dressed in shooting clothes, a shotgun over his shoulder, proudly holding up a brace of pheasants. On the far wall facing the door was a painting by an artist I was familiar with and when Agnes paused for breath I mentioned it.

"I see you have a DuPont, Mrs Whittingstall. I've recently acquired one myself."

"I beg your pardon?"

"The painting on your wall back there, a Pierre DuPont?"

She glanced behind her then shrugged elegantly.

"It's my husband's. I know nothing of it. Now if there is nothing else …"

"Just the apple pie and scones," said Agnes raising her basket with a smile.

"I'm afraid I don't like apple pie, or scones, and my husband is unable to eat them. In fact, I believe I've just heard his bell. If you'll excuse me …"

And with that she shut the door.

Agnes and I looked at each other in mutual shock at her rudeness.

"Oh dear," she sniffed, the sparkling of unshed tears in her eyes.

"Don't let her upset you, Agnes, not everyone is as gracious or generous as you. Come on, I think afternoon tea is in order, and I believe there is a lovely little tea shop on the promenade which has just opened."

We were halfway down the drive when we were met by the postman who was delivering a letter.

"Good afternoon, Miss Bridges, Miss Shepherd," he said, tipping his hat. "A lovely day for a visit, isn't it?"

"It is a lovely day although it was rather a short visit. I'm afraid I should have called ahead, we caught her unexpectedly," said Agnes dejectedly.

"Oh, I wouldn't worry too much, Miss Shepherd, she's a bit of a strange one, very private. Well, I'll not keep you. You have a good afternoon."

We said our goodbyes and carried on to the car, but not before I had seen the return address of the letter he was delivering, nor the black cat with purple collar sitting on the garden wall, eying the house with haughty disdain. It appeared as though Phantom didn't like Mrs Whittingstall much either.

CHAPTER EIGHT

I returned home in the early evening having had a lovely afternoon with Agnes. She had cheered up enormously and insisted I take the pie and scones home.

"It would be such a shame to waste them and we already have far more than we can eat ourselves," she said.

So of course I acquiesced, the tempting smells had been making my mouth water all afternoon.

I found Mrs Shaw in my office, working on the compendium, but of Aunt Margaret there was no sign.

"Has my aunt not returned yet?"

"She telephoned earlier to say she would be staying on for dinner and not to wait up. She sounded in high spirits."

I smiled to myself. Knowing my aunt as I was beginning to, I wouldn't be surprised if the sedate game of canasta had turned into a rousing game of poker, to which half the hotel had been invited.

"Oh, and this came for you. Special delivery."

Mrs Shaw handed me a large cardboard folder. Quickly untying the red ribbon I carefully opened it and removed the handwritten note. It was from Sergeant Baxter.

"Mrs Shaw, come and look at these."

"My goodness, they're wonderful and perfect for the compendium. He certainly is a man of many talents," she said as she peered over my shoulder at the exquisitely rendered drawings.

"He is indeed. He's as good a detective as he is an artist too. His note says he's been spending some time in various parts of London, drawing from life."

"Well, he's certainly captured a broad representation of people, that's for sure. From the wealthy having a constitutional around Hyde Park, to the poor of the East End and everything in between it looks like."

"Criminals come in all shapes and sizes and from all walks of life as Sergeant Baxter well knows. I think he's done an exceptional job and I shall call to tell him so in the morning."

But as it happened I didn't get the chance, for he telephoned me first thing the next day with the news we had been waiting for.

"I received the results from the laboratory this morning. We were right, Miss Bridges."

"Where was it found?" I asked.

"I don't want to say more over the telephone, but I'm booked on the next train and will be at Linhay station at ten thirty."

"I'll have Mrs Shaw meet you and bring you back to the cottage, we can discuss it in more detail here. I must also thank you for your splendid drawings, they are absolutely perfect."

"Well, I used a bit of artistic license; hopefully the models won't recognise themselves if they chance upon them."

"I doubt they will, you've done a remarkable job. The way you caught the sneer of the lip on the bespectacled gentleman and the shift of the eye in the angry young man were astonishing, I …"

"Miss Bridges, are yer still there? 'Ello?"

"Yes. Yes, I apologise, Sergeant, something just occurred to me."

"About the case?"

"I'm not sure. I have a feeling I'm on the cusp of something but the pieces are eluding me at present, it's quite maddening. But never mind I'm sure it will come to me soon. I'll see you shortly, Baxter, and thank you again."

Shortly after eleven o' clock Sergeant Baxter and I were seated in the drawing room while Mrs Parsons served tea.

"There, I think that's everything," she said, eying the tray with satisfaction.

"Thank you, Mrs Parsons."

"Oh, and while I remember, I've cleaned your good black coat. Goodness knows what was on it but it's all come out now and is as good as new. But you left this in the pocket, it's a good job I didn't dunk it in a bowl of suds otherwise it would have been nothing more than a soggy mess, and that would have ruined your good coat and no mistake."

She delved into the front pocket of her apron and handed me a plain brown envelope, sealed but devoid of any writing.

"Right, if there's nothing more, I'll go and prepare some lunch, then I'll be off."

"Yes, of course, thank you, Mrs Parsons."

I eyed the envelope in confusion.

"What is it?" asked Baxter.

"I've no idea. It's certainly not mine, I've never seen it before."

I retrieved the letter opener from the table and sliced open the envelope. Then carefully withdrew the folded paper nestled inside and opened it.

"Oh, my word! I think you had better take a look at this, Sergeant."

Baxter peered over my shoulder and read the note. It wasn't handwritten but instead made up of letters cut from newspapers and magazines, which in itself was unusual. But it was what the words themselves said that were cause for concern.

'ASK JB WOT THE VICAR SORE IN THE STABLE.'

"JB must mean Jocasta Blenkinsop," I said.

"I agree, especially as it also mentions stables. Miss Bridges, you need to think back. How and when were this note slipped into your pocket?"

I sat and sipped my tea while I thought.

"The only time I have worn that particular coat since I've been living on Linhay was at the memorial service for Father Michael, so it must have happened then. But there were so many people there, where on earth do we start?"

"I doubt it were inside the church. Nearly everyone arrived afore we did and I were next to you the whole time. No it musta happened when we were all congregatin' outside. There were quite a crowd and we were jostled a few times if memory serves."

"Yes, we were but one in particular sticks in my mind. Do you remember I was bumped into quite sharply and would have fallen if you hadn't caught me? I think it was then, in fact I'm quite sure of it."

"Can you recall what the person looked like?"

"A young girl, pale with freckles and red hair. On the plump side and definitely in service by the cut of her clothes, and the atrocious spelling in the note would bear out that thinking."

"Well, she shouldn't be too 'ard to find. Are you thinking what I am? That she's in the employ of the Blenkinsop's?" asked Baxter.

"I think it most likely. I mean if she is responsible for the note then it would make sense. I can't imagine many people would refer to the lady of the household as JB, it's overly familiar but it is something the staff would do her behind her back."

"We need to pay another visit to the 'ouse, but I don't want to show our 'and too soon. Any ideas?"

"I think the simplest approach would be to make an appointment."

"You do?"

"I'll telephone now and say I wish for her advice about my walled garden. When we're there, while I keep her occupied you can make an excuse to leave the room, then find and talk to the girl."

"I must say I'm glad yer on the right side of the law, Miss Bridges, you'd make a fine criminal."

"Why what a lovely compliment, Sergeant."

The telephone call was short and sweet, and I returned moments later to Baxter who was just polishing off a last mouthful of apple pie.

"Well, Sergeant, all the subterfuge is completely unnecessary. Jocasta is currently in London with her husband and won't return until tomorrow evening. I've taken the liberty of arranging to see the housekeeper. She's expecting us in half an hour."

On the journey to the Blenkinsop's house Baxter confirmed what I already knew; it was the tea found in Father Michael's cupboard which had tested positive for the poison.

"We've found a set o' prints too, so we'll be able to match 'em with a suspect when we 'ave one. You mentioned he ordered 'is tea in specially, d'you know where from?"

"Yes, Carnaby's Emporium. It's in a small town called Broughton not far from Sheffield. It's where Aunt Margaret lives actually. I visited the emporium last time I was there."

"How is yer aunt by the way? Is she still with you, I didn't see 'er this mornin'?"

"Oh yes, she's still here but she was up and out early. She has some friends staying at the hotel and had made arrangements to spend the day with them. Baxter, do you think it's possible the poison was introduced into the tea at Carnaby's before it was delivered to the vicarage?"

"I find anythin' is possible when it comes to murder, Miss Bridges, it's staggerin' the lengths some people will go to. We'll keep it at the back of our minds but I think the best course is to follow up clues nearer to 'ome first, rather than tearin' all over the country."

"Yes, I suppose it's not the best use of our time. Nonetheless, if it's all right with you I think I will speak to Aunt Margaret and see what she can find out. She's one of their best customers and I suspect she knows the owner."

"It can't do any harm, and the more we know the better; we'll be prepared should a visit be required."

"My thoughts exactly. Now I think I'll drive around to the servants' entrance," I said as we reached the turning for the Blenkinsop's house and started up the drive.

"Catch 'em unprepared," Baxter nodded approvingly.

"You never know what we may find."

I parked the car a reasonable distance from the door so as not to announce our arrival too soon, and just as I had switched off the engine a pale young girl with freckles and tendrils of red hair escaping from her cap came out into the yard carrying a bucket overflowing with dirty water.

"That's her. She must be the scullery maid," I said.

"We're on the right track then, Miss Bridges. Let's make the acquaintance of the 'ousekeeper then we can ask to speak to this maid. What were the 'ousekeeper's name again?"

"Mrs Brown."

By the time we reached the door to the kitchen the maid had disappeared, but we were greeted by a footman named Johnson who had been taking a quick break to smoke a cigarette around the corner.

"Here to see Mrs Brown, you say? I'll take you to her office if you'd like to follow me," he said amiably.

We followed him through the busy kitchen and down a long hallway, where open doors showed a range of servants hard at work polishing boots, ironing laundry, mending clothes, cleaning silver and a vast array of other duties needed to keep a large household running smoothly. Presently we came to an unremarkable door, where the footman knocked once and upon hearing a reply opened it.

"Visitors, Mrs Brown. A Miss Bridges and a Sergeant Baxter."

"Of course, do come in and have a seat. Johnson, go and ask Tilly to prepare a tea tray please."

Once Johnson had left in search of Tilly, Mrs Brown turned back to us. She was a neat woman of middling height and middling age, wearing an old fashioned brown house-keeping dress and a chatelaine at her waist.

"You're a tad early, I'm afraid you've caught me balancing the housekeeping."

Indeed there was a large ledger open on the desk in front of her filled with columns of neat writing.

"It seems to me the cost of groceries goes up every week, but only the best will do for Mrs Blenkinsop. Always been that way, always will be. Now what can I do you for you?"

I let Baxter take the lead.

"Mrs Brown, thank you fer seein' us at short notice. We're investigatin' the death of the vicar over at St. Mary's, no doubt you've heard about it?"

"I should say so, it's been the talk of the village since it happened. Such a tragedy and a man of the cloth too. I assume it's something suspicious considering you're here?"

"Only insofar as he was quite young, Mrs Brown. We have to investigate all sudden deaths as you probably know. Did you know Father Michael?" I asked.

"I'm sorry no, I didn't. I worship at St. James's, you see."

"But some of the staff here attend St Mary's? I believe I recognised your scullery maid in the yard just now."

"That would be Betty. Yes, she attends St Mary's along with several of the other staff. But I doubt she will be much help, head in the clouds that one. Mooning about all over the place imagining she's in love with every young man who sets foot in the place. It's her age I'm afraid, but what can you do? Although I must admit her work has improved somewhat since Dawkins has gone. Of course that infatuation was going nowhere, he was completely out of her league, although she couldn't see it. But then again I doubt she'll amount to much, not the brightest button in the tin I'm afraid."

"What can you tell us about this Dawkins?" asked Baxter, who was scribbling notes in his black book.

"He was one of the grooms. An exceptionally handsome young man, personable, had a way with the horses and was very good at his job by all accounts. I don't oversee the riding school employees but of course he came up to the house for his meals, and was always very polite. He was a popular member of the staff but … "

"What is it, Mrs Brown?" I asked.

"Well, I always found it rather odd that Alfred would have taken the position in the first place. He's strictly middle class you see, from a good family and very well educated. He always carried a book in his pocket and I'd often find him reading Shakespeare or Dickens. You would have thought it would have driven a wedge between the other staff and him, wouldn't you? But it was never the case. He had no airs or graces and preferred to be called Alfie. He'd also muck in doing any job that was needed and do it with a smile on his face. But by the same token he never hid where he came from, nor his education. He was simply perfectly at ease with everyone and they with him."

"It seems odd considering all you've just said that he would no longer be working here. Was he dismissed?"

Mrs Brown paused here for a moment as though trying to think of a suitably tactful reply.

"To be honest, we all thought it was a bit strange when he left, but you can't know what goes through a young man's mind, can you? According to Mrs Blenkinsop, he had found a better position elsewhere."

"She came and told you that herself, did she?" I asked.

"Yes. Gathered us all in the kitchen yonder and announced that he had left the previous evening. We didn't see him again."

"When were this?" Baxter asked, still furiously scribbling.

"Toward the end of September. But how does this have anything to do with the death of the vicar?"

Baxter smiled genially.

"We're not sure it does, Mrs Brown, just getting the facts straight is all. Can you tell us if Father Michael ever visited 'ere?"

"I believe he came to see Mrs Blenkinsop two or three times when he first arrived, although he did have a tendency to turn up unannounced on that bicycle of his so it could have been more. Church business I supposed, she's heavily involved with the fundraising and does the flowers, you see. Although I hadn't seen him for a long time before... well before he passed on."

"Thank you, Mrs Brown," I said. "I think that's all for the moment. Now we'd like to have a word with Betty, in private. Would you like us to use another room or can we remain in here? I don't want to put you out of your office if it's inconvenient."

"Oh, er, of course you can stay in here. I need to speak with the cook about tomorrow's menu anyway. But are you sure it's Betty, you wish to speak to? She's just a simple scullery maid, I doubt she knows anything of use."

"Quite sure, Mrs Brown, thank you."

"All right, well, I'll send her in and find out what's keeping Tilly with the tea."

••‹‹◇››••

Tilly came in not long after Mrs Brown had left and laid the tea tray in silence. Giving a small curtsy she left as quietly as she had arrived, and Baxter and I were left alone while we waited for Betty.

"So what are yer thoughts so far, Miss Bridges?"

"I think after we have spoken to Betty, we need to find the groom Dawkins. There is most assuredly more going on in that regard than at first appears."

"They're my thoughts too. I 'ave a nasty feeling we're about to find out something that'll blow this case wide open."

I sighed heavily. "A possible motive you mean?"

Baxter nodded.

I began to pour the tea, my mind in a whirl, when the door suddenly opened and Betty entered. She was even younger than I had first thought, thirteen or fourteen perhaps, certainly no older.

"Sit down, Betty," I said without preamble, indicating Mrs Brown's recently vacated chair. She hesitated for a moment, then did as she was told. "I'll come straight to the point." Reaching into my bag I removed the note and laid it on the desk in front of her. "You slipped this into my pocket at Father Michael's memorial service the other day. Why?"

"Twern't me, miss."

I had been prepared for such a denial after the description of the girl from Mrs Brown.

"It seems you haven't been as clever as you think you have, Betty. You see I recognise you. Bumping into me as harshly as you did nearly made me fall so I was bound to look to see who was responsible. Plus of course, Sergeant Baxter and myself are detectives, very good ones in fact, and I'm sure the fingerprints on this note will undoubtedly match yours. Did you know fingerprints can be taken from notes such as this and matched to a specific person? No two prints are the same, you see. I learned that in my previous murder case. A case which I solved by the way. Now do you want to try again? What does this note mean and why did you put it in my pocket?"

At my deliberately stern pronouncement Betty's plain plump face crumpled and she dissolved into floods of tears. I fished in my bag for a handkerchief, which she filled noisily then tried to return.

"Do keep it," I said.

"She took 'im from me. He loved me and she took 'im from me," she suddenly blurted out.

"Who do you mean, Betty? Mrs Blenkinsop?"

She nodded.

"Who did she take from you?"

"Alfie," she wailed amid another bout of tears.

I looked at Baxter who shrugged and nodded for me to continue. Obviously dealing with hysterical young girls was to be my job.

"Do you mean Alfred Dawkins, the groom?"

She nodded again and looked up at me. Her pale skin had broken out into ugly red blotches and her eyes were swollen from all the tears. She looked positively wretched.

"Look, just tell us exactly what happened, Betty, from the beginning."

"I saw 'em together. T'were me afternoon off and I was just comin' round the corner of the 'ouse when I saw the vicar leavin' the stables. He looked like he'd seen a ghost, so I sneaked round the side and that's when I saw 'em. They was undressed and had been lyin' in the hay. The mistress grabbed a blanket and ran to the stable door. She must 'ave seen the vicar cyclin' away 'cos she came back and said to Alfie to get dressed quickly and leave, and to keep 'is mouth shut. Next day he was gone."

I glanced at Baxter's notebook while Betty recovered herself and saw him underline the word motive twice.

We'd eventually extracted information from Betty which led us to believe Alfred Dawkins was currently employed at the Hardcastle Livery Stables, situated on the northern side of Linhay. So we said our goodbyes and with an air of gloom set off to find him.

"It all fits," said Baxter a while later.

"I know."

"Once we've got this Dawkins's statement we'll 'ave to formally interview Mrs Blenkinsop."

"Yes. She's back from London early tomorrow evening. I suppose we'll have to do it then?"

"We'll 'ave to make sure we're there when she arrives, no doubt 'er staff will mention our visit if they get to 'er first. I only 'ope Betty keeps quiet like she promised."

"I'm quite sure she will, Baxter. Don't forget she saw Jocasta and this Dawkins in the stable herself, yet she hasn't mentioned it to anyone. The only time she has broken her silence was when she found out Father Michael was dead and she made contact with me via the note. Even then she tried to do it anonymously."

"Well I 'ope you're right."

"Jocasta is coming in on the quarter to five train by the way, perhaps we could contrive to be at the station to meet her? By coincidence naturally. Of course we'll have to let her driver know not to pick her up."

"Leave it with me," he said, and we once more lapsed into silence, each of us with our own thoughts.

The more we'd talked to Betty the more pity I had felt for her. She'd been brought up by a drunk and absentee father, who had finally met his maker by way of two bottles of cheap whiskey and the river two years ago, her mother having passed on when she was just six. The Friends of St Mary's had taken it upon themselves to find her gainful employment to avoid the orphanage, or worse, a Public Assistance Institution. Which up until five years ago was aptly named The Workhouse. Jocasta had stepped forward with a position of scullery maid and Betty had been in her employ ever since.

However, I was having difficulty uniting this plain simple girl with the description Mrs Brown had given us of 'the exceptionally handsome' Alfie Dawkins, and so had asked...

"Betty, did you and Alfie have an understanding?"

At her look of incomprehension I tried again.

"I mean to say did you think that you and Alfie were a couple?"

She looked up at me coyly through swollen red-rimmed eyes, and short lashes so pale they were almost invisible and said...

"I think so, miss."

"And what made you think so, Betty?"

"He were nice to me, miss. He talked to me when he come up to the 'ouse, and he brought me a posy once, daisies and the like from the back field."

"I see. And did he talk to the other girls or bring them posies?" I asked gently.

She shrugged, a sullen look on her face.

"S'pose so. But mine were nicer and he talked to me more."

I'd left it then, no longer wishing to pry into the heart of a young and impressionable girl, who had been so devoid of love and affection for most of her life that she'd latched onto the first person who showed her any true kindness.

Baxter's voice when he suddenly spoke made me jump, as I'd been completely lost in my thoughts.

"We're here, Miss Bridges."

The Hardcastle Livery Stables was a very well patronised and thriving business, catering to the rich and famous who paid a weekly fee for their horses to be taken care of, and who occasionally visited when a suitable gap in their social calendar allowed. It was run in the main by a manager, the owner being a foreign gentleman who rarely set foot in the country, and he came out of the office to greet us as we pulled up.

"Good afternoon, may I help you?"

Baxter introduced us both and explained why we were there.

"Alfie Dawkins? Yes, you'll find him over in the stable block. Not in any trouble, is he? I don't employ trouble-makers here."

"No trouble, we just 'ave some questions regarding 'is previous employer."

"All right, well just go through the archway there and follow the path round to the right. The stable block's at the end."

We thanked the manager and proceeded to the afore-mentioned block, where we found an athletically built youth in shirtsleeves grooming a beautiful bay mare. There was no doubt this was Alfie Dawkins, Mrs Brown's description had been highly accurate. He was perhaps twenty years of age, six feet tall, with jet black hair styled slightly longer than was fashionable, and which flopped over his forehead momentarily hiding deep brown eyes. Kind eyes, filled with humour and intelligence. He flashed a friendly smile on our approach, displaying a set of perfectly straight white teeth. This was a young man who was completely at ease with himself. A modern-day Adonis who would have caused the heart of the most stoical old maid to flutter, but I believed he truly had no idea how breathtaking he was.

"Alfie Dawkins?" inquired Baxter.

"Yes, Sir?"

"Sergeant Baxter, and this 'ere is Miss Bridges. We'd like to ask you a few questions about Mrs Blenkinsop. I understand you were employed by her previously?"

"That's right I was. Is she all right, Sergeant?"

The concern on his face was genuine and I saw immediately he had cared for Jocasta a great deal.

"For the moment she is, son. Can you tell me the circumstances which led to your dismissal from Briarlea?"

"I'm sure you know the circumstances, Sergeant, otherwise you wouldn't be here. But I wasn't dismissed. I chose to go."

"You did, did you? And why was that? You 'ad a good job there, a regular wage and plenty of scope for promotion. Why give it all up voluntarily? What made you do it?"

"To save the reputation of a woman you'd come to care for. That's right, isn't it?" I said to the youth.

"Yes, Miss Bridges, it is. Jocasta had everything to lose whereas I could pick up and start again elsewhere. As long as I'm working with horses and in the fresh air, I'm happy."

"How did it happen, Alfie? The affair I mean," I asked.

He glanced into the yard and I saw it was beginning to fill up with other workers.

"Let me put Acorn back in her stable then perhaps we could take a walk?"

Baxter and I agreed and soon we were walking through open fields while Alfie talked.

"I grew up in a house of women. My mother and three sisters, two older, one younger. My father works on the railways so is out from dawn 'til dusk, and you can't grow up surrounded by females and not learn something about them. I've always had an affinity with animals, especially horses. I don't believe there to be a more majestic creature on earth, so when the job came up at Briarlea, I immediately applied and got it, much to my father's chagrin unfortunately. It was like a dream come true being paid for doing a job I loved most, but I soon realised how lonely Jocasta really was. We became friends to start with, you see. I know how ridiculous that sounds, the lady of the house becoming friends with a lowly groom, but that's how it happened. Forgive my crudeness, Miss Bridges, but it wasn't all rolling about in the hay. In fact it wasn't about that at all really, she needed someone to talk to and I was a good listener. She started to seek me out especially, oh, just to talk about the school and the horses and the general running of things to begin with, but then it became more personal. You see she was surrounded by the best that money could buy and if she didn't have it she could simply purchase it. But the one thing she really wanted couldn't be bought for all the money in the world."

"Love," I said simply.

Alfie nodded.

"She told me she married young, and although her husband was twenty years older than her, she loved him. The early years were very happy ones for her, especially with the birth of her sons, but as time went on things changed. Mr Blenkinsop started spending more time in London, her boys were sent away to school and suddenly she found herself in a big house all alone."

"So she tried to find things to fill her time, like the riding school and the rare plants and getting involved with the church?" I asked.

"Yes, but it didn't fill the void."

"You're a very astute and well educated young man, Alfie," I said.

"My father is a clever man, Miss Bridges. My mother is a private music teacher, she doesn't need to work of course, it's for the sheer joy of it. And my sisters are all academically and artistically inclined, as well as being avid bookworms. Some of it was bound to rub off on me."

"What exactly is your father's position with the railway, Alfie?" I asked.

"He's Chief Mechanical Engineer with Southern Railway."

"I see. A high level managerial position with considerable responsibility. How does he feel about you working as a groom? You mentioned he was rather put out at your securing the job at Briarlea."

"I suppose it's natural for all fathers to want their sons to follow in their footsteps, and mine was no different. But from the moment I could walk I've been happiest outdoors among the animals and nature. Mother thinks I was born with the soul of a nomad or a gypsy and I think she's right. My father was somewhat disappointed initially, but even he could see how miserable I would have been if he'd forced me. He's come round now and is perfectly accepting of my working with horses. Especially considering my younger sister Emily is showing signs of being very interested in engineering."

"Do you attend church?" asked Baxter.

If Alfie was surprised at the abrupt change in subject he didn't show it. Instead he spread his arms wide.

"This is my church, Sergeant Baxter. We're all God's creations, are we not? From the lowliest beetle to the King of the land. I don't need a building to worship in to be a good Christian. Many people do and that's their way, it's just not mine."

It struck me then how much Aunt Margaret and this young man had in common, and if circumstances had been different I'm sure they could have found themselves in an odd sort of friendship.

It was a second or two later as Baxter and I kept walking that we realised Alfie had stopped, so we turned around. He eyed us thoughtfully for a moment then spoke.

"Well, I'm certainly slow on the uptake today. You're here about the death of the vicar, aren't you?"

He indicated we should make the return journey to the stables, so we continued to walk back the way we'd come.

"Yes, we are. Did you know Father Michael?" Baxter asked.

"Never had the pleasure."

"We 'ave been led to believe the day afore you left Briarlea for good, Father Michael chanced upon you and

Mrs Blenkinsop together in the stables. Can you shed any further light on that, son?"

"Not really, I didn't see him myself. Jocasta said she heard a noise so she grabbed a horse blanket and went to the stable door. She returned saying she'd just seen the vicar bicycling down the drive and she was convinced he'd seen us. We parted ways, but that night she sought me out in floods of tears, terrified her husband would find out. I calmed her down and explained that for her sake it would be best if I left. She disagreed to start with, but we talked it through and eventually she came to realise it was the only option. I haven't seen her since.

"Do you know … " he continued as we neared the stables.

"One of the jobs we have is to get rid of the mice and rats? They come in for the horse feed and make their little nests in the hay, if you don't do something about them you're quite overrun in a matter of weeks. It was the same up at Briarlea, but instead of putting down poison Jocasta made these little traps that would catch them unharmed, ingenious little device actually. Then she'd drive up to the woods or down to the river and set them free. She said they were God's creatures as much as we were and what right did we have to kill them?"

He stopped as we approached the stable bay where he'd returned the mare earlier, and looked at us both in turn.

"If you think Jocasta had anything to do with the death of Father Michael, you're wrong. Someone who couldn't even bring themselves to kill a rat could never hurt another human being."

CHAPTER NINE

I t was early evening by the time I returned to the cottage after dropping Baxter off at Elsie's boarding house, and I was absolutely famished. I'd had nothing to eat since the mid-morning tea and my stomach was literally growling in complaint.

I found Aunt Margaret in the small sitting room waiting for me.

"Ella, there you are, dear. Did you have a successful day?" she asked, laying the book she had been reading on the side table.

I flopped down in a chair suddenly exhausted.

"Well we certainly know a lot more now than we did, Aunt. I'll explain everything shortly, but I must eat first, I'm feeling quite faint with hunger."

"Yes, I thought that might be the case, dinner will be ready in ten minutes so you just have time to change."

I scurried upstairs and came down ten minutes later to the sounds of clinking crockery coming from the dining room.

"Salmon-en-Croute, new potatoes in herb butter and a medley of vegetables," my aunt announced, lifting various lids.

"My goodness, did Mrs Parsons make all this?"

"Of course not, dear, I had it delivered from the hotel. I fancied something a little different and the chefs there are quite excellent. There's treacle tart for desert."

"Oh, Aunt Margaret, I feel quite ashamed. I've been neglecting you terribly, haven't I?"

"Absolute nonsense, I'm having a perfectly lovely time. However, please promise me that when this case is over you will make a concerted effort to find yourself some proper staff? You need a full-time cook, a housekeeper and a maid, you're becoming far too busy to manage everything alone and Mrs Shaw will be leaving soon."

"Oh dear, yes I suppose she will be now John has been found and the news leaked to those that were a threat. I hadn't given it much thought to be honest, she's become rather a fixture around the place."

I ate with unseemly gusto as I mused on how to broach a particular subject with Mrs Shaw. It had been on my mind since I'd found out her true purpose for being here, but I'd come up blank as to the best way to ask, it was such an unseemly subject.

"I know what you're thinking," my aunt said.

I laughed out loud at the pronouncement knowing full well she probably did.

"Do tell."

"Mrs Shaw's wages. You were paying her as your housekeeper before you knew who she really was, but she was also being paid by the Home Office."

I stared open-mouthed.

"How do you do that?"

"It's a gift, dear."

"You'd make a lot of money as a fortune teller you know."

"It's uncanny you should say that ... but no, that's another story. Rest assured it's all been quite above board, the wages you paid have all been deposited back into your bank account and Mrs Shaw has all the necessary receipts."

"Well, that is a relief, I was worrying about how to raise the subject. Thank you, Aunt Margaret."

"Think nothing of it, Ella. Now tell me where have you got to with the case."

I informed her of how the poison had been found in Father Michael's special supply of tea, and explained in detail the interviews with Mrs Brown, Betty and Alfie Dawkins. Over coffee and a digestif in the sitting room, my aunt gave me her thoughts.

"From what you tell me it's looking increasingly worse for Mrs Blenkinsop. She had the means at her disposal in the form of the poisonous seeds, more than enough opportunity with both her work at the church and as the vicar's housekeeper, and now it seems you've discovered the motive. Her affair with the groom should it come to light would mean the loss of everything she holds dear, her marriage, her children, not to mention her reputation. It was Father Michael who discovered them together and now he's been murdered. But even in the face of all this you're still not convinced she's guilty, are you?"

"No, I'm not. It's all circumstantial at best, and if you take Jocasta out of the picture as a suspect then I think it could quite easily be someone else who killed Father Michael."

"Well, who are your other suspects?"

"There is no one else unfortunately. But why wait so long to get rid of him if he posed such a threat? He discovered her infidelity last September, yet he wasn't killed until the following May."

"But he had been away for most of that time, had he not? Perhaps this was his reason for going, he needed time to think what he should do about his discovery. Perhaps he approached her on his return and told her his conscience wouldn't allow him to remain silent? Remember, Ella, lust is one of the seven deadly sins and each one goes against the root of Christianity. Adultery wouldn't be something Father Michael would take lightly."

"No, of course it wouldn't, but I feel as though I'm missing some crucial clue. Doesn't it seem a little too convenient that someone would break into Jocasta's greenhouse and steal the poisonous seeds? Then there is the tea. It's a Carnaby's blend, did I tell you that?"

"Yes, you did, but it's delivered countrywide, Ella. In fact I hear they may soon start supplying some of the larger London department stores, it's very popular."

"What can you tell me about them? Would it be possible, for instance, to poison the tea prior to it being shipped out?"

"I sincerely doubt it. The company is owned by the Fortnum brothers, whom I happen to know quite well, and the entire process is a heavily guarded secret. I've had the privilege of touring the factory and believe me the security is akin to that of the palace. No it's entirely impossible for someone to have tampered with it there."

"Well, I suppose that means it was someone either with legitimate access or who broke into the vicarage … Oh, my goodness, I've just remembered something."

I stood up and began to pace while I put my thoughts in order. Occasionally glancing at Phantom who was sitting staring at the black cat in the painting Pierre DuPont had gifted me.

"Aunt Margaret, do you remember me telling you I nearly ran over Agnes outside of St Mary's?"

"I do."

"Well, that was the first time we met. I also met Jocasta for the first time then too."

"Yes, and you helped with the flower arrangements, correct?"

"That's right, but we also had several hot drinks. It was so cold in the meeting room as the boiler had broken down and we needed something to warm us up. However, the tea had run out so Jocasta pinched some from the vicarage. Agnes and I had coffee but Jocasta drank the vicar's tea. However the most important clue is that she was perfectly fine afterwards."

"So it didn't contain poison then," my aunt said, quickly grasping onto the salient point.

"Exactly. But a few days later at the meeting for the fete committee, Agnes was terribly upset as she had forgotten to purchase more tea, so once again Jocasta purloined some from the vicarage. I remember quite clearly there were only three people who drank the tea that night. Jocasta, Anne, and Mrs Fielding."

"All of whom subsequently became quite poorly. That is very interesting, Ella."

"Isn't it? So the poison must have been introduced during the time between my first visit to St Mary's and the fete meeting. And if Jocasta knew there was Ricin in the tea then surely she would never have drunk it?"

"Well, it seems unlikely, but then again it's a clever way to cast suspicion elsewhere."

"Perhaps, but even if she was prepared to take a small amount of the poison herself, she would never risk her friends. Mrs Fielding is elderly and the poison affected her much more, she was quite seriously ill for a while. All of them have been visited by Doctor Wenhope since, and they all seem to be recovering, thank goodness."

"I think you're correct, Ella. But if Jocasta didn't poison the tea then who on earth did? And more to the point, why?"

The next morning with nothing much to keep me occupied until Baxter and I went to the train station to collect Jocasta, my aunt and I took a leisurely breakfast together then a walk around the garden.

"I'll be leaving tomorrow morning, Ella. And before you say anything I genuinely have had a lovely time. The cottage is adorable and the island quite enchanting, in fact I shall be visiting more often from now on."

"You know you're welcome any time, Aunt Margaret, it's been wonderful having you here, even though I've not spent as much time with you as I would have liked. Oh, and while I remember please do thank your housekeeper for the donations, it was very generous of her."

"I will. She'll be pleased to know they were such a valuable contribution."

"Aunt Margaret," I said, stopping and taking both her hands, "I can't thank you enough for being here and supporting me during the last weeks. When the news of John came through it was such a shock, and I don't think I would have managed at all without you."

"Oh, my darling girl, you are my family and I love you dearly. Of course I would take care of you. I'm just glad I was here with you when it happened. But take it from me, you are stronger than you know and don't ever forget it. But by the same token, have a good cry if you feel like it, there's no sense bottling it all up. Now, is there any news on when the extension to the Church will be built?"

"I'm afraid it's all rather up in the air at present with the loss of Father Michael. Plus of course, Jocasta was steering the committee, and while you and I know what's about to happen no one else does. Without Jocasta the building may not go ahead at all."

"So you're quite sure an arrest is imminent even after what we realised last night?"

"I don't think there will be any alternative considering the mounting evidence against her, but I will bring Baxter up to date before we interview Jocasta this evening and see what his thoughts are. I'm rather hoping we can avoid putting her in prison while we exhaust all other avenues."

"Like a house arrest you mean?" asked my aunt.

"Yes, something like that. Of course it will all depend on what she says. If she does break down and confess well … "

"She'll only do that if she is guilty and you've quite swayed me to your way of thinking, my dear. She does have much to lose but I'm not wholly certain she would commit murder to save it. What do you know of her husband? Could he have found out about the affair and murdered Father Michael, to save his wife?"

"It will be a question to put to her of course, but according to Alfie Dawkins, they never met unless they were absolutely certain Hubert Blenkinsop was in London. I don't see how he could have found out. But even if he did and decided not to confront his wife about it, how would he know the vicar had been a witness? No, the more I think about it the more I'm convinced that he was unaware of their liaisons."

"So we're back to square one with Jocasta being the only viable suspect," my aunt said with a sigh.

"I'm afraid we are."

At four thirty on the dot that evening, Baxter and I were sitting in the car at the station waiting for the four forty-five from Waterloo. I'd explained the poison had been added to the tea in between my first two visits to St Mary's, and who had drunk it.

"So we could easily 'ave been investigatin' four suspicious deaths rather than just one?" he said with a disbelieving shake of his head.

"Yes. Including that of our prime suspect. I've taken the liberty of speaking with Doctor Wenhope to confirm poison. He has been treating them all anyway, but he'll do some follow up visits now he has a correct diagnosis. However, he told me he thought the danger had passed so they must all have only ingested a small quantity. When he said that I realised he was right. At the fete meeting I distinctly remember Anne adding so much milk to her cup there was barely room for the tea. Mrs fielding drank just under half and then spilled the rest, and Jocasta was so busy talking she barely drunk any."

He made some notes in his little book as I stared out of the window watching a car pull up and park not far from where we were.

"I say, isn't that Jocasta's driver?" I asked.

Baxter glanced at the car and nodded.

"It is. I'll go and 'ave a word while you go to the platform to meet Mrs Blenkinsop."

A few minutes later the train pulled into the little station amid gusts of billowing steam and Jocasta stepped down lightly onto the platform, an overnight bag in her hand.

"Jocasta," I called, and standing on tiptoe waved over the heads of the alighting crowd.

"Ella, what a nice surprise. What are you doing here?"

"I've come to meet you."

"You have? Well, that's very thoughtful but how did you know I'd be here?"

"I spoke to your housekeeper yesterday and she mentioned it. Come along, the car is this way," I said and quickened my step in an attempt to avoid more questions.

We walked through the station building and out the other side towards the car, where Jocasta immediately spied my companion leaning against the door. Her countenance stiffened slightly and a wary look appeared in her eye briefly, but she carried on gamely.

"And Sergeant Baxter too. Well, what a welcome committee, I feel quite honoured."

"Mrs Blenkinsop," Baxter said in greeting, and helped her into the rear of the vehicle.

Once we were all settled I set off towards Briarlea.

"So how was London?" I asked.

"Busy, noisy and quite dirty. It's easy to forget all that discord exists when living here, it catches me by surprise every time I go."

"Was it a special occasion?"

"The birthday of a friend of my husband's. Dinner, theatre and dancing, the usual sort of thing when you go to the city."

"It sounds wonderful," I said.

"Yes, it does, doesn't it?" she replied in a way that made me think she hadn't enjoyed it at all. "So why are you really here? I assume you have news of Father Michael's death?" she continued.

"That's right, Mrs Blenkinsop. There's some new information come to light and we wanted to keep you updated," answered Baxter smoothly, while my stomach churned.

"I see. Well we can speak in the drawing room, we won't be disturbed there."

"Can I get you a drink of something?" Jocasta asked as we settled into the drawing room.

She approached the drinks cabinet and after some musing decided on a stiff gin and tonic. Baxter and I both declined the offer of alcohol.

"But I wouldn't say no to a coffee if there is one?" Baxter said.

Jocasta rang the bell and a moment later a butler appeared.

"You rang, madam?"

"Yes, could you ask Tilly to bring coffee please."

"Certainly, madam," replied the butler and with a stiff bow disappeared.

Leaning against the sill of the large window, glass in hand, Jocasta turned to face us.

"So what is this new information you mentioned in the car?"

Baxter cleared his throat, then said, "We spoke with Alfie Dawkins yesterday, Mrs Blenkinsop. We know about yer affair."

I watched Jocasta like a hawk as this news was imparted but she remained quite still, staring into midair but seemingly seeing nothing, her face inscrutable. Eventually she took a sip of her drink and turned to look out of the window.

"It was only a matter of time before you found out, I suppose."

"Do you understand the implications of this, Mrs Blenkinsop?" Baxter asked.

"I'm not a fool, Sergeant Baxter," she said softly. "Of course I understand. It's a motive."

At that inopportune moment there was a knock at the door, and the maid entered with the coffee.

"Just put it on the table, Tilly," instructed Jocasta.

Tilly did as she was told, then quietly retreated.

Still intent on the view of the terrace and gardens beyond the window, Jocasta began to speak in quiet tones as though to herself.

"Have you ever felt as though you were a stranger in your own life? Going about things day to day but never really feeling as though you belong? Practically invisible but for a series of titles and associated duties; wife, mother, Mrs Blenkinsop, but never Jocasta, never me. No one ever saw me until Alfie. You've met him of course so you understand what a remarkable young man he is. An old soul in a young body is how I referred to him. He understood me better than anyone else ever has and immediately saw how lonely I was."

She sighed heavily and took another sip of her drink. I saw Baxter put down his notebook and take a breath and quickly stayed his arm before he spoke. He looked at me quizzically and I gave a slight shake of my head. I realised this was the first time Jocasta had ever spoken so openly and I didn't want any interruptions. She would get to the point eventually but it was important she got to it in her own way, regardless of how roundabout it was. Baxter seemed to realise what I meant and settled back with his coffee as Jocasta continued.

"I married too young, you see, to a man who was a friend of my father's and twice my age. And while it was quite wonderful in the beginning it didn't take me long to realise what a horrible mistake I had made. But of course by then it was too late, we already had one child and the second was about to be born. With two sons, Hubert had done his duty and his life was once more his own. It was the oddest feeling but I felt like a widow even though he was still alive. For the sake of the boys we've kept up appearances but the marriage has been over for a long time now."

She shook her head and realising her glass was empty went to refill it.

"But of course you want to know about Father Michael. I wasn't one hundred percent sure he had seen us that day, you know. I saw him cycling away but that wasn't to say he'd stopped by the stables. I became certain, however, the following Sunday when the subject of his sermon was sins of the flesh, he looked at me directly several times and I knew without a doubt he'd been there. So I waited until the service was over and everyone had left, then I went to speak with him in private."

"You did?" I asked, momentarily forgetting my decision to keep quiet at this revelation.

"I can see you're surprised at the news, but it wasn't as though it would make any difference. My marriage was already over, Alfie had gone and our affair ended, it was the right time to clear the air. My only concern was for my children and I knew Father Michael would never speak of our conversation."

"But 'ow could you be so sure?" asked Baxter.

"Because it happened within the sanctity of a confessional, Sergeant, and he would have been prohibited from repeating it."

"So you see I had absolutely no reason to kill Father Michael as my secrets were safe," Jocasta continued. "I will also tell you plainly now that I did not do so, you will need to look elsewhere to find your murderer. However, there is something else I can tell you that may be of help."

"And what is that, Mrs Blenkinsop?" asked Baxter retrieving his notebook.

"The father and I talked briefly after we had left the confessional, and he appeared to me to be quite overwhelmed with worry about another matter entirely. Eventually after some gentle encouragement he intimated he had recently lost a friend, a man he had held in great esteem. I could see he blamed himself but I didn't understand exactly why until he said, 'The devil comes in many guises, if only I'd recognised sooner he'd taken her to his side he might still be alive.' And that was it. After that he made me promise not to give in to further temptation and seek forgiveness from God. Which I did."

We sat in silence for a moment while Baxter and I digested this information.

"What do you believe he meant by that, Mrs Blenkinsop?"

"Well, I'm no detective but, and I've thought about it quite a lot since, I think he had information about a crime against a man he considered a friend, by a woman he knew. Possibly a spouse and probably a murder. Father Michael hadn't been here long, remember, so I'm quite sure it must have happened in his previous parish, although where that was I haven't the foggiest. But I think this must have been the reason he left and why his previous posting was deliberately kept quiet."

Baxter and I excused ourselves while we went out through the French windows onto the terrace. We needed to discuss this new information further and in private.

"Do you think she's telling the truth? We only 'ave her word the conversation with the vicar took place," Baxter said as we sauntered to the end of the terrace where we could still see Jocasta seated in the drawing room, but wouldn't be overheard.

"Well, I'm considered a bit of an expert at spotting the art of a lie. Oh! That's perfect," I said scrabbling in my bag for my notebook.

"What is?"

"It's the perfect title for the compendium, The Art of the Lie, especially with your wonderful illustrations. I knew it would come to me eventually."

"I see. But do you think we could get back to the case?" Baxter asked, smirking.

"Of course. Well, I have to say I do think she's telling the truth, there were no indications of subterfuge in her mannerisms, and what's more I don't think she murdered Father Michael. However, as she is our only suspect I'll understand if you want to arrest her, although I'd prefer it if you didn't. I'm not sure her reputation would ever recover if she's hauled in for killing a priest even if she is subsequently found innocent. It hardly seems fair to do that to her."

Baxter looked at me in amusement.

"And what would you suggest instead?"

"Well I was talking to Aunt Margaret about it last night…"

"You were, were you?"

"Yes, she's an extremely good listener and very clever at this sort of thing. I wondered if some sort of house arrest would be an option? Perhaps we could arrange for a plain clothes detective to stay here for a while under the guise of a family friend to save face, while we follow this new lead?"

Baxter laughed.

"Well, you've certainly thought this through, I'll give you that, and it might be possible, but I'll have to speak to my superiors, it's a bit above my pay grade.'Owever, there's a bit of a problem as far as I can see."

"Oh?"

"Just where exactly is this new lead?"

I sat on the terrace wall thoroughly deflated. Without the Archbishop of York, who was not due back for a while, we had no idea where the vicar's previous parish had been. With such little factual information to go on it would be impossible to know where to start.

"I suppose the only thing we can do is to petition the church for the information. They've obviously kept things quiet to protect Father Michael, but now he's dead I don't suppose they'll mind sharing what they know. But I have no idea how to go about it, have you?" I asked Baxter.

"None whatsoever, and my Super is dealin' with that side anyway. But I'll speak to 'im when I call about the plain clothes man we need 'ere. Come on, we'd better tell Mrs Blenkinsop what we're planning."

Jocasta greeted the news of her house arrest and the presence of a plain clothes detective living in her house with incredible grace.

"I wouldn't have gone anywhere of course, there's nowhere for me to go, and I must be here for the boys, they need their mother. But I do understand until the real killer is found this is the best option, and I appreciate you taking my feelings and reputation into consideration."

"Will yer husband be agreeable?" asked Baxter.

Jocasta sighed and rose once more to stand at the window.

"I very much doubt he'll find out, Sergeant. You see I asked him for a divorce while we were in London and he said yes. I'm quite sure there is a mistress or two in the city who will jump at the chance to take my place."

I expressed my sorrow at her news but she waved my comment away.

"Don't worry, Ella, it's something we should have done a long time ago. At least now I'll have the chance to be happy in the future. Now is there anything else?"

"There is just one thing, then p'raps I could use yer telephone?" said Baxter.

"Of course there's one in the hall."

"Much obliged. Now, can you tell me who knew you kept poisonous seeds on the premises?"

"Goodness, probably the whole village, if not the entire island. I speak at the Linhay Horticultural Society quite often, you see, and always take samples of seeds and plants with me. It's held at the village hall and is always full to capacity."

Baxter sighed and I saw he scribbled, 'between four and eight thousand depending on time of year,' in his book. The population practically doubled when the tourist season was upon us and I realised it would be impossible to follow this line of inquiry.

"Thank you, Mrs Blenkinsop. I'll use the telephone now."

I took the opportunity to use the powder room while Baxter was making calls and returned mere moments before he did.

"Right, that's all sorted. There'll be a plain clothes man arriving at Linhay train station at ten tomorrow mornin'. He is to be yer third cousin twice removed on yer mother's side. Name o' Charles. I trust yer driver can pick 'im up?"

"I'll see to the arrangements after you've left, and thank you both again," Jocasta said as she showed us out.

"So they're gettin' a divorce. A sad business. I only 'ope it works out the way she wants it to. While the grass might be green on the other side of the fence she may well find it's no greener than what she has now, only a different shade," Baxter said as we got in the car.

"Or she could discover a verdant oasis where she is no longer invisible and taken for granted," I said.

"Well, there's always that I suppose, and I agree she 'as been treated a bit shabbily by 'er husband if what she says is true. Well we've done all we can 'ere fer now, if you could take me to the station I'm headed back to London. Apparently there's a mountain of paperwork to complete fer the acquisition of a plain clothes baby sitter."

I smiled at Baxter's faux grumpiness, then putting the car into gear started the journey to the railway station. As I drove, my thoughts turned to how little real progress we were making on the case. If the church were unable or unwilling to give us the information we needed then we would soon find ourselves with no way of moving forward, and that worried me greatly. However the elusive memory, a vital clue I had been chasing for days, was about to make itself known, and it came from a source I had been unwittingly ignoring; my dear cat Phantom.

CHAPTER TEN

arly the next morning I took Aunt Margaret to the station where she had a ticket booked on the first train out.

"Thank you, darling, it's been wonderful. I should be back home in time for afternoon tea, I'll telephone you to let you know. Best of luck with the investigation, it will all work itself out soon you'll see. And do keep me posted on developments if you can."

"I do hope you're right, Aunt Margaret, we seem to have reached a brick wall at present."

"Well, you know where I am if you want to talk things through."

A shrill whistle and clouds of steam signalled the train's imminent departure, and I stood back as the wheels began to turn and the train chugged slowly out of the station. Aunt Margaret slid down the window and waved briefly before disappearing into her carriage.

My next few hours at home were filled with tasks I needed to catch up on, 'The Art of the Lie,' was coming along nicely and Mrs Shaw wholeheartedly agreed with the new title. I caught up on some correspondence then took a walk in the gardens.

It was a beautiful summer day with a clear blue sky and not a cloud in sight. I hadn't seen Tom for days but he'd managed to clear an impressive amount of dead shrubbery along the wall of the enclosed garden, and eventually a large wooden gate had been revealed. It was terribly exciting but I was under strict instructions not to interfere, and I was quite happy to leave him to it. The key to the gate had been unearthed in one of the out-buildings, and I could hear Tom's cheerful whistle now, alongside the excited yips of Digger his little dog, emanating from beyond the wall as they worked.

I spent a very pleasant half hour sitting on the bench at the end of the garden, watching a pair of swans glide majestically up and down the river, and several ducks waddling in the reed bed on the opposite bank. I could hear a woodpecker hard at work on one of the trees in the woodland across the water, and to my immense joy a sleek otter popped his head out of a cleverly concealed holt for a moment, then vanished as quickly as he'd appeared. It was quite the most perfect and magical time with thoughts of murder pushed to the far recesses of my mind, and I felt quite rejuvenated by the time I returned to the cottage.

It was early afternoon, I'd taken my coffee into the sitting room and once again I found Phantom staring at the painting from Pierre.

"Dear, Phantom, I realise that you cats were worshiped as Gods by the early Egyptians, but this really is taking your narcissistic tendencies a little too far, don't you think?" I said to him as I moved closer to study the painting in more detail. "Although I do agree it is a very good likeness … Oh!"

I barely noticed the coffee cup slip from my hands and crash to the hearth breaking into smithereens, as the elusive clue finally rushed forward to the forefront of my mind.

"Oh, Phantom, you've been trying to tell me for days, haven't you?"

Phantom finally looked at me then jumping down from his perch disappeared through the wall into the garden. His job was done.

"Miss Bridges, are you all right, I heard a crash?" Mrs Shaw said as she rushed into the room.

"I'm fine, Mrs Shaw, I just dropped the coffee cup. Sorry, I need to call my aunt urgently."

"Actually that's what I was coming to tell you when I heard the crash. She's on the telephone now."

"She is? Goodness, she seems to be able to read my mind from a distance too," I murmured, dashing into the hall and picking up the receiver.

"Aunt Margaret, I need … "

"Ella, listen to me, you need to come at once. I've just spoken to my housekeeper."

"That's just what I was going to say."

"It was?"

"Yes, and I'll be bringing Sergeant Baxter."

"I was going to suggest that myself."

"I also need you to do something for me."

I explained to my aunt what I wanted and she agreed immediately.

"What time will you be here?" she asked.

"I'll telephone Baxter now and ask him to meet me off the train at Waterloo, but it will be quite late. I doubt we'll get to Broughton station much before eleven tonight."

"My driver will be waiting for you both. I'll see you soon, Ella."

I telephoned Baxter as soon as I had disconnected from Aunt Margaret, and once I had briefly explained how the pieces were finally fitting together he agreed to the journey at once.

"That's an excellent bit o' detective work, Miss Bridges, well done. But time is of the essence if what yer tellin' me is right, and a man's life is at stake. I'll get a plain clothes man to get over there and watch the 'ouse urgently. See you soon."

True to her word, Aunt Margaret's driver was waiting at Broughton train station when we arrived, and by eleven fifteen we were all comfortably seated in the parlour.

"Is Pierre here?" I asked.

"No, dear, you know what he's like with, er, crowds. But he sent what you asked for."

I shared a smile with my aunt, understanding immediately Pierre's reluctance to meet yet another member of Scotland Yard.

"Who's Pierre?" asked Baxter.

"Pierre DuPont." I said.

"The artist? Well I never. 'Ow is he involved in this mess?"

"You've heard of him?" I said somewhat surprised.

"Indeed I 'ave. I've long bin an admirer of 'is work, Miss Bridges. Once upon a time I fancied I'd be lucky enough to own one of 'is paintings, sadly the more popular they are the further out o' my reach. But 'ow on earth is he involved with this case?"

Aunt Margaret interrupted at this point.

"Before you get to that would you mind listening to what my housekeeper has to say? The poor dear has been waiting up for you."

Mrs Shipley came into the parlour, full of her usual cheeriness and bright smile, despite the lateness of the hour.

"Miss Isobella, how lovely to see you again so soon."

"Hello, Mrs Shipley. This is Sergeant Baxter."

She greeted Baxter then at my aunt's urging began her tale.

"When your aunt returned home this afternoon she passed on your thanks regarding the donations for your May Day fete. You are very welcome, by the way. Now I believe she told you we wouldn't be needing them this year but not why?"

"I wasn't aware of it until you told me today," said my aunt.

"No, I realise that, I apologise," said the housekeeper.

"No need to apologise, Shipley, I was just explaining for Ella and Sergeant Baxter."

"Do go on, Mrs Shipley." I said.

"Well, the reason we no longer needed them was because we weren't having a fair this year, because our vicar had left unexpectedly. It was at the end of July last year and he just up and disappeared, none of us had any inkling. He didn't even say goodbye. We all thought it terribly odd at the time. Of course there have been a number of rumours since, some complete nonsense of course, but the general consensus is that he found out something about one of the parishioners which caused him to go. But one of his friends died around the same time so it could just as easily have been that."

"Mrs Shipley, what was the name of this priest?" I asked.

"Oh, of course, I apologise. It was Father Michael."

··«‹◆›»··

Mrs Shipley could tell us nothing more and so retired. She didn't know who the deceased friend had been but the description she gave us of her Father Michael fitted ours perfectly, and none of us were in any doubt it was the same man.

"Well, we're certainly gettin' somewhere now," Baxter said with relief in his voice, then added ... "All we need now is to find the woman Father Michael mentioned to Mrs Blenkinsop, and we should be able to wrap this case up."

"I believe I can help with that. Aunt Margaret, do you have the painting and drawings Pierre sent over?"

My aunt nodded and collected a parcel from the sideboard. Bringing it over, she unwrapped it carefully and laid the contents on the table in front of us.

"Good god!" Baxter exclaimed, in a very unbaxter-like way.

"Awful, isn't it?" I said.

"Well, it's a remarkable bit o' work, very well done, but it is quite 'orrible. What on earth pointed you in the direction o' this?"

"My cat."

"I didn't realise you had a cat."

"Well, he's not really mine, he appears and disappears when he feels like it."

Baxter nodded knowingly. "The wife and me 'ave a stray as well, turns up when he feels like it, fer food mostly. But back to this paintin', can you explain how it all fits together? How yer've come to the conclusion you 'ave?"

"Well, it all started when I came to visit Aunt Margaret the other week and we visited Pierre DuPont's gallery."

"He 'as a gallery here?" asked Baxter with extreme interest.

"He does, and no doubt you'll be able to visit tomorrow. Anyway it just so happened this painting was in the window. It wasn't supposed to be, Pierre was quite cross when he realised and removed it at once. But of course I'd seen it by then and once seen never forgotten, however it got pushed to the back of my mind until I received your note with the drawings for the compendium."

"Right. And 'ow did that 'elp exactly?"

"Your note mentioned you'd gone out and drawn real people. I've never really thought how artists paint their subjects before, but of course it must be like that. Regardless, it suddenly dawned on me you'd need to have a real person to sketch to start with."

"And you think Mr DuPont based this paintin' on a real person?"

"Oh, I'm sure of it, I recognise her, you see. But I asked him to also send preliminary sketches if he had any just to make sure. I presume those are in this portfolio."

I untied the ribbon holding the portfolio together and opened it with extreme care, the sketches as well as the painting itself were worth a lot of money. Inside were several loose sheets of paper each with numerous pencil studies of the same woman.

"Yes, this is definitely her. I thought originally I must have seen her at St Mary's but it was one of those elusive memories that I couldn't quite grasp. I realise now the painting was what I was remembering."

"But this is your suspect?" asked my aunt.

"Yes, it is. You see I've met her since on Linhay."

"So you know who she is?"

"I know who she is now, but not who she was when she lived here and that's the proof we need. Did you ask Pierre those questions I gave you on the phone when we spoke earlier, Aunt Margaret?"

"I did and I wrote down his answers."

She reached over to retrieve a writing pad and tearing off the top sheet handed it to me. Baxter and I read in silence for a moment.

"I'll visit this place Nell Bank tomorrow," Baxter said pointing at one of the answers.

"My driver can drop Ella and myself in town then be at your disposal for the rest of the day, Sergeant. You'll have the furthest of all of us to travel," Aunt Margaret offered. "Now I think we'd better turn in, it's very late and we have an exceedingly busy day ahead of us tomorrow."

She was right, for if everything went according to plan, tomorrow we would catch a murderer.

The next morning was a flurry of activity as Aunt Margaret, Baxter and myself made our plans. Baxter was to go to an address at Nell Bank to see if he could obtain both a name and more information, then onto the local police station to discuss a suspicious death. After that he would visit a company of solicitors in Sheffield, the address of which I had given him previously.

Aunt Margaret was to visit the local paper, to read any applicable news reports in archived publications around the time of Father Michael's disappearance. And I was to return Pierre's artwork and to see if he could give us anything more about the muse he used for his painting, 'From Mistress to Wife.'

We would all meet up later at the art gallery.

I waved goodbye as the car containing my Aunt and Baxter drove away, then with the little bell signalling my arrival entered the premises.

I was greeted by a tall heavyset girl in a black dress with white apron, and a mass of blond hair piled on top of her head in a complicated arrangement of thick plaits. Which gave the impression she wore an upturned wicker basket on her head. Blue eyes the size of dinner plates turned to greet me and a smile broke out through rose-coloured lips which lit up her whole face and made her eyes shine in a remarkably mischievous way.

"Good morning, welcome to the DuPont Gallery. May I be of assistance?"

"I'm here to see Monsieur DuPont. My name is Ella Bridges."

Before the girl could reply the man himself appeared from beyond the curtain. He was wearing a floor length apron which was so covered in splotches of paint it was difficult to know what its original colour had been. Upon his head was a French beret in midnight blue velvet, and he had a paintbrush stuck behind one ear.

"Meez Bridges, how deeelightful to see you again," he said as he bowed to kiss my hand.

"Bonjour, Pierre."

"Hilda, bring tea immediately. We will take it in the studio. Chop chop," he said, clapping his hands.

Hilda rolled her eyes and with a smile at me said to the little man, "Be polite or I shall hide your ladders."

I stifled a surprised laugh as she disappeared toward the kitchen. Pierre took my elbow and gently steered me toward the back room, shaking his head in mock exasperation.

"Mon Dieu! But it is difficult to get good staff nowadays."

Safely seated in the studio, which to my eye was every bit as confusing and disorganised as the shop, and with tea on a low table in front of us, I explained the reason for my visit.

"Firstly, I would like to thank you for the loan of your painting and sketches."

"Think nothing of it. Were they of help?"

"Very much so. Indeed your paintings have provided a vital thread throughout this latest case."

"And just what is this case you speak of?"

"Murder, Pierre. I am investigating a murder."

"Sacre bleu! But this is most horrible to hear, Maggie mentioned nothing of this on the telephone. And you wish for my help in some way? But what can I do? I know nothing of this murder?"

"Can you tell me more about the woman you used for this painting?" I asked, indicating the two-faced woman which I had unwrapped and placed on a convenient easel just moments earlier.

"It is she who is dead? Ah, no … I see now, it is she who is the culprit, no?"

I nodded.

"It does not surprise me so much actually. You can see how I painted her, so different from my usual work, yes? This is how she appeared to me, beautiful to look at but with a core of evil and rotten to her soul."

"Can you tell me from the beginning how you came to meet her?"

"Of course, but I did not really meet her until a long time after the portrait was finished, when she visited the shop unexpectedly. But I will begin at the beginning and tell you what little I can."

Pierre's tale began on a warm day in Spring of the previous year. With an urge for fresh air he'd taken his sketch book and pencils to a little park opposite St. Paul's church in Broughton, and had settled himself to an afternoon of sketching. He had been there perhaps two hours, and filled several pages with drawings when this woman had appeared and sat on a nearby bench. At first he'd simply watched her, she seemingly oblivious to his attentions, then he felt a compulsion so strong to immortalise her he became almost afraid. But he was powerless to the stop the impulse and page after page he filled with her image, pencil flying over the paper as though with a life of its own. Eventually, much later and completely exhausted he had laid down his pencil and closed his eyes.

"When I opened them she was standing but a short distance away, observing me," he said with a shudder.

"What did she say?" I asked.

"Nothing at all, but her face for an instant ... malfaisant! You understand? It was pure evil. Then the mask came down again and she simply turned and walked away."

"Had she seen your drawings?"

"I'm sure of it."

"What happened then?"

"I gathered up my work and proceeded in the same direction."

"You followed her? Why?"

"Alas I do not know. It was as though my actions were not my own, like being a puppet whose strings were being manipulated from elsewhere. I have never felt anything like it before or since, and I never wish to again. It sounds fanciful, does it not? But it is as exactly as I have explained."

Pierre had continued to follow the woman unobserved to an affluent part of the town, where she had disappeared through the gate of a large house.

"Nell Bank," I said.

"Oui, just like I told Maggie."

"So when did she come to the shop?"

"Not until June. It was a horrible shock to hear the little bell then find her standing there. She demanded to see the painting I had done of her. I had finished it of course but I told her it did not exist. That I had returned with the sketches but they had amounted to nothing."

"And did she believe you?"

Pierre gave a shrug.

"I did not know and I did not care. I offered to give her something else instead and when she informed me of the illness of her husband, I found something suitable and she left. I have never seen her again."

"This is why you were upset the day I came to find Hilda had displayed the painting in the window?"

"But of course. I had lied and said it did not exist. What would have happened if she had seen it?"

"You have no more need to worry, Pierre. She no longer lives in Broughton, she has moved to Linhay."

"Such a relief I cannot tell you!"

"I'm glad you are relieved and thank you for telling me it all. I realise it must have been quite an ordeal. Now I need to tell you my aunt will be here shortly along with my colleague."

"Another policeman?"

"Yes. I thought I should tell you in case … well, never mind. But he is a great fan of your work and has been looking forward to visiting the gallery and meeting you."

"Then we shall make him feel quite at home, mon amie."

The bell above the shop door tinkled the arrival of newcomers, and a moment later Hilda popped her head through the curtain.

"Visitors to see you, Oh Mighty One," she said with a cheeky glint in her eye.

"Less of your impudence, wench, or you will find yourself on the streets," Pierre replied.

"Yes, My Lord," said the girl with a giggle, and disappeared back into the shop.

CHAPTER ELEVEN

"Ah, Maggie, you look as lovely as ever," Pierre said with a bow and a kiss of her hand. "And this must be the colleague of Miss Bridges, no?"

"Sergeant Baxter, Mr DuPont. It is a real pleasure to meet you at last."

"Likewise, my dear Sergeant. Now, say nothing more!"

Aunt Margaret and I stood to one side while Pierre dragged his stepladders in front of Baxter, and peered deeply into his eyes. Baxter shot a worried glance at me and his eyebrows rose high enough to disappear beneath his hairline, as a blush crept across his cheeks. I couldn't help but grin.

"Mmmm. Most interesting," the dwarf said.

Grasping Baxter's hands he turned them this way and that, examining them first close up, then at a distance.

"Yes, it is as I thought. Remain still please."

Jumping off the ladder he wandered around the perplexed sergeant, studying him from every angle until he declared himself done.

"A man after my own heart. I have the most perfect piece for you, my dear Sergeant."

I had assumed it would take some time, as it had with me, for Pierre to find a gift for Baxter. But I was wrong. With a flourish he pulled a small frame from the rear of the chaise-longue just seconds later.

"Eh voila!" he said and thrust the painting into Baxter's hands.

"Well, I never. How did you know?" he said, staring at Pierre in astonishment.

"What is it? Do let me see," I said, moving to Baxter's side.

The painting was exquisite. A small tow-headed boy sitting on the stoop of a step, his tongue caught between his teeth and a look of fierce concentration on his face as he bent over a little drawing pad, sketching in perfect detail a Robin Redbreast perched atop a milk bottle.

"It's simply perfect, isn't it?" I said.

He looked at me with a questioning raise of an eyebrow.

"I never said a word, Baxter. Truly."

"Then how?" he said, once again addressing Pierre.

The little man gave a depreciating shrug.

"It is easy to identify a fellow artiste. Would you not agree? Now I'll have Hilda wrap it for you."

As we were leaving Baxter turned to the dwarf and shook his hand.

"It's been a real pleasure to meet you, Mr DuPont. I'm more grateful than words can say. If there is ever anything I can do fer yer in return … "

"As a matter of fact, there is something, Sergeant."

"Yes?"

"Catch this despicable murderess, for she is evil through and through."

"I 'ave every intention of doing so, sir. You can count on it."

"I presume my aunt told you to accept a gift from Pierre if he offered?" I asked Baxter as we settled in the car.

"Yes indeed, said he'd feel mortally wounded if I refused, 'though she warned me it might not 'appen. He's very particular 'bout who he gifts his paintings to, I feel very honoured."

My Aunt nodded.

"Perfectly true, it's very rare for him to bestow his work on strangers and you have both been honoured. He must think highly of you."

"How does he do it, Aunt Margaret? Find the most perfect painting for the person?"

"Honestly I have no idea, darling. He says it's a gift and I don't question it. Now I thought we'd visit the tea rooms on the way home and discuss our findings. There are some private booths at the rear which will be perfect for our needs. I find myself in dire need of sustenance."

Ensconced in a booth at the rear of The Lilly Tearooms, the table groaning with more food than the three of us could possibly eat, we shared what we had learned.

I began by relaying the story Pierre had told me, how he'd eventually followed our suspect to a large house at

Nell Bank and culminating in her visit to his shop some months later.

"Goodness, poor Pierre. I had no idea," my aunt said.

"How did you get on at the newspaper?" I asked.

"Quite well, as a matter of fact. I only found the one article pertaining to a gentleman's suspicious death at the correct time, a man by the name of Redmond. Here, I was able to clip it."

She laid the newspaper clipping on the table and Baxter and I quickly read it.

"Not much to go on 'ere, but it mentions he lived at Nell Bank, so it must be the same man," said Baxter.

"Well, I also managed to find the reporter and he was much more forthcoming."

"That's excellent work, tracking down the reporter," said Baxter.

"Well, I'd like to take credit, Sergeant, but sadly I cannot. It's a small town newspaper and there are actually only two reporters. Both of whom happened to be in the office when I arrived, so it was quite simple to find the right one."

"Was 'is name Briggs, by any chance?"

"Why yes, it was. How did you know?"

"And did you explain yer were workin' with a Scotland Yard detective who was at that very moment on 'is way to Nell Bank?"

"Of course, I could hardly waltz in there asking questions without some form of legitimacy."

"And after you imparted this information did he then excuse himself to make a brief telephone call?"

"Sergeant Baxter, you really are quite the tease. Who did he telephone?"

"The daughter from Mr Redmond's first marriage. She was waitin' outside the 'ouse when I arrived."

"So all my snooping was superfluous?"

"On the contrary, it was invaluable. 'Ow else could we 'ave flushed out the daughter? But I apologise for interruptin', please carry on."

My aunt, quite amused at Baxter, continued.

"I have made some notes of the pertinent facts…"

She informed us Mr Redmond was a man who had always been in excellent health. He had a love of the outdoors and was involved in various gentlemanly sports such as shooting and fishing. He was a regular member of St Paul's church, a keen gardener and had won many a rosette for his produce at various village shows. All this, until a fall had necessitated a hospital stay for a broken leg, after which he had never quite fully recovered. But according to the reporter Briggs, he had fallen in love with his young nurse and married her not long after his release.

"After that he became almost a recluse apparently. I also managed to obtain this, it's the original from the newspaper so I will need to return it, but this is Mr Redmond."

Aunt Margaret handed us a photograph, as soon as I saw it the connections became clear and I knew we had the murderer in our sights. It was of an elderly man in tweeds with a cane, standing in front of a floral display and holding up a first prize rosette. My aunt also had another interesting morsel to share.

"Mr Redmond had a hothouse and grew many interesting specimens. Some of which were poisonous."

At this point I began to panic that we may be too late.

"Baxter, we need to move on this now before there is another death. We can't get back to Linhay in time, so you must make some telephone calls."

"Miss Bridges, no need to fret it's already in 'hand. By the time I had spoken to the solicitor I knew we 'ad our murderer, so made haste to Broughton police station where I made the calls and put things into action. I daresay there's already bin an arrest. I also made sure Doctor Wenhope was present and informed it were likely a case of prolonged poisoning he'd need to treat. I expect there'll be a message left at your Aunt's 'ouse when we return."

"Oh, thank goodness."

"'Ow did you know about the Will, by the way?" Baxter asked.

"I saw a letter when I visited. I didn't know it was about a Will at the time of course, but as things went on I remembered it because it was from Sheffield."

"Well, we've done all we can. I only 'ope we were in time to save 'im," said Baxter.

I fervently prayed we were too.

There was indeed a message at Aunt Margaret's when the three of us returned. The arrest had gone according to plan and the poisoned victim had been rushed to hospital. It was touch and go as to whether he would make it, but he was under the best care possible and it was now in the lap of the Gods.

The packets of seeds stolen from Mrs Blenkinsop's greenhouse had been found on the premises, along with a copy of a new Last Will and Testament giving everything over to the murderer. And fingerprints taken had matched those on the box of tea at the vicarage.

By the time I returned home the news of the arrest had spread through the village like wildfire, and everywhere I went shocked locals and visitors alike were huddled in small clusters discussing the news in hushed tones.

Jocasta had telephoned to inform me her resident detective had left, and to thank me again for my tact. And Agnes, in an unusual show of fortitude, had called and asked if she could come for lunch. I had naturally said yes and she appeared on time and with a freshly baked peach tart.

"Mrs Whittingstall!" exclaimed Agnes as she sat across from me at the outdoor table.

It was another beautiful day and I had decided the informal setting of the garden and dining al fresco was a perfect idea.

"I simply can't believe it. It's such a shock. But tell me, Ella, how on earth did you put it all together?"

"Well, it all started when I happened to see a ghastly painting on a visit to Aunt Margaret a few weeks ago. It's very difficult to describe to one who hasn't seen it but suffice to say it lingered in my memory."

"And this was your first clue?"

"It was, although I didn't realise it at the time, nor for quite a while actually, but that's by the by. Do you remember when you and I first met, Agnes, we were leaving St Mary's and a woman rushed down the path and bumped into me?"

"Yes it was Mrs Whittingstall, so I found out later."

"Well, I happened to look back at the church that day; it seemed to me as though she were running away from something. What I saw was Father Michael and he looked in a state of shock. Of course I realise now they must have recognised one another."

"From when he was at the Broughton Parish, you mean?"

"Quite right. You said yourself you'd never seen Mrs Whittingstall at St. Mary's prior to that incident and Father

Michael had been away for a long time, returning just moments before in fact. I doubt either of them realised the other was now living on Linhay. It must have been a dreadful shock for both of them to come to face to face that day, and I'm afraid the vicar was in terrible danger from that moment on."

"But how did you know it was Mrs Whittingstall who had murdered Father Michael?"

"Well, it was a case of lots of little things which eventually made me see the bigger picture. Much of it when you and I went to visit her actually."

"I shudder when I think of that visit, it was quite horrid. But how did it help? We never even set foot in the door so you can't have seen much."

"I saw what I needed to, Agnes."

I explained the things I had noted. The photograph of the gentleman in tweeds with his pheasants which had turned out to be Mr Redmond, and the cane in the umbrella stand which also belonged to him, I said I had filed away for future reference, not being able to attach much significance to them there and then. Of course this was a small tarradiddle on my part, however I wasn't about to add visitations from his ghost into the conversation. But I did share my observation of the Pierre DuPont painting on the back wall, and the return address of the solicitors I had seen on the letter the postman was delivering.

"I remember you mentioning the painting, but thought you were trying to make polite conversation under remarkably strained circumstances," Agnes said.

I smiled.

"Perhaps I was at the time, but it was another little clue to add to the others. Of course the real break came when my aunt telephoned about her housekeeper and insisted Sergeant Baxter and I went up there post-haste."

I relayed to Agnes all that had gone on in Broughton and the subsequent proof we had found which led to the arrest of Elizabeth Whittingstall. Previously known as Elspeth Redmond.

"Oh dear, it's all rather dreadful, isn't it, Ella? I can't imagine what Mr Redmond's daughter must have felt not only having lost her father but her entire inheritance, including her family home to this evil woman. But how do you prove murder so long after the fact?"

I looked down wondering how to explain gently to Agnes what Baxter had told me earlier. But I need not have worried about her sensibilities as she grasped the truth almost immediately.

"He's going to be exhumed? How utterly ghastly. But I suppose it must be done for the family's sake. I wonder what actually happened between Mrs Whittingstall and Father Michael, do you know?"

I shook my head.

"I don't think we will ever know for certain, Agnes, but here is what I think happened. Mr Redmond was a good friend of Father Michael's, someone he held in great esteem and presumably spent a lot of time with. But all that changed when his new wife came on the scene and succeeded in isolating him from his family and friends. Of course we think now she was slowly poisoning him and preventing anyone from realising the truth of what was happening. Sadly she was very successful in that regard. However I believe Father Michael was suspicious and not realising how truly dangerous this woman was, eventually made a dreadful error in judgment when his friend died. He met with her and accused her face to face of murder."

'Oh dear, I'm sorry. I thought I had come to terms with it but hearing this…" said Agnes, fishing for her handkerchief as tears coursed down her cheeks.

"Don't worry, Agnes, it's delayed shock, it happens like that, catching you unawares at the least expected moment," I said gently, taking her hand.

She nodded and blew her nose.

"Please carry on."

"Are you sure?"

"Yes, I need to know."

"All right. Well there isn't much more to tell but Sergeant Baxter is still up in Broughton and has found out something else. Shortly after the funeral of Mr Redmond, according to witnesses, his widow visited the church and went to confession. It is our belief she must have confessed to Father Michael that she had murdered her husband and…"

"He couldn't tell anyone," finished Agnes, a look of anguish on her face.

"No, he couldn't. It was a cruel and evil thing to do but she is an evil woman. I'm quite sure she deliberately told him in order to gloat and prove she had got away with it. And I'm sure this is what had been troubling him for so long and the reason he took his sabbatical."

"Why did she do it, Ella? Murder her first husband and try to murder her second?"

"For the inheritance. It was greed pure and simple."

Agnes sat back and sipped her tea in contemplative silence for a while before asking a final question.

"She won't get away with it, will she, Ella? She's going to be sent to prison for the rest of her life, isn't she?"

"She might not go to prison, Agnes. Baxter has heard rumours of an insanity plea. If she is found to be mad then she will be incarcerated in an asylum. But you have no need to worry, I can assure you she will never be a free woman again."

Agnes nodded then, accepting of my word. I was under no such illusion, however. I felt sure a plea of insanity would be thrown out as the crimes had been premeditated, very carefully and cleverly worked out. No, Baxter and I both agreed that the reprehensible Mrs Whittingstall would be hanged from the neck until dead.

The next day I decided to ride over to St Mary's. Propping my bicycle against the wall just inside the lych-gate I walked leisurely up the path toward the entrance. I had come to light a candle for John.

He'd been buried properly this time, in the grave where I thought he had rested for the last two years. I had not been allowed to attend, done as it was under cover of darkness and in secret, however I had been assured full protocols had been observed. I frowned at the ludicrous, impersonal language which had been used, but understood it to mean a vicar had been present along with a few members of MI5 who were his friends, and a proper burial had taken place. I was still coming to terms with how I felt about it all, but was comforted in the knowledge he had at last found peace and had been laid to rest properly. I would visit one day but for now I would light a candle to remember him by and say a prayer.

Half way up the path I noticed a figure standing by the far wall and stopped to greet him. He raised his cane in acknowledgment, nodded his thanks and with a slight shimmer the ghost of Mr Redmond vanished completely.

The temperature inside the church was a welcome respite from the heat of the day, and I stood for a moment cooling down while my eyes adjusted to the dimness. When I was quite sure I wouldn't bump into things if I moved, I collected a candle and lighting it set it with the others. I stood for a moment watching the flickering flames then moved to sit on a pew at the front. There were already several others sitting in quiet contemplation, no doubt including Father Michael in their prayers. Agnes had informed me his funeral was to be held the next day, presided over by the Archbishop of York, and I had already noticed on the way in the sexton hard at work digging the grave.

Several minutes had passed before I felt the presence of someone sit behind me and lean forward. It was Jocasta.

"I'll be in the meeting room. Come and have a cup of tea with me when you're ready," she whispered.

"All right. Just give me a moment and I'll be along," I whispered back.

In the meeting room I found Jocasta putting the finishing touches to the church flowers for Father Michael's Funeral. Stacked along one wall were numerous wreaths and bouquets expressing the sorrow and heartfelt loss of a man, who although hadn't been at St Mary's long, had become a friend to many.

"Is tea all right or would you prefer coffee?"

"Coffee please."

"I must admit this business nearly put me off tea. Although I've brought my own with me this time. I feel awful about what happened. If I hadn't filched the vicar's stuff, poor Anne and Mrs Fielding would have been fine."

"You can hardly blame yourself, Jocasta. You didn't lace it with poison."

"No, I know but I can't help it."

"Well, in that case let's blame Agnes," I said.

"Why would we do that?"

"Because she was the one who forgot to buy more."

"But that's just silly. It's hardly her fault."

"Just as silly as blaming yourself. It wasn't your fault either."

Jocasta looked at me for a minute then burst out laughing.

"Ella, you have no idea how glad I am we met. Come on, let's go and sit outside in the sunshine."

Once again we moved to the bench where we had sat when I first visited St Mary's. It seemed a lifetime ago, and Jocasta obviously had the same train of thought.

"Gosh, it seems ages since we first sat here. Such a lot has happened since then. I spoke to Agnes last night by the way, she told me what you'd discussed over lunch. I hope you don't mind?"

"Of course I don't mind, it's hardly a secret now. Besides I expected her to considering how close you are."

"Poor Agnes, my dearest friend and I've treated her abominably. I feel horribly guilty about it."

"Agnes will forgive you, Jocasta. In fact I doubt she thinks there is anything to forgive. She probably thinks the same way I do, that you tried so hard to be someone your husband wanted, you lost sight of who you really are."

"No wonder you're such a good detective. Alfie said something similar actually, how did he put it? Something about the hardened shell I had built around myself being a reaction to my unhappiness, he's terribly intuitive. He was right of course although I shan't use it as an excuse."

"You've seen, Alfie, then?"

"Yes, a couple of days ago."

"Will he be moving back to Briarlea?"

"There's a huge amount to be sorted out before then, not least a divorce and an agreeable settlement, which I confess I am dreading having to go through. But Alfie is hugely supportive, we're just taking it one day at a time and enjoying each moment. If he does come back it won't be as a groom however, I'll never go skulking around like that again. I have well and truly learned that particular lesson."

"Well, if he does return, in whatever capacity, might I make a suggestion?"

"Of course?"

"That you find a new position for your scullery maid, Betty? She is very young and impressionable and thinks herself not only in love with Alfie, but that her feelings are reciprocated. I think it will make things terribly difficult for you and Alfie, if he returns and she is still there. It's not her fault, she had a terrible start in life and was on the receiving end of some awful abuse as you know. But I believe she would benefit from another position where she will have a good mentor. She missed so many of her early life lessons and I worry about what she may become."

To my surprise Jocasta put down her tea cup and enfolded me in a hug.

"Gosh, you're such a good egg, Ella. I'm so glad we're friends, and yes I shall find somewhere perfect for Betty."

Releasing me and reaching for her tea, she went on to ask if there had been any new developments in the case.

"Actually I spoke to Sergeant Baxter this morning and there's a few things come to light that make him believe Mr Redmond wasn't her first victim."

"Good heavens, that's shocking news! Thank goodness you caught her when you did, Ella, it sounds to me as though she would have just carried on marrying and murdering if you hadn't. It's peculiar the way things work out, isn't it? Father Michael knew she was guilty and had wanted to stop her. In his own way, desperately tragic though it was he has done just that."

CHAPTER TWELVE

Two days after the funeral Mrs Shaw and I finished 'The Art of the Lie.'

"It's excellent, isn't it?" she said.

"It really is, Mrs Shaw, we should be jolly proud of ourselves. I can't thank you enough for all your help. I shall of course give you credit on the cover."

"Actually I'd rather you didn't if you don't mind. But I would very much like a copy once it's printed if that's possible?"

"That's more than possible, Mrs Shaw, you deserve it."

We were just packing it up ready to send to Uncle Albert when Mrs Parsons came bustling in, a look of barely suppressed excitement on her face.

"Whatever is the matter, Mrs Parsons?"

"Miss Bridges, Mrs Shaw, I wonder if you have time to come down to the kitchen for a moment?"

"Yes of course. But is something the matter?"

"Not at all, Miss Bridges," she said enigmatically, then bustled off towards the back stairs.

Mrs Shaw and I shared a puzzled glance and then followed.

In the kitchen we found Tom standing to attention with Digger at his side. Everything became clear then and I felt the immediate prick of tears spring unbidden to my eyes.

"Oh, Tom. Is it finished?" I breathed.

He nodded, a huge grin plastered on his face, and reaching into his pocket handed me an enormous wrought iron key. I looked at Mrs Shaw, then at Mrs Parsons, then finally back at Tom.

"Well, what are we waiting for? Let's go!" I said to them all, and raced out into the garden, Digger hot on my heels and the others not far behind.

I ran across the lawns with the exuberance and excitement of a child who had awoken on Christmas morning to find Father Christmas had visited. The weeks since John's telephone call had weighed heavily, as though a huge invisible millstone had been placed around my neck, forcing me to stoop lower and lower until I barely had the strength to lift my head. But with John now at peace and the murder of Father Michael solved, the weight had been lifted. Of course a telephone call barely two hours later would put a stop to all that, but for the moment I felt free and as light as a feather.

I stopped in front of the huge gate and taking a step forward read aloud the engraved plaque which had been placed there.

'To think or reflect is to step aside from events. To give up the world for a space of internal quiet, as if you have entered a walled garden.'

I gently traced the letters with my finger and thought how utterly perfect it was.

"Do the honours then, Miss Bridges," said Mrs Parsons who had come up puffing and panting behind me.

I lifted a shaking hand and inserted the key into the lock. With a clockwise twist I heard a click and slowly pushed open the gate. I stood on the threshold for a moment, then took a step inside.

"Oh, my goodness," whispered Mrs Parsons behind me.

"How splendid," said Mrs Shaw.

It could have been the inspiration for Frances Hodgson Burnett's novel so completely magical was it. I turned to Tom who was waiting in his usual quiet way.

"It's more than I ever dreamed possible, Tom, you have worked miracles here, it's as though we have our own slice of Eden. A simple thank you just doesn't seem enough for the oasis you have created but know I will be forever grateful for what you have done, it's exactly what I need. But please understand, this is as much your garden as it is mine and you must treat it as such."

Tom grinned and nodded, then beckoned for us all to follow and we began to explore in earnest. There were two things I had noticed immediately upon entering, the first was the long greenhouse which ran the entire length of one wall. Freshly painted in dark green with white window frames on an old red brick base, it had two steps leading up to an interior full of everything a gardener could possibly need, and I couldn't wait to begin work.

The second was in the absolute centre of the enormous space, a huge old weeping willow tree whose frond like branches fell to the ground like a living waterfall. It must have been planted many years ago and been growing all this time, just waiting for someone to rediscover it. But the real magic was inside. A secret within a secret.

As I stepped through the leafy curtain into the cool space below I saw attached to the strongest branch a simple rope swing, with a sturdy wooden seat. On the opposite side was an iron table and matching chairs with rose patterned cushions. To the rear of the enormous trunk, suspended between two thick branches, to my delighted surprise was a hammock in a thick and colourful striped fabric, upon which rested several cushions.

"Well, I never," said Mrs Parsons coming up behind me and gazing at the hammock.

I laughed and pushing my way back through the branches went to explore further in the sunshine. There was a huge herb garden in the shape of a cartwheel made from woven willow, and further along several strawberry planters, their luscious red fruits ready for picking. There were rows of to-mato plants with marigolds planted between, and I smiled remembering Jocasta's tip which Tom apparently already knew. Along the walls were trained trees, their wares in abundance, three kinds of apples and two sorts of pears. Plums and damsons which would fruit later in the year, and even a medlar, unusual in that it provided its fruit in winter. Various beds showed redcurrant and blackcurrant bushes, alongside blackberries and gooseberries, as well as my favourite raspberries. And further along the large leaf and red stalks of rhubarb were apparent.

Through a magnificent avenue of white rose arches, their branches heavy with creamy white blooms, I discovered an entirely separate section of the garden and was amazed to find a row of beehives. I had been aware of their gentle buzzing in the background, and had watched as they flew from plant to plant feeding on the nectar, but had never thought they were housed here.

"Mr Honeycoat looks after the hives. It's a bit of a specialist job, you see, and Tom prefers to look after the plants. But you need them for pollinating so I asked Mr Honeycoat if he'd help out, everything else was a secret from me though. That's all right, is it?" asked Mrs Shaw.

"Of course it is, Mrs Shaw, it's a wonderful idea. Sorry, did you say Honeycoat? And he keeps bees?" I couldn't keep the smile from my voice but she smiled along with me.

"I rather think he chose his profession to go along with his name, but there's no doubt he knows what he's doing. You'll have jars of fresh honey before you know it. In fact you'll have far more of everything than you'll ever need, Miss Bridges," she said looking around the garden with a frown as it dawned on her just how much food there really was here.

"Yes, I've just come to realise that myself. I also realise Tom will need help if this venture is to be successful. We don't want to waste anything but there's enough here to feed the entire island, and I don't think it's possible to pick, bottle, pickle, bake, cook and eat everything fast enough. I know he can't possibly have done all this work alone too."

"Well, he did do a lot of it and he was in charge. He had a very definite plan of how it was all to be and woe betide anyone who deviated from it. But I confess his brothers did help, and a couple of their friends when it came to the heavier labour, but they are trustworthy types. I knew you wouldn't want strangers traipsing about the place so kept it in the family, as it were."

"Your family is a credit to you, Mrs Parsons, please thank them for me and tell them they are more than welcome to the fruits of their labour whenever they want it. I wonder if you would also help me find some extra staff to work under Tom? Perhaps another two or three, if you have time?"

"You leave it with me, Miss Bridges," she said, then wandered off to inspect the cabbages.

I had barely seen Mrs Shaw since we had entered the garden but she eventually caught up with me by the runner beans, their bright orange flowers already beginning to show.

"Tom has worked absolute wonders in here. You must be very pleased."

"Oh, I am indeed, it's surpassed everything I had hoped for. I've barely had time to look at everything even though we've been here for ages."

"Did you notice the sundial?"

"No I didn't, where is it?"

"Over near the salad beds, it seems to be very old. I also spied some statuary near the potato patch you may want to have a look at."

"I must have missed that too. Is this goodbye by any chance, Mrs Shaw?"

"It is, Miss Bridges."

"Can you not stay for lunch?"

"I'm afraid not, I'm due in London shortly."

"Ah, news of your next assignment?"

She nodded.

"Well, let me walk you back."

And we left Tom and his mother chatting together by the cold-frames, while we returned to the house.

"Will we meet again, do you think?" I asked her as we stood in the hall by the front door.

She paused for a moment.

"If I ever find myself in this neck of the woods, Miss Bridges, I'll be certain to pay you a visit," she said.

I think we both knew it would be highly unlikely but left it at that.

"Well goodbye, Miss Bridges, and best of luck."

"Goodbye, Mrs Shaw, and thank you. For everything."

She turned and was halfway down the path when she stopped and looked back.

"Oh, and while I remember, when it comes the time for you to purchase a motor car, go and see Simpkins, at the garage here. He knows what he's talking about and will get you a good deal."

"I'll do that," I said.

As I waved a final Goodbye to Mrs Shaw I heard the telephone ringing in the hall.

"Hello?"

"Isobella, is that you?"

"Mother?"

"Oh, thank goodness. Listen do you think you could come right away?"

"To France? Yes, of course but what's happened, are you all right?"

"Not really, dear, no. You see I rather think I'm about to be arrested."

ABOUT THE AUTHOR

J. New is the author of The Yellow Cottage Vintage Mysteries, traditional English whodunits with a twist, set in the 1930's. Known for their clever humour as well as the interesting slant on the traditional whodunit, they have all achieved Bestseller status on Amazon.

J. New also writes the Finch and Fischer contemporary cozy crime series and (coming in 2021) the Will Sharpe Mysteries set in her hometown during the 1960's. Her books have sold over one hundred-thousand copies worldwide.

Jacquie was born in West Yorkshire, England. She studied art and design and after qualifying began work as an interior designer, moving onto fine art restoration and animal portraiture before making the decision to pursue her lifelong ambition to write. She now writes full time and lives with her partner of twenty-one years, two dogs and five cats, all of whom she rescued.

If you enjoyed the first three books in the *The Yellow Cottage Vintage Mysteries*, please consider leaving a review on Amazon.

If you would like to be kept up to date with new releases from J. New, you can sign up to her *Reader's Group* on her website www.jnewwrites.com You will also receive a link to download the free e-book, *The Yellow Cottage Mystery*, the short-story prequel to the series.

Printed in Great Britain
by Amazon